Scream
and
I'll Kill You

Alexander (Lex) von Rudloff was born in Pretoria, South Africa on 18th August 1951. He was educated at Christian Brothers' College and graduated in English Literature and Political Science at UNISA. He found his opposition to the apartheid system leading him into exile in Botswana in 1973 where he obtained citizenship in 1978. After teaching for seven years and a long career in the construction industry, he began writing, and was the scriptwriter of the successful Setswana television drama series, RE BINA MMOGO in 2005. He now writes full time, supplementing his income with consultancy work. He and his wife live with their young son Kabo in Mokatse, a small traditional village in the Kgatleng District of Botswana, about thirty kilometres northeast of Gaborone.

He has two grown-up sons: Otto lives in Gaborone with his wife and their young son, and Munaf lives and works in Canada.

He is the Chairman of CamelThorn Media Trust.

In his spare time he enjoys painting and making music.

http://www.alexandervonrudloff.com/

Scream
and
I'll Kill You

Alexander von Rudloff

Libros
INTERNATIONAL

Printed and bound by Jakaranda Printers.

ISBN
978-1-905988-41-9

Published by Libros International

www.librosinternational.com

Acknowledgements

I would like to thank all those who read early drafts and assisted me with helpful suggestions and advice: Norm Forshew, André de Jongh, Ruth Curran-Crawley, Zaza and Annalee Curran, Bob Patterson, Clive Grantham, Denis Crampton, Doni von Rudloff, Batsho Dambe-Groth, Frans van Heerden, Tim Morton, Kgafela Kgafela, John Hinchliffe, Brian Costas, Ernst Engels, Mmamosese Tladi and Glen McVeigh. Pete Moore enhanced the readability of the book with great wisdom and the lightest of editorial touches. Also, my thanks go to John Mole for his advice and encouragement, and to Ollie Groth for his generosity and unending indulgence. Finally, my undying appreciation to my dear wife for her patience and support, and to my children for putting up with me!

For Ims

Zero

Despite the Germanic origin of his family name, Maurice Anthony Wentzel was as English as could be. Rugger, beer and seducing horsy debutantes were his preferred amusements, and he exuded the compelling bouquet of self-assured public school gentry.

His breeding, education, financial background and social station were impeccable. His friends would have called him supremely confident, if a bit loud. The rest of the world would unanimously have thought him arrogant and stuck-up, the epitome of an upper-class prick. He was enjoying life at university; the parties were wild and the girls attractive and generally very willing.

None of this mattered to him at the moment, as he stared wide-eyed at the ceiling, waiting for death. He strained futilely against his bonds and the gaffer tape gag.

He could still see the horrifying sight of the gloved hand holding up his blood-gushing genitals for him to examine. The blood had caked across his face where they had smeared his ruptured scrotum, and he could still smell the nauseating odour of his own raw flesh; still taste his own blood. The pain was excruciating. It would no doubt get much worse before it was all over.

Apart from the soft rumble of traffic along the Tottenham Court Road, and the faint reverberation of the windows as a tube rattled along the Central Line far below, the only sound he could hear over his own sobbing, snotty nasal breathing was the steady drip-drip of his blood into the bucket they had placed under the table beneath his mutilated groin.

In the morning when Roger had told him that the girl had been raped, he didn't make the connection at first. It took a little time, through the hangover and splitting headache for

Maurice to comprehend that *he* was being fingered as the culprit. There had been talk of arrest and charges, frantic thoughts of scandal, of Daddy, and of prison. A miasma of panic and despair had enveloped him.

What a relief when he got the text message inviting him to her flat to 'talk it over'! Surely she'd understand that a bloke can't just stop in mid-flight simply because someone changes her silly damned mind...

He remembered knocking on her door. After that, events had taken on a totally surreal hue.

Hours later when he regained consciousness the pain seemed to have abated. Alone in the dark he thought he must have been hallucinating, he was sure he had an erection, though he knew it couldn't be possible.

One

Dear Anton.

There is a notion that the character of a newly created soul is the product of the circumstances of its conception; that the soul of a new person is a consequence of the spiritual gush of its parents' orgasmic fusion. I hope my conception was not like that, but there is a bit of background to the story.

My grandmother was a person of no account. She was unmarried, and as such had the status of a child. The only saving grace was that she bore two children, and this elevated her to a sort of semi-adult, permitted to socialise superficially with her peers.

She remained rigorously excluded from matters of family, clan or tribal decision-making. At weddings or funerals, when the elders would meet to negotiate the bride price, or plan the funeral proceedings, she would remain at the cooking fires with the young girls. Her first child was my mother.

My grandmother discovered the facts of life the hard way. Various reasons had prevented her thus far from attending 'bojale' – the female initiation ceremonies. Many of her peers had done so and were now women, but each year since she had reached a suitable age, she had been prevented from going for one reason or another. Last year it had been the floods, and bojale had been postponed. The year before that she had the mumps.

She was a late developer, and up to her twentieth year had not an inkling of the reproductive process.

One day, when she was helping with the harvest at the family fields, she had a sudden sensation of a very private wetness. To her horror she discovered that she was bleeding. She went down to a muddy pool in the otherwise dry sand-riverbed, and washed her soiled underthings.

The bleeding did not stop, and the bloomers, as they were in those days, needed repeated washing. She had a rising feeling of panic. The more she washed them the more the persistent bleeding soiled them. She was sure she was going to die from some unspeakable disease.

Her elder sister, noticing that she had absconded from the work in the field, followed her to the pool, and when she saw the blood, angrily called her and said they should go immediately to their mother.

They walked the distance to the village in silence, the elder leading the way purposefully. When they reached their homestead, she motioned for her sister to sit on the ground outside the gate, while she went into the yard.

There followed a long muted discussion between mother and daughter, until at last the neophyte was summoned with angry tones. She sat down and greeted her mother, who dispensed with any formalities.

'You see what has happened!' she barked in the voice usually reserved for admonishing a child for some heinous mistake. 'Now, after this, if you lie with a boy you will become... like that! Do you hear? Go back to your work.'

My grandmother had departed from this, her first and last sex education lesson, totally bewildered and confused. She was mortified that her most private, secret body part had invited such humiliation.

However, a few days later the bleeding had stopped and she slowly regained her composure and self-confidence. She had no clue what her mother had been alluding to, except that the term 'like that' was often used to refer obliquely to someone who was pregnant.

But 'lying with a boy' meant nothing to her. She puzzled over the warning. After all, she had lain with many boys. She had slept on the floor in a huddled group of brothers and cousins since she was weaned and no longer slept with her mother.

She had lain in the grass on lazy hot afternoons with the same brothers and cousins and friends while out collecting firewood or herding goats.

What about it? None of it made sense to her. She had no idea what her mother had been talking about. Although she had witnessed dogs, chickens, goats, cattle, lizards, birds, and countless other species copulating in pursuit of their natural urges, she had never even conceived of the thought process which would have allowed her to extrapolate the same activity to humans.

In her culture one did not speak of such things, and the naïve girl failed to make the connection. Had she gone to bojale, all the secrets would have been revealed to her, but a child had no need for such weighty information, and she remained just that, a mere child.

Even the half-overheard gossip of scandals about young girls being 'spoilt' and becoming mothers before they were married or even fully grown up had not excited a logical thought process within her innocent mind. She knew nothing.

As fate would have it, she made the cognitive connection soon enough. A week after the bleeding incident she accompanied the rest of her family to a not-too-distant neighbouring village to attend a relative's wedding. As a young girl, or woman as she in fact now was, albeit unknowingly, she busied herself with the countless chores involved in preparing for a large social gathering.

For some days leading up to the wedding feast she and her peers cooked, cleaned, swept, washed, peeled, looked after babies, fed toddlers, collected water, served tea and performed a myriad of other tasks, morning till night.

Late in the evenings, with the jobs done, they went off to sing and chat in the moonlight, usually on the bare rocks of an outcrop not far from the wedding homestead. The moon was waxing and almost full, and the children were safe from unexpected encounters with snakes and other perils, and were free to wander and play till weariness overtook them in the early hours.

One night she and her friends were sitting in their usual place practising their wedding songs. Some older boys were with them, and among them was a youth whom she knew distantly. He seemed to be watching her constantly while she sang and laughed, and his look gave her a queasy feeling, as if his eyes were drilling into her.

She felt uncomfortable. No one had ever made her feel so uneasy merely by looking at her. In fact, she had never noticed anyone looking at her like that before. But despite her uneasiness, she felt a strange compulsion to steal glances in his direction, a fact he seemed to notice, and to appreciate.

As the night wore on, he found an opportunity to speak to her without the others hearing. 'When are you going to give that thing to me?' he asked. She was bewildered. The tone of his voice was conspiratorial, and he clearly didn't want the others to overhear him.

'What thing?' She found herself using the same secretive undertone.

'That thing you have, which is mine. I want it very much,' he said.

'Why are you troubling me? I don't have anything of yours. I don't know what you are talking about. What is this "thing"?'

'I will show you. I will show you under that morula tree over there.' He indicated with his head. 'I will go and wait for you there.' With that he got up and wandered off in the opposite direction to that which he had suggested.

She watched him leave. She felt peculiar. A slight sweatiness was on her forehead, her heart was pounding in her ears and her breathing was unnatural.

The others seemed not to have noticed her hushed conversation with the youth, and had begun singing another song. What he spoke of was very confusing to her. Although she knew him vaguely, there was no occasion she could remember that he had given her anything.

How could he want something of his back? What could he mean? While she sat and pondered she noticed his silhouette as he walked away from them. He seemed to be veering off to one side, so that while he had left the group as if to go in the direction of the homestead, he was now describing a wide circle through the bush and heading towards the morula tree.

Other than snakes and scorpions, there was very little to fear in those parts at that time. The community was widely dispersed over the countryside, and each family had a village homestead, some fields for ploughing and raising crops, usually with some rudimentary accommodation, and a cattle post, similarly equipped for an extended sojourn.

These three dwellings could be as much as a day's walk apart, though it was usually the cattle post that was further from the village than were the fields. All the children grew up in an environment in which moving from one dwelling to another was commonplace.

Every person met along the path was a kinsman, and there were no apparent dangers. Children as young as five or six would routinely commute between the village and the fields, and boys particularly got used to the long trek to the cattle post from an early age. Unlike amongst the neighbouring Bapedi, witchcraft and ritual murder were almost unknown, and consequently, even small children wandered far and wide without supervision.

It had been more than a generation since the last lions had been seen in this part of the country. Crime of any kind was almost non-existent. The girl felt no apprehension as she stood up from the rock, determined to find out what 'thing' of this boy she had.

She was excited, though. The conspiratorial whispers, the penetrating look, her own strange reaction, the palpitations and breathlessness were all inexplicable, but curiously enticing.

On leaving the group she surprised herself by also going in the direction of the village, with just a casual 'I'm coming' over her shoulder to her friends. She was even more surprised to notice that, almost involuntarily, she had adopted his subtly deceptive style. She also took a wide circuitous detour to the morula, but in the opposite direction.

The degree of her subterfuge amazed her, but by now she had fully entered into the conspiracy. She was off to a secret meeting, and that was that! She had absolutely no idea what she was going to be shown, but this game was exciting!

He was waiting at the morula. The enormous umbrella canopy cast a deep shadow, and she could barely make him out leaning casually against the great trunk of the old tree.

He came forward and grasped her by the hand and pulled her towards him. She was strangely calm and unfazed by this. She spoke in the same undertone they had used earlier, although no one could have heard them.

'What thing of yours do I have?' she asked.

Suddenly things began to move very fast. In one movement he pulled her closer, so that she was standing against him. One arm encircled her and held her to him. He bent down and said quietly in her ear, 'This!'

In the same movement his free hand grabbed her squarely by the vulva and his finger pressed inwards so that there was no doubt. Her head reeled.

Ever since she was a little child and learnt to wash herself, no one had ever touched her there. Now, with her heart pounding and her legs trembling, this man was fondling and pressing and pushing.

He lifted her skirt, and pulled down the waist of her bloomers and put in his hand so that his fingers were against her exposed flesh. Before she knew it his finger was sliding into her, and tremors gripped her.

She moaned involuntarily. She couldn't think. Her mind seemed to have frozen. Her body was no longer in her control, and she sank down onto the soft leaf litter beneath the tree as he lowered her.

She lay on her back and he kneeled beside her. There were explosions happening inside her head. He pulled off her bloomers and spread her legs apart and kneeled between them. He was pulling at his belt.

The next thing she knew, he was lowering himself on to her, and she felt something hard against her thigh. For a moment she didn't know what it was. Hard, but somehow also soft. He shifted his position and it pressed against the very centre of her privacy, pressed and pressed and then there was a sharp pain, and he entered her.

Realisations tumbled through her head. All of a sudden she knew exactly what was happening. All of a sudden she understood sexuality and reproduction and what dogs and chickens did. Connections, previously absent, abruptly and simultaneously became a firework display of cognitive pertinence within her head.

It was all happening at once. She had seen donkeys with erections, little baby boys with tiny erections, yet she had never, in her childlike ignorance comprehended the obvious.

As he stroked back and forth, in and out, one half of her beamed with the clarity of her awakening, of understanding that which for so long had remained hidden. The other half of her wanted to scream, to flee, but no words came, and she couldn't have run had the devil himself been after her.

She knew that this was bad, was wrong, she knew that trouble was sure to come of it. Now, instantly she knew why this was a secret, never spoken in the open. Now she knew!

Almost to the day, nine months later, my mother was born. The old lady's words had proved to be prophetic. 'If you lie with

a boy you will become like that!' She had lain with a boy – once
– and she had indeed become like that.

Maybe it was in recognition of the bright light of comprehension on the night of her conception that her mother called her Phatsimo[1] – One who shines.

---

[1] Pronounced 'Pah –TSEE-moh'

TWO

I finished reading and put down the exercise book. I was stunned. She had told me she would write it all down, and I had expected a couple of paragraphs covering her entire life history. This was half of a forty-eight-page exercise book, and she hadn't even been born yet!

In fact, there was an entire generation still to come. But it wasn't just the amount of detail that floored me, it was the style, she seemed to be an outsider looking in, like a social anthropologist, rather than the subject of the text. There was much more to this Kelly Modise than I could have imagined. Clearly more than just a sexy butt and a pretty face. For sure.

I looked out over the balcony. From where I sat I could see the sea between the beachfront hotels. A dark line of casuarina trees fringed the beach on the opposite shore of the bay, sweeping off towards Pointe aux Canonniers.

The usual afternoon shower was squalling in from the interior of the island, but the people on the beach didn't seem to notice. These showers were usually brief, and barely took the edge off the oppressive heat. I picked up the exercise book and began to read the next passage.

As I read, my mind wandered from the neat handwriting on the page, and I found myself going over the events of the last three days. Yes, it was just three days! Three life-changing days. Today was Saturday. Three days ago I hardly even knew Kelly existed.

On Thursday I had been in court in Johannesburg, as I had been for more than a month before that. The case had been occupying my attention absolutely.

It, and I, had been in all the newspapers and on TV every day for weeks. Every evening there had been a gaggle of reporters waiting for me on the steps of the Supreme Court. I had become quite used to TV cameras and microphones being shoved at me while I gave the latest update on the progress of the trial.

My client was becoming something of a folk hero, a *cause célèbre,* and I had been basking in the reflected attention. Not that I wasn't something of a celebrity myself, but this was something else entirely.

Nozipo Nxumalo[2] stood accused of perjury and defeating the ends of justice. Though not usually extraordinarily newsworthy charges, in this particular context the trial was at the very centre of the national debate. That the case was being heard in the Supreme Court rather than in the magistrate's courts was in itself significant. The fact that I - supposedly one of South Africa's better-known human rights lawyers - was defending her added to the hype. The media circus that surrounded it was a reflection of the profound emotions that it stirred.

I felt that if ever the justice system in South Africa had miserably failed someone, it was now. Few cases in recent times were as transparently iniquitous, so unjust and unfair.

Through prejudice, abuse of power and deceit, the victim had been transformed into the culprit. The innocent had been made guilty. When I undertook the defence of Nozipo, I did so knowing that I was defying the establishment, but my anger at the injustice overcame any caution.

I stood up and leant over the railings of the balcony, gazing past the palm trees and white hotels, out across the turquoise lagoon. Beyond the distant line of breakers was the ultramarine of the Indian Ocean, bespeckled with white horses. Despite a faint, unobtrusive hum of traffic, it was very peaceful, very laid-back. Oh what a difference from Johannesburg, Nozipo, the trial, suddenly all seemed so remote.

But then again, I mused, if it hadn't been for Nozipo's case, I probably would never have met Kelly. My heart skipped a beat

---

2 The 'x' is a click, made with the tongue against the forward ridge of the palate. The click slips seamlessly between the 'N' and the 'u' (pronounced *oo*). The second syllable, 'MAH' is stressed.

at the thought. I was smiling to myself as I looked up and down the road below, but there was still no sign of her.

The sun was getting low over the lagoon, and the oppressive heat of the day was beginning to subside. *Where was that girl?* After all, she had said she was going for a walk, not for a bloody hike around the island!

I was beginning to miss her; yet she had only been gone a few hours. I reflected that that was something of an admission: known her for only two, three days and missing her already. Yes, only three days!

Three days ago I hadn't even spoken a single word to her. I had still been wholly immersed in Nozipo's perjury trial - a defence advocate, totally involved in my work. I had been a simple, uncomplicated single man, as innocent as could be, with no hint of romance on the horizon.

I fetched myself another cold Phoenix from the fridge and went back to the chair out on the balcony. I picked up the exercise book, and was about to start reading again when a shout on the street below distracted me. I peered over the railings, hoping that it would be Kelly, but it was just some local youths having a bit of fun, and I returned to my seat.

Despite allegedly being on holiday, I couldn't stop thinking about work. Every time I thought of Nozipo and of the circumstances that brought her to the dock to face these spurious charges, my blood boiled.

After all, I privately acknowledged, it was my anger that fuelled the dedication to my work. I began thinking about it yet again, the blue exercise book in my hands forgotten for a moment.

At the start of our association five months ago, when I had taken her on as a client, she had given me a fairly thorough account of her recent history.

Nozipo was a Zulu. She was twenty-five and an orphan, having lost both her parents at an early age. A distant cousin of her mother had informally adopted her, and she grew up relatively securely in Kwa-Mashu, near Durban.

After finishing high school, Nozipo was fortunate to be placed with another relative, this time in Johannesburg. This gentleman, Jabulani Zulu, whom Nozipo called 'Uncle Jabu', was a legendary figure in The Struggle. He and Nozipo's father were comrades in the early days of the liberation war, and trained together in Tanzania before the latter died in an apparent road accident near Arusha.

Jabu had played a vital, if not widely publicised role in the negotiations that brought about the New South Africa. The former senior intelligence officer of *Umkhonto we Sizwe*, the military wing of the ANC, had been instrumental in thrashing out backroom deals with the SADF military intelligence brass – deals that had been crucial in peacefully welding together the new South African National Defence Force from the old guard, the former 'homeland' armies, and their erstwhile adversaries, the liberation forces.

Many expected Jabu Zulu to reach the very top. During the first post-*apartheid* government, he had been deputy Director General of intelligence and was mooted for a cabinet post. At the first opportunity however, he put politics aside and opted instead for the much more rewarding field of Black Economic Empowerment. Under the BEE banner, Jabu had become a multi-millionaire in less than ten years, sat on numerous corporate boards and was one of the ANC's most successful economic appointees.

The glamorous and effete Gladys Ntombi Dladla-Zulu was Jabu's wife of twenty-odd years. She had managed the metamorphosis from working-class exiled war hero's wife to high-society hostess with aplomb and style.

She had borne him three sons: Phumzile, 22, who was rumoured to be living in Botswana, out of reach of the long arm of the vehicle recovery unit of the South African Police, and the twelve-year-old twins, Thando and Siphiwe, who both attended St Jude's Diocesan Sc

Gladys had welcomed the poor orphan into her home and treated her more like a sister than an adoptive daughter. With

Phumzile gone and the two younger boys absent so much of the time, Gladys unwittingly diverted much of her maternal energies towards the bright, amenable young woman from her husband's clan. In fact, despite the differences in their ages, Gladys and Nozipo had grown very close. What had been a major catalyst for this intimacy was the tragic news that Nozipo had received two years ago: she was HIV-positive. Gladys had comforted, counselled and supported her throughout.

Then, a year ago, an extraordinary thing had happened. Gladys was away in London at their Bloomsbury Square flat, shopping and spending half term with the twins. Jabu and Nozipo were the sole occupants of the grand Houghton residence. It was a Sunday evening, and the staff had all retired. The eight-bedroom mansion was isolated behind the latest security installations in its large grounds.

It was very quiet and peaceful. Nozipo was relaxing on her bed, watching her usual reality TV channel. She had bathed and was in her nightdress and dressing gown.

Suddenly, Jabu appeared in the doorway. He had been out at some function, and was still in his tuxedo, though he had removed the jacket and loosened his bow tie. She instinctively pulled the dressing gown more tightly around her, and covered her knees.

He never visited her in her room in the guest wing, and they generally met in the kitchen, dining or living rooms. What made it even stranger was that he was carrying a bottle of *Bollinger* and two glasses.

As was usual for the household, he addressed her in English.

'Thought you might like to join me for a drink.' He seated himself uninvited on the foot of the king-sized bed, arranging the bottle and glasses on the small, glass-topped occasional table that he pulled towards himself. 'Haven't really celebrated the African Mutual Securities deal yet, and what with Mama away.' He busied himself with the foil and untwisted the wire.

He smiled as the cork popped, and dribbled a few drops of foam on to the carpet for the ancestors.

'Au! But Uncle Jabu... you... You know I don't drink alcohol!'

'Aw, come on, just this once. Anyway, it's not really alcohol... this is just champagne. French. Very expensive!' He put on a pouting, rich-man expression - one eyebrow up, the other down. 'Don't deny your old uncle every little pleasure! *Toe*! Just one sociable drink! To celebrate!'

He paused, and his look was meaningful. 'After all...' The rest was unsaid, but Nozipo instantaneously felt the weight of obligation - after all, she owed Uncle Jabu and Auntie Gladys everything. He poured them each a glass and handed the flute to her. She accepted it reluctantly. The TV was too loud. She grabbed the remote and set the volume right down. He raised his glass, and she did likewise.

'African Mutual!' His tone was as for a diplomatic banquet, his toastmaster's voice.

The bubbles tickled the back of her nose, and she had to struggle not to cough. But the second sip tasted better, and she tried to be less hostile. In any case, Uncle Jabu had always treated her like his own daughter, giving her everything she needed.

'Yes,' he continued, 'this little deal is going to be worth a lot of money. Look at me!' He patted his chest. 'I'm sixteen million rand more valuable than I was this time last week! And that's just the beginning.

'This stock is going to...' he searched for the word, 'soar!' He smiled with satisfaction. 'Isn't that great?' He paused, grinning knowingly to himself. 'I mean it's great for the Africanisation of capital!' He tried to sound magnanimous. 'That is why we do it, after all! Here, let me top you up.'

She proffered her glass, maybe a little less reluctantly. The *Bollinger* was going straight to her head.

'You must tell me what I should buy Mama to surprise her when she gets back.' He was still using his 'posh' voice. 'I find it so difficult! I mean, what do you buy the woman who has everything?' He guffawed at the cliché.

Nozipo looked at him. His head was tilted back, and his rich, deep voice reverberated off the ceiling as he laughed - too loud - at his own joke.

He was well into his fifties, and his hair, which he kept very short, was past the salt-and-pepper stage, and was now uniformly grey. The finely clipped moustache, too, was going white. His face had lost the striking good looks of his youth, and his very dark complexion had lost its lustre.

The patina on his forehead that reflected the light of the chandelier was only a thin overlay of sweat on the dull skin, not any inner glow. His neck seemed to have disappeared entirely, and in this posture the skin of the back of his head described multiple, improbable rolls over his collar.

A middleweight boxing champion in his youth, he had once had a very athletic, if stocky body, but now he looked paunchy, and his belly stretched the fabric of his shirt.

The room was large and luxuriously furnished. Nozipo could see herself in the long mirror on the opposite wall. She had never regarded herself as being pretty. She was just a simple, dumpy, rural girl with a nose that was too wide, hips that were too broad, and big, ugly feet.

Her hair was in disarray, and in the dressing gown, she cut a thoroughly unglamorous figure; in her opinion totally out of key with the brocaded wallpaper, crystal chandeliers and deep-pile carpets. She felt a twinge of embarrassment that her uncle should choose to pay her a visit while she was at her least presentable.

'What do you think of that new Audi, the sporty one? You think she'd like that? Or the new Jag?' He looked at her. 'Or maybe she's had enough cars. Maybe something else.'

Jabu leant across towards her, and unceremoniously grabbed her calf. 'And you? Would you like me to buy you a new car? That old Corolla is pretty out of date, hey!'

Nozipo's heart stopped. This was most unlike Uncle Jabu. He had always been the perfect gentleman towards her. He had never laid a hand on her. Now, all of a sudden, he was groping her leg. He seemed to be making some sort of pass at her. She flinched involuntarily.

'Come, come! Don't jump like that.' He tried to smile reassuringly as he put his glass down on the table and shifted closer to her, without releasing his grip on her leg.

'Don't pretend you have not been aware all these years that… that I find you… er… desirable!' As he said this last word, confirming her worst suspicion, his hand shifted from her calf to her thigh, and he leant even closer.

'But, Uncle Jabu! No!' She shrunk away. The headboard behind her made escape impossible. His hand slid up her thigh and started searching, rummaging, while with the other hand he grabbed her arm and pulled her towards him.

'No! Please, Uncle Jabu, please!'

Suddenly, there was anger in his eyes. 'You ungrateful little bitch! You think you can refuse me? You think you can tell *me* "no"?' He pulled her roughly towards him, dragging her into a prone position diagonally across the bed, and threw himself on top of her.

'After all I've done for you!' He was shouting now; flecks of saliva struck her face. 'All these years of free board and lodging, free school fees at college, countless holidays, free petrol for your free car! After this you want to tell me "no"? *Me*?'

She wailed. 'Please, Uncle Jabu! I'm begging you…'

Jabu straightened up, and for a moment she felt relief. But suddenly he slapped her violently across the face. The blow caught her across the cheek and nose, and was hard enough to make her nose start to bleed.

He clicked his tongue as one would to a dog. 'I will not be denied!' He was shouting now. His eyes were bulging. 'You slut!'

Jabu pushed up her nightdress and ripped off her panties. He was panting with anger and exertion. He forced her legs apart roughly and began to undo his trousers. Nozipo froze. She was helpless. She didn't know what to do or how to react. The shock of what was happening had numbed her, and she couldn't think or make any voluntary movements.

As he tried to enter her, she suddenly found her voice. There was a note of pure panic in it. 'A condom, Uncle Jabu! You must use a condom!' she stammered. 'AIDS! Uncle...you know I'm...'

'Fuck you!'

When he had finally finished he straightened up, adjusted his clothing and looked for his drink. He noticed that his glass was empty and he reached for the bottle to refill it. Nozipo's glass had fallen on to the carpet and he retrieved it and filled it as well, thrusting it into her hand.

She wiped herself with tissues from a box on the bedside table, and curled up against the headboard. He resumed his original seat at the foot of the bed. He drank in silence. Nozipo drank too; the now-warm champagne the only comfort within reach.

There was a long silence. Nozipo was almost motionless, except for an uncontrollable, involuntary trembling shiver. She thought of going to the adjacent bathroom but couldn't make herself move, afraid of what he might do.

She felt as if in a dream. Nothing was real, and she could have pinched herself until she bled and still have felt nothing. As a sort of displacement reflex, she mechanically reached for the remote, and raised the volume on the TV.

She remembered that once he began to settle into his rhythm he became almost tender, whispering apologies into her ear and doing his best to make this rape transform itself, midstream, into gentle lovemaking.

When he noticed the blood on her face, he reached across to the tissue box in order to wipe it, making cooing noises as he did so, gently kissing the bruised cheek. She had the feeling that by the time he reached climax he had convinced himself that they had indeed been making love... that this was consensual sex.

Her state of numbness was such that she felt no surprise when she saw him take a blister pack from his trouser pocket. As he pressed out a pill, she could read the 'Viagra' trade name clearly on the back of the pack. He swallowed the bluish diamond-shaped tablet with the last of his *Bollinger*. Next, he searched his trouser pockets again and placed a small folded piece of white paper, a two hundred rand note and a platinum *Diners Club* card on the glass table.

Then, as if it was the most natural thing in the world, he unfolded the paper, shook some white powder onto the glass and began to chop some lines.

Nozipo was totally naïve about drugs. She had never considered using any substance, and had never before witnessed what she now saw, except in the movies. She had never dreamt that her respectable uncle could possibly be involved in such things. But such was the state of her ego, so subjugated was her will, that when Jabu had finished the process, snorted a line and peremptorily proffered her the rolled-up banknote, she dutifully crawled across the bed to the table and without demur sucked the white powder into her nostril.

After the initial cold, sharp, burning sensation, a subtle sense of contentment contrived, along with the champagne, to make her stop shivering; like an accident victim on the side of the highway who is comforted by a stranger's jacket around her shoulders, as she waits for the ambulance.

The reality TV show had reached the point where the bachelorette contestant had to ditch one of her potential suitors. There were superficial interviews with all eight aspirants, and one-dimensional soundbite observations from the bachelorette about the 'totally awesome' date she had with each, and how 'incredibly much' they all meant to her.

Both Nozipo and Jabu seemed to be engrossed. In her numb state, she found herself easily slipping into the ersatz reality, her present plight temporally shelved. Eventually the blond bimbo of a contestant made her choice, and there was a tearful farewell as the unlucky wannabe stud was obliged to take his leave from the romantic island.

When the channel went into an ad break, Jabu picked up the credit card and began to scrape together the makings of another couple of lines. This time, Nozipo found herself watching the process in fascinated anticipation. Despite herself, despite the circumstances, the cocaine had made her feel better, more in control.

She almost eagerly bent over the table when it was her turn.

No sooner had she done so than Jabu looked her straight in the eyes.

'Now, my little girl, we're going to do it properly, neh! No silly nonsense this time.' He wagged his finger. 'Do you hear?'

He got up and dimmed the lights, then proceeded to undress himself. He yanked his unresisting victim to her feet, and removed her dressing gown and nightdress, so that she was completely naked. Then, he pulled back the bed covers, and guided her into bed.

She didn't resist him. She didn't feel him. Her shame, her hurt and horror, her disillusionment in mankind were so immense that she let it all just wash over her, as an exhausted shipwrecked swimmer in the middle of the vast dark ocean might give up and slowly allow herself to sink beneath the waves.

But Nozipo had surprised herself. First thing on Monday morning she had gone to the Houghton police station and had made a complaint of rape against one Jabulani Benedict Zulu.

In a plastic bag she carried the tissues with which she had wiped up his fluids.

Three

I was not involved in the rape trial. Well, in any case, not directly. I didn't manage to attend any of the court sessions. The public gallery, which I would have had to use, was full to overflowing every day of the trial, and I hadn't had a day off from work, anyway.

I followed it very closely in the press and on TV though, as did almost all of South Africa. Everyone seemed to be involved to some extent or another in the acrimonious debate that had raged around it.

The media circus began as soon as the rape charges hit the headlines, and didn't let up until the verdict, seven whole months later. Then there was a brief pause before the perjury trial started, and the spectacle begun anew.

From Day One of Jabu Zulu's rape trial there were massive demonstrations and counter-demonstrations outside the court. The police were forced to separate the opposing camps in an attempt to maintain order.

The larger and more vocal group comprised Jabu's supporters, mostly from his clan, and all stalwart ANC cadres, who vehemently protested the charges against one of their revered leaders. It was tantamount to blasphemy to besmirch the character of a national hero with trumped-up allegations that had obviously been framed to undermine him and his political affiliates.

Across the police lines were an assortment of women's groups, anti-violence and anti-rape coalitions who equally vehemently protested against the abuse of power by a man who should know better, and against the ignorant, blind, tribal, party loyalty of the defendant's supporters.

The slogans, the banners, and the interviews with various demonstration leaders mirrored the processes that were taking place inside the court. Each morning and evening, as Jabu arrived, or left the courthouse, flanked by a phalanx of his security goons, the chanting, the cheering and the acrimonious jeering from across the police lines reached fever pitch. Groups of his supporters, some with assegais, shields and tribal headdress, toyi-toyed in the street, blocking the traffic and looking almost like a regiment on a war dance. The TV cameras, local and international, had a feast.

Some of the slogans of the demonstrators reflected the divisions within the ruling alliance, which was beginning to show fractures as the three main components, the trade union movement - COSATU, the communists – the SACP, and the ANC strained with the tensions of a fifteen-year marriage of convenience.

Within the ANC itself were diverging tendencies; the traditional Charterists with their enduring belief in the pure uncompromising democratic principles as enshrined in the historical Freedom Charter on the one hand, and the more modern pragmatists, the apologists for corruption and for failed 'brother' regimes like Mugabe's across the border, on the other.

Within these were the subdivisions of tribe, particularly the long-established rivalry between the two major Nguni groups, the Xhosas and the Zulus. Inside these were further subdivisions of district and clan.

The Zulu nation itself is divided into two diametrically opposed and bitterly alienated groupings. Those who support the ANC and its affiliates on the one hand could be characterised as seeing themselves as South Africans first and as Zulus second. The majority of rural Zulus however, staunch supporters of Mangosuthu Gatsha Buthelezi's Inkatha Freedom Party, see themselves as true Zulus, heirs to Shaka the Great, and inherently superior to all other peoples.

The acrimony between these two factions is only slightly less intense now than it was at the height of the Zulu civil war in the eighties and early nineties, when Buthelezi allied himself to the shadowy 'third force' of the *apartheid* regime in his desperate attempt to marginalize the ANC support within the tribe and to maximise his stature and importance in any future dispensation.

Inkatha claimed to embody the true Zulu ethos and allied itself to the royal house. Jabu Zulu, as the name attested, was a member of the royal family, and some saw his involvement with the ANC, and consequent rejection of Inkatha, as a betrayal of his clan and noble lineage.

Jabu himself was thoroughly pragmatic, the realities of high finance and *realpolitik* having long since supplanted the principles that guided him through the early years of The Struggle. His name spoke for, and embodied his tribe. His heroic career as a freedom fighter and commander stirred deep passions within his zealous following.

Before the trial could get started, the defence petitioned the court to dismiss the charges outright on the grounds that they were spurious, baseless, malicious and deliberately calculated to destroy the political and corporate career of their client.

It was only because of the corrupt nature of the National Prosecuting Authority, and of the obvious political mischief-making of the Director, that these charges were framed in the first place. It was common knowledge, they contended, that the Director of the National Prosecuting Authority himself was under investigation for alleged corruption and political manoeuvrings. The Honourable Mister Justice Albertus 'Lappies' Labuschagne denied the application, and the trial got under way.

The prosecution team consisted of two young, inexperienced, overworked and underpaid lawyers, Ndipo Mokalanga and Neo Motsumi. Despite perpetual sleep deprivation and a ridiculous workload, they had built up a convincing case, based on Nozipo's blow-by-blow testimony and backed up with the forensic DNA evidence of the semen in the plastic bag of tissues.

Traces of cocaine on the glass table and the empty champagne bottle added to the weight of substantiation. The medical reports, with photos of the bruised cheek and blue-green discolorations on the thighs completed the picture, and gave the specifics of Nozipo's story consistency and credibility.

Jabu's blue-chip defence team, led by Oxford-educated senior counsel, Advocate Ishmael Patel, barrister and State Advocate - the South African equivalent of a QC - consisted of lawyers who were all much more experienced than the two prosecutors. All four of them, supported by a dedicated staff of legal secretaries and paralegals back at the office, had only one case – The State vs Jabulani Benedict Zulu – on their plush desks.

They also earned between five and ten times as much as their harried 'learned friends' at the opposite table. They all knew too, that Jabu Zulu had enormously deep pockets and that a hefty cash bonus would inevitably come their way - off the books and tax-free of course - should they succeed in clearing his name.

They challenged every State witness, questioned every piece of evidence, and sought every opportunity to get the case thrown out. At one stage, the judge warned them against deliberate time-wasting, particularly when they tried to cast doubt on the validity of some of the forensic evidence on the grounds of the totally specious allegation that the State Pathologist, a Xhosa, was a Mbeki loyalist and may have been persuaded to falsify the DNA results.

Despite the best efforts of the defence, the prosecution's case proceeded fairly predictably, and Nozipo acquitted herself very satisfactorily on the stand. When it was her turn to be cross-examined, however, the gloves came off and the true drift of the defence's case began to become evident.

'Ms Nxumalo.' Ishmael Patel had an excellent command of language. Though he was at his most eloquent in Urdu and Hindi, his English was cultured, precise, and superbly enunciated. A Durban native of Gujarati origins, he was equally articulate in Zulu, Arabic, French and Afrikaans. Behind the beak of a nose and sunken, sallow cheeks, lay a razor-sharp mind.

He quizzically furrowed his brow and regarded a point in the ceiling above the judge. 'Do you have a fiancée?'

The prosecutors looked at each other with undisguised dismay. Although it was inevitable that the defence would exploit Nozipo's sexual history, they had somehow hoped that she would escape. Nozipo shook her head. Ishmael Patel ignored her, looking condescendingly at Justice Labuschagne, making it clear that he had not seen her and that his question remained unanswered.

'Ms Nxumalo,' the tone was acerbic, the voice unnecessarily loud, 'you will do the court the courtesy of answering my question!'

'N… No,' she stammered. Despite all the mental and emotional preparation, her pulse rate was way up. Round One to Ishmael Patel.

'Thank you!' Patel leant forward deliberately across the table and placed a bony hand on the polished surface. He softened his tone, sounding almost avuncular. 'But you have… er… had a boyfriend or two, have you not?'

'Ye… Yes.'

'Well, is it two? Three, maybe?'

'I… I'm not sure I…'

'Come, come, Ms Nxumalo, we are all adults here. How many boyfriends have you had? Hmm?'

'Objection, my lord!' Ndipo Mokalanga was on his feet. 'This is totally irrelevant to the case. The complainant is not the one who is on trial here! My learned friend knows full well that he is harassing the witness!'

Patel raised his hands, palms upward. The gesture eloquently expressed contrived exasperation. 'My Lord, we are not harassing the witness. Relevance will be self-evident.'

Justice Labuschagne leant forward on the bench. 'Counsel may continue,' he looked at Patel, 'but keep it to the point.'

'Thank you, my Lord.' Patel returned to his soft, familial tone. 'Let me put it another way, Ms Nxumalo. You are not a virgin, are you?'

'Objection, my lord! Objection!' Ndipo's angry voice was thin and reedy and a poor match for Patel's resonant oratory. 'How can a rape complainant possibly be a virgin? My learned friend is not being serious!'

'I'm sure we all know what counsel for the defence means.' Judge Labuschagne was getting impatient. 'Go on, Mr Patel.'

'Well, Ms Nxumalo… let me rephrase the question…' Patel smiled patronisingly at the young prosecutor, and his delivery was slow and deliberate, '… a year ago, *prior* to the events in question, were you a virgin?' and out of the side of his mouth, '…happy now, Counsel?'

Nozipo was doing her best not to let Patel's line of questioning get to her, but there was an involuntary tremble in her voice. 'No, I was not a virgin.'

'And how many years ago did you have your first, er… experience?'

'Objection!' Ndipo's tone was shrill. 'What possible relevance has…?'

The judge snapped at him, 'Come now, Mr Mokalanga. I've already given my ruling. You will let the witness continue!'

Nozipo looked at her hands. It was clear she was not enjoying this. Patel looked at her with exaggerated patience. Eventually she mumbled, 'About seven or eight years ago... I think.'

'And in those seven or eight years, you have had how many lovers?

'I… I don't know… '

'Approximately then…?'

'Maybe… er…' She lapsed into silence, the awkwardness of the situation was rapidly becoming too much for her.

Patel's voice became a notch less gentle. 'Five? Ten? More than ten?' He paused. 'Twenty?'

There was a flash of anger in her eyes. 'No! Not twenty!'

'Well?'

'Maybe seven… probably seven… excluding the rape!'

'Alleged rape, Ms Nxumalo! *Alleged* rape!'

Nozipo looked down. The muscles of her jaw twitched. 'Yes, excluding… excluding that.'

Patel cupped his chin in his hand as he slowly shook his head, miming bitter disappointment. His tone was mournful as he muttered, almost as if to himself, 'An unmarried girl of what… twenty-five! Hmm. Already been intimate with seven different sexual partners. Allah!'

He let out a deep sigh, raising his eyes as if appealing for the Almighty to have mercy on this poor sinner, and shook his head again.

Suddenly his voice rose. 'Pray tell the court, Ms Nxumalo, are you still, er… going out… er… with any of these… er… seven gentlemen?'

'No.'

'Aha!' Patel knew he had made his point. 'So these were all just *casual* sexual encounters, were they?'

After the lunch recess, it carried on.

'Ms Nxumalo! On the evening in question, you were in your room in the Zulu home. Were you not?'

'Yes, I was.'

'And was the door locked?'

'No.'

'Was the door closed?'

'No, it was not.'

'Aha! Would you please describe to the court what you were wearing?'

There was a disturbance as some spectators in the public gallery shuffled to their seats, late on their return from lunch. Justice Labuschagne frowned and held up his hand towards Nozipo so that she would wait for the noise to subside.

'I was in my nightie… I had just had a bath.'

'You were wearing a nightdress? What else?'

'And a dressing gown.'

'Pray, continue'

'A panty…'

Patel nodded towards his colleagues at the defence table with him. One of his juniors, Craig Kravitz, jumped up on cue and took his place beside Patel. He was holding a shopping bag.

'My Lord! Defence exhibits thirty-nine, forty and forty-one…' The judge's clerk rose to pass some papers and photographs up to the bench. Kravitz reached inside the shopping bag, and withdrew a chiffon nightdress. He held it up for the court to see. Any neutral observer would hardly have described the style of the nightdress as being overtly sexy or revealing. It was just a regular - if fairly expensive-looking - nightdress, with a bit of lace around the neck and on the hem. Ishmael Patel, now sounding almost like a lingerie salesman, continued, 'Attractively cut nightdress, in pale blue…' He put his hand under the garment, and held it in such a way that his wrist and his watch were clearly visible through the fabric. 'Very revealing… er… transparent… Next!'

Craig Kravitz held up the dressing gown. It was of the same material as the nightdress, and both garments appeared to be part of a set. The dressing gown too, could not reasonably have been described as being overtly sexy, but Patel applied the same transparency test, and used the same smarmy tone of voice.

'Alluringly translucent! Similarly see-through…Next!'

The white panties were full-cut and conservative. The fabric was plain except for a small pink embroidered heart on the part that would have covered the pubic mound.

'These are your clothes… the ones you were wearing on the night in question… are they not?' Patel fingered the heart with his long, bony digit. His repugnance was palpable.

'Yes… They look like them…'

'A transparent negligee… a suggestive pink heart…' The icy tone was back. 'Do you consider these to be suitable attire for a young lady who is a houseguest in somebody else's home?'

'Well… er… I was in my room…'

'In your room with the door wide open! Indeed! In a transparent nightdress, with an inviting heart on your underthings!'

There was giggling and whispering in the gallery. Craig Kravitz folded the garments and returned them to the shopping bag and then ostentatiously handed the bag to the court orderly before sitting down.

Ishmael Patel drank slowly from a glass of water. 'Ms Nxumalo!' He took another sip, and wiped his thin lips with the back of his bony hand. 'You say in your testimony that my client, Mr Zulu and his wife, housed and fed you, gave you the free, unfettered use of a car. Do you not?'

'Yes.'

'And that Mr Zulu provided you with a monthly stipend of …er,' he picked up his reading glasses and elaborately set them on the beak of a nose as he referred to his notes, 'eight thousand rand.' There were some gasps and whispers in the gallery.

'Yes.'

'Your monthly allowance, your pocket money, was eight *thousand* rand! Eight *thousand* rand a month!' He let the substance of the sum sink in as he slowly placed the spectacles back on the desk. 'Now, would you agree…?'

He deliberately cleared his throat. 'It would appear would it not,' he cleared his throat again, 'that all your needs,' he counted them methodically on his long, bony fingers, 'board, lodging, transport, college tuition fees, textbooks and stationery, holidays with the family, trips to London - Paris - New York, most of your toiletries, your personal satellite television, your own private telephone, your cell phone…' Patel paused for breath, '…that these were all covered by my client's generosity, er… and by the generosity of his wife?'

Nozipo wasn't sure about the question. In the briefings, such as they had been, the prosecuting team had drilled her about not having to give opinions, to only give facts. She looked for guidance at the prosecutors. Neo Motsumi seemed poised to object, but then she shrugged as if deciding to let it go, glanced at her colleague, and lowered her eyes.

Nozipo had a sense of foreboding. 'Yes.'

'With every imaginable expense taken care of, please tell the court what you do with your pocket money of eight,' the emphasis was heavy, '...eight thousand rand a month!'

The question was unexpected and Nozipo looked across the court at Neo again. They hadn't rehearsed this one. Anyway, the drained young prosecutor had been so busy with this and her other twelve cases, that with all the interruptions, she and Nozipo had only had about ten minutes together. That was weeks ago. The attractive young prosecutor stood up.

'Relevance, my lord?'

Judge Labuschagne dismissed the objection with a grunt and with a wave of his hand and another grunt indicated to Nozipo that she should answer.

'Er...' Nozipo was unsure, glancing from the judge to the prosecutor and back again. 'Well...'

Patel was quick to maximise her discomfort. 'Ms Nxumalo, please answer the question!' He inclined his upper body towards her, and raised his voice a notch. 'What does a twenty-five-year-old student do with eight,' he paused, 'thousand,' again, 'rand – a – month? Please, please. Do tell the court!'

'Er... I suppose I buy clothes... I save some... CDs...' Nozipo was on the defensive, and it showed. '... I give some to charity...'

Patel cut her short. 'You suppose you buy clothes! Hmm!' He reached for his glasses and picked up a file from the table. 'My lord, defence exhibit thirty-seven-point-one to thirty-seven-point-eighty-two.' The judge's clerk handed the judge some documents.

Patel continued, 'I have here copies of some invoices signed by you. That is your signature, is it not?' He handed the sheaf of papers to the court orderly, who stepped forward and held them up in front of her nose.

'Yes.'

The orderly returned the invoices to Patel who quickly summarised them. 'These invoices are from er... Foschini, the year ended er... last July... er and I quote... total sum seventeen-thousand-four-hundred-and-twenty-seven   rand. Here Edgars, er... sixteen-thousand-eight-hundred rand. Er... Stuttafords. Nine-thousand-four-hundred-eighty-two rand.' He returned the papers to the table and removed the glasses.

'These accounts are in the name of Mrs Ntombi Zulu... You had signing powers on these accounts?'

'Yes, I did.'

'Indeed you did! And you bought clothes! Indeed you did. In the year leading up to the events in question, you bought clothes... or rather, *you were bought* clothes on your benefactor's account, to the value of...' he checked his notes, '...of forty-three-thousand-seven-hundred-and-nine rand and eighty-five cents, and yet you say you used your stipend to buy clothes! That's a lot of clothes for a young woman!'

'Yes, but I also donate...'

Patel held up his hand peremptorily. 'Please, please! You are here to answer my questions, not to make speeches!'

Patel cleared his throat. His tone feigned patience. 'Ah! CDs. You bought CDs. Yes, I'm sure you did. And how many CDs did you own in July last year?'

'I... I'm not sure.'

He picked up the file and using the indexed tabs, paged until he found what he wanted. 'My lord, defence exhibit forty-six, inventory of the complainant's bedroom. South African Police Service; Prosecutions Division, dated... etc. etc.'

He turned to Nozipo. 'There were exactly twenty-seven CDs in your bedroom in July last year. Ah yes, and four in your car. Thirty-one in all. That's about what? Two-and-a-half... you'll note I'm being generous here... three? Three-and-a-half thousand rand's worth?'

Nozipo looked at her feet.

'Well?'

'I suppose so...'

'Hmm! You suppose so indeed! Three-and-a-half thousand rand! How many years did it take you to build up this... er... collection?'

'I don't know, a few years, I...'

'A few years to build up a music collection of thirty-one CDs! What, one a month? Two? Three a month? One hundred, two hundred... not even three hundred rand spent each month on CDs? That leaves a bit of change from eight thousand rand, does it not, Ms Nxumalo? A bit of change!'

Patel paused as if searching his memory for some distant object.

'Ah yes, and saved! You *saved* your stipend of eight thousand rand a month. Hmm?' The putting on of the glasses was more elaborate that ever. He paged the indexed file. 'My lord, defence exhibit sixty-point-one to sixty-point-twelve. First National Bank Savings Account statements in the name of the witness, Nozipo S Nxumalo, freely given upon request by the defence under attached instruments, etc. etc.'

Nozipo remembered giving her permission. At the time she couldn't see how it could possibly compromise her, and she had wanted to be seen to be cooperating.

'These are your savings bank statements, are they not?' He handed them to the orderly who crossed the floor and gave them to her.

'Yes.'

'And this is your only savings account, is it not?'

'Yes. I only have that and some credit cards...'

'Thank you! We will concern ourselves with the savings account. Few people manage to save on their credit cards!'

There was laughter in the gallery. Even Justice Labuschagne smiled. The prosecutor looked at Nozipo nervously. Ishmael

Patel ignored the levity and continued. 'Would you be so good as to read out the amounts in the deposit column, for the period ended July last year.' He held up a photocopy of the statement and indicated to her the relevant column to illustrate his request.

Nozipo felt flushed. There were only three entries on the page in the deposit column. At this moment they didn't make wonderful reading.

'Eighteen-hundred rand.'

'Do go on!'

'Five hundred rand… One thousand rand.'

'Well?'

'That's all…'

'That's all! That's all? So, in a year when you received ninety-six thousand rand - correct me if my arithmetic is awry, but I do believe it is indeed ninety-six thousand rand that you received in monthly stipends over that year - you managed to save, what is it?' He furrowed his brow theatrically, 'Three-thousand-three-hundred rand. That's three-thousand-three-hundred out of a possible ninety-six thousand! Is it not?'

Nozipo's responses had become mechanical. 'Yes.'

'Ah! But let us not forget the other three-and-a-half-thousand for the CDs. Well, that totals up to… hmm… a bit short of seven thousand rand. By my reckoning, there are some eighty-nine thousands unaccounted for, are there not?'

'Yes, but… But I also…'

'Thank you! Just answer the question please. And that's just for the one year, is it not?'

'Yes, but… But I…'

'Yes. I'm sure it is.' He paused, and his change of tone heralded a change of tack. 'My Lord, with the court's permission, allow me to show the witness some video footage… Lights please!'

Nozipo glanced at the prosecutors, who seemed as nervous as she. They both turned towards the nearest screen, as did Nozipo. She had a strong sense of foreboding.

There were five TV monitors in the courtroom, and in one of them Nozipo had a good view of a shot showing her amongst other students at college. She cringed at the sight of herself unselfconsciously slouched on a bench in one of the corridors, worrying a spot on her chin, staring into space. Many other students were passing up and down.

There was no soundtrack. The video was grainy and the camera unsteady. It was all shot from below waist level, suggesting that the footage had been unobtrusively taken a by mobile phone camera held by someone sitting on a bench diagonally opposite.

Suddenly, a dreadlocked man was in the picture. He approached Nozipo and passed her a package, a small plastic bag. She accepted it and peeped inside, as he bent to whisper something into her ear. Immediately, she realised what the bag contained, she hurriedly and furtively stuck it deep into the pocket of her jacket as the Rasta man turned and left.

The grainy piece of video ended. Nozipo was stunned. What she, and the court, had just seen looked exactly like a clandestine drug delivery. She knew at once that she had been set up.

She remembered the occasion. It was a few months ago. She had been waiting for her next class when fellow-student Ras-Jay had come up to her.

'What-a-go-on, mah sista? Hey, Maria asked me to give you this.' He had handed her a small package, a pharmacy plastic bag, and leant closer to whisper conspiratorially. 'She said she didn't want her mother to find these, so please keep them safe for her!'

She had taken the package and looked inside. It contained three or four packets of condoms. Instinctively she had immediately put them out of sight in her pocket. Before she could ask for more details about her friend Maria's need for this unusual assistance, Ras-Jay had disappeared.

Ishmael Patel cleared his throat theatrically. 'Thank you! Lights!' He continued in an almost melancholy tone, 'Ms

Nxumalo, it would appear that we have very likely just witnessed the sort of transaction that accounted for your eight-thousand rand stipend! Have we not?'

Nozipo felt her anger rising. 'No! No! You don't understand…'

The whispering in the gallery became a hubbub. Patel raised his voice.

'The cocaine that was found on the glass table in your room was yours, was it not?'

'No! No, it was not!'

The clamour got louder.

'Order! Order!'

'You deliberately misled the court by falsely accusing my client of drug taking! Did you not?'

'No! No! No!' Nozipo's voice was a shriek.

'Objection!' Neo Motsumi's voice was too small to be noticed over the uproar. The courtroom was in turmoil now.

A court orderly barked, 'Silence in court!'

Even Judge Labuschagne had raised his voice. 'Order! Order! I will have order!'

'Objection! Objection, my Lord!'

Patel's voice rose above all others, 'These allegations of rape are all a pack of lies, are they not?'

'No! *No*!'

'I have no further questions, my Lord.'

The court was adjourned for the day amid scenes of pandemonium.

Four

I remembered how the Press went berserk after Patel's stellar performance. Only one or two journalists from the more serious papers went against the flow and suggested that the defence was playing a dirty game. The majority of publications and the headline TV reports sensationalised the events in court and related Patel's annihilation of the complainant at face value, without apparently noticing his cynical manipulative purpose.

In almost all the reports, Nozipo was portrayed as a cheat and a liar, a drug-taking, husband-stealing golddigger who would clearly stop at nothing to destroy the man who so selflessly provided for her all these years.

Poor Ndipo Mokalanga and Neo Motsumi! I still empathised with the two young prosecutors - their case was so persuasive, their cause apparently so just, they should have had the upper hand. Yet they had been completely out-manoeuvred and outplayed by Patel's enormous experience and subtle guile.

There was a suggestion of surrender in the air when the prosecution rested its case first thing the following morning.

'Mr Patel?' Judge Labuschagne's raised eyebrow in the general direction of Ishmael Patel signalled the commencement of the case for the defence.

Patel nodded and sprang out of his seat, suddenly much more youthful and eager.

'My Lord, we call Mr Jabulani Benedict Zulu to the stand.'

There was a buzz in the gallery, and the prosecution team exchanged a mumbled discussion, while Jabu was sworn in by the registrar. To many it may have appeared to be bravado, even reckless stupidity, but to Patel it was a carefully calculated strategy.

He knew it was a risky manoeuvre. Putting Jabu on the stand would allow the prosecution to cross-examine him, under oath, but Patel had reason to feel supremely confident as he began his questioning.

What was more alarming was that for the first time since the trial started, Gladys Ntombi Dladla-Zulu was in court. She sat in a prominent seat in the front row of the public gallery, dressed in a striking Senegalese outfit, looking more like an African Queen than the wife of a rape defendant.

She exuded an air of total confidence, as if to affirm that the ridiculous charges faced by her husband ought to have no effect on her serene composure or her unqualified support.

For his part, as he took the stand, Jabu wasted no time in looking across the courtroom at his wife, clearly determined to demonstrate his total confidence in her support and her belief in his unsullied innocence.

'Mr Zulu,' Patel's self-assurance was palpable. 'Did you, or did you not, rape this... er... the complainant, Nozipo Nxumalo?'

'I most certainly did not!' The rich baritone boomed confidently across the courtroom.

He was immaculately groomed, dressed in the sort of tailored dark-blue suit and subdued silk tie that he would wear to an African Diamond Corporation, or Southern Financial Systems board meeting. His cufflinks glittered with a conspicuous hint of sumptuousness.

Patel lowered his voice. 'Did you, on the night in question, have... er... sexual intercourse with her?'

Jabu looked directly at Gladys as he answered the question. She in turn, looked directly back at him. Neither flinched or betrayed the slightest discomfort. 'Yes, I did.'

There were audible gasps in the public gallery. The prosecution team exchanged nervous glances. This wasn't expected! Where was this heading?

'You say you and the complainant did have sexual intercourse? Is this correct?'

'Yes. We made love that evening.' The whispering and nervous giggling got louder

'Silence in court! I will have order!' Judge Labuschagne's voice was firm.

Ishmael Patel continued, 'I see. Thank you, Mr Zulu. You say you and the complainant made love. Would you like to tell the court how this …er …romantic event came about?'

He couldn't resist sneaking a glance at Gladys Zulu in the gallery. 'I am sure we all appreciate the very personal and sensitive nature of this matter, but in the circumstances,' he nodded obsequiously at the judge, 'I'm sure the court would be much obliged.'

'Certainly, if I must.' Jabu was rock-steady, clearly very well rehearsed. 'For years, I think nearly five years, my wife and I have cared for Noz... er, the complainant. We have catered to her every material need, provided her with accommodation in our own home, given her money, transport… everything.

'My wife, in particular,' he looked lovingly at her, 'has gone out of her way to befriend her and to provide her with emotional, as well as material support. All this while, as we have striven to care for her, at every opportunity she has fluttered her eyelashes seductively at me behind my wife's back. I always did my best to ignore her provocation,' Jabu paused and looked at the judge with an expression of utmost innocence, 'but she intentionally targeted me when my wife was absent, when I was at my most vulnerable.'

Jabu paused dramatically, looking down at his hands. After a moment, he looked up at Gladys and continued. 'While my wife was away in England last year, she deliberately flaunted her body at me - dressed only in a nightdress, mind you!' Jabu theatrically threw up his hands. 'I am a man, after all! What was I to do?'

Patel interjected. 'She deliberately exposed herself to you? She overtly invited you to have sex with her?'

'Objection! Counsel is leading the witness!' Neo Motsumi, the prosecutor, was on her feet.

'Sustained.' Judge Labuschagne made a show of frowning at the advocate for the defence.

Patel ignored the slap on the wrist, and nodded at Jabu. 'You were saying...'

'Yes, exactly! She invited me! I am ashamed to admit it, but in a moment of weakness I yielded, but which man,' he glanced at Patel and then looked the judge squarely in the face, 'which man wouldn't?'

'The complainant has accused you of rape,' Patel continued. 'Why would she want to seduce you and then do such a thing?'

'I think that is obvious.'

'Objection, my lord!' Neo Motsumi was on her feet again. 'Inference.'

'Sustained. The witness will be more specific.'

Jabu seemed to be expecting the objection, and didn't miss a beat. 'I mean, I think it is obvious that, er ...certain elements have been, er ...manipulating her. The whole thing was a deliberate plot to try to destroy me.'

The judge leant forward. 'Would you like to elaborate, Mr Zulu?'

'My Lord, I believe she was influenced by my political enemies; dark forces that wish to damage the unity of the ruling party by dragging my name through the mud. My Lord, I will only go as far as to say that there are certain elements that are trying to marginalize my followers within the party. You will understand that I am able to say no more than this.'

The defence continued in the same vein throughout the remainder of the day. The drugs had been planted, the bruises self-inflicted. Nothing was real; all was fabrication. Jabu denied rape, denied everything. His counsel guided him through a carefully constructed annihilation of Nozipo's character. Jabu also denied drug taking, and with some confidence.

The prosecution was only too aware that certain forensic samples, including Jabu's blood and urine samples for drug analysis, had gone missing from the police forensics lab during the investigation. Then again, I remembered thinking at the time, if one still had a finger deep inside the intelligence community, it wouldn't be a very difficult thing to arrange.

They played it well. Jabu responded to Patel's questions by addressing his testimony directly at the judge, and maintained an air of affronted injury throughout. The Honourable Mister Justice Albertus 'Lappies' Labuschagne was only a year older than Jabu.

Though they were raised on diametrically opposite sides of the *apartheid* gulf, their age and gender, and the recently imposed comradeship of their joint participation in the affairs of the ruling classes, gave both a clear acknowledgement of their fraternity.

Throughout the process Gladys Zulu maintained a regal air, never flinching at the revelations, always smiling benignly at her husband and making it clear that she at least had no doubts of his total innocence.

Finally, the charade that was the case for the defence came to an end. Ishmael Patel settled himself on his chair with satisfaction. He was supremely confident about the cross-examination. These lightweights weren't going to disrupt his case.

With a look of encouragement from her colleague Ndipo Mokalanga, Neo Motsumi rose to her feet.

'Mr Zulu.' Neo's voice was no match for Patel's sonorous tones. It filled only a small portion of the void left after his 'Thank you! No further questions, my Lord!' had faded away.

'Mr Zulu, you accept that you and Ms Nxumalo had sexual intercourse on the night in question. May I ask you, were you aware at that time that Ms Nxumalo was, er… is… HIV-positive?'

Jabu's disapproval of being asked questions of such an intimate nature by a younger person, a girl for that matter, was clear for all to see. He couldn't hide the wrinkled brow and cynical sneer.

'Yes, I was aware.'

'How did you know that she was so?'

'My wife…' he looked across at her and echoed her smile, 'my wife had informed me some time, er… maybe two, three years ago that Noz... er Ms Nxumalo had HIV.'

'And did you use a condom on this occasion?' Jabu was visibly affronted by the question. This was just too personal! He would have loved to slap the little bitch across the mouth for her impertinence. He struggled to maintain his self-control and took a deep breath.

'No.' The court was hushed. Everyone was on the edge of their seats.

Neo continued. 'In her evidence, Ms Nxumalo stated that she asked you to use a condom before… before sexual contact, er… took place. Is this true?'

'She may have made such a suggestion, I do not remember.'

'You will forgive me for asking, Mr Zulu. Why would you regard it as unnecessary to use a condom when having sexual relations with a person whom you know to be HIV-positive? Would you not consider this to be highly risky behaviour?'

Jabu's patience was being tested, and it showed. His tone was terse. 'I have explained to this court how the girl provoked me, time and time again. Whenever my wife… my wife who treated her like a younger sister, for that matter… when my wife was away she came after me in her nightdress…' Jabu swallowed hard. He looked down as he gathered his thoughts. Neo looked at him enquiringly.

'Well… eventually, when I finally succumbed to her relentless flirtation, I went to my room and er… and I put on some … *Vaseline*.' Jabu made a gesture of rubbing something on to the back of his hand. 'Then, I went to her rooms.'

He took a deep breath and looked imploringly at Patel, and then at the judge. The presence of his wife in the courtroom was no longer a comfort to him, and he studiously avoided her eye.

Neo was clearly unsatisfied with his answer. 'I'm not sure I understand. You "put on some petroleum jelly"? Mr Zulu, I have asked you why you found it unnecessary to use a condom and you reply that you went to your room and applied some petroleum jelly? Where? To your hand? I'm sorry, could you please elaborate? I'm not sure that I see the connection.'

'Objection! Irrelevant! Counsel is badgering my client!' Patel needed to rescue Jabu from himself. He was clearly getting very angry.

Judge Labuschagne seemed as confused and as intrigued as the prosecutor. He looked at Jabu. 'Overruled. The witness will continue.'

Jabu was sweating now. Discussing these matters, particularly the intimate details, in public, in front of women and young people - in front of his own wife - went against a lifetime of conditioning. It was totally in opposition to his culture, the way he was brought up.

He stumbled on. 'I… er… covered myself… er… my private part… in *Vaseline*… er… as a protective barrier…'

There were gasps of disbelief around the court, and one or two people in the gallery laughed out loud. Gladys sat impassively, her expression betraying nothing.

'Silence!'

Neo was no less taken aback. 'Mr Zulu, are you telling the court that you applied a layer of petroleum jelly to your…' she had to steady herself, 'to your penis… er… before having sex with an HIV-positive woman… as a means of preventing infection?'

Jabu could have throttled her. 'Yes.'

Neo's face betrayed total amazement. The thin veneer of legal professionalism slipped, and she was a schoolgirl once more, scandalised, wide-eyed and fighting back the giggles. She had to steady herself on the corner of a table with one hand, as she held the other firmly over her mouth.

She solemnly stared at the floor, careful not to catch anyone's eye. With a supreme effort she regained her composure, took a deep breath and continued, 'Are you telling the court that it is your belief that petroleum jelly provides effective protection against HIV infection?' She couldn't resist a glance at Gladys. 'Condoms are superfluous, are they? *Vaseline* does the trick! Is this what you are saying?'

The air of ridicule in the courtroom was palpable, even to Jabu. He felt very foolish, and tried to recover. He had to raise his voice against the hubbub. 'Immediately I left her room I took a hot bath. With *Dettol!*' The shrieks of laughter were audible even outside the courtroom.

Despite the manoeuvrings of Ishmael Patel, despite the aspersions cast upon Nozipo, by the time the defence had finished presenting its case public opinion had swung heavily against Jabulani Benedict Zulu. His diehard supporters aside, South Africa condemned him unequivocally.

The more cautious argued that the prosecution case was inherently flawed, that it relied too heavily on the main witness and that she had been discredited. The press had concentrated more on sensationalising the steamy details of what had happened in the bedroom than on the ebb and flow of legal argument, and by and large, the general public had nothing but sympathy for Nozipo.

An informal radio station phone-in poll was five-to-one in Nozipo's favour. The papers were unanimous. Jabu had not done himself any favours. "WHO NEEDS CONDOMS? - ZULU GOES FOR *VASELINE*" ran one headline in the *Sowetan*. "ZULU KNOWS BETTER - IT'S *VASELINE* AND *DETTOL* FOR ME!" trumpeted *City Press*. Even *The Star*, generally more staid than the others, was unequivocal: "ZULU SHOOTS HIMSELF IN FOOT!"

It was very bad exposure for Jabu, very poor public relations. Here was a pillar of society, an influential millionaire who had everything, being seen to have taken advantage of an orphaned, powerless houseguest, a friend of the family, almost his own daughter. It was tantamount to incest. He had no shame for his conduct, even in the presence of his wife, the likely victim of his reckless selfishness.

Jabu's supporters appeared to be becoming more and more isolated, outflanked by events. The corporations he represented, such as they could, cringed in embarrassment. Many would move to suspend him as soon as he was found guilty.

Here was a man of power and persuasion who clearly did not champion the nationwide drive towards safe sex and condom use, even in the face of a known case of HIV infection. The press did not hesitate to compare him to the President, who had caused such a stir in the nineties by questioning the very link between HIV and AIDS. But Mbeki had been forced to take many a backward step since then.

Now Jabu Zulu too was making a monumental fool of himself, and the shortcomings in the Government's AIDS policy were being put back in the spotlight.

Some senior ANC personalities, former comrades and colleagues, began to distance themselves from him, like rats abandoning a sinking ship. Only his diehard supporters failed to let the State's persuasive case, or their hero's idiocy, diminish their blind, unqualified loyalty. Such are the realities of South African 'democracy', however, that these supporters, particularly in rural KwaZulu, still numbered in the hundreds of thousands, if not in the millions.

After five weeks of argument and counter-argument, of bitter allegation and counter-allegation, South Africa waited with bated breath for the verdict. The facts of the case seemed to be clear to most. To me, they were crystal: Jabu had forced himself upon Nozipo, and then with his lawyers had fabricated an outlandish pack of lies in a palpable, transparent attempt to discredit her. Where incontrovertible physical evidence against him existed, it was simply destroyed. Nothing could be simpler.

The judgment was lengthy, broadcast live on radio for the world to hear. I still now remembered phrases old Lappies Labuschagne used:

After all the accused and his wife had sacrificed for the poor orphan... Total lack of respect for her host's feelings... Parading, partly dressed... Deliberately targeting him, flaunting her body… A loyal, faithful husband pushed to his limits... Had she planted the drugs, as alleged by the defence, it would be a matter for the National Prosecuting Authority to consider… Investigate a possibility that the course of justice has been deliberately perverted…

And finally: Not guilty on all the charges!

That was five months ago, but I still felt embarrassed to be a lawyer, a man, a South African - embarrassed to be an African - after that hateful day. The feeling that I - and the whole of South Africa - had been cheated wouldn't go away.

The thousands of Zulu supporters who thronged the streets around the Supreme Court on the day of the judgment didn't know it, but they too had been cheated. Cheated of any innocence they may have had left, cheated of any hope in the survival of the rule of law, cheated of any justice in the future for the meek amongst their children.

It was less than a week later that Nozipo was arrested and charged with perjury and defeating the ends of justice.

Five

Nozipo had spent two nights in the Northcliff police cells before she was bailed. The vindictive nature of the charges against her quickly became clear when her bail was set at twenty thousand rand. Murder suspects routinely were expected to post two or maybe five thousand. Twenty thousand was way over the norm, and announced clearly where this case was coming from.

The NGO South African Women Against Abuse - SAWAA - managed to raise the money from friends and sympathisers to get her out, but it took two days. That was not soon enough for Nozipo.

Northcliff was not unusual amongst police stations in that a *de facto* segregation policy existed in the staffing arrangements. As a simple deterrent to racial bickering, the roster was designed to keep officers of different complexions apart wherever possible.

Therefore, on a night that the police out on patrol were black, the station was manned by whites. On another, when the black officers were in the charge office, whites, by and large, were on the beat. It was a simple arrangement that made the station management's task a lot less complicated.

It was on Nozipo's second night in the cells, when, accompanied by taunts about Jabu and his long black *Vaseline-ed* dick, a laughing blonde policewoman sexually assaulted her, in a desultory fashion with her nightstick, while a plainclothes male colleague held her down.

'As long as these blerrie kaffirs give each other AIDS, and all die like fokken flies, who are we to complain, hey, Piet?'

The legal practice of Mokoena and Venter was the ideal firm to defend Nozipo and indeed, hers was exactly the kind of case upon which Solly Mokoena, and particularly I, had built our reputations.

When Christine April, an attorney associated with ARCSA - the Anti Rape Coalition - phoned me on another matter, the conversation quickly came round to Nozipo and the outrageous charges she now faced. Christine had the latest update on the situation.

'It's pretty bad news for her, Anton. Her State-appointed *pro Deo* defence advocate is that incompetent Mtshali fellow. He'll never give the case what it deserves. Scared to death of the establishment, he is! She hasn't got a chance, poor thing!'

I hadn't hesitated. 'Send her to me. We'll do it for her *pro amico*.'

'I'll tell her. She'll be chuffed!'

Nozipo of course no longer had the financial support of her erstwhile benefactors, and was unemployed. Mokoena and Venter were not going to realise a single cent from the case, but that was the way we often worked. This was going to be a long, time-consuming trial. Times were hard, and Solly wasn't overly impressed with my decision. 'As long as you also do a case or two that'll pay the bloody rent!'

Nozipo's case wasn't going to pay the rent. That was for sure. What it did do was to advance the reputation of our firm as a unique, caring, sincere practice that put the rights of the innocent above mere cash - great for a particular idealistic status but pretty uninspiring for the bank manager, or for my ex-wife.

Christine phoned me back later that day.

'Hey, Anton! When I told Nozipo that the great Anton Venter was prepared to defend her for free she was ecstatic! You should have seen the smile on her face! It's the first good news she's had in a long while.'

'Oh well, it's what we do. I'm not so sure that I go along with that description, though. "Great" is a bit much!'

'Depends where you're coming from, I suppose,' Christine countered. 'Many who know about these things would suggest that, after George Bizos, you are South Africa's most noteworthy defender of human rights.'

'Hold on there, Christine.'

She laughed at my discomfort. 'Okay, but Nozipo's damn lucky to have you in her corner, and she knows it!'

I guess Nozipo, like most clients, must have been a bit apprehensive when she came to my office for the first time. The building in Eloff Street was run-down and dirty, with winos sleeping on garbage in the lobby. The lifts were usually out of order, and it was an unpleasant climb up the stairs, with menacing-looking characters loitering on the landings. The modest third-floor suite of offices was dingy and dilapidated, with cracked frosted glass and peeling carpet tiles in evidence.

It was a far cry from your average South African law firm. Most practices had fled the city and were housed in modern high-security garden office parks in the suburbs; rolling lawns surrounding koi ponds with fountains, and original sculpture, and designer furniture in the swish reception areas.

Abigail 'Abby' Zwane, a handsome, stout woman of indeterminate middle age staffed the reception desk. Through the open door of my office I could see her point an apprehensive young woman towards a torn leatherette chair.

'You must be Ms Nxumalo!' I heard her say. She smiled. 'Have a seat.' She got up and came through to my office

'Nozipo Nxumalo's here, Anton.' Abby was the firm's only employee and did all the secretarial work for Solly and me, most of the research and almost all the running around. The two partners made their own coffee, and clearly no one had time to do any cleaning.

'Thanks, Abby. Give me a couple of minutes, will you?' I was at the point of finishing a quick DIY manicure, and there were nail clippings all over my desk pad.

Abby smiled indulgently and returned to reception.

'Mr Venter won't be long.'

I got up off the leather and beech swivel chair that was so old it had moulded itself to my habitual slouch, and began quickly to straighten out the office. It was piled high on all sides with legal files bound with pink ribbon, piles of books and cardboard boxes.

I cleared some old law books off the visitor's chair, emptied the ashtray, and hastily swept the nail clippings off the desk and into the overflowing wastebasket.

I caught sight of myself in the dusty framed mirror behind the door. I had never been able to see why, but I had been told more than once - teasingly, I must add - that women swooned when they spoke of Anton Venter.

Ridiculous! I had to duck slightly to see my face in the mirror - one of the drawbacks of being just a little under two-metres tall. When I swept the longish, dark-brown hair off my forehead, I noticed that the hairline was definitely receding, and there were a few streaks of grey, especially at the temples.

The overall impression was distinctly unkempt - a trip to the hairdresser was long overdue. What had once been called finely chiselled features were now, at best, leathery and rugged, and the laughter lines around my eyes were beginning to verge on the geological.

With my jacket off, the remnants of an athlete's body - at least a rugby player's body - were dimly discernible under the cotton shirt. I never wore a tie in the office, and the chest hair that peeped through the open neck was also no longer uniformly dark.

My overall verdict: rather dishevelled and past my best. It was obvious that there was no woman pampering me!

Why did friends tease me about women swooning?

I have to admit that I quite like my eyes - sort of greeny brown and, at least to me, sincere-looking. Maybe one could say the mouth is a bit severe, but that impression lasts only as long as I don't smile, and usually that isn't for very long.

Nozipo looked up from the dog-eared magazine she was perusing when I came into the little reception area. I thrust out a hand.

'*Saubona* Nozipo! *Kunjani*?' My isiZulu is heavily accented and, typical of the average suburban white South African, doesn't go beyond the most basic greeting, a fact that embarrasses me no end.

'Nice to finally meet you! Come through, please!' I led the way down the short corridor to my office. We sat down.

'Hope you don't mind if I smoke?' I jumped up and opened the window, as I made my un-PC request. It always made it difficult for them to refuse.

She probably did mind, but then again she knew she wasn't paying. 'No, please…go ahead.'

'Coffee? Tea?'

'No thanks.'

I noticed her examining my hands, as I took a cigarette from the pack of Marlboro's. I have strong square wrists and long, powerful, pianist's fingers. I've been told my hands are attractive, but then again, I wouldn't know. They just look big and hairy to me. Anyway, I don't look at hands that much. I'm an old-fashioned tits-and-arse man.

I lit up with a battered old Zippo, settled back in my chair, and smiled at the nervous young woman in front of me. 'You've been having quite a difficult time, haven't you, my dear?'

Six

Despite the continuing hype surrounding the trial, The State vs Nozipo Sibongile Nxumalo turned out to be no more than a rehashing of The State vs Jabulani Benedict Zulu, with the boot, so to speak, on the other foot.

Much of the evidence was a repeat of what had already been heard, yet the story had lost little of its popular appeal, and raised the media temperature almost as much the second time round. Reports of the day's proceedings still made all the front pages, still headlined the TV and radio news bulletins, and the public reaction was as intense as before.

The demonstrations outside the courthouse in support of Jabu were a bit smaller, however, as his name was no longer directly on the line. But the support for Nozipo had grown, and one could say that the balance of power in the street and on the Supreme Court steps had shifted in her favour.

The prosecution case had produced no startling new evidence, and to the public eye, at least, it looked for all the world as if the State, as a vehicle for the vindictiveness of Jabu Zulu and his affronted clique, was bent on revenge rather than on administering justice.

The judge, Ephraim Mazibuko, who had a sound pedigree in human rights issues, was also far less likely to be as sexist or as biased in favour of the establishment as Lappies Labuschagne had been.

Yes, I reflected, the trial was going well. Well for myself as well as for Nozipo. I knew I would feel enormous satisfaction if I got her off. My faith in the justice system would be restored after the debacle of Jabu Zulu's acquittal.

If the State were to lose its case, it would be a damned good lesson for those who thought they could conduct personal political vendettas through the courts. I was confident that Judge Mazibuko was as aware as I that the charges of perjury and defeating the ends of justice against Nozipo Nxumalo were trumped-up and baseless.

The trial had been going well and was rapidly coming to a conclusion. Then, on Thursday, it had taken a totally unexpected turn.

I had just begun my second, and final, day of summing-up - the last arguments before judgment would be delivered. The prosecution case was full of holes, and the prosecutor, Jonas Moyo, had not made a particularly strong impression in his summary.

I felt supremely confident as I probed and nudged at the weaknesses of the State's case, which rested almost entirely on the spurious assertion that Nozipo, the supposed cocaine addict, had been persuaded by persons unknown to betray her host and guardian in order to destroy his reputation. She had done this in order to obtain money to buy drugs.

I was sure that I could prove that Nozipo had never touched cocaine prior to the night of the rape - when Jabu Zulu had coerced her to partake. I reminded the court of the evidence of no fewer than eight character witnesses who had all asserted Nozipo's naivety with regard to drugs. I reminded the court too that Nozipo's doctor, the counsellor who had assisted her to come to terms with her HIV status, and her church pastor had never had reason to suspect that she could plausibly be a cocaine user.

During the trial, the prosecution had returned to the specious analysis of Nozipo's finances to corroborate the allegation that she was a heavy drug user. This line of reasoning had been much to the detriment of Nozipo's credibility as a witness for the prosecution in Jabu Zulu's rape case.

In that trial, the defence strategy had been successful because Nozipo never had the opportunity to explain how she spent her allowance. Each time she had attempted to explain, Ishmael Patel had cut her short with a 'just answer my question please'. The impression had been created that she was a spendthrift - one with an expensive habit at that.

This time around she and I had been prepared however, and now I reminded the court how my witnesses, particularly Nozipo's aunt, the coordinator of a crèche for AIDS orphans in Durban, had testified to the fact that Nozipo supported a string of good causes in Kwa-Mashu.

Far from financing a drug habit, her sizeable monthly stipend had been feeding, clothing and educating unfortunate children - a fact that had been deliberately obfuscated by Ishmael Patel at Jabu's trial.

I had focused the second part of my summing-up on the fact that at no point in the trial had the prosecution been able to identify the shadowy person or persons on whose behalf Nozipo had allegedly been acting. I once again posed the question: who had allegedly encouraged Nozipo to seduce Zulu and then to cry 'rape'?

It was clearly very convenient for the rehabilitation of Jabu's good name after the scandalous rape trial that he be seen to be the innocent victim of an evil conspiracy. But, I reminded the court, no evidence of such a conspiracy existed.

My third area of emphasis was on Nozipo's character and her behaviour as a houseguest. Here too, I had produced a number of character witnesses.

One of these, Annah Tshabalala, an employee at the Zulus' Houghton mansion, had been asked to describe Nozipo's habits around the house in the days and weeks leading up to the notorious event.

I reminded the court that her evidence all pointed towards the accused being a model houseguest, modest and private, the very antithesis of the seductive predator that the prosecution - like Ishmael Patel in Jabu's trial before them - tried to make her out to be.

'My Lord, Ms Tshabalala clearly described the accused's demeanour in the presence of her host. The accused, Nozipo Nxumalo, was never seen to display even the slightest hint of seductive behaviour. On the stand, Ms Tshabalala repeatedly stated that the accused's clothing was at all times both modest and ...'

At that moment a uniformed policeman unexpectedly entered the court through the side door and made his way to the judge's registrar's desk. He reached up to the bench to hand the judge a folded piece of paper. Seeing that the judge's attention was diverted, I stopped in mid-sentence.

A strange look came over Mr Justice Mazibuko's face. He got up without a word and made for the door. The accused, counsel, and the public scrambled to their feet in observance of the customary protocol as he left the court, and then all at once, started asking one another what had happened. For a few moments confusion reigned. The unprocedural exit of the judge was extraordinary.

A few minutes later, Annemarie du Plessis, the judge's registrar, who had followed him out, came back into the courtroom through the door behind the bench and stood beside the judge's vacant chair. She called for attention. Her ashen face attested to the fact that she had just had a terrible shock.

'Ladies and gentlemen... Counsel...' The hubbub subsided. 'Ladies and gentlemen.' Her voice was unsteady. 'Due to unforeseen circumstances court will adjourn until Monday week, ten days from today. That's on... er... the twenty-seventh. Nine o'clock.'

Everyone in the courtroom started talking at once.

'Excuse me...' She hadn't finished. 'Counsel...' She looked at Jonas Moyo, the prosecutor, and then at me, 'chambers please.' She hurriedly gathered up the judge's notebook and a few papers, and left the way she had entered.

When Jonas and I entered the judge's chambers we expected to find him seated behind his desk, but the only person present was Annemarie. She was clearly in a state of shock.

I looked around, mystified. I saw that Jonas was as confused as I was. His big, round face registered perplexed incomprehension. I'm sure I must have looked just as bewildered.

'What's happened, Annemarie?' I asked.

She looked at me, her tearstained face filled with horror. 'Nomsa has been hijacked! Oh Anton, they shot her!' Nomsa Mazibuko was the judge's wife.

'My God! Is she okay?'

'No. She's dead… she's dead, Anton!' Annemarie was in tears. Jonas looked dazed.

Within a minute I was back in the courtroom. I looked blankly ahead as people moved towards the exits, and court personnel gathered up their files and papers. Groups of people stood around asking one another what was happening.

Nozipo, sitting in the dock near me, was clearly as surprised as anyone else. One got used to the sedate, predictable procedures surrounding the daily court process. This circumstance was exceptional. She noticed that I was back and looked at me expectantly. There was no point in withholding the news from her, I thought. It would be on TV within the hour anyway. I walked across to her, crouched beside her and quietly told her what had happened.

'Au!' Nozipo jumped to her feet, 'No, Anton, no! Don't tell me!' She stood with her hand over her mouth and stared at the floor in front of her. I put a comforting arm around her and patted her shoulder. After a few moments, she regained her composure and went to tell her support group of family and friends the appalling news.

I returned to my desk and sat down. *Fuck me!* I thought. My carefully prepared and deftly orchestrated arguments had dissolved into a maelstrom of disconnected ideas and incomplete phrases that were racing around my head. *Poor woman! Poor man*!

I knew the judge reasonably well. Although he was fairly recently appointed to the bench, he and I had met numerous times over the last decade, each involved in human rights legal issues of one form or another. I had only met Nomsa once, at a cocktail reception to celebrate her husband's appointment.

The meeting had been brief, and I couldn't recall her face. I had a memory of a large, genial, middle-aged woman who had appeared very humble and unsophisticated - clearly immensely pleased for her husband but somewhat out of her depth at a function attended by legal luminaries and government bigwigs.

Suddenly I was aware of someone standing next to me. I looked up and found myself looking at the girl. My heart leapt unbidden into my mouth.

Seven

I had noticed her there most days the last two or three weeks. She had been attending the trial, sitting every day in the same seat in the public gallery. How often she had been coming initially I couldn't say, but for the last few days I was acutely aware of her presence, and of catching her eye far too often. She had jet-black, wide-set eyes that seemed to bypass mine and penetrate the inside surface of my skull when she met my glances.

I felt myself looking at her in that certain way: the way a man looks at a woman. I had never before allowed myself to do that, at least not as an adult. Notwithstanding my somewhat gushing, progressive 'New South Africanism' and my efforts for The Struggle through my professional activities, that part of me had been so tightly welded shut that what I found myself doing these last few days was totally out of character.

I am the son of a *Dominie*, a minister of the Dutch Reformed Church, the *Nederduitse Gereformeerde Kerk*, the spiritual stockade - the *laager* - of the Afrikaner soul and the philosophical abode of *apartheid*.

When I was twelve, we lived for a year in the little farming community of Mooinooi, west of Pretoria, where my father was the locum pastor. There we had a housemaid called Agnes, whose seventeen-year-old daughter, Eileena, came to stay with her mother during the December school holidays.

Thanks to the inequity of the *apartheid* education system, she and I were both about to begin high school in January - despite the five-year difference in our ages. Eileena and I became playmates, innocently spending our time in youthful diversions like shooting lizards with my pellet gun, gorging ourselves on tart catawba grapes or stealing ripe, succulent peaches from *Oom* Stoffel Janse van Rensburg's orchard.

Once or twice, lying under the shade of the old mulberry tree in the corner of the garden by the compost heaps, looking at her pleasant face and laughing about something silly, I had noticed myself feeling a sort of affection for her, but it was a fleeting thing.

One Sunday afternoon after our usual family Sunday dinner, the telephone rang, and after a grave, hushed conversation my father hurriedly left the house with a solemn face and drove away.

My big brother, Willem, who was doing his national service, was away 'on the border', and my fifteen-year-old sister, Antjie, was going through an insufferably prissy stage of her life, so feeling bored with my own company, I went to the servant's quarters to look for my friend. I was carrying my pellet gun. Maybe we could shoot the mousebirds that were stealing the mulberries.

The servant's quarters were at the bottom of the garden, screened from the main house by the citrus orchard and a split-pole fence, and consisted of a swept-earth compound with a tiny, one-roomed house and outdoor cooking hearth.

Inside the little bedroom, reminiscent of a prison cell and barely big enough for a single bed and a chair, there was a stub partition wall, demarcating a 'bathroom' area with a drain in the bare cement floor beneath a single cold tap and one of those toilets with two curved wooden strips instead of a proper seat. As you entered the bedroom from outside, the partition hid the toilet and 'shower' from view, affording the occupant a modicum of privacy.

Agnes was in the main house doing the dishes, and I expected to find Eileena when I entered the little building on the run, calling her name. In two strides I was across the room, to a point where the partition didn't obscure my view of the bathing alcove.

Eileena was standing in a small galvanised tub, naked except for see-through wet cotton panties. Her dark skin glistened with soapy water, and her upturned breasts, like dogs' noses, were the most beautiful things my twelve-year-old eyes had ever beheld.

She smiled and carried on washing, as she would at her home in the presence of a younger brother, unruffled by my intrusion and blissfully unaware that, at that instant, our friendship changed forever.

The air rifle fell clattering to the floor. I stood there open-mouthed, ogling her body, fascinated by her breasts and the contoured mound of transparent wet cotton, and became aware that I was getting an erection.

'I'm coming' was all I could muster before I fled, ears bright red, to the safety of my bedroom.

My mother had a German friend in Pretoria who passed on old copies of *Stern* magazine to her. The lingerie adverts were much more daring than those in *Woman and Home, Die Huisgenoot* or *Rooi Rose*, even *Personality*.

Maybe it was a question of rhythm or the logistical problems of page-turning to look at all the best pictures at once, but the few experimental attempts at masturbation I had thus far had in my young life had never reached a proper zenith. Once or twice I had experienced a sort of a tingling rush, but never the real thing. Pietie Nievoudt said it felt like you had shaken a bottle of *Pepsi* and shoved it up your arse as it frothed.

But that afternoon it came naturally. As I ejaculated, eyes screwed shut to recapture every detail, the vivid fantasy in my mind was of Eileena peeling off the wet panties, and beckoning for me to come to her.

As the feeling faded and I lay on my bed panting with the overwhelming power of it all, I realised what a fool I had been, running away like that. Who knows what might have happened had I coolly stayed, leaning against the wall, admiring her assets?

I had barely tidied up and buttoned myself when my bedroom door flew open and Antjie unceremoniously burst into the room.

'Anton! Where is my ruler? Hey? I know you've got it. You're always taking my stuff!' Before I could summon a riposte she was rummaging through the things on my table.

'C'mon, I know you took it! Where is it, Snot-Nose? I'm sick and tired of you just going into my room and taking my…'

She found the ruler, snatched it up and spun on her heel scowling at me on her way to the door. She stopped and stared at the floor under the bed. She seemed about to say something, then arched her eyebrows and stormed out.

I leant over and looked under the bed. A large wad of damp sticky toilet paper stared back at me. The tips of my ears burned with mortification. It was too late to make a big issue of sneezing and sniffing and blowing my nose - Antjie was already out of earshot. Would she understand what it was that she had seen? Could she? How could a girl possibly know anything about such a secretive male affair?

As I scrambled to collect the toilet paper, I noticed that one of my mother's *Stern* magazines had slipped down between the bed and the wall. I had wondered where that magazine had disappeared to.

I recognised it immediately as one, which in addition to the alluring lingerie adverts, also had an article on naturists in the Netherlands. In its matter-of-fact German way, the article was uncensored, and there were full frontal shots, albeit grainy black-and-white shots, of totally naked people.

One photo, in particular, had captured my attention. It showed a group of tanned, leathery, middle-aged sun worshippers. In the background of the shot were some younger folk playing volleyball, amongst whom was a truly luscious young girl, captured in mid-leap. Her youthful breasts were as if afloat, her legs widely parted, so that despite the graininess of the photo, one could quite clearly discern the inner surface of her buttocks through her legs, beyond her pubic hair. It was a picture that had enthralled and fascinated me.

Refreshing my memory of the magazine's contents, it didn't take me long to begin thinking of Eileena again. I resolved to place myself in harm's way, to see if there might not be a favourable outcome. I made a quick detour to the loo to get rid of the wad of toilet paper and slipped out of the kitchen. Agnes, I noticed, was still in the scullery.

With revitalised and refreshed ardour I made my way back to the servant's quarters, hoping to find her as I had left her, but by then, of course, she was fully dressed, outside in the compound, combing her hair. Her demeanour showed that she was ignorant of my new interest in her, and she chatted away as before.

My pellet gun had been retrieved and was leaning against the split-pole fence. Little did she know that I could now see right through her clothes and that my thoughts were not those of the innocent playmate she once had till a few minutes before. I was determined to recapture the moment. I tried to be masculine and cool. Super cool.

'Show me your tits again.'

She was surprised at the atypical question, but didn't seem to be offended. 'I wasn't showing you anything!'

'Well, you didn't hide them. You didn't chase me away. Please, just once.'

'Why do you want them? They're just breasts. All women have them. At home in the village no one notices them if I'm washing. They're just breasts, after all. Or, do you white folk think they're something special?'

'Very special! *Ag* please, Eileena, quickly before Agnes comes.'

She frowned. Her tone was slightly patronising. 'Is that all you want? Just to look at my breasts?'

'Yes. Can I touch them?'

She looked at me for a moment. Her expression softened. 'Come on then, you crazy boy.' She giggled. 'Let's go to the tree.'

She led the way through the orchard and the vegetable garden to the mulberry tree. Feeling self-conscious and guilty of my secret purpose, I clutched the pellet gun with a hunter's intent, as if any casual observer should know that I was still as innocent as ever, and that those thieving mousebirds were in for it.

There, behind the compost heaps, she sat down and unbuttoned the front of her dress, exposing the two wondrous cones that shimmered with freshly applied glycerine. I sat down next to her and reverently cupped them, then stroked and moulded them in my hands. The dark, pointed areolas changed shape as her nipples became more defined and turgid. I was in heaven.

Despite my very recent self-abuse, my twelve-year-old dick was throbbing as if it would burst. I rubbed and fondled, dry in the mouth and with a ringing in my ears. When I dared look her in the face she was smiling.

'This is where you should touch a girl to make her feel good.' She took one of my hands and guided it up her skirt. Her legs opened, and my fingers were directed inside her panties and into a wondrous hairy world of warmth and moist mystery. My fingers quickly found their unsupervised way around the folds and crevices and deep into her wet inside.

Her breathing came in shallow gasps, and her eyes closed. A new smell, one that I had never in my life been conscious of before filled my nostrils, and like the stirring sight of blood to a warrior in battle, it seemed to amplify my lust. As if responding to a command, she arched her back to pull off her panties, and manhandled me in between her legs. Together we grappled with the buttons of my khaki shorts, and in a moment I was free. She pulled me towards her, one hand grabbing and guiding.

'Anton! Anton! Where are you?' It was Mammie calling from the stoep.

Pappie was back from his errand. His face was terribly sad and strained. He had obviously told Mammie whatever it was that had happened, because she too had an expression of horror. Neither noticed that I was breathless and flushed, or that the buttons of my fly were done up wrong.

I was surprised to find that I was not specifically needed for anything in particular; Mammie just said that she wanted me home. I went to my room with a mixture of relief and desperate disappointment, only to masturbate again immediately I shut the door. My mind reeled with what might have been, with what, sure as hell, was going to happen the very next chance I got.

As I wiped up the evidence I heard a vehicle pull into the drive. Through the lace curtains I could see Sergeant Nievoudt walk to our front door. My curiosity was aroused and for a moment I stopped thinking about the warm wet depths that I had so nearly plumbed.

I heard the policeman and my father go into the study. I darted into the adjoining empty dining room, and stood at the open window, behind the long drapes. I knew that on warm days like this, the study windows would be open and I would be able to hear what was being said. Sergeant Nievoudt was talking. There was a strange tone in his voice.

'We have taken the body down. The mortuary van from *Brits* should be here soon. I telephoned them from his farm. I must be getting back out there.'

'You sure it was suicide?'

'No doubt, man! *Dominie*, what a terrible two days. Yesterday, his wife comes to me and reports that she caught him red-handed, lying *kaalgat* buck naked with the kaffir *meid* in her *kraal*, and today the man is dead!

'With a blerrie kaffir, pardon my language, *Dominie*! You know, I hadn't even finished typing up his arrest warrant for the immorality case when they called me this morning, and now I've got to change it all for a suicide docket. Suppose now I'll have to let the kaffir girl go, too. What a day!'

'How can I best help?'

'I don't know, *Dominie*. I mean, how do you comfort a woman whose husband has done such a disgusting thing? I'm glad I haven't got your job, *Dominie*!'

Later that night, I heard Mammie talking to Pappie.

'If you or Willem, or God forbid, Anton, could ever do such a thing, I would die!'

Ever since that moment, I was unable to even consider crossing the race-sex gulf. Notwithstanding the New South Africa being more than a decade old and despite my close working relationship as a human rights lawyer with a myriad of women of all shades, in this one respect the Calvinist cast of my upbringing had not yielded.

I had never allowed myself to take that leap, not even in the flightiest fantasy. After more than a year - when we had left Mooinooi and moved to Pretoria - the overpowering guilt of my near betrayal of the reproductive purity of the *volk* eventually subsided, and I was able to sustain an erection again. But now, the mental pictures that fuelled the wrestling bouts with my penis were of big-breasted, airbrushed white women in cowboy hats that I had seen in Willem's *Playboy* magazine, not of Eileena.

Even thirty years later I knew that there was just no future in it. Me, take a black woman to Zeerust to meet my parents?! My mother would have a stroke on the spot! There would be no way, no time, to explain.

But that didn't alter the fact that I was very single. The divorce was six years old, and I was letting life pass me by. Two short-lived, unsatisfactory liaisons were all I could show for six whole years of solitude.

I only got to see the children on alternate weekends. Work took up a lot of my time, but the lonesomeness of my solitary existence was palpable, and celibacy certainly didn't come naturally.

Over the last couple of days, the glances that I had wilfully been stealing in court were replaying themselves unbidden over and over in my head. I was undeniably attracted to this girl. But in my replays there was still no way out for Mammie and Pappie, no going back to the moment under the mulberry tree at Mooinooi, the day *Oom* Sakkie van Zyl hanged himself in shame...

The eyes! From close up, she was stunning. She had very dark skin. Her slight and petite body was superbly proportioned. Her sensible skirt and blouse, appropriate for a day in court, obscured what promised to be a stunning body.

I caught my eyes tracing the relief of her sculpted collarbone and the deep hollow at the base of her throat. She was stroking a faint scar on the left side of her neck with her fingertip. I noticed as she opened her mouth to speak, that she had a quaint light and dark patterning on her gums. She had pristine white teeth.

How long had I been staring at her? Had my mouth been open all the time?

'Hi.' The smile was all I could notice. She held my gaze. 'Sorry to bother you, but do you know what's going on?'

Her accent took me totally by surprise. She looked South African, but the voice was English. Had I met her in the dark I would have sworn she was white. The way her lips curled around the words somehow made the smile all the more bewitching. I was aware of my pulse in my ears.

'The judge's wife has been murdered.' My mouth was suddenly dry and I had to pause before continuing. 'A hijack, apparently. I haven't heard any details yet.'

Her hand went to her mouth. She looked at me, her eyes wide.

''Kin' 'ell! When?'

I took a sip of water from the glass in front of me. 'This morning, I think.'

'Jesus Christ! Cry the beloved fuckin' country. Only in bloody South Africa!' The way she said South Africa sounded more like 'Sahffafricah'. Sahf London, I thought!

'Yes, it's depressing, isn't it?' I concurred.

She seemed to check herself.

'Sorry.' She put out her hand. 'I'm Kelly.' The smile was back.

'Anton. Anton Venter. Glad to meet you.' Her hand was small but the handshake was firm.

Close up, she was utterly stunning. An absolute doll! Her face was fringed with short, stylish dreadlocks. The eyes were so bold as to be plain inviting. Her full lips and large, brilliant teeth interacted seductively as she spoke.

I was still slouched in a chair, looking up at her. I caught myself as my eyes were drawn to the curve of her hip, her flat belly, where the rounded contour of her thighs stretched the fabric of her skirt across the void... With an act of will, I raised my eyes.

'Seen you here quite often. Do you know Nozipo?' I indicated towards Nozipo and her supporters gathering at the demarcation fence. 'She a relative?' I felt I had to make conversation to cover for my undisguised ogling. *Idiot!* I thought. It sounded like one of those 'do you come here often?' openers.

'Yeah, we've been helping her, arranging bail, accommodation... that sort of thing. The organisation I'm with is involved with abuse victims. Counselling, shelters, legal aid... stuff like that. We're following the trial; observers, like. Also come to listen to you. You're quite famous, you know!'

'Which organisation?' I dodged the hero-worship angle.

'SAWAA. South African Women Against Abuse.' Her look was right at me, seemingly unconnected with the words.

'Oh ja, heard of it. You must know Allison Bagwasi, then. Is she still there?'

'You mean Allison de Groot. No, she left to go to Holland with her husband. Must be a year ago. Very committed lady!'

The court was almost empty. It dawned on me that this was the moment. *Flee, Anton. If you don't, there's no telling how much shit you're going to be in.* I got to my feet.

'Well, nice meeting you.' I went round the desk to get my things. That sounded too abrupt, too final. Almost rude. I felt I had to soften it.

'Maybe we'll get a chance to chat about the trial sometime. Could turn out to be quite a landmark case for women's rights. That's if old Justice Mazibuko finds for us, as he ought to.' *Idiot again! If the decision is to walk, then walk. That was a bloody invitation. What are you doing?*

'Really! Yeah, that would be wicked. I'd love to…when would suit?'

Oh fuck! That's done it. Anton cornered by a groupie. A black groupie! This is going to end in tears. But I heard myself continuing.

'Can I buy you a cup of coffee? The Brasilia is just around the corner.'

'Sure, I'd like that. I've just got to catch up with someone. I'll meet you outside.'

She smiled and turned to go. Tiny as her body was, it had all the sensual motion of a tall, willowy model. Smooth. Yet she looked somehow strong and wiry beneath the elegance. Tight. An athlete? Maybe.

She pushed open the low swing gate to the public gallery and walked towards the exit. What a perfect arse! At the door she turned and smiled. She saw that I was still looking at her. I saw that she saw… she knew… we both knew.

The Brasilia was an anachronism. That sort of inner-city coffee and toasted sandwich emporium, with its *Formica* tables and dated cruets was a thing of the past. But the Brasilia seemed to have taken the drastic changes to Jo'burg's central business district, from 1970s haute shopping precinct to today's cell phone-snatching, mugger-ridden informal street market, in its stride.

It was still unchanged, selling the same old tasteless cappuccinos and greasy toasted ham and tomato, and continued to be faithfully supported by the lawyers and ancillaries from the Supreme Court opposite.

I found her waiting near the Brasilia, after I managed to extricate myself from the scrum of journalists, smaller than usual due to the untimely recess. I fielded the questions about the day's events with a wordy version of 'No comment!' and made my getaway.

Thankfully, the demonstrators too were almost absent. They had also been taken unawares by the mid-morning adjournment. I took her elbow to steer her through the traffic, as we crossed to the café, and found a table.

To say that we clicked would be an understatement. She clearly admired my work and seemed to know an embarrassing amount of detail about my cases. I drank my espresso in a cloud of infatuation. This beautiful, desirable girl was hanging on my every word. Yes, we did talk about The State vs Nxumalo, but most of me was somewhere else, worrying myself with the same vicious circle, searching for a way out.

Each cycle ended with my mother's voice. 'If you or Willem or, God forbid, Anton could ever do such a thing, I would die!'

But then, I would catch Kelly's eye as she made some witty, erudite comment in her quirky south London accent, the pink tongue, white teeth, luscious lips… and the circle commenced anew.

Her cell phone rang. She answered it. It was the office. She had to go.

'Sorry I have to rush off like this! Thanks so much for taking the time.' Her wondrous eyes mimed: 'Well, what's next?'

I knew I shouldn't. 'Got a cell number? I could call you. We didn't really cover any of the technical aspects.'

'Cell? Oh yeah, mobile. Keep forgetting, sorry. Here, I'll write it down. 'Fraid I don't have a card.'

She opened her bag and scribbled on a day-glo yellow *Post-it* message pad.

'There you go.' She tore off the page and handed it to me. 'I'd really appreciate it. Cheers.'

I was alone in the noisy coffee bar. In my hand, a brilliant yellow square, with neat, italic script; *Kelebonye Modise,* and a cell number. I put it in my pocket, took up my things, and headed for the door.

Eight

The lunchtime traffic was heavy and the usual inner-city chaos reigned supreme. I did my best to thread the Audi through unpredictable minibus taxis and heavy trucks, each observing a different set of rules amid throngs of pedestrians. Downtown Jo'burg had become a real African city. Welcome the Third World! I headed for home, to the northern suburbs, to more familiar, manicured, orderly streets.

The one o'clock news on the car radio headlined with the Mazibuko hijack murder. There were no more details except that the attack had apparently taken place in the driveway of their Rivonia home. *That's less than two kilometres from my place!*

The next story was of a breakthrough arrest in the serial murder case that had been getting a lot of headlines lately. Some sick individual had been torturing and mutilating seemingly random male victims, and then murdering them.

The 'Castration Murders' they were called. No two cases were alike, except in their end result - a dead man with no testicles or penis attached. The method was different in each instance. The killer seemed to delight in devising a different technique for each victim.

And the police now finally had a suspect in custody.

I had been following the story extremely closely, both because of my professional interest, and also because the detective in charge of the investigation was a good friend from my university days. Christo and I had discussed the case often. In fact, in many ways, I had become Christo's unofficial collaborator, his personal sounding board for new ideas and theories.

Also, I had to admit that I was not entirely immune to the sensational characteristic of the murders. My association with the investigation went back more than two years - I had been staying with Christo in Cape Town when the first body was found, and had been in on the early hypotheses that guided the initial futile search for the twisted, perverted killer.

When more murders occurred, the investigation had taken on a new appearance, and the manhunt became nationwide. What was undeniable was that the murderer was determined to eke out the maximum pain and suffering from each of his victims.

What was baffling was that the victims all suffered their pain and death alone: the killer would construct an elaborate apparatus, almost like one of Heath Robinson's mythical contraptions, set the mechanism in motion, and depart. He never stayed to observe his handiwork, never actually watched his victim suffer and die.

The physical evidence that had been garnered from the murder scenes was paltry, to say the least. Whoever this guy was, he was good. Forensics had been having a torrid time. Hours and hours of backbreaking crime scene searches had revealed practically nothing.

The murderer seemed never to put a foot wrong, never to make the slightest slip-up, never to shed even a hair off his head to gratify the guys from the lab. They had a few shoeprints, a few tyre tracks, the odd bit of circumstantial evidence that could just as easily be leading them away from the real killer as towards him.

The investigation was relying on a few very particular pointers. The physical circumstances of the crime scenes, the way each of the victims had been silently overpowered and conveyed to the execution site, the size of the shoeprint - all these pointed to a very strong, powerfully-built man.

There was no indication of his race, his age or any other elementary parameters. The police psychology unit had profiled a killer who was probably gay - very likely a gay who was still deep in the closet - though they couldn't say for sure.

Whatever was driving him was very precise and very specific: his victims all had to experience slow, deliberate emasculation before they died. The psychologists said that the murderer was likely to have a fixation about mutilation. Maybe self-mutilation.

So, the police had been looking for a big guy of indeterminate ethnicity with maybe a predilection for studs, earrings and tattoos. Maybe. Not a lot to go on.

I put the cell phone into the hands-free rack and punched Christo's number. The ringing phone displaced the news through the car speakers.

'*Ja Poepol!* Did you hear the great news?' Christo sounded celebratory.

'Arsehole yourself!' I teased back. 'Howzit *Bra*? Well done! You think it's him?'

'Blerrie hope so, Anton. This case has taken so much out of me, man! I need a fokken break!'

'But is it the guy?'

'*Ja*, Anton, I think we've got the bastard!'

'*Goedgedaan*! Well done, Chris!' There were phones ringing in the background.

'Hey cheers, Anton. Got to go, man. Catch you later.'

'Cheers, Christo.' I hadn't the chance to tell him about the hijack.

The news on the radio returned. '…and police have so far made no arrest in the Malmesbury baby-rape investigation, though Western Cape Police spokesperson, Captain Hester van Biljon, announced at a press conference this morning that the police are following a strong lead and that an arrest is expected soon.

'The investigating officer have issued a identikit of the wanted suspect. Age about twenty-two, he are about one-comma-seven-five metres tall and have a shaved head, and are of light complexion.

'He also have a rope tattooed around his neck, with the words "born to hang" as well.

'Members of the public is requested to contact their nearest police station if they has any information about the suspect. In the meantime the seven-month-old victim remain on a critical condition in hospital.

'Captain van Biljon, spokesperson for the Western Cape police, ending that report. Now the business news: the rand fell sharply against the major currencies in early trade…'

Cry the beloved country, indeed!

Bang! She was back! Suddenly, right at the forefront of my consciousness, gorgeous and desirable and maybe within reach and, *oh fuck*, what would my old folks say? My heart missed a beat as I recalled the bright yellow square in my pocket.

Tyres squealed and a hooter blared. A black BMW had missed the Audi by inches. Someone shouted obscenities, and I heard the words 'fucking stupid white man!' I had gone through a red light.

Twenty-five minutes later the yellow square was on my kitchen table. It had lost none of its intensity, and admonished me as I moved around sorting out some lunch.

Esther was nowhere to be seen. I never usually came home at this time of day, so she'd probably taken advantage and was having a nap or something. The dogs were happy to see me, even if the domestic help had gone AWOL.

But the bit of paper wouldn't let go of me. What was I thinking? There was no way I could start a relationship with her. I had never been able to conduct a secretive, private affair. If I fall for a woman, that's it. I can only function in an all-in, committed, transparently public relationship.

There is no way I could get it on with her and not eventually have to take her to Zeerust. I couldn't bear the thought of the old people finding out through the gossip grapevine. I could just picture it: some well-meaning *Oom* Hennie or cousin Marikie meeting my parents at a church braai and asking with feigned innocent curiosity, 'What's this now with Anton and a kaffir *meid*?'

The fact that I totally opposed their view from an ideological perspective did not diminish the fact that I strove to be a loving and dutiful son, who tried his best not to hurt his parents.

The marriage to Hannah had been bad enough for them. 'Why does your son need to seek out a damned Jew for a wife? A nice, God-fearing, wholesome, Christian, Afrikaner maiden not good enough for him, heh? And what's going to happen with the children?'

The divorce, though it must have been almost as much of a relief for them as it had been for me, also rocked their steady, pious, rural lives. *'Could have told you, Dominie. The Lord didn't bless their marriage. Those Jews should stick to their own nation. And now what's going to happen with the children?'*

They were both in their late seventies now. They were just too old to change. Pappie had never really been a racist. He was a compassionate, if paternalistic, loving human being. But he had nevertheless functioned within the system all those years, even if he had taken some criticism for being too soft on 'them'.

Their workers always said that he was much respected in their community. But Mammie was just a dyed in the wool Afrikaner, and while she probably didn't hate black people, she sure as hell didn't love them.

In her opinion, and she had few political opinions, *apartheid* was the right thing, because it sought to keep the races apart, just as God had created them apart. She would have no means of understanding, no frame of reference. She *would* have a stroke.

The day-glo caught me again as I went back to the kitchen to refill my Coke. I went to open the fridge, and then it suddenly struck me. It must have been the postcard on the fridge door that set the ball rolling. By the time I had dropped a couple of ice cubes into the glass, the plan was fully fleshed out, all the details were in place.

Mauritius! I'll take her to Mauritius! That way I could safely find out whether this mad attraction was real or just cunt-struck, *poesbedonnerd* lunacy.

If it was just a heady mix of forbidden fruit and unsatisfied lust after years of celibacy, we could go to Mauritius, fuck ourselves stupid, acknowledge our incompatibility, and come home. No harm done! No one need ever know. I wouldn't tell any friends. No need to tell my sister, Antjie. Life could just go on as before.

If, on the other hand, there was something serious, and we came back from Mauritius deeply in love, well then I would just have to figure a way to tell my parents. But this would give me the chance to find out. Incognito, as it were.

I had nothing on my desk except the Nxumalo case, and that was now postponed for ten whole days! The office wouldn't need me. Anyway, I hadn't had a break for months, probably the best part of a year. Kelly had been at the trial every day, so presumably she had planned to continue being there. Would I be hoping for too much if she also happened to find herself with an unexpected free week on her hands?

I was excited. This was a good plan. Where to start? Phone her? Phone the travel agent? Phone the office? Confide in someone? Stop and think? Have a cigarette?

I sat on the couch and smoked. Probably call her first. None of the other calls made any sense if she said no. I got up to fetch the damned yellow square and sat down again.

But what about sex? Safe sex? In this day and age you can't just find someone new and go right ahead and have a bonk. Not having been an active participant for the last few years didn't stop me from knowing that sex could now mean death and that bedroom politics had changed irrevocably from what they were in my day.

And I couldn't deny that I had always felt, as many white South Africans seem to, that the whole AIDS thing was a black thing. Or a gay thing. Somehow it didn't seem to feature in my circles. And what if I were to suggest a condom? It's a bit like saying 'you black girls are filthy. Could catch something evil off you'.

How do people get around the implicit insult of suggesting using a condom? And what if I didn't mention a condom? Would she? If she did would she be saying 'Protect yourself, baby, you've got no way of knowing the places I've been.'

Or, would she be saying, 'I don't trust *you* and the places *you've* been'? How do young people these days handle the dilemma? I lit another cigarette and looked at the square of paper.

I had already made up my mind to cross the rickety bridge of telling my parents if, and when, I got to it. That seemed to set a precedent. We'd just have to cross the condom bridge if, and when we came to it, too. *Anyway, she may be black, but she's English. Not much AIDS over there.* I mentally kicked myself for the political incorrectness of my line of thinking. HIV is a human problem. End of story!

The Coke wasn't hitting the spot, so I got up and fetched a beer. I never usually drink alcohol during the day. *What the hell, I'm on bloody holiday,* I thought. I went outside on to the stoep, and lit another smoke. Wow, I was stoked up! I tried some deep, slow breaths to settle myself, took a good swig, and dialled the number, only to be connected with a disembodied computerised voice.

'You have reached the voice mailbox of... *Kelebonye*,' - oh, that voice! The computer voice continued, '...Please leave a message after the tone. After recording your message, you can press the hatch key for further options or you can just hang up.'

Just hang up! Now!

'Speak slowly and clearly after the tone... BEEEEP.' *Hang up, you fool!*

'Hi, Kelly, this is Anton. I just wanted... I mean Anton Venter, from court this morning...' *Why didn't I hang up while I had the chance?* 'I was just wondering... er... I just wanted to... er, I mean... don't worry, I'll call later.' *Cut!*

I was sweating. My heart rate was in the two hundreds. It was like being sixteen again and phoning Magdalena van Wyk to ask her to the high school matric dance. *What an ass!*

Here I was, at a not so well preserved forty-two, having nerves about phoning a girl! Anyway, it's probably a blessing. This hare-brained Mauritius scheme is way out of line. Behaving like some James Bond playboy.

The thoughts somersaulted around as if in a tumble-dryer. Maybe I could just phone her later and say I called to tell her I was sorry, I'd be out of town for the next few days, and we will have to postpone the continuation of our discussion on the trial. That would let me off the hook.

She's probably got AIDS, anyway. And Mammie would have a stroke.

Gradually, I calmed down and returned to my customary, rational state. Of course it was a ridiculous, off-the-wall idea. Anyway, what if I was misreading the signals? Nothing she had said or done overtly suggested anything other than an interest in the legal aspects of women and abuse, coloured with a bit of misplaced admiration. Professional admiration.

I was confusing her respect for my legal reputation with romantic intent. I was sure to find that out as soon as I made any sort of move on her. *Stupid randy old bastard! She's young enough to be my fucking daughter. 'Piss off, Granddad! You've got to be joking! Dirty old sod!' Or, something like that. That's what she'll say! What the hell, it was fun for a few minutes*. I had been quite carried away!

The cell phone rang. I looked at the screen. It was her. The tachycardia instantly returned. I took a long, slow swallow of beer.

'Hello?'

'Hiya, Anton! You awright? Got your message.' The voice was cool and confident, totally at ease. 'Sorry, I must have been on the line when you rang.'

'Thanks for phoning back, Kelly.' *Take the plunge.* 'I just had a thought. You know the case has been put off for more than a week?'

'Uh-huh.'

'Well, I feel I could do with a break. You see, the postponement took me totally by surprise. For the first time in ages I don't have anything else on my desk at the moment, so I was thinking of getting out of town for a couple of days.' *Phew,* I got through that all right. I still had an out: sorry, I won't be able to discuss the case with you…

'And…?' Her tone was difficult to fathom. Was that an 'And what the fuck has that got to do with me?' or an 'And you were asking what I'm doing for the next few days?'?

I continued to plunge.

'I was wondering if you, like me, were at a loose end with the trial on hold and all… I mean if you are also free for a few days you might want a break from sunny, sinful Jo'burg. You know…the crime capital of the world, and all that. I was wondering if you would like to come with me.'

There was silence at the other end. Bloody idiot! I thought. You've blown it. Here comes the 'Fuck off, you dirty old...'

'Where to?'

'What?'

'As in out of town to where?'

'Oh, I don't know. Mauritius, maybe. I was thinking Mauritius. Maybe...'

'Fuckin' 'ell!'

'What?'

'You asking me to go to Mauritius with you?' There was incredulity in the voice. I grimaced at my rising embarrassment and discomfiture. *Blown it, you old fool!*

'When?'

'Huh?'

'I said, when. When do you want us to go?' My heart leapt. Us!

'Dunno, I haven't checked the flights. Sort of a spur-of-the-moment kind of idea. The way I'm feeling right now, I wanted to be on the next flight.' I didn't say *I wanted us to be on the next flight,* but I had wanted to. 'Let me phone my travel agent and see what I can find out. Can I call you back in five?'

'I haven't said I'll come.' There was an uncomfortable silence. 'But phone me.' The line went dead.

My first reaction was relief. I had done it! I had actually propositioned a stunning woman, a girl probably half my age, and got away with it! *I will phone you, lady!*

Jessica, at Travelexec, was her usual breezy self. 'Oh hi, Mr Venter. Howzit? Good, no fine. Mauritius? Today! Let me see… South African Airways to Kuala Lumpur, eighteen-forty, that's twenty-to-seven this evening… just let me check that it does call at Mauritius… yes, Mr Venter, one business class return? Should I book it to the firm as usual? Have you got an order number for me?'

'No, Jessica, make it two economy returns, and I'll give you my personal credit card number.'

''Right you are then, Mr Venter, two economy returns, Venter, A Mister. And the other party?'

'Oh yes, hang on.' The yellow paper, where the hell is it? Panic. Okay.

'Modise, K Miss. That's M-O-D-I-S-E.'

Slight hesitation. When she continued there was a new tone to her voice. 'Right you are then, Mr Venter. I'll have the tickets ready for you at our customer service counter at Jo'burg International. And your card details please.'

I told her.

'Thank you for doing business with Travelexec, Mr Venter. Have a good day! Bye for now! Thank you.'

Despite Jessica's poorly disguised distaste of my choice of travel companion, my confidence was growing. I dialled Kelly's number.

'Hi, Anton.'

'We have to be at the airport in just over two hours.' I was flowing now, not planning to miss a beat, and hoping she wouldn't interrupt. 'Where can I pick you up?'

'What time is the flight?'

'Six-forty.'

'I'll meet you at departures by five. What's the flight number?'

I told her.

'I'll see you then, then.' She was gone.

Nine

Before leaving for the airport, I phoned Abigail, my secretary, to tell her I would be out of town for a few days, and to ask her to take messages, unless it was very urgent, and then she could give them my cell number. Solly was in Botswana doing an appeal, so there was no point in phoning him.

From the moment I put the phone down, things started to go wrong. Esther was not having a nap, was not in her annexe, and was nowhere to be found. I needed to tell her I would be away, and give her some instructions and some cash to ensure that there would be enough dog food.

I packed and waited for her, and was in the process of composing an angry note for her, when she finally arrived back from visiting someone in the neighbourhood. Quite unreasonably, I gave her hell for not being there when I needed her, and then got ready to leave. My excitement was showing.

In quintessential fashion, I forgot to phone to say goodbye to the girls. I remembered as I merged into the heavy evening traffic on to the freeway, but delayed until the end of the track that was playing on the radio: *Melodi* by Matlhatini and the Mahotela Queens, probably the archetypical *mbaqanga* song - the greatest of all time. Definitely one of my *Desert Island Discs*.

When it ended, I dialled Hannah's home number with the usual dread. These calls never went well, even after six years. Rachel, the younger at nine, was the one who answered.

'Hello, sweetheart... how's school?'

'Hi, Dad. We've got half term. We only go back next Wednesday.'

'That's great! What do you plan to do?'

'Is that Dad?' I could hear Margot, the twelve-year-old, in the background. 'Remind him about Sun City.'

Sun City?

Then, Margot was on the line. 'Daddy, when are we leaving for Sun City? Can we leave tomorrow? Can you finish work early?'

'Sun City?' I was blank.

'Remember, Daddy, you said next half term you would take us to Sun City. Remember?'

'Yes, darling, now that you mention it… But why didn't you remind me. I didn't remember it was half term! I've got to go away this weekend.'

'Oh, Daddy, you promised!' There was rising emotion on the line. Rachel heard that we weren't going and started to cry.

'You promised. You promised, Daddy, you promised!'

'Sorry, my girls. We never confirmed Sun City. You should have reminded me. Something came up quite suddenly.'

'What came up?' It was Hannah. The voice was ice. 'I'm sick and tired of you, Anton. Every time you promise the kids something, you forget, or something "comes up". It's just not bloody good enough. What's come up that's more important than your children?' I hated the way she said 'bloody'. More like 'bladdie'.

'Well, er…' The whole thing, the traffic, the trial, the hijack, the crazy romantic getaway, the forgotten half term, everything was suddenly too much for me. All at once, I felt very tired.

'It's a woman, isn't it?' *Where did that come from?* 'Well… isn't it?'

'Look, Hannah, I'm sorry I forgot the half-term arrangement. The girls should have reminded me last weekend when they were here.'

'*Last* weekend? They were with me last weekend. You had them the weekend *before* last! *This* weekend is *your* weekend with the kids. Starting tomorrow! Can't you even bladdie count? Don't you have a bladdie calendar?'

'My God, Hannah, I'm sorry! I'll make it up to them. I promise. It's just… I've been so busy.'

'Anton, your promises are worse than useless. Where is it that you suddenly have to go that's more important than your children?'

I hesitated. Lying to Hannah was a useless enterprise. She had always had a way of getting the truth out of me, or confronting me with it later. But I tried, at least in part.

'I've got to pop over to Mauritius. It may take a few days.'

'Why Mauritius? Doesn't sound like work to me. It's a woman, isn't it! Tell me! Admit it, Anton! It's a woman, isn't it!'

'I've got to see a potential witness for one of my cases,' I lied. Then I slipped back on to the firmer ground of half-truth. 'Yes, I probably will take a bit of a break while I'm there.' It felt better, telling a little truth. I lied on, 'but the trip is essentially for work.'

'What nonsense, Anton. It's a woman! I can always phone your secretary and confirm if it's work!' She raised her voice for the children's benefit. 'Girls, forget about Sun City, your father has got a dirty weekend planned with some or other floozy. A peroxide-blonde Goy slut, no doubt. He can take her to Mauritius but he can't be bothered to remember that he has children.'

Hannah was very dark and thought she had too much hair. It was always blonde Goyim I was supposed to be spending my time with, instead of the girls. More specifically, it was Christian Afrikaner blonde Goyim with minimal body hair. Hair was a big thing with Hannah.

'And another thing. The bladdie maintenance cheque hasn't come through yet, Anton. I don't have to remind you again that the agreement is "on or before the seventh" of each month. Bladdie cheapskate! Every other bladdie advocate in town seems to be able to make real money, but no, not you, you've got to take all those bleeding heart legal aid lost causes.

'You're always on the bladdie TV, the damn Press makes you look like some bladdie saviour of the world! Tell them you can't even pay for the upkeep of your own kids! You make me bladdie sick.' She was shouting now. 'Go to bladdie Mauritius with your slut. The children don't want you, Anton. They don't need you.'

The radio took over again. This time it was some tuneless R&B crap that sounded more like three singers independently practising their scales in different keys at dissimilar tempos than real music. I punched the button for the next channel. Supertramp: *The Logical Song*! More essential desert island stuff! This was going to be a good day after all!

The traffic on the airport freeway was a nightmare, and I was now well behind schedule. Supertramp reached the 'Take it, take it, take it, yeah!' and the incredible sax solo. I decided on impulse to take the off-ramp into Kempton Park and to zigzag my way to the airport that way.

I tried to promise myself to do better as a dad. I managed to keep all my other appointments, thanks to an electronic organiser and an excellent, if shared, secretary.

I had always balked at logging my parenting weekends on to the organiser, thereby somehow downgrading my paternal commitments to mere business appointments, with a reminder set fifteen minutes before. But maybe it was the only way I could ameliorate my adherence to the 'alternate weekends' clause in the custody settlement.

Kelly was at departures, just as she said she would be. I barely made it by five, and she was there waiting for me. I found her at the 'Passengers Only Beyond this Point' security barrier where one has to show a ticket before one can proceed to the check-in counters.

She was dressed in wonderfully tight, faded jeans, a T-shirt and sandals. An ostrich eggshell necklace went beautifully with the dark skin of her throat. She had very little luggage.

It took me till after we had checked in to relax and realise that I had no more responsibilities, and that the conveyor of the airport system could take over and make the decisions for me. We settled down in the designated corner of the only bar with a smoking section. I got us a couple of beers, and we could sit down for the thirty-minute wait to board the flight.

I could hardly believe what I had done. Here I was, single and sex-starved, in the apparently willing company of the most desirable woman imaginable, off on an open-ended, lust-filled adventure. We hadn't even discussed a possible return date yet. She seemed totally at ease with the whole situation.

'So, tell me about Kelly.'

''Kin' 'ell! Where to start?' She didn't seem to mean to start.

'You English? British, I mean?'

'Sort of. I've got dual citizenship. UK and South African.'
Sahffafrican.

I nodded at the passport on the table. 'I see you're a South African today.'

'Yeah. Gissa a fag…Ta!'

'Sorry, I didn't realise you smoked.' I leant forward to give her a light.

'Don't really. I'm an occasional smoker, I suppose.'

'Me too: *any occasion*.' Schoolboy humour. 'Age? I'd hazard a guess in the twenty-five region.'

'Twenty-five! You must be fuckin' joking! I'll be thirty-one in a couple of weeks.'

I was aghast! She didn't look thirty. For that matter, she didn't even look twenty-five. In fact, put her in a high school uniform and she wouldn't stand out. I had been more inclined to say twenty-two but was trying to cover for what I perceived to be cradle snatching. Thirty-one sounded much better already. Only an eleven-year gap!

'You're forty-two.'

'How did you know? You're spot on. Shit, I thought I looked more like fifty-two! The cares of life!'

'I'm pretty intuitive. It's a female thing. You wouldn't understand.'

'I'm sure I don't. I'll just put it down to a damned good guess. Lucky.'

'Don't be a wally!' Her chuckle was bewitching. 'I looked in your fuckin' passport while you were getting the drinks!'

My cell phone was a camera phone - not the latest model, but nevertheless an entertaining plaything. I'd had it only a few weeks, and had hardly used the camera facility yet.

I was in the process of taking a couple of shots of her smiling shyly at me when the phone burst into life, the buzz of the vibration alert almost knocking it out of my hands. It was Christo.

'Excuse me a minute.' She smiled permission.

'Howzit *Blikpiel*?'

'Tin cock, yourself! Hey, Anton man. Sorry I cut you off at lunchtime. The office was a blerrie zoo!'

'That's okay, Chris.'

'Hey man, I hear your judge's wife got killed. Shit story, hey?'

'Yeah, I was about to tell you when you dropped the phone on me. *Ja*, your typical suburban hijack. The guys panic, and the poor old woman gets shot. I'm just guessing though. Haven't heard any details.'

'No, I hear it was something like that. *Ag* man, there are twenty hijacks like that in Gauteng every blerrie day. It's just when you know the victim personally.'

'Brings it home, hey!'

'What pisses me off is that it's totally blerrie unnecessary.'

'What do you mean?'

'Man, it's the fokken insurance companies. Before they started insisting on immobilisers on all vehicles, the guys would just steal the blerrie thing with a bent piece of wire. They didn't need to have you or your wife and kids fokken sitting in the car.

'Now, since the introduction of these blerrie immobilisers, the only way to steal it is with a gun so they can get hold of the remote. That's why nowadays they have to kill you to get your car. In the old days, they just stole the blerrie thing while you were safely somewhere else… asleep in your bed, or wherever.'

'I hadn't thought of it like that.' Food for thought. 'So what's new with your suspect? Going alright?'

'*Ja*, we're just waiting for DNA results to confirm, you know. Should be in a couple of days. We'll get an order to hold him until then.'

'DNA? Did you guys find any stuff on the bodies? At the crime scenes? I thought you said forensics hadn't found anything. I remember you saying that whoever he was, the guy was a pro.'

Kelly was looking straight at me with her enormous, stunning, eyes. I smiled a 'Sorry, it's work, won't be long' smile. She smiled back. 'Take your time.'

'No, well apparently they did get a tiny bit of skin from under one of the corpse's fingernails. That was more than a year back. Lucky enough we kept it. At the time it was too small to test, but the forensic lab's just upgraded to this new DNA process. The new equipment is so sensitive it can get a profile from the minutest blerrie sample. Latest technology from America.'

'*Ja* well, Chris, hope the results confirm that you've got the right guy in the cells, then you can take a holiday!'

'No, it's the blerrie guy all right. Fits all the profiles: small-time cocaine and ecstasy dealer, and gay porn movie actor from Cape Town. You know, part-time model, hairdresser, occasional male prostitute; that sort of thing.

'Name of Sylvester Cupido. Coloured. Tattoos and piercings all over his body. Been done for aggravated assault with intent, in the early nineties for biting off some other *moffie's* schlong during a drugged-out homo orgy. Got five years. I'm sure it's the guy. Some sort of sick weirdo who gets his kicks from torturing guys and castrating them. Cuts off their fokken *piels* too.'

'You forget you've told me all that before. Besides, you're forgetting you took me to an autopsy! Didn't you?'

'*Ag ja*, man… Sorry! I suppose I'm a bit fokken excited! How's the "State versus Nxumalo" going? Apart from the judge's wife being murdered, I mean. Any idea whether you're going to win? You going to get her off? What are the chances?'

'Not bad. I think the judge will come our way. He's got the right background, you know, human rights and all that.'

'*Ja*, you blerrie ANC guys, all hugger-mugger together! Happy families, hey!'

'Fuck off, jealousy will get you nowhere!'

'Jou poes!'

I lowered my voice slightly. 'Fucking cunt yourself!'

'Hey, Anton, where are you? I'm just getting out of the office. I could blerrie murder a couple of cold ones! Can we meet at O'Hagans? I'll buy you supper. I could fill you in with the details?'

'Sorry, Chris. No can do. I'm at Jo'burg International. Got to catch a flight. Give me a call when you get your DNA results. Cheers, Boet.'

I ended the call quickly before Christo could ask where I was off to, and switched off the cell phone.

'Sorry, that was a policeman friend of mine. Work stuff.'

'The little I overheard sounded a bit like my work, too. What's it about? A rape? Murder? I heard you say something about forensics and DNA.'

'No, not a rape. It's this gay serial murder thing that's been in the news. You must have heard about it. You know; the castration murders?'

'Er… oh yeah, that!' She appeared to have heard something about it. 'You say your mate's on the case?'

'Detective Inspector Christo Januarie. *Ja*, he's been heading the investigating team. They seem to have made a breakthrough. Got a suspect in custody. Apparently, they've found some of the murderer's DNA on one of the victims. They're just waiting for the results.'

Her expression was strange. Ugly, even. She looked away. In a fidgety, unconscious way, she rubbed the scar on her neck with her fingers. Well, I thought if you work for an NGO involved with violence and abuse you're bound to have had experiences that hurt. Maybe something awakened a memory.

'Hey, we're boarding,' she said.

I looked at the monitor. A gate number was flashing.

As we left the bar I felt a hand on my elbow. I turned.

'Hello, Anton my boy!' An unmistakable rich, cultured voice - a well-educated Afrikaner, with impeccable English. 'Long time no see!' It was Judge van Jaarsveldt. 'Where are you off to?'

'Oh hello, Judge. Yes, off to Mauritius for a few days. And you?'

At that moment Mr Justice Etienne van Jaarsveldt became aware that Kelly had stopped and turned towards me, and was waiting for me. That we were together. His face assumed an expression of profound distaste. Like someone had smeared shit in his nostrils.

'Er… Kelly Modise… Mr Justice van Jaarsveldt.' I ventured a stammered introduction.

Van Jaarsveldt ignored her extended hand. He looked at me with his old mouth twisted in disgust, turned and stalked away.

I was outraged. I wanted to go after him and tell him to fuck himself. Kelly looked at me and winked. She didn't seem flustered at all.

'Getting a taste of the Old South Africa, are we, Mr Venter? Some of us live through it every fuckin' day.'

Cry, the beloved country.

* * * * *

On the plane, I gradually regained my cool. I had a double whisky and soda in my hand. The sun had set and the twilight outside the window was sublime. Next to me, in the window seat, was the most extraordinary little woman, smiling, joking, flirting.

97

She had a G and T 'wiff ice an' a slice' in one hand, and had taken my free hand in the other. She seemed to have accepted her role as my female companion without declaration or ceremony. It was as if the looks exchanged in the courtroom and a cup of coffee, combined with my Mauritius invitation and her acceptance, were sufficient cause.

Her body language was open and accepting. Her eyes betrayed no restraint, no hint that this was a provisional acquiescence; that she was still weighing me up. Our conversation was spontaneous, whether we touched on abstractions, or trivia.

Her witty, profane, incisive discourse went straight to the point, and she seemed to catch the drift of what I was saying before I finished saying it. We were getting on. Well!

'Tell me, isn't Modise a Tswana name? Are you a Tswana?'

'Jesus! You fuckin' Dutchmen could never get it right! Yes, Modise is a *Se*tswana name. Yes, I am a *Mo*tswana.' She was almost shouting. 'My relatives are *Ba*tswana! Not fuckin' Tswanas!'

I was taken aback until I saw the facetiousness in her eyes. 'And *you*, Anton Venter, should know better!'

'Why me? Why me in particular?'

'Because you come from a Setswana-speaking area! By rights, you should be fluent. If it wasn't for the stupid history of this fuckin' country!'

I was aghast. 'What Tswana… Sorry, *Se*-tswana area do I bloody come from?'

'Madikwe. Your ancestors couldn't be bothered to pronounce it correctly and called it "Marico". You know, Kwa-Bahurutse… Zeerust.'

'How the hell do you know I come from Zeerust?' Now I was the one raising my voice. 'Anyway, I don't. My parents live there. I grew up all over the place, mostly in the Cape and in Pretoria. How the fuck do you know my old folks stay in Zeerust?'

She put down her glass, and took my face in both her hands. Her eyes were unblinking.

'Do you think I'm fuckin' stupid, or somethin'? You've told me nothing about yourself. I mean, would I be here, in this plane, on my way to Mauritius with you, if I hadn't done some research? Would I be holding your hand if I thought there was a Mrs Venter at home waiting for you? Or do you think I habitually sit in courtrooms flirting with any old, good-looking advocate, brilliant or not? What kind of girl do you think I am?'

With that she pulled me towards her and kissed me… really kissed me.

Most of the passengers were bound for Kuala Lumpur, and only a few disembarked at Mauritius. It was well after midnight when we made our way through an almost empty Plaisance Airport, and found a taxi. I suggested that we would just get to a hotel, any hotel on the northern coast, and then look for a villa or a studio apartment in the morning.

No sooner were we in the taxi than Kelly complained of feeling ill.

'Sick as a fuckin' parrot. Sorry, mate.'

She asked the driver in seemingly flawless French, to stop so that she could open the door and throw up into the gutter.

'Fuckin' airline food! These cramps are killing me. Can we get somewhere quickly? I'm going to have a shit very, very soon.'

Our first night in the island paradise was spent in the dingiest little hotel in the industrial town of Curepipe. It was the sort of hotel frequented by Indian travelling sewing machine salesmen on a shoestring budget. But it had a bathroom. And a bed. Two separate beds actually, but it made no difference. Kelly was completely out of it, and we finally fell asleep just before dawn.

When I awoke she was already washed and dressed. She looked as beautiful as ever and had apparently fully recovered. The holiday mood was heavy in the already hot, humid air.

Jo'burg, the trial, Hannah, and hijackings were a world away. She noticed I was awake and came to the bed and ripped the covers off me.

'C'mon, lazy bones. I think I've found us an apartment. Mont Choisy. Two minutes from the beach. Let's get there. This hotel stinks. Literally!'

I was still half-asleep. I was bemused. I had expected that I would be making all the arrangements.

'Have you been here before? Mauritius, I mean.'

'No.'

'Then, how did you know that's exactly where I was thinking of looking for a place? There, or Trou aux Biches.' I sat up. 'How did you get to find it anyway?'

'I went for a walk, and met this taxi driver. It's his brother's place. We spoke to the brother on the phone, and, well, that's it. Cheap, too.'

'You're amazing!'

'I thought we could have more fun if we didn't waste time looking for somewhere to stay. Come on. Get up!'

'Something I need to know. I'm not being silly, but I need to know.'

She looked at me enquiringly.

'There's no bloke waiting back in South Africa for you? Or in the UK for that matter?'

'Would I be here if there was?' Her look was very direct and candid. 'I'm not that sort of girl.'

Two hours later we were across the island, ensconced in our studio apartment with the deposit paid, a fridge full of beer, and snacks, bread and cheese in the little kitchen. I couldn't have found a better place myself. It was perfect, with a wide view of the sea, air-conditioning, the lot. Not only that, but it cost about half of what I had been expecting to pay.

Now, there was no obstacle to our incipient intimacy. The taxi driver, who helped with the bags and groceries, and the apartment complex caretaker had each accepted their gratuities and withdrawn. The apartment door was closed and locked in deference to the caretaker's warnings, bizarre as they appeared to us Jo'burg types, of likely thieves in the area. We were alone, and spontaneously fell into each other's arms.

We kissed passionately and clung to one another with a ferocious agitation. The difference in our stature, and the consequent mutual discomfort in the region of the neck, precipitated an expeditious and inevitable collapse on to the bed.

As we strove to accommodate each other comfortably without interrupting our embrace, our thighs intertwined and I could feel her urgency, as the pressure increased between our groins.

One of her arms, low around my back, tightened in concert with the pulsating grinding of her pubis. I slipped a hand under her T-shirt and cupped her round, bountiful breast. Her nipple was swollen with expectancy.

My fingers traced a line down her cleavage, across the flat, firm belly which fluttered lightly under my touch, and around her waist and down the back of her shorts, across her bare buttocks. Only the thin thong of her G-string interrupted my meander across the malleable flesh and lustrous, satiny skin.

As my fingers dipped further around the sonorous curves, her pelvis thrust more and more explicitly against my pulsating rigidity.

We paused for breath, and to readjust trapped limbs, and rolled slightly apart. The caresses became easier, less constrained as we lay side by side. My hand, still within her shorts, migrated around the point of her hip, and then, slowly and reverently down the junction of her thigh and *mons*.

The tiny G-string was soft and unrestrictive, and moved easily aside as my fingers explored so that, all at once, my hand was cupping the fullness of her mound and the very tips of my fingers discerned a warm wetness. The wing beats of the heavenly host wafted down on us.

We remained at that pinnacle of exploratory closeness for a mere instant. Further downward progress of my seeking hand was curbed by the tightness of her shorts. I slowly extracted it across the, for me, unfamiliar texture of her African pubic hair - memories of Eileena and the mulberry tree - and began to disengage the button of the waistband.

'Not now! Let's go for a swim. I'm aching to get into the sea.'

An hour later, I felt better. Her bubbly enthusiasm about Mauritius, the sea and the beach, as well as her continued flirtatious warmth all contrived to salve my bruised ego and strained gonads.

I couldn't help questioning though how she could be so intimate without concurring that the consummation of the electric tension between us was urgent and imperative. *Well, tonight, I suppose*, I thought. I resolved to read all the signals closely to save myself another aching letdown.

'So what else did your research about me turn up?'

She smiled guiltily. 'Not that much. You're divorced with two daughters, Margot, and Rachel, twelve and nine. Your wife lives in Honeydew and maintenance costs you a packet.

'You work in a small practice, only two partners, yourself and the senior partner, Solly Mokoena. You tend to concentrate on cases with a human rights angle. Also give a lot of free advice.' She gazed wistfully past me out over the lagoon, a look of delicious naughtiness in her eyes. Her finger traced the little scar on her neck.

'Where did you get all this?'

She ignored the question.

'You're very good-looking, rather sexy, quite famous...mmm, what else? Your wife is a total pain in the arse. Manic depressive but won't admit it.'

'*Ex*-wife!'

'Okay, ex. Anyway, you're scared of her, ex or not!'

'Fuck! Where do you get this from? I'm not bloody scared of her.'

'Apparently, you jump if she phones you,' she giggled.

'Who's been telling you all this? I bet you it's Solly. I'll have his balls on fucking toast! Slow roasted!'

Kelly laughed. 'No, not Solly. Haven't even met him.'

'Then who? Abby?' The thought of Abigail giving out my personal details horrified me. It would be completely out of character.

'Who's Abby?'

'Abigail Zwane, my secretary. Er... our secretary. I mean Solly's and mine. Was it Abby?'

She ignored the question. 'Oh yes. I also know that you are single, like. I mean you're not in a relationship.'

'I was rather hoping I wasn't. Not *not* in a relationship, I mean. Or is that jumping the gun?'

She mimed an elaborate gesture of reassurance, and leant across the beach towel and kissed me. As she pushed herself back, her retreating hand briefly pressed on my dick. With a quick squeeze through my shorts her fingers transmitted an encouraging validation.

'You may be, Anton Venter! You may well be.'

Oblivious to the promenading tourists, the large Hindi families, with mothers and grannies in their saris, wallowing cacophonously in the shallows and the vendors selling shells and straw hats, we submersed ourselves in our embraces. I was falling in love!

This time it was I who broke off the clinch and suggested a swim. But I had an ulterior motive. Our caresses continued in the relative privacy of the water. The lagoon was shallow and warm. We could touch and caress and mock-couple in weightless concealment within metres of the innocent holiday crowds around us.

We pressed and wriggled, touched and explored. I had a throbbing erection worthy of my years of abstinence. I started to calculate the chances of actually getting laid in the water in front of so many unsuspecting people.

While I was still working out the mechanics of such an enterprise, Kelly manoeuvred herself behind me, and as we sat in the chin-deep Indian Ocean, looking out to sea, she eased my penis out of my shorts and began to stroke me with purpose.

Her legs were parted and wrapped around me, as she sat behind me with her body pressed against my back. I was able to slip one hand into her tiny bikini - but as I found her clitoris she wriggled free and moved out of reach. As she did so she twisted my head around with her left hand and smothered any possible verbal retort with kisses, her right hand all the while maintaining the rhythm.

To all intents and purposes, we looked like any innocuous couple sharing a quiet moment. No one took any notice of us. Below the surface we were carrying on like a pair of heavy-petting high school kids till I shot my milky load into the sea. She continued to tenderly rub me, till she felt the last ejaculatory spasm die away. Then, she leapt off, swimming like a dolphin with her sexy butt wiggling up and down through the water. She surfaced some distance away and turned and laughed.

'Looks like you really needed that!' She launched herself backwards, arching her perfect body in a back dive and swam off. *God, she's beautiful!*

Later, we sat at a kerbside table of a small restaurant having a late lunch. I was itching to return to the question of who was her informant, but felt that would get us back on to the subject of me. We had hardly talked about her.

'Tell me more about you.'

'What?'

'Are you a lawyer? Are you married? Have you got kids? Why do you have an English accent and a South African passport? Where have you been all my life? I have not done any research, unlike some people!'

'Not married, not an attorney, no children… How do you know you're not taking an enormous risk? I could be an evil, scheming Jezebel looking to get hold of your money, for all you know!'

'Well, tell me your evil schemes, then. I'm all ears. If you're looking for money, you've come to the wrong address. If you want the money I earn, go see Hannah. If you want the money I used to have, go see Hannah. Jezebel and Hannah. What a team! Sounds sort of biblical. Makes sense.'

My tone changed, as I tried to bring her back to my original question. 'Come on. Tell me. Just start at the beginning and tell me everything.'

She was silent. After a second she averted her eyes and looked down at her fingers toying with the edging of the tablecloth.

'C'mon, Kelly. Like, where were you born? Where are your folks? Surely you can tell me that? Just start at the beginning.'

Her jaw was tight, and her fidgeting fingers betrayed her discomfort. When she raised her face her eyes were wet. I reached across the table to squeeze her hand. She squeezed back and looked at me.

'Sorry, mate! Didn't mean to… Look, I've been through some heavy shit in my life and it's not easy for me to talk about it. Okay?'

I held her hand in silence. The prawn curry arrived and broke the spell.

We had just got up from the table when she returned to the subject.

'Look, Anton, I'll tell you what. I'll try to write some things down. Maybe I'll be able to do that. That way you may get some of your questions answered.'

She was serious enough about her suggestion to steer us to the local supermarket where she bought not just one, but a handful, of school exercise books.

On the way back to the apartment I realised the obvious: Nozipo must have been the one who had been pumped for all my personal details. I even remembered the day she had been in my office for a briefing and Hannah and I had one of our regular rows over the phone.

I hadn't realised that I had 'jumped' when Abby put through the call, though. I resolved to be more careful about what personal matters were discussed in front of clients in the future, however sweet and innocent such clients may appear. I also reminded myself that women have their own networks.

Ten

Kelly and I seemed to have somehow settled our terms of engagement. The remainder of that afternoon we lazed around the apartment like an old couple who had been together for years. I lay on the bed and started on the latest John Grisham that I had bought at Jo'burg International, while Kelly sat at the little table on the balcony and busied herself over her exercise book. We each had a Phoenix at our elbow, and I had an ashtray balanced on my stomach. It was very restful. It felt very natural. I looked over at her. Yep, I was in love. Like I had never, ever been before.

My heart missed a beat when I suddenly thought of Zeerust.

Later, after dinner at a gaudy Chinese in nearby, touristy Grand Baie, where the food was totally uninspiring, we snuggled together in the back of the taxi. The beer, wine and *Remy Martins* were having their effect, and our hands began their furtive wandering. By the time we reached Mont Choisy we were steaming hot.

She surreptitiously readjusted her clothing, while I paid the cab driver, and we rushed into our apartment, kicked the door shut behind us and fell straight into a fiery embrace.

'Got to pee,' she said as she broke off and went to the bathroom. She unwound her sarong, threw off her top and stepped out of her G-string on the way to the loo. I removed my jeans and shirt and lay on the bed in rapturous anticipation.

She came out of the bathroom naked and beautiful. She knelt over me and ripped off my boxers, and traced a line of kisses down my chest, tickling me with her 'dreads'.

She moved down over my belly, and over my instantaneously responsive manhood. Then she went down on me. I twisted myself under her, pulled her down on to me and tried to reciprocate, but she squirmed out of reach, and I let it go, concentrating instead on the skilfully applied pleasure that was on offer.

I caressed her thighs and buttocks, and inevitably found my way to her very centre. She was wet under my touch. All the signals were *Go*! I disengaged myself from her lips and turned around to face her. She was panting as she kissed me and tugged me towards her.

As I was at the point of entering her, she slammed her legs shut and twisted away. It came as a total surprise.

'I can't! I'm sorry. I'm just not ready.'

'What's the matter?' For whatever reason, I felt instantly blameworthy. 'Did I do something?

'No, it's not you. Really!' She was crying, and concern and tenderness outweighed my carnal distress.

'Do you want to tell me about it?' I held her close.

There was no response. Her body trembled silently, as the sobs wracked her petite frame. I held her as tight as I could.

She was up before I was. I awoke to the sight of her, dressed only in a pair of shorts, performing the unhurried, ethereal moves of Tai Chi. I knew better than to interrupt, and I propped my head up on the pillows to watch and marvel.

It was clear she was a serious practitioner. Her wondrously supple body floated through the form, as if she were under water. When she had completed the series of moves and postures, she stood in a relaxed stance and performed some breathing exercises, followed by a two-minute meditation posture.

Only when she was through did she acknowledge my presence, and blew me a kiss. Then, she started press-ups, first on her fists, then on two fingers, followed by one-arm press-ups, also on fists and then just two fingers. She went on and on, as if there was no physical effort. I wasn't counting, but there must have been over a hundred of them, all told. She wasn't even sweating.

She came over to the bed, and sat down next to me. Her breathing was as natural as if she had been reading a book. She kissed my forehead.

'We going to the beach, or what?

'I'd love a cup of coffee first.'

In spite of the disappointment of last night I couldn't resist the two perfect breasts. I noticed for the first time that they weren't exactly perfect… the left nipple was not quite in the centre of the areola. She playfully slapped my groping hand away.

'C'mon, Casanova, enough of that! I'll get you some coffee if you get your lazy arse out of that bed!'

A minute later she opened the bathroom door and leant against the frame. I was in mid-shit, usually a very private moment for me. The little room was rich with my alimentary vapours, my face felt as if it was flushed with effort. I was sure I betrayed my self-consciousness. She appeared not to notice.

'How d'you like your eggs?' She seemed not to mind the stink.

'Nnn… cooked, if possible.' Splosh.

'Wally! How cooked?'

'As they come, thanks.' Her expression told me that she didn't mean to be trifled with. 'Okay, then! Fried? Sunny side up?'

She walked off. I had lived with Hannah for seven years, but she had never casually stood at the door watching me defecate while discussing the breakfast menu. This was all new for me. In a weird way, it felt good to have so few barriers. Sort of insinuated there was scant terrain for secrets or deceit.

'C'mon, boy, breakfast's ready.'

Half an hour later as we were doing the washing up together, I impulsively slapped Kelly on the bum. Her reaction was lightning-fast. She swung round and grabbed my hand with both of hers, and twisted it upwards.

Before I knew it I was on my knees, my face grimacing in agony at the sudden sharp pain in my wrist. The flash of what looked almost like anger left her face. She smiled, then, seeing I was really hurt, her expression showed concern

'Sorry, mate, didn't mean to hurt ya! You okay?'

I was amazed at her strength and her incredible speed. 'You almost broke my fucking arm… I was only being affectionate.'

'I know… sorry. Don't know my own strength!' She knelt in front of me and massaged the injured wrist. Our eyes met, and we kissed, passionately, embracing each other, kneeling on the kitchen floor.

Later, as we lounged on the beach, familiar, close, and conspicuously in love, we chatted blithely about anything and everything except sex. I didn't venture on to the obviously sensitive terrain of what had happened last night. Kelly, for her part, showed no sign that anything untoward had happened at all. She sat in bikini and straw hat, her notebook on her knee, pen poised.

Had we spent a long night of fervent fornication her demeanour could have been no more intimate. I couldn't help but grapple with the enigma. She was an eager, enthusiastic partner. She initiated much of the action. Last night's escalation of our intimacy to oral sex had been her doing, not mine.

She betrayed no hint, up to the final moment, that she was anything but a spirited participant. I couldn't believe that there was a deliberate, premeditated cock-teasing operation afoot. Yesterday's hand-job in the sea was hardly cock-teasing strategy.

She really appeared to be as deeply in love, and as brimful with passion, as I was. Her lovemaking seemed so fervent, so natural. She went along with every nuance of eroticism and then demurred at the point of entry. It baffled me.

For the first time since it had crossed my mind on the couch at home, I thought of HIV. It amazed me that the subject had not even entered my head these last two days and nights. Could that have something to do with it, I thought? Was she worried because we weren't attempting to have safe sex?

I found myself countering with a torrent of arguments: she would have suggested a condom if that were the problem; she could hardly be called shy! She would not have sucked my dick if she had any fears. Her tears last night had been pitiful. Surely they were genuine. The physical signs of her sexual excitation were bloody real enough!

The memory of her exquisite little pussy cupped in my hand, the remembrance of her turgid wetness, her erect clitoris and engorged labia against my finger, as she played sword-swallower with skill and eagerness was enough to make me all hot again. Pandora's box opened and exposed. I rushed for the sea.

I tried to displace my reawakening sexual arousal with hard swimming and stroked my way purposefully out into the lagoon. My wrist still hurt from this morning's rough and tumble in the kitchen and I gave up and lazily coasted instead.

As I floated in the tepid, glassy-smooth water, watching her bent diligently over her writing, I wondered what trauma it had been that hurt her so. I assumed the most likely explanation was that she must have been raped. That's hardly unlikely in South Africa. One rape every twenty-something seconds, say the statisticians. And that's only reported rapes.

And why else would she be the director of a women's anti-abuse NGO? Well, hopefully it will all come out in the text, I mused. She seemed pretty busy. I was looking forward to reading it.

I didn't have to wait long. We lunched on delicious, spicy stuffed roti from a stall and pineapple and litchis from a beach vendor. I returned to John Grisham, and she to her writing.

'Just about done. I'm going for a swim and then I think I need a long walk. Alone. Gissa fag.' I resisted the tendency to petulance. Unsuccessfully.

'Can we at least swim together?'

'Of course, you wally.'

After the swim, she very deliberately tossed the exercise book on to the beach towel.

'I'll see you back at the apartment.' A kiss, and then she leant forward and whispered in my ear.

'Love ya!'

I sat watching her incredible legs, as she walked off along the beach.

The sun was hot, and without Kelly for company, the beach lost its appeal. The blue school exercise book beckoned. I gathered up our things and walked the short distance to the apartment.

Its balcony was in shadow and the fresh air seemed much more attractive than the air-conditioned indoors, so I settled down on one of the loungers in anticipation, with Kelly's book, my smokes and a beer from the fridge. Maybe I would understand.

I flicked through the pages. The entire forty-eight page exercise book was filled with Kelly's neat, italic script. Wow! She had been busy! I hadn't anticipated this. I was expecting few paragraphs about her life from her birth up to now.

I took a sip of beer, lit a smoke and opened the book. I was touched with the 'Dear Anton' at the beginning, as if it was a letter to me personally rather than the diary or journal that I had expected.

As I read the story of her grandmother's sexual awakening under the morula tree I got the feeling that Kelly was going into much greater detail that I had planned for. It was obvious that she wanted to establish a theme that I immediately suspected was going to be repeated further into the story: a thesis that male sexuality generally expresses itself with scant regard for the concerns and needs of women, and that society fails to equip women to deal with this masculine self-centredness.

The birth of Phatsimo, Kelly's mother, suggested a change of pace in the story. Maybe I'd soon be reading about Kelly herself and the things that had hurt her so.

I fetched another cold beer and gave in to the impulse to peek over the balustrade. *Of course she wouldn't be back yet!* I chuckled to myself at my crazed obsession with this wonderful new friend and returned to the exercise book in anticipation.

The genealogy of my family is complicated by two factors. Firstly, the nuclear family and all the social clarity it creates in defining individuals and their place in the larger social grouping has been absent from my family for three generations. Secondly, the women in my line have compounded the confusion by calling one another by annoyingly bewildering nicknames.

Thus, my grandmother is known to me as 'Mama', her elder sister Mmamoratwa - my great aunt - as 'Nkoko' or 'Granny' and her younger sister Florence - my other great aunt - as 'Ausi' or 'Sister'. My own mother I call 'Mmane' or 'Auntie'. This confuses a lot of people, but it's just the way it is.

My great-grandfather Kabelo Modise married my great-grandmother, Motsei Sikwane in Rustenberg in 1942, thereby bringing together two lines of the Kgatla nation: he was from the Pilane clan, then based in the area north and west of Pretoria, and she from the Kgafela clan in Botswana. They were the last in my line to be married and to raise a family in the conventional sense.

The fathers of the subsequent generations have all, one way or another, disappeared into the night, leaving - by way of parental input - only their genetic endowment and nothing more.

Kabelo and Motsei had two sons - both of whom died in early childhood - and three daughters. My grandmother, who was later to be impregnated by the unnamed youth under the morula tree in the moonlight, was their middle daughter.

My mother, Phatsimo, was a deaf-mute. At least, she started out that way. The social ideology of her community relegated her to nothing more than an unfortunate piece of human baggage, unworthy of any attention except the barest necessities for her continued existence.

Her development was arrested and she never came out of herself. Even her mother dismissed her as worthless. Her childhood was spent on the fringes of the family. She never carried water or collected firewood with the other children, and her complete lack of any sort of education kept her from the other chores of her age group and gender. No woman ever trusted her with a toddler, and she never had the opportunity to learn to cook.

Her incapacity and the unenlightened response of her family and the community around her had contributed to her severe autism, and she existed apart, in a small, silent world of her own. She cooperated with the day-to-day requirements of her survival, readily led by the hand with which she could feed, wash and relieve herself. She spent her time in her private, silent world, ignoring those around her and in turn being totally ignored.

Even as a baby, she had been unable to vocalise at all. She had a vocabulary of grimaces and open-mouthed silent screams that conveyed variously pain, frustration, unhappiness, fear, and delightful smiles when a thing pleased her. She was capable of an involuntary whimpering hum, which appeared to have no relevance to the circumstance: she appeared to be unaware of it and the particular position of her throat muscles that occasioned it.

As she grew older however, the expressions became less noticeable, and by the time she was five she had ceased to communicate to the outside world at all.

My grandmother's second child was a boy, who was named Steven. No one ever was told who the father of this second child could be. Like the other phantom fathers in our family, he had simply been 'run over by a train', and that was that. Although my grandmother, many years after the event, personally recounted to me the story of my grandfather meeting her under the morula tree that moonlit night, she never alluded to the identity of Steven's father nor to the occasion of his conception. The family therefore secretly supposed that, whoever he was, Steven's father had managed to coerce my grandmother into everlasting silence.

It was a matter of considerable interest to the community when my grandmother's younger sister, Ausi, suggested that Phatsimo should go to the city where she could be helped. So it came about that, when she was about twelve years old, her aunt, having returned from a two-year sojourn in the city, managed to convince the family to send the girl to obtain a cure for her condition.

Neighbours were eloquent in their condemnation. No one thought it was a good idea. The girl was blighted, the Lord had made her so for His own good reasons, and meddling was not recommended. These newfangled big-city ideas were dangerous. Furthermore, Ausi had taken on a new 'town' name. Apparently she was now called Florence. This was also unpopular with the kinsfolk.

But Florence persisted, and eventually got her way. The pair duly departed after the Christmas holidays, and Phatsimo's life was to change forever.

In the city, Ausi, or Florence, had become involved with one of the very many small churches that had sprung up in the drab and dusty shantytowns and townships that surrounded the segregated suburbs and the city proper. Her particular choice was the Church of the Twelve Apostles of Zion Faith Healing Christian Fellowship Church, which consisted of the Bishop and a flock of fewer than twenty faithful followers, all but one of whom were women.

In common with many of the ladies of the congregation, she had a somewhat more than spiritual affiliation with the Bishop, of which the Bishop's wife had an inkling of suspicion, but no proof. The wife often chastised herself for harbouring such unchristian thoughts about her husband, and like good wives everywhere, preferred the blissful peace of ignorance, and did not more thoroughly investigate some of the more private prayer meetings her husband conducted with members of his flock from time to time.

The sole male in the congregation was a microcephalic fellow with the head the size of a large fist and a perpetual dribble, who had managed to inveigle himself into the role of lay-preacher and general assistant to the Bishop. He was known as Stompie. No one knew his real name.

Four features were essential, in the Bishop's thinking, to attest the august personage of his office. The first had been provided to him by Providence: a full head of white hair, and a goatee to match. Another was a black Homburg hat -"Like Churchill's!"- the third a dog collar with a purple bib, and the fourth, a black overcoat. The Homburg had been acquired long before the church had been established.

The Bishop worked in the suburbs as a 'garden boy' and one of his former employers had given him the well-used hat as a 'Christmas-box' years before. It was faded to a gunmetal-grey colour, and the ribbon had lost its sheen, but perched on the Bishop's crown it still conveyed the necessary degree of olde-worlde elegance that his rank required. The dog collar and bib were home-made: a scrap of purple satiny material and an old detachable shirt collar adapted to be worn back to front.

The black overcoat had not been that easy. The Bishop had needed to employ his imagination to convert an old khaki army-surplus greatcoat into the ecclesiastical garment his dignity demanded. He had replaced the brass buttons with black ones he had bought for the purpose. An attempt to dye the coat had failed miserably. An expensive outlay on proper black fabric dye had produced a nauseating baby-shit olive green when overlaid on the military khaki. The dye had been much too expensive and he had had to dilute it with much too much water, cancelling its effect.

He finally got round the problem. His wife worked as a labourer at a timber treatment factory. There, eucalyptus poles that were destined to carry power and telephone lines, or to be used as fencing posts, were treated in great tanks of hot steaming creosote. The good lady had managed to procure a can of it at her husband's request, and with a thorough soaking the coat had taken on a very credible black shade.

An unlooked-for by-product of this process was the smell. It permeated the compound and followed the Bishop wherever he went. He was denied access by the bus conductors and the taxi drivers, and had been forced, therefore, to wear the coat only for ceremonial occasions. But even when he went to work in the city, dressed in his everyday clothes, the sharp odour, which seemed to have impregnated his skin, clung to him and attracted odd looks from passers-by.

The Church of the Twelve Apostles of Zion Faith Healing Christian Fellowship Church met in a temple, which was also the Bishop's dwelling – a collection of mud-brick and rusted corrugated iron buildings surrounding a small bare-earth courtyard with a gaggle of grubby babies and toddlers in the care of older children, scattered about at random.

A hand-painted sign in green lettering on a flattened-out bulk peanut-butter tin nailed to a post proclaimed the church premises. The post was topped with a flag of what had once been white cloth. The sign had been painted by the Bishop himself, and in common with so many signwriting efforts by semi-literate souls, the letters got smaller and smaller towards the end as the available space ran out, so that while the words 'Church of the Twelve Apostles' were boldly scripted in letters as big as your hand, the word 'Fellowship' was so small and cramped as to be almost illegible.

The lettering of the last 'Church' was so tiny that the brush strokes were fatter than the letters, and it came out all smudged – a sort of green blob in the lower right hand corner of the sign.

It was because of this that the he had augmented the signage with a cardboard flap nailed to the same post just below the first sign, with the important-looking anagram 'C.T.A.Z.F.H.C.F.C.' in yellow lumberman's crayon.

To this place, my mother was brought. It so happened that Florence had lodgings with the Bishop's family, and Phatsimo shared a single room with her aunt and a number of the Bishop's children.

The journey from the sparsely populated fringes of the desert to the metropolis appeared to have an effect on her. As the trip progressed she became less withdrawn, looking with alert eyes from the bus at the passing vehicles on the road. She gazed with apparent comprehension at the surroundings as the mud huts of home gave way to concrete and steel.

The bustling shantytown, with its busy comings and goings and crowded squalor also seemed to create some impression. Florence noticed a glint in her eye that she had never seen since Phatsimo was born. This encouraged the aunt. Signs of hope! She added special prayers for Phatsimo's healing to her daily devotions.

On the evening of the second day after her arrival, Phatsimo was led into the Bishop's compound for the faith-healing service that was to cure her of her affliction. The women of the full congregation sat in a semi-circle on the earthen courtyard, legs straight out in front of them, backs straight, as was the custom.

After a long sermon by the Bishop, a reading by Stompie, in his high-pitched voice, all interspersed with hymns, she was led by Florence to the lectern. The Bishop stood over the frightened little girl in the open patch at the centre of the semi-circle and, as he raised his hands in supplication, his rich, resonant baritone rose and fell in theatrical cadences.

Many times he had practised this sort of thing in front of his shaving mirror, and knew too well the impression he was making on his flock. Lit from below by a couple of storm lanterns as well as from the side by one hanging from a clothes line, casting his profile into relief, he cut a dashing figure in his black coat and purple bib. His white hair shone like a halo. Even the circling moths and midges swirling around his head seemed to enhance the effect.

He had some holy water, seawater that his Madam had brought back from the coast for him, with real sea sand and a few shell fragments at the bottom of the corked Coke bottle. He opened the bottle and raised it above his head, like a Catholic priest with the chalice, and intoned a chanted consecration. Then he sprinkled a few drops in the dust as a benefaction to the ancestors and poured a few drops of the precious liquid into his palm. Into this he breathed and spoke a few final murmured incantations, and then rocking back her head with his other hand he emptied the sanctified liquor into her mouth. The last drops were massaged on to her mute throat.

The congregation leaned forward in anticipation. Phatsimo was suddenly more animated. The water was disgusting and she wanted to retch, but was too paralysed with terror. After a moment she regained some composure and her habitual shutters slammed shut, and she subsided into her silence and appeared as before. The disappointment in the congregation was palpable and the Bishop sensed it. Faith healing was a delicate business.

He had had some noteworthy successes. One particular healing had made an indelible impression on his congregation, and had been instrumental in bringing his church into being.

He had always liked the sound of his own voice and had dabbled in lay-preaching, ever eager to volunteer a prayer over a corpse at a funeral, and was sure he could make a good living as a priest. But it was only after he had contrived a healing that he had been able formally to establish the Church of the Twelve Apostles of Zion Faith Healing Christian Fellowship Church.

At that time, the Bishop had begun a liaison with a lady from Mozambique. As a recent immigrant, she was not known in the shantytown community where he lived, and one day, while lying in bed together, they hatched a plot. She would arrive at his home feigning a condition, he would 'cure' her, and he would become famous. In his mind he could visualise a great congregation and an overflowing collection basket.

So, one day the Mozambican had shuffled up to his gate. Her left arm was scrunched up under her armpit, with useless fingers dangling limply. Her left leg was clearly paralysed and she walked with obvious pain. Saliva drooled from her mouth, and her head was held at an uncomfortable angle. The Bishop's wife, deeply moved by pity, had invited her into the compound. The afflicted woman said that she had had a dream, in which her deceased grandfather had told her to seek healing from this place. There was a man here who could cure her.

The Bishop's wife had been thoroughly duped, and had played right into their hands. She called all her friends to witness the healing that was going to take place. On the appointed day, with spells, prayers, herbs and mystical signs, the Bishop had driven out the demons, and after collapsing to the ground with a cry, the crippled woman had risen up, delivered of her affliction. The incredulous witnesses became the founding congregation of the new church.

Regrettably though, over the years that followed, the church had barely grown at all, despite the Bishop's ambitions, unless, of course, one considered growth in the form of the three children he had sired with the Mozambican, and half-a-dozen more with other members of his flock.

Standing over the mute, autistic Phatsimo, the Bishop considered his options. He knew he had taken on a huge challenge, and had hoped that the otherwise normal-looking girl would react to all his mumbo-jumbo and that he would be able to claim some credit, even if it was only for a partial cure. He had hurried into acquiescing to taking on the healing of Phatsimo. His motivation had been to further his sexual activities with Florence, who he sensed was becoming less enthusiastic for his company. Helping her with her niece would score him a lot of points, and would guarantee continued favour for months, if not years, to come. But apart from the brief animation induced by the stale seawater, Phatsimo was visibly unchanged. He needed more time to contrive something that would mollify the expectant congregation.

The Bishop announced that the next stage of the healing required isolation, and he took her by the hand and led her into one of the small one-roomed buildings. He left her there, and returned outside to instruct Stompie to read a passage from the Bible, the bit about Jesus casting out the demons into the herd of swine, and to follow this with a number of hymns. He then went to his own room to collect some necessary items: methylated spirits, candles and a jar of a home-made herbal infusion. He then solemnly returned to the girl. In the bare little room, dark except for a smoky oil lamp, the Bishop placed her prone on a mat on the floor.

Stompie's high-pitched, reedy-thin voice could be heard outside as he began the lesson.

The smell of the old man's creosote-soaked coat enveloped her like a choking fog. The Bishop lit four candles, which he placed on the corners of the mat. Then he smeared some of the herbal medicine into the deaf ears, and began massaging the methylated spirits on to the mute throat.

He loosened the collar of her dress so that his massaging was less restricted, and noticed for the first time that this little girl already had the beginnings of a woman's figure. Her small breasts were a pleasing, rounded shape. All of a sudden his massaging took on a different hue.

The Bishop would never have considered himself a paedophile. He had never interfered with young girls, and although his harem had a wide age distribution, his youngest mistress had been well into her twenties when he first began with her. The thought of seeing sexual attractiveness in a child had never occurred to him, and he had never conceived of such a thing, even hypothetically.

But here he found himself in a strange and powerful position. He had her alone, in protected privacy. He knew that no one outside would dare to interrupt the faith healing. The girl herself was a deaf-mute, and her autistic state would guarantee the secrecy of the act that he felt creeping into his mind. He felt a powerful stirring in his loins, and realised that he was in the grip of an entity greater than himself.

With his mind swayed by his gonads, he continued the masquerade of his healing massage, by degrees extending the area under his hands. Her dress was an old cotton housemaid's overall, with buttons all down the front, so he was able to expose her body without changing her prone position.

His massage took his hands down her belly and he removed her underclothes, amazed that a girl of such slight stature already had pubic hair. He looked at her in the candlelight, and wondered why it was that he found her so desirable. His own taste in women tended towards the buxom.

He had a weakness for heavy thighs and well-developed buttocks, and could not for the life of him understand what white men saw in the bony, gaunt models he had seen paraded in magazines and on billboards. But here he found himself being aroused by this skinny wisp of a girl.

The old man bared himself and forced himself on to her. She had seemingly taken notice of neither the massage nor her disrobement, but now, as he forged ahead, driving her legs apart with his knees and thrusting his penis against her virginal smallness, she began to squirm and look wildly about her. He thrust and thrust, but her wriggling made it difficult to direct his pressure on the vital spot.

As they battled, his coat rode up over his shoulders, so that it formed a tent over their heads. The smell was overpowering, and she couldn't find her breath. He was having trouble subduing her flailing arms and at the same time trying to wedge her legs apart. She seemed to have enormous strength for such a small person.

Unwittingly, the Bishop's boots made contact with the bottle of spirits, which fell over and disgorged its contents on to the hem of his coat. Her foot knocked over one of the candles. Before long, the spirit-soaked creosote impregnated coat was on fire. The flames began to spread towards her naked leg.

All this struggling proved to have an incredibly arousing effect on the Bishop. He was ready to ejaculate by the time he eventually managed to enter her tight vagina. As he did, she felt a searing pain in her groin. At the same instant the flames reached her exposed skin.

There, in the moment of claustrophobic agony, of violation and flame, my mother screamed.

As the singing in the yard rose and fell, and the dark, noisome room filled with creosote fumes and smoke from the Bishop's burning coat, her hitherto silent voice found itself. She screamed and screamed, long, high and full. She screamed again and again. Overcome with shock, the Bishop leaped up, found his clothing on fire, tucked away his protruding immodesty and ran out into the yard followed by an enormous ball of orange flame and black smoke.

The awestruck congregation descended on him to free him from his flaming garment, and within seconds Phatsimo emerged, still screaming. Her open dress had also caught alight and no one thought her state of undress the slightest bit strange under the circumstances.

The shack burnt to the ground. The thanksgiving went on into the small hours. The Bishop, his composure and dignity fully restored (the damage to his ecclesiastical garment notwithstanding) presided over a success that would be talked about for years to come. Phatsimo was no longer mute. Praise be the Lord and Hallelujah!

Strange how history repeats itself. Maybe it was just that the female line of my family was unusually fecund, but just as had happened to her mother on the night of her first sexual encounter, it happened to Phatsimo. The Bishop was my father, and that was the night of my conception.

I put down the exercise book. I was stunned. I had finished the whole book and *still* she hadn't been born yet! Kelly's writing style was so unexpected. Looking at the bubbly, youthful girl, one would hardly suppose her capable of it.

I reminded myself that she suggested she write it all down, that what she wanted to tell me was too painful for her to say out loud. But thus far there was no hint of the pain, of the things she clearly found so difficult to speak of. Well, I reflected, perhaps it would come out in her next chapter.

The theme though, was the same throughout: men behaving badly.

Eleven

Despite regularly leaning over the balcony and searching the road below, I missed her approach. The opening door of the apartment took me by surprise. She was back from her walk. She looked hot and sweaty, and still utterly lovely. She came out on to the balcony.

'Hiya. You 'right?' She bent over and kissed my forehead. I squeezed her hand. 'I'm knackered! I'm going to have a shower, and then, Mr Venter, I would appreciate an invitation to dinner. I'm fuckin' starving!'

With that she wandered through the apartment, shedding sandals, shopping, sling bag, sunglasses, watch, straw hat, her tank top, shorts.

'Want a beer?' she called.

'Cheers.' She brought it out to me, wearing the tiniest G-string, which came off halfway to the shower. I followed her to the bathroom door, sipping from the cold bottle of Phoenix.

She got into the shower, leaving her beer balanced on the edge of the bath. She didn't draw the shower curtain, and I stood in the doorway, leaning against the frame. I had never been in the presence of someone so self-assured in their nudity, male or female.

She was all at once unbelievably sexy and at the same time totally innocent. I was trying to get used to having her around. She was perfectly proportioned, with breasts like ripe peaches. Her body was firm and athletic and, though tiny, she moved with incredible elegance and fluidity.

I was utterly besotted by her. But we still hadn't had sex. That will come, I told myself. I could wait. She was soaping her crotch. I hoped I could wait!

'Read your writing,' I ventured, 'the story of your mother... and the bishop! Remarkable.'

'I saw a nice-looking restaurant on my way back.' She clearly would not be drawn. 'Sort of place with no obvious tourists. Not far. Perhaps we could go there.' She was leaning back, legs parted, to let the shower get the soap out of the perfect little triangle of hair.

I really hoped I could wait!

'Sounds good to me. Where did you go? It was quite a walk!'

'Shit! All over the place. I walked along the beach, down past the big hotels, all the way to Trou aux Biches. Some fancy places along there! Really larney, like you South Africans say.

'Then I walked inland between the sugarcane fields, all the way to Troilet. There's a little market there. I got lazy and caught the bus back, and then pottered around the shops around here, what's it, Mont Choisy?' She trailed on, as women tend to do, about the wonderful bargains in the factory shops.

We hadn't yet had sex. She seemed to make nothing of it, and was light and breezy and intelligent and beautiful and witty.

And naked.

Kelly finished her shower and I my Phoenix. I was hungry too, and an early supper seemed a good idea. Having just read the astonishing story of her conception, I was eager to exploit some of the events as openers for probing more about her. As I watched her towel herself, I couldn't deny that my main motivation was to solve the puzzle so that I could make love to her. If only I could dislodge the obstacle. Whatever it was.

The restaurant was just as she described it: definitely not touristy. The few foreigners there were French, and the remainder of the clientele was Mauritian. There was neither a South African in sight nor in earshot. Nowhere was there a painting of a dodo.

We found a corner table and ordered beers, while we looked at the menu. We chose a mix of Chinese and Indian: spring rolls, prawn curry, spicy chicken with cashew nuts, dhal, raita, roti, and glutinous rice.

I lit a cigarette and pondered how to get on to the subject of her life.

'Is the bishop still alive?'

She smiled. 'No, he died many years ago. But we're not going to talk about that. I'll write more tomorrow, and you can read for yourself.'

'It's just that I was expecting a couple of pages summarising Kelly from birth to today. I wasn't expecting so much detail, or such brilliant prose. You write fucking well.'

She smiled again. Bashfully. 'Why don't you leave off me and tell me a bit about Anton?'

'Okay, but it's totally boring.'

'I'll be the judge of that.'

'Okay, okay.'

So, over the spring rolls, I started.

'I am the third of three children. My brother, Willem, died a couple of years ago. Antjie, my sister, is married with three children and lives in Somerset West, near Cape Town. My parents, as you know, live in Zeerust. My dad is a retired Dutch Reformed minister. He's not your run-of-the-mill fire-and-brimstone arch-conservative, though, that said, he did manage to co-exist with such for more than forty years.'

Kelly finished her spring roll and propped her chin on her fists, her beautiful eyes wide and steady, watching every word. I carried on, 'I really can't tell you about *my* conception.' We winked simultaneously, then laughed.

'I can only presume that it took place in the missionary position under the covers of the marital bed in Stellenbosch, probably in total darkness, and, seeing that they shared the room with their two children, in total silence as well. In fact, my parents were doubtless fully clothed in pyjamas and nightdress, with only the essential parts bared for the occurrence!'

She giggled. 'You're kidding.'

'Well, I'm not sure that I am. I never saw my mom and dad getting dressed together, or in the bathroom together. Even at home, she always locks the bathroom door. I don't think I'm far off the mark. You know, in the seventies there was a weird

Afrikaans pastor called Gert Ysel who announced that the drought that year was caused by girls wearing mini-skirts. And people believed him!'

She laughed out loud.

'I swear! God gets angry when the hemlines go up, and then he punishes everybody by withholding rain. It's fucking logical.

'In an interview he even said that when his wife died, her body gave off a sort of holy light because in fifty years of marriage he had never seen her naked.'

The main course arrived. The prawn curry was very spicy, and delicious.

'So, you were conceived in Stellenbosch in the dark, through the flies of your father's missionary pyjamas. In dead silence. And…?'

'And, born in Pretoria. But there is a bit of a story to that. My dad was late in going to university. He was well into his thirties. He and my mother had lived on a farm before that, where he was a sort of farm manager.

'They were desperately poor, with two small children. Nevertheless, my dad decided to become a pastor, and enrolled at Stellenbosch University to do an MA in theology. In those days, it was a five-year course.

'He must have been in his third year when I came along. They were living in shared student accommodation, a sort of commune-type arrangement, where each student had his own room, and meals were shared in the kitchen.

'My old folks, my brother and my sister all lived in one little room. My dad was working at the local bistro - the steakhouse hadn't been invented yet - as a waiter during the evenings and on weekends to keep them afloat. He also took holiday jobs. You haven't fallen asleep?'

'No, go on, I'm riveted.'

'Anyway, things looked increasingly desperate. The part-time jobs weren't bringing in enough to meet all the family's needs, and gradually the little money they had ran out.

'My dad didn't know what to do, but then one day, one of his professors told him that there was a certain Doctor van der Merwe who was very rich and had sponsored needy students in the past. At first, my dad was very reluctant. He had made the decision to study, and he felt it was incumbent on him to earn the money needed to do so.

'But his back was against the wall. He couldn't go to a bank to borrow money, as he had no permanent job, and he was over the age limit for the usual theology bursaries offered by the church or the university. There was no way he was going to let his wife go out to work. After a month of soul-searching, during which the cash crisis worsened, he eventually decided to approach the good doctor.

'Apparently, Dr van der Merwe lived in Pretoria. My dad was a very retiring man, and was unable to compose a letter to his potential benefactor. He said it felt cheap to write a begging letter to a stranger.

'The only way would be to go to Pretoria and to ask him face to face. So at the end of term, my dad dumped the whole family into the aging *Vauxhall*, and headed for Pretoria.

'Their housemates put together a farewell supper the night before, and they drove off one Saturday morning, into the unknown, with half a tank of petrol and a few coins. My heavily pregnant mom asked herself how they would even get to Beaufort West, let alone Pretoria. She had no idea. "The Lord will provide," said my dad.

'They did manage to get to Beaufort West, but the fuel gauge was on "E". When they stopped at the petrol station, my dad got out of the car to go to the loo. An insect flew into my mom's eye and when she pulled down the sun visor to use the little vanity mirror to get it out, thirty rand fell into her lap. The Lord had provided! In those days thirty rand was a fair bit of money, more than enough to get them to Pretoria.'

'Where the fuck did the money come from?' Kelly looked engrossed.

'It turned out later that the students who shared the house with my parents had passed a hat amongst themselves, and knowing that my dad would never accept charity from them, they had hidden it in the car.

'Anyway, they continued on their journey. In those days it was almost unheard of to drive from the Cape to Pretoria in one day. Even driving fast, it was a solid fifteen or sixteen hours. By the time they got to Johannesburg it was already after nine at night.

'By rights, they should reach Pretoria in another forty-five minutes, but there was a massive storm, and the rain was lashing down. My dad had never in his life been to Jo'burg, and had only ever been to Pretoria by train.

'Somewhere they took a wrong turn. The road signs in those days were fairly rudimentary, and after driving around Jo'burg suburbs for an hour, they were totally lost. My mom pleaded with him to stop and ask directions, but my dad was determined to find Pretoria himself. After all, it was the capital city of his country. He wasn't some foreigner, a stranger, needing to ask directions to the capital! Stubborn bugger, my old man.

'The rain lashed down, the visibility was atrocious, the children were cranky after a marathon day in the car, and my mom was in tears. She was eight and a bit months' pregnant.

'At one stage they were so lost that they found themselves back in the veld, seemingly in the middle of nowhere. My dad finally capitulated and promised that the next place they reached that had a light on, he was going to stop and ask directions.

'Eventually they came to a suburb, where there were big, new, expensive-looking houses. Everything was in darkness. It was already past eleven. Finally they came to a grand mansion, with an expansive lawn, and a big curved driveway leading to a *porte cochère* at the front door.

'There were lights on in the house. They stopped outside in the road with the rain thrashing down, while my dad composed himself to intrude on strangers so late in the night. There was someone looking out through the curtains. At least they were awake.

'My dad drove our clapped-out car up the grand, sweeping driveway, and stopped under the portico. He got out and rang the bell. Almost immediately the door opened, and a middle-aged man in a claret dressing gown and slippers stood on the threshold with an enquiring expression.

'"Can I help?"

'"Sorry to trouble you so late at night, *Oom*. I'm afraid we are lost."

'"Where are you heading?"

'"Monument Park, in Pretoria."

'"Well, this is Monument Park. You look as if you have travelled far."

'Over my father's shoulder the man could see the mud-spattered *Vauxhall,* the two children in the back, and the pale, drawn woman in the front. In the lights of the portico he could see her face was wet, glistening with tears.

'"Yes. We came from Stellenbosch this morning."

'"That's a long journey. Look, you have to all come in for a cup of tea. You must be exhausted!"

'"*Oom* is very kind. We really don't want to impose."

'"No, no. You must all come in. At least for a cup of tea."

'My dad turned around and motioned to my mother to get the children out of the car. The man continued, "Where exactly are you headed?"

'"It's a long story. You know, I am a student, a theology student at Stellenbosch, and what with a family and all, I'm finding it hard to make ends meet. I'm looking for a certain gentleman. A doctor, here in Monument Park... Doctor van der Merwe. One of my professors suggested I speak to him. He told me that in the past he has occasionally helped impecunious students with their tuition fees..."

'"Pardon me interrupting you," said the man, "but I insist you all come inside. You can tell me the rest while we have a cup of tea."

'So my dad helped my mom and the children out of the car and the family shuffled forwards awkwardly, acutely conscious of the lateness of the hour and the incongruity of their grubby, creased, travel-worn poverty in these posh surroundings.

'"Sorry, I haven't even introduced myself. I am Gerhardus Venter."

'The man in the doorway extended his hand. "I am pleased to meet you."

'As my mother shook the gentleman's hand, her waters broke all over his slippers.

'"Mrs Venter, you are welcome. It seems you have arrived just in time. Come inside. I am Anton van der Merwe. Doctor Anton van der Merwe. You are welcome!"'

'What?' Kelly was amazed. ''Kin' 'ell! You telling me they like, stumbled right into the bloke!'

''Strue as God! As you can imagine, my dad went a little nuts, prancing about in uncontained excitement, as the puddle grew on the doormat.

'"The Lord has guided us, my wife. Oh, let us give thanks. Come children, come greet the doctor. Oh Lord, you are truly my shepherd!"

'I was delivered in the spare bedroom fifteen minutes later.'

* * * * *

It was a short journey back to the apartment. I switched on my cell phone. I had been keeping it switched off, usually checking for messages only first thing in the morning when South Africa was fast asleep, and the necessity for explanations of my whereabouts unlikely.

Within a few seconds I had four text messages. The first was from Hannah. '*Daddy, why do you always make me sad?*' Probably Rachel. The second was from Antjie. '*Tried 2 phone. only got yr voicemail. where r u? need 2 talk re pa, Luv.*'

The third was from Solly. 'Sent you an email. Please read it v urgent + revert. Watch it - Mauritian chicks got crabs, may bite! Pee in sea for me!'

Christo had also sent me one: *'V. interesting new developments. Call me'*. There was nothing much to cheer about in that lot, though at least Christo seemed to be on to something. I tried to get hold of Antjie, but her phone was off and I left a message on her voicemail.

I sent a reply to Solly saying I'd check his email in the morning, and one to Christo telling him I'd call him on Monday, and by the time I was finished, tiredness or moodiness had overcome Kelly, and she was in bed, eyes shut, with her back to me.

Strange, I thought. She had been her usual bubbly self right up to when we got back from the restaurant. When I slipped naked and hopeful into bed, I noticed she was still dressed in T-shirt and shorts. *Don't even try*, I thought.

As I lay in bed, I couldn't stop thinking about Antjie's message. I hoped Pappie wasn't sick. Come to think of it, I couldn't remember him ever having been sick. Apart from the hip replacement fifteen or so years ago, I couldn't remember a time when he'd been troubled by anything worse than a bad cold. It was difficult to imagine him really sick. Then again, he was nearly seventy-eight. Getting close to his mortal limit, I supposed.

Kelly was fast asleep, and was snoring softly. I got out of bed and went out on to the balcony. The moon sparkled in reflection out on the lagoon. Despite the sound of the occasional scooter or car, it was extraordinarily peaceful. A far cry from Jo'burg. I tried Antjie's number again.

'Hello?'

Although we grew up in the same Afrikaans-speaking home, we always seemed to speak to one another in English these days. 'Hi, Sis. Got your message. What's up? How's Pappie?'

rings.'

I had mentally rehearsed an answer, but before I could deliver it she continued. 'Not a big crisis. Mammie phoned to say that he had a fall this morning. He's fine, nothing broken. He's spending the night in hospital as a precaution. They took him to the Ferncrest in Rustenberg by ambulance. The doctor thinks he probably had a little stroke, but doesn't think it's serious.'

'A stroke!'

'*Ja*. But Mammie says he's fine. They'll do a MRI scan tomorrow.'

'Shit! That's terrible! Is Mammie okay?'

'No, she's fine. I'll be there in another three hours or so. I left as soon as she phoned.'

'You driving? Where are you?'

'Just past Kimberly. Johann and the kids are at home, so I'll probably stay in Zeerust for a couple of days 'til we hear more about Pappie. You know how Mammie hates to be alone.'

The thought of my sister driving fifteen or sixteen hundred kilometres at the drop of a hat, alone, at night, made me feel all the more guilty about my self-indulgent getaway. But that was typical Antjie. Intrepid and capable!

She visited the old folks about ten times more often than I did, despite the fact that I lived only a three-hour drive away. Exemplary daughter. I could just picture her, streaking through the Northern Cape under this same moon, on her way to comfort her old parents. Probably doing about one-eighty in the BMW, she would have her .38 on her lap, cocked and on safety, and the emergency number already keyed into the cell phone so she could call for help with the touch of a single button if needed. She knew how to survive in South Africa!

I felt I had to tell her. 'Look, I'm a bit far away at the moment. Looking out over the clear Indian Ocean as we speak, in Mauritius. Taking a bit of a break while my trial's on hold. Did you hear the judge's wife got killed in a hijack on Thursday?'

'*Ag* no! Was that *your* judge's wife?'

'*Ja*, shit happens! Look, I'll be in Jo'burg in a couple of days and I'll pop down to Zeerust as soon as I get back.'

'Don't rush, I can handle it. Doesn't sound too serious. I'll get in touch if there's anything...' she paused, 'you know...'

'Thanks, Sis!'

'You enjoy your break. Don't worry about Pappie. He'll be fine.' Her tone changed. 'What's her name?'

'Whose name? Who said I was with a woman?'

'No one.' She giggled. 'Just wishful thinking, I suppose. It would hardly be too soon! What's it now, six years since the divorce?'

I knew I couldn't lie to her. Never could. 'No, you're right as usual. Her name's Kelly.'

'She nice?'

'Very.'

'Where's she? She there with you now?'

'She's asleep. It's after midnight.'

'Off to bed with you too, then! Let me concentrate on the road. Love you.'

'Love you too, Sis. Bye now, drive safe. Love to the old folks.'

When I awoke, Kelly wasn't there. I called her name, but there was silence. I jumped out of bed and I saw the note. 'Didn't have the heart to wake you. I'll be on the beach. Not where we were yesterday, the other one, with the trees. See ya! XXX.'

I looked at my watch. It was past eleven. I had struggled to fall asleep after the call to Antjie. I couldn't stop feeling guilty about being in Mauritius when I should have been racing to Zeerust like my sister.

The more I thought of Mammie, sitting up alone waiting for Antjie to arrive, praying for her husband of half a century, and him lying in a strange, unfamiliar hospital bed, the more uncomfortable I felt with the circumstances I was creating.

I was falling deeply in love with Kelly. That much was clear. Nothing so far had suggested that we would not continue seeing each other after we got back to Jo'burg. There was still no way I could imagine my parents finding out about her. I hadn't even had the guts to tell Antjie that Kelly was black.

Sometime during the night Kelly awoke to find me staring at the ceiling. I told her about my dad and the call to Antjie. She snuggled up to me comfortingly, and went straight back to sleep. Sometime in the wee hours, I finally fell asleep.

After a shower and a cup of coffee I felt better. I tried Antjie's number, but all I got was her voicemail. The landline at Zeerust just rang and rang. They're probably on their way to Rustenberg, I thought. I could try later.

I decided to look for an Internet café on my way to the beach so that I could get hold of Solly's 'urgent' email. I tried a couple of the hotels, and found a connection at a little travel agency in the lobby of the Hotel Royale du Maurice.

The news wasn't good: *'Howzit Partner? Got some bad news. I know you're on leave, but I'm going to need you to be back latest on Wednesday. The Tsotsetsi appeal has been re-scheduled to Thursday, and what with my niece's wedding I'm not going to be able to make it.*

'We can't really ask for a postponement – you know the Appeal Court roll is pretty tight - so I'm going to have to ask you to go. Abby will arrange your flight and hotel, so don't worry about that side of it. I've sent you some notes so you can start familiarising yourself with the arguments. Give you something to do besides chasing pussy. Please confirm. Solly.'

I had a coffee at the hotel while I waited for the attachments to be printed - over a hundred pages, all told. Thanks, Solly!

Benjamin Tsotsetsi was a South African who had been sentenced to death in Botswana on a murder conviction. Solly had defended him at his original trial four years ago, and was a member of a relatively high-powered legal team for the appeal.

The on-again-off-again appeal had been going for the best part of three years. Solly was right. We really couldn't ask for a postponement because of a wedding and a fling in Mauritius. The Botswana Court of Appeal only sat for a few weeks a year, and the condemned man was relying on Mokoena and Venter to get the sentence commuted to a custodial term.

Then again, I knew how serious an uncle's role was in a traditional African wedding. There was no way Solly could not be in ThabaNchu for the delivery of the cattle for *bogadi* - the bride price. There wasn't any getting out of this one. Before I left the hotel I sent Solly a reply. I'd be in Jo'burg latest on Wednesday. As an afterthought I added: *'Tell Abby not to worry about the flight. I'll go by road.'*

It's only a four-hour drive from Jo'burg to Lobatse, the seat of Botswana's High Court, and Zeerust is on the way. *Two birds with one stone,* I thought. *Maybe three even? Nah! Anyway, it's much too bloody soon. Only known her for what... four days?*

I tried Antjie's number again and this time I got hold of her. She and Mammie were at the Ferncrest in Rustenberg. Pappie had had a restful night, and the doctor reckoned that he could go home after they had done the scan. Mammie was fine, and I felt a lot better when I put down the phone.

I tried Hannah's home number, hoping against hope that I might speak to the girls without the customary quarrel with their mother. There was no reply, and with a sinking feeling I dialled Hannah's cell phone instead.

'Hold on.' Not so much as a 'hello!' There was a pause as she passed the phone to Rachel.

'Hello, Daddy! How's Mauritius? We're at Sun City with Mom and Uncle Ivan.' Ivan Zuckerman was Hannah's socially inadequate younger brother.

'Hi, Rachel! How's Margot? You girls having a good time?'

'She's gone on the big water slide, you know, the *very* big one. I'm not going on it. They say under-tens aren't allowed. Daddy, we went on a game drive and we saw *seven* lions. And a rhino! It was awesome, Daddy, you should have been here!'

I was relieved to hear that the weekend had apparently turned out successfully, even if I had miserably failed to do my part. I listened to more of the wonderful adventures they were having.

'Okay, darling! Listen, make sure you tell Margot and Mom that I have to go to Botswana on Wednesday, but I'll be back on Friday night, so I'll pick you girls up on Saturday morning. Okay?'

'Okay, Daddy, love you!'

'Love you too, darling… give my love to Margot! Say hi to Uncle Ivan… Bye-bye.'

'See you on Saturday.'

I felt a whole lot better after the call - my guilt temporarily stilled. On the way to join Kelly at the beach, I picked up some cold beers, cheese, olives, ham and a fresh baguette from the supermarket. It was Sunday, and there seemed to be half of Mauritius enjoying the sun and sea. I had to walk the entire kilometre length of the crowded beach and back before I found her sitting in the shade of the casuarina trees that fringe Mont Choisy beach, busily bent over her blue exercise book.

She smiled her beautiful smile when she saw me, then laughed to see me all sweaty after my long search up and down the crowded beach, my awkward cargo of beach towel, groceries, metre-long baguette and a sheaf of papers weighing me down.

A frown. 'How's your dad?'

'No, he'll be fine. Just spoke to my sister thirty minutes ago. I promised her I'd get down to see the folks during the week.'

I noticed that she had started on a third exercise book. While we ate our lunch, I picked up the full second one and started reading, despite the fact that I knew I ought to read Solly's hundred pages first.

Twelve

Phatsimo's stay at the Church of the Twelve Apostles of Zion Faith Healing Christian Fellowship Church had ended only two days after the momentous event. The situation had become intolerable for all concerned.

Despite the miraculous circumstance that had been witnessed by more than twenty astonished congregants, the rejoicing had diminished, slowly at first, but then more abruptly and finally so that by dawn despair and depression hung over the compound like the heavy stench of the creosoted coat that had almost expired in the event.

The reason for this was that, having found her hitherto mute voice, since the healing Phatsimo had not ceased to employ it to its maximum capacity. She screamed until, through sheer exhaustion, she fell into a stupor and slept.

The morning after the healing, Phatsimo had woken early and begun to scream. She screamed continuously and with passion; loud, shrill, and unmodulated. She seemed never to run out of breath. Her eyes were wild and dilated. And she screamed and screamed and screamed.

By the end of a stressful day, (it was a Sunday and almost everyone in the neighbourhood was home and becoming annoyed) all agreed that Phatsimo should leave. The Bishop - who strangely seemed to be most affected by the unrelenting noise - even went as far as to donate the six rand that Florence would need to take the girl back to the village, and to return herself to the city. Hasty preparations were made, and early on Monday morning Florence and the shrieking Phatsimo were on their way to the bus depot.

Phatsimo had hardly left the Bishop's compound before the screaming stopped. A few paces down the path, the girl closed her mouth and lapsed into her former, silent, withdrawn self. Florence was relieved that she would not have to suffer the embarrassment of travelling with a mad girl all the many hours to the rural areas. Soon they were on the bus and Florence had an opportunity to reflect on the weighty events of the previous thirty-six hours.

She knew she had witnessed a rare and special thing. She had seen the Lord at work, with her very eyes. Too bad that the innate sinfulness of the congregation had prevented Him - as the Bishop had explained to them yesterday to the backdrop of incessant screaming - from completing a perfect cure.

But the fact remained that, until that moment, no sound had ever issued from the girl since she was born. God had palpably intervened, and had laid His fiery finger personally on her niece. That much was indisputable.

She realised that the bishop was indeed a strange and powerful man, and that he clearly had the hand of Jehovah on him. She smiled indulgently to herself when she suddenly realised that her lying with him must surely be sanctioned, and that, by association, she herself was divinely touched. The Lord indeed worked in mysterious ways!

She was rudely awoken from her reverie as Phatsimo, in the seat next to her, suddenly began to scream as she had before they left the bishop's home. There was no warning, no introductory whimper: just an instantaneous switch from utter silence to wide-eyed, full-volume screaming.

There seemed to be no reason for the sudden outburst. The passengers in the bus were alarmed and the driver looked back over his shoulder in concern. Various passengers got up and tried to calm the girl, one old lady offered her a stick of sweet-reed, and another a Chappies' bubble gum. Florence cuddled her as one would a small child who had fallen, but it was to no avail. The screaming was unrelenting.

Then the bus managed to overtake the big lumbering truck in front, and as it pulled back into the lane ahead, Phatsimo's screaming stopped as abruptly as it had begun.

Some hours from the city the bus pulled in at a lay-by at the side of the road. In those days there were no facilities for travellers. The toilets at the filling stations in the towns and hamlets were all reserved for white people. The passengers disgorged from the bus, climbed over the roadside fence and headed for the bushes to relieve themselves; men off in one direction, women in another.

Florence was large and unathletic, and she and the girl approached the fence with the intention of clambering over the flexible, tensioned jackal-mesh next to a fence post, where the undignified exercise would be less wobbly and precarious. The diagonal stays of the post would also give Florence a positive foothold as she swung her leg over, modestly tucking her skirts between her thighs as she did so. Phatsimo was about to grab the pole to follow her aunt when the screaming started again, and she recoiled from the fence.

Florence was disturbed. This was alarming. For no apparent reason, the screaming would start and stop at the oddest moments. As they reboarded the bus, the truck they overtook earlier lumbered past.

She knew it was the same truck, because it was loaded high with telegraph poles, and the load had shifted to one side, so the truck had a recognisable tilt. At once Phatsimo started her screaming. By the time they were underway, she had fallen silent, but when they slowed down behind the truck again, further along the road, waiting for an opportunity to overtake, she was at full volume. After passing the truck, she was quiet again. Suddenly, Florence realised what it was. Creosote! The merest whiff and Phatsimo screamed.

The homecoming was a strange affair. The first reaction had been one of surprise to see them back so soon, for they had been gone less than a week. Phatsimo's mother was enthralled and amazed by the account of the fiery intervention.

The kinfolk assembled and were, in turn, told the momentous news. The fact that the girl had lapsed into her habitual silence took nothing away from the account of the dramatic visitation by the hand of God.

In fact, Florence was able to demonstrate the miracle. She took Phatsimo and her mother for a walk out of the village to where the local headman had built himself a cattle-crush out of treated gum poles. Their approach was from downwind, and before they even reached the structure, to the mother's amazement, Phatsimo began her shrieking.

Indeed, the Lord worked in wondrous ways.

It was almost six months after the flaming appearance by the Holy Spirit at the Bishop's sanctuary that Phatsimo's mother began to question herself about the girl's figure. There was a distinct swelling of the belly, which had one not known any better, one would almost liken to that of a pregnant woman.

* * * * *

The Kgatla nation is the largest Setswana-speaking tribe. Colonial boundaries cut it in two, and today about a third of Bakgatla are citizens of Botswana, while the remainder are South Africans and populate what was formerly the western Transvaal, now the North West Province, Limpopo and even as far as Gauteng and the Free State.

In the years before The Struggle, before the nascence of the fortress mentality of "total onslaught" that characterised P.W. Botha's regime, the border was indulgently porous, and kinsfolk moved between the two sovereign states with unrestrained ease.

Kabelo Modise, my great-grandfather, was from the Bakgatla-ba-Pilane clan, which is based north of Pretoria. Both my grandmother, whom I called Mama, and my mother, whom I call Mmane, or "maternal aunt", consequently also belonged to this branch of the Bakgatla.

Mama's mother, my great-grandmother, however, hailed from Mochudi, in the then Bechuanaland Protectorate. Today Mochudi is the capital of Botswana's Kgatleng District and is the seat of the Kgafela branch of the Kgatla royal family - the paramount chiefs of all Bakgatla.

When the fact of Phatsimo's pregnancy became apparent to the community, to avoid disagreeable questions and snide remarks, Mama decided to take her to her aunt in Mochudi, and that is where I was born. So, in addition to my UK and South African passports, by birthright I could also claim Botswana citizenship.

In those days, almost all births took place at home. Most old women were de facto midwives, and western medical assistance from a clinic or hospital was resorted to only in emergencies.

One would have supposed that Phatsimo's tender age, for she was just thirteen, and her tiny frame, should have qualified her as an emergency-in-waiting. However, on the momentous day she found herself with her mother and great-aunt at the lands, three hours walk from the Deborah Retief Memorial Mission hospital, in Mochudi.

As Phatsimo's arduous labour continued through the night, panic set in, and at first light Mama left the remote homestead to look for transport. As luck would have it, when she reached the road, the first vehicle that she hailed, stopped. The car was driven by an Afrikaner man, who was travelling to Mochudi who, when told that there was a sick child, readily agreed to manoeuvre his car down the narrow, rutted footpath to the homestead, where the two women helped Phatsimo, wrapped in a blanket from head to toe, into the back seat.

Gynaecological affairs are very private in Setswana society, and are exclusively female turf, so the women took care not to alert the gentleman as to the very private nature of the child's medical emergency.

He was no doubt surprised, when halfway to the hospital he was urgently and peremptorily requested to return them to the lands. The kindly man was surprised that the critical medical emergency had apparently resolved itself, and with a bemused expression he made a U-turn and returned his charges to the humble, little mud hut beside a giant morula tree in the middle of nowhere from whence he had collected them.

He may have noticed that as the passengers disembarked they formed a huddle, shielding the little girl from his view, with one of the old women bent over, supporting the folds of the blanket between the girl's knees. Both Phatsimo's health and my life were put in danger by this strict adherence to culture and taboo. I unwittingly participated in the deceit. Apparently, I was as mute throughout the whole process as my mother.

Perhaps it signified something that I was born on the move: a portent of the gypsy lifestyle that I have come to lead.

If any single event contributed most to Phatsimo's growth and development it was the birth of her only child. I am her only child because she was surgically sterilised immediately after my birth. She was obviously handicapped, and when news of my arrival spread as far as the hospital, Mama was directed by the nurse to consent to Phatsimo having her tubes tied.

Both Mama and Mmane displayed their exceptional fertility by conceiving on the occasion of their first sexual encounter. I did not. This is not necessarily because I do not share their fecundity, or because the man involved was sterile, but because I was four at the time.

I hesitated before I looked up at her. The last sentence I had read horrified me, even though it did not come as a complete surprise. *Four! Jesus!*

She seemed so relaxed and intent on her writing. When she sensed me staring, she stopped. In stark contrast to the last paragraph I had just read, her face was serene and gorgeous, her look warm and tender.

'Why don't you go for a swim? Won't join you, though. My ancestors have slaughtered a goat.'

I raised my eyebrows in incomprehension. She smiled.

'Got my period this morning.'

I should have been disappointed that the ancestors' goat, as she put it, had been slaughtered in the middle of our supposedly dirty weekend, but I was more relieved than anything else.

There was obviously a lot more of this deep girl that I needed to fathom before I was going to feel comfortable pursuing my passionate intent, and a short enforced break from the tension was, under the circumstances, convenient.

The feelings I was beginning to have for her were unlike any I had ever experienced. The spark between Hannah and me had been a short-lived, feeble flash that I had mistaken for the real thing. This was something completely different. I felt I could wait as long as necessary. Anyway, I mused, Hannah had got her period on our wedding day, so I wasn't cut out to ever have a proper honeymoon, or whatever one would call it. I would wait.

'What are you waiting for, you sweaty boy? The water looks wicked. Don't hang about on my account.'

She was right. The sea looked appealingly inviting. I swallowed the last of my Phoenix, buried my half-smoked Marlboro in the white coral sand and gave Kelly a peck on the cheek.

The sea was lukewarm and tranquil. I floated in the clear, turquoise lagoon, lying on my back, buoyed up by the salt water. The surface was like a millpond and there was barely a ripple. I closed my eyes against the glare of the sun and soon found myself almost dozing as I floated.

How does one get over a thing like that, I thought? How does one reconcile that kind of violent trauma with the idea of using the same organs - fundamentally the same process - to give and to receive gentle affection? Can a person - particularly a woman - ever recover from something like that? I couldn't even begin to comprehend.

What I *could* comprehend was my anger. No form of violence filled me with more intense rage than the violation of the innocent. I had no answer for the question: What goes on inside the head of the perpetrator? What would the abuser say, for example, if midway through the commission of the horrific deed, all the lights were suddenly turned on and a jury of his peers were to surround him and ask him - his dick buried deep in a bleeding wound, the terrified child screaming for mercy - 'What the hell are you doing, man?'

What answer could he give? What goes on inside the head? I could not imagine.

In a dispassionate way, I felt that I could put myself in the shoes of almost any other criminal. A 'there-but-for-the-grace-of-God-go-I' kind of comprehension was possible for me for crimes of passion, crimes of greed, of neglect.

I could imagine becoming angry enough to kill, desperate enough to steal, drunk enough to drown the kid in the bath, or to run over the innocent pedestrian. But this? This was something different. No matter how arousing the naughtiness, how exciting the wickedness, how alluring the forbidden-ness of the sexual temptation, I could just not conceive of maintaining an erection in the face of such pitiful misery and terror. How do these men do it? I found it simply impossible to put myself into the child rapist's head.

The psychologists, I reminded myself, say that it has nothing to do with sex. It is about power. That may well be so, I conceded, but the commission of the act nevertheless requires an erect sexual organ to fulfil the power purpose, still requires sexual stimulation, titillation and orgasm. These have need of a certain state of mind, and it was this state of mind that I found impossible to fathom.

Of course, today there is another dynamic: child rape to purge the blood, child rape to cure one of HIV. The perception exists - amongst exactly which sectors of the population is difficult to ascertain, but it appears not only to be the very rural, uneducated castes - that sex with a virgin is a cure for AIDS.

Many social commentators and observers contend that the sudden increase in child and baby rape in the last decade can be ascribed to this belief; after all, the younger, the more surely a virgin. Thus, the sudden rash of rapes of infants and toddlers.

Poor Kelly though had been raped long before anyone had ever heard of AIDS.

A shout shook me from my reverie. Despite the calm surface of the lagoon, I had all this while been riding a subtle current that had conveyed me almost as far as the reef, two hundred metres from the beach. When I raised my head and lifted my ears clear of the water I could hear the crashing of the surf on the reef's outer edge.

The shout I heard was a fisherman in a boat hailing another wading amongst the coral outcrops. Despite the distance I had drifted, the water was no more than chest-deep, and I could easily wade towards the small fishing boat, though I was careful not to stand on any of the black spiny sea urchins scattered on the sea floor. One misstep meant hospital and an end to the holiday, as many a vacationer had discovered to their acute discomfort.

'*Bonjour*! Er… got any fish… er… *poisson*?' Neither of the fishermen spoke a word of English, not untypical for this peculiar little nation where English is the official language and the majority speak only Creole, or Creole and French. My French didn't go beyond the most basic '*Bonjour Mademoiselle, voulez vous coucher avec moi ce soir?*' so the conversation was conducted largely with hand signals. The upshot was that I purchased three small silver bream-type fish, and alternately swam and waded towards shore with them, waving at Kelly to attract her attention.

With more sign language she got the message and waded out towards me in her shorts with her purse held aloft. Standing in knee-deep water we exchanged the three fish for the required rupees, and I made the return journey to the fishing boat on the reef. A well-placed photographer would have captured an astonishingly surreal shot of a tall suntanned white man, glittering fish in hand, bending forward to interlock tongue and lips with a diminutive black woman, head precariously tilted to reach, both seemingly adrift in the turquoise ocean - like something off an early Pink Floyd album cover.

I pride myself as a cook. Not that I usually bother. At home, alone, I am happy to subsist on snacks, sandwiches and TV dinners, beans out of a can or a quick fry-up. But when the mood takes me, I am an accomplished chef. I have no specific specialty but my curries are pretty good.

Here in the tiny kitchen in the apartment, with the three fresh bream, garlic, ginger, fiery bird's-eye chillies, newly-picked coriander, tomatoes, dried cumin, a can of coconut cream, an iniquitous fresh masala paste, and Pakistani basmati rice I was in my element. Kelly was happy to leave it to me and to just chill.

But I was still unable to get it out of my mind...

I looked through the bead curtain of the kitchen, through the living room and out on to the balcony to where she was leaning over the balustrade, gazing at the twilight over the bay.

She looked so calm, so comfortable, her elbows on the rail, her beer balanced beside her, and a wisp of smoke from her cigarette rising in the warm, still air.

I just couldn't rid myself of the image of this vulnerable girl having been violated like that. I pictured her as a little four-year-old: tiny, she must have been, for even as a grown woman she was small. What man did such a thing? How did he do it? Did he lie on top of her? Did he use her like some sort of masturbatory glove, an object, with which to stimulate himself?

Did he close his eyes and pretend he was copulating with a grown woman? Did she bleed? Did she scream? Why had no one heard, and come to her aid, and saved her? How could the bastard have damaged such a beautiful girl? I felt my rage rising again.

And what would I do if I could witness such a thing? What if I were to walk into a room and find a grown man in the act of raping a four-year-old? What would I do? I had often asked myself that question. Whenever I had heard of or read of one of these horrific child or baby rapes a train of thought was set in motion inside my head - an unnatural, uncontrollable fury.

Whether it was South Africa, like the recent case in Malmesbury, or Belgium, where paedophilia seemed to be endemic, or Craig Sweeney in Wales, or that slime ball Ian Huntley, in Soham, it made no difference to the way I felt.

Now, with Kelly there in sight, the anger was much more focused, more personal. That swine had even affected *me* with his deed.

Yes, I challenged myself. What would I have done... what would I do if I caught the scoundrel in the act?

The sweat was pouring off my forehead, and it wasn't just the heat of the stove. My hand was shaking as I stirred the pot. I wondered if I would be able to control myself. Would I kill the piece of shit on the spot? Rip off his dick and chuck it on the ground for the dogs to eat? What would stop me doing that? What would stop me tearing the scum apart?

'What's up? You look like you've just seen a ghost!' Kelly's face, serene and beautiful, was a stark contrast to the dark, evil mental space into which I had drifted. Sudden concern showed in her eyes. 'You okay, luv?'

'I'm fine... but I'd be better if you'd opened me another beer.' I tried to look cheerful, to hide my agitation. Unsuccessfully.

'What's up, Anton?' She touched my arm. 'You don't look right.' She maintained eye contact as she fetched me a beer and opened it. 'Did I do something? Should I have offered to help with supper...?'

'Don't be silly... No, it's nothing... just...' I struggled for the right words '...you know, your diary... life story... thing.' I shrugged. 'It's just a bit overwhelming, I suppose. Difficult to understand... some of the things you've been through... even more difficult to talk about it without sounding patronising...'

No sooner were the words out of my mouth than I knew I shouldn't have mentioned the subject, even if it had meant being a little dishonest. Kelly's face immediately betrayed deep disquiet, her eyes shifted from side to side as if she didn't dare to focus on anything, let alone to look at me, lest the thoughts that came to her were to take hold.

For a moment the tension in the room was acute. Neither of us moved. But then Kelly bowed her head, placed my beer on the counter and shuffled, face averted, towards me. She snuggled her head into my chest and slipped her arms around my waist. I wrapped my big arms around her and we stood frozen in a moment of intense closeness, of unspoken empathy.

The moment would seemingly have lasted forever had the rice not started to burn.

Though I say it myself, the fish curry was delicious, and the rice wasn't spoilt. When we had finished eating, we sat on the balcony under the tropical stars, finishing our last beers and smoking. Our chairs were facing each other and her feet were in my lap. It was very peaceful, very relaxed... very close.

'Why don't you check how your dad is? Bet you there's a text from your sister.'

I got up and fetched my phone, and switched it on. Immediately, there was the double beep of an incoming message, followed a second later by another.

The first message was from Antjie. I read it out aloud. 'Pa much better. Going home tomorrow. Relax and enjoy yourselves. Love.'

'That's a relief!' Kelly looked genuinely happy. 'Now you don't have to worry so much.'

'True, but I really must get to Zeerust. Anyway, that's already arranged. I'll drop by on my way to Botswana on Wednesday. Which reminds me. We must go to the travel agent in Grand Baie tomorrow morning and organise our flight.'

Kelly had a naughty look on her face. 'Why did your sister say, "enjoy *yourselves*"…in the plural, I mean? Have you told her about me?'

'Well…' I immediately felt guilty. Antjie had intuitively known that I was in Mauritius with a woman, but I had deliberately avoided saying much about it.

'She sort of guessed I wouldn't come to a place as romantic as this on my own…'

'So what did you tell her about me?'

'That you were gorgeous. And that you were sleeping.'

'And that I am… you know… not your average Afrikaner… white girl?'

''No… I didn't get round to that.'

'Didn't get round to it? My foot!' Her tone was only half-joking.

We both knew that this was not going to be the end of that particular topic.

The other text message was from Christo. *We got a breakthrough on the case. Need to tell u about it. I said bloody well phone me, Poepol!* I knew I should have. Now was too late, it was already past two in the morning in Jo'burg. I promised myself to do it tomorrow.

Thirteen

We had fallen asleep in each other's arms, still fully clothed, on top of the bedcovers. Maybe it was a mosquito, maybe something else, but I was suddenly awake and couldn't get back to sleep.

The text message from Christo was playing on my mind. It was tantalizing. After all the ups and downs, there finally seemed to be some kind of a breakthrough. I wondered what it might be. I was sceptical though about the suspect Christo had told me of on the phone at the airport on Thursday.

I just couldn't see how the gay drugged-out weirdo with the tattoos and body-piercings could be the culprit. The murders were too widely dispersed across the whole country: it seemed too big a stage for him.

The suspect Christo described sounded too local, too 'Cape Town' to have been able to orchestrate such professional killings over such a wide area, and to have left no trace.

Despite all the sensation surrounding it, the case was baffling. During the last two years a total of six seemingly unconnected male victims had been discovered in different parts of the country, murdered and disfigured. The *modus operandi* was different in each instance, but the results were essentially the same: genital mutilation followed by a horrifying, painful death.

The detective work had been a slow, unrelenting, unrewarding grind, with false lead after false lead being faithfully but futilely followed till it petered out. On the surface it seemed straightforward enough: a serial killer with an idiosyncratic predilection on a depraved mission. But that was where the straightforwardness ended.

Very early on the possibility that these were ritual, or *muti* murders was dismissed out of hand. One of the hallmarks of ritual murders was that the body parts were cut off and taken away to be used in the making of *muti* - magic potions. In all these cases, however, the excised body parts had been left on the scene, and nothing had been removed. *Muti* murder it definitely was not.

Two years of painstaking detective work, thorough forensics and careful investigation had produced almost nothing. The murderer had left nearly no clues for the police to go on.

The murder scenes were as clean as could be. From six murders, six different murder scenes, the police forensics had a total of two partial shoe prints, a few nondescript tyre tracks and a miniscule tissue sample that only now, years after the event, was about to give up a DNA profile - a DNA profile that could turn out to be the murderer's, and then again could turn out to be the victim's own, his wife's or even his dog's. Apart from that - nothing.

The one assumption that remained unchallenged was that the same individual had committed all six murders: all the evidence, such as it was, pointed to a lone operator.

Criminal psychologists were called in to construct a profile of the killer. Nothing they came up with made the investigation team's job any clearer. The killer evidently got his pleasure by slowly torturing men to death, always castrating them and mutilating their genitals before they died.

The motive was obscure, and the investigating team had fallen back on the assumption that he killed for the fun of it, for pure sadistic pleasure. The preponderance of opinion was that there was a homosexual angle to the crimes. At least two of the victims were known to be bisexual.

The details of the first murder stuck in my mind more than the others. This was because I was in Cape Town when the body was discovered. I had gone to The Mother City to deliver a paper to the South African Human Rights Forum, an annual conference that brought together activists from all related disciplines in a sort of celebration of South Africa's new freedom... freedom to discuss openly the subject that for so many years had been shrouded and outlawed.

Christo was a detective with the Cape Town Serious Crimes Unit then, and it was he who had led the crime scene investigation. He later was to head the special unit that was established to solve the murders. It came to be known informally in police circles as the Castration Unit.

When in Cape Town, I almost always stayed with Christo. On this trip, arriving as I did on a Sunday, Christo picked me up at the airport. It was one of those impossibly clear days, and from the air I was able to see the whole peninsula laid out before me like a relief map. When I came through the gate my friend was there with his habitual beaming smile. We hugged.

'*Ja Poepol! Wat sê jy*? What's up?' Christo was big, round and reddish, with very short, crinkly ginger hair - one of those people of totally indeterminate genealogy. One could only assume that his ancestry included Khoi-khoi, Malay, Xhosa, Dutch, British, French, Chinese, Indian, and probably anyone else who had visited these shores in the past three hundred and fifty years. He prided himself in being a representative of almost the entire human race, and liked to say that the *apartheid* term 'Coloured' - for mixed race - had been coined just for him.

'*Niks, Blikpiel, ek sê fokkol!*' The Cape accent came back to me reflexively. 'Fuck-all to say, Tin-dick!' We immediately settled into the almost schoolboy vulgarity that characterised our close, affectionate relationship.

Christo's car, an old Toyota Cressida that had probably once been beige, was battered and dirty, a typical policeman's car. Cape Town drivers and the salt-laden southeaster explained the dents, the rust and the dirt. Pathetic pay, ridiculously long working hours and never having enough time off accounted for not getting it fixed or cleaned.

'Have to pick up the kids at Hout Bay on the way,' he said, as he dumped my bag in the boot. Hout Bay is on the way from the airport to Claremont like Dublin is on the way from Tel Aviv to Rome, but I knew that was how it is in the Cape. In this city with an enormous rock in its centre, no journey is convenient, though almost all are spectacular.

Cape Town has the most beautiful setting of any city in the world, I reminded myself. Many cities would like to lay claim to the title, but Rio, Sydney, or any of the other contenders simply cannot get near the variety that Cape Town has to offer.

It has two oceans, and this makes it unique. Although the official boundary of the Atlantic and the Indian Oceans is at South Africa's southernmost point, Cape Agulhas, hundreds of kilometres to the south-east, any fool can tell you that the greenish, warm False Bay surf at Fishhoek is not the same ocean as the ball-freezing blue Atlantic at Kommetjie, just fifteen minutes away across the spine of the peninsula.

As we drove down the freeway from the airport, the spectacular mountain in front of us, I reminded myself how much I missed living here, how drab and boring Jo'burg is in comparison.

As I looked, the famous tablecloth began to materialise, as if by magic, out of what had been crystal clear air, and to drape itself over the mountain.

'So, how's the family?'

'The kids are great! Can't say the same for Charmaine, though. Fokken driving me up the blerrie wall!'

Charmaine was Christo's wife. They had been together for about ten years, and it had been stormy almost from the start. I never really liked her and always secretly wished that they would part - for my friend's sake. I never had a good feeling about her.

Christo eased the Cressida into the fast lane. Typical for him, he was doing one-forty in an eighty zone, one hand on the wheel. He was one of those people who believed that seat belts were a mere decorative accessory. 'How are your beautiful girls? Haven't seen them for, must be nearly two years now. Growing up, I'm sure.'

'They're good, as good as they can be, living with that bipolar bitch of a mother of theirs!'

'*Ja*! I always told you that woman was trouble. After all, you *mos* didn't want to listen, did you?'

I was quick to jump in. 'And you still don't want to fucking listen, do you!'

Christo's silence was as close as he could get to admitting that I was right.

Our route took us through Kirstenbosch, right next door to Claremont, our eventual destination, and then up through the pass of Constantia Nek.

I love the mountain. I had done lots of climbing on it during my days at Stellenbosch, and I knew its gullies and folds, faces and crags like the back of my hand. As we drove up the zigzag road to Constantia Nek, the hot, sunny day dissolved into almost impenetrable mist, so thick that Christo had to put on his lights to be visible to the other drivers. Suddenly, it was cold and damp, almost dark.

That was why I loved Cape Town so much. The sea and mountain combine to produce an incredible variety of settings and mini-climates, so that on a typical summer's day, a short drive can separate a bakingly hot, windless beach with perfect surf from a squall with foam-flecked wind and stinging sand, or misty mountain gullies from clear summit views. All one needs is a car, and one can experience the proverbial four seasons in one day – every day.

As we crested the summit of the Nek, rounded the little traffic circle and started down the other side, the mist got whiter and brighter so that we had to screw up our eyes against the dazzle. Then, the mist was gone and we were driving under the azure sky down towards the sparkling Atlantic, Hout Bay harbour far below.

'It's the blerrie drink man, Anton! Every fokken day she winds up blerrie pissed as a fart. The drunker she gets the more fokken crap she talks. Man, I'm worried for the kids, you know. It's not right that they should have to hear stuff like that every fokken day. Out of their own mother's mouth, for that matter! I'm fokken sick of it now, you know.'

It was clear that Christo was hurting. I could offer nothing more than a sympathetic look.

'I mean, I can handle it, you know, if she fokken insults me or calls me by my mother's whatsit or whatever. I can just fokken ignore it, know what I mean? But not in front of the blerrie kids, man! It's just not fokken right, you know?' There were tears in the big man's eyes.

'Have you tried talking to her folks? You know, maybe they can knock some sense into her.'

'They've all long since blerrie washed their hands of her, you know. Anyway, they are Moslems, *nê*. Once she decided to marry me, a fokken non-believer, a *kefir* - I'm *mos* a Methodist - they fokken said goodbye. Now, with the drink and all, none of them wants to blerrie get involved.'

We pulled up outside a suburban house in the beautiful upmarket little village of Hout Bay. 'Anyway, enough of that crap now!'

Bianca, who was nine, and six-year-old Eugene, 'Genie-Boy' had been spending the weekend at friends. As I watched them come out to the gate with their hosts, I mused how Cape Town had changed in the last few years. Ten or fifteen years ago it would have been almost unheard of for coloured kids to be invited to spend a weekend with white folks. Times have changed, I reflected.

The face of the city has altered radically since the onset of democracy. It used to be a white town, on the fringes of which there appeared to be a minority of coloureds and a smattering of blacks.

Without the *apartheid* barricades, the true complexion of Cape Town becomes visible. It is a vast coloured city, with a minority of whites and another fast-growing minority of blacks. The blacks though, I thought as we drove past one of the informal squatter settlements on the edge of Hout Bay - tin and cardboard shacks in the dust, with fluttering discarded plastic bags adorning the Port Jackson willows - still get the thinnest edge of the wedge, *apartheid* or no *apartheid*.

Charmaine Januarie had a glass in one hand and a lit cigarette in the other, as she kissed me at the front door of the modest red-brick house in Selous Road. She had put on a lot of weight since I had last seen her. The smile was still there, but there was bagginess round the eyes, and an air of general debauchery about her that I hadn't noticed before.

The smile was spoilt a bit. The four false teeth that replaced her upper incisors no longer fitted too well. Like many girls who had grown up in the Cape Malay tradition, her incisors had been filed down to stumps. Like many women, she now wore false teeth, but hers looked very plastic. They had become stained with nicotine and no longer matched her real teeth. Her gums had shrunk back from the plate, leaving an obvious gap.

Bianca, a fair-skinned, sweet, self-confident little girl with almost straight, blonde hair, showed me to the spare room, and Genie-Boy rushed to try on the new Spiderman playsuit he'd just received from his favourite uncle.

In contrast to his sister, Genie-Boy was dark of complexion and had pitch-black curly hair. He didn't look at all like his father, but bore a striking resemblance to Abie Philander, who worked with Charmaine at a Goodwood clothing factory.

That was a bit of history, I reflected, that didn't need re-awakening. Christo had faced charges and had almost lost his badge, and Abie had spent a few weeks in hospital with multiple injuries when the truth had come out. Poor Genie-Boy knew nothing of the fuss, and the love Christo showed him would ensure that he would never feel himself any less a flesh-and-blood Januarie than his sister.

Sure enough, Christo's description of his wife's drink problem wasn't exaggerated. She had apparently said she would make supper, but it was already getting dark, there was school for the children tomorrow, and it was clear that nothing was happening in the kitchen. Nothing, that is, except regular replenishments of the glass that seemed to be welded to her hand.

Christo suggested that he and I should pop out to the local *KFC* down to supper Charmaine was sozzled. He opened a bottle of red wine and offered her a glass, probably hoping to get her off her diet of triple brandies and Coke, but she immediately became abusive.

'You know I can't drink that crap. You fucking *poes*!' Christo poured himself and me a glass, pretending not to have heard.

Without provocation, Charmaine continued, 'Hey, Anton!' She was loud enough to be heard by someone on the street outside. 'Tell your fucking stupid fat friend to fucking stop trying to fucking tell me what to do! D'you hear? He doesn't know his fucking place! Thinks he's fucking special or something!'

She turned to Christo. 'You just listen to me, mister fucking policeman... fucking detective fucking sergeant... cunt... Leave me a-fucking-lone! I'll drink whatever I fucking like, d'you hear me? ...Hey? ...Hey?' She clicked her tongue. '...*Jou ma se moer!* ...Your mother's fucking dirty cunt!'

Bianca and Genie-Boy kept their heads bowed, doing their best to concentrate on the fried chicken. It was clear to me though that this was not an unusual situation for them.

The unprovoked abuse continued throughout the meal. The children, cowed and frightened, finished their food and scampered to their room. I cringed with embarrassment and Christo tried his best not to be drawn, but eventually he snapped. He banged the table with an enormous fist.

'Enough! Charmaine, that's blerrie enough. For Christ's sake, sweetheart, blerrie shut up!'

She jumped up, staggering and lurching, triumphant that she had needled him into reacting. Her voice had risen to a shriek, and her dentures flew out of

to the floor as she yelled: '*Ga' naai jou ma... in haar gat!* Go fuck your blerrie mother in her arse! *Sy's seker daaraan gevoond...* After all, she must be fucking used to it! She fucking gave birth to you, you piece of shit! S*y het mos 'n stuk stront soos jou aan die lewe gebring! Gaa!*'

She flung her plate at him. It barely missed his head, and smashed into a thousand pieces against the wall. 'Go to fucking hell, you arsehole!'

Mercifully, Charmaine staggered off to bed after the plate-throwing incident, and Christo and I settled down on the stoep to finish the bottle of wine, and to luxuriate in the peace and quiet. I could find no words of consolation for my friend, but hoped that my being there was some comfort.

There was a rush in the morning, with children to be got ready for school, and the one small bathroom was barely adequate. Charmaine was very quiet, almost contrite in her bearing, and did her best to make up for her performance of the previous evening by cooking a proper breakfast and by calling everybody 'My sweetie'. After breakfast she left with the kids, both still visibly shellshocked, and I got a lift into town with Christo.

On the way, Christo's cell phone rang. 'What? Say that again!'

It was clear to me that something serious had happened.

'Jesus! …Okay, okay, I'll be there in twenty minutes.'

When he finished the call, Christo turned to me. 'Hey, mate, I'm going to have to drop you off near a taxi rank or something. Got to rush to a murder scene, up on De Waal Drive. Apparently some bloke has been found hanging from a tree, naked, with his goolies cut off.'

Christo chuckled irreverently. 'Poor bugger. She must have been blerrie damn hungry!'

The Human Rights Forum conference only started at nine, and I had ample time to make my way to the venue, despite being unceremoniously dumped on the side of the road by Christo.

'See you this evening, *Poepol*! Have a good conference!' Tyres squealed as Christo threw a U-turn through the traffic and headed off towards the slopes of Devil's Peak, to where the macabre scene awaited him.

That evening I approached the house in Claremont with considerable trepidation. I was not looking forward to a repeat of last night's degrading performance, yet I was reluctant to abandon Christo by moving to a hotel. I still had a number of friends I could bunk with in Stellenbosch, forty kilometres away. I could even have gone to stay with Antjie and Johann in Somerset West - it was only a little more than an hour into town from there – but I felt Christo needed all the support he could get. As I alighted from the taxi outside the Januarie home, I saw Christo on his way out of the front door.

'How was the conference?'

'A bit dreary... not quite what I had hoped for.'

'Sorry! Hey, Anton, I just have to rush somewhere. Look, let me grab you a beer and you can come along. Then I can tell you all about it in the car.'

Without waiting for a reply, Christo snatched my briefcase, disappeared into the house and returned in seconds having substituted it for a six-pack from the fridge. We got into the battered Cressida and headed up Lansdowne road.

'Where are we going, by the way?' I asked, as I opened myself a can.

'Wynberg. To the police mortuary. I want to catch the autopsy.'

'Charming!'

'*Ja*. Let me tell you about this stiff we found this morning. Apparently an old couple had just parked their car, you know, in that little lay-by on De Waal just before the last right-hander by the pedestrian bridge.'

I nodded.

De Waal Drive winds along the flanks of the mountain, well above the last line of urban development, into the city from the University of Cape Town and Groote Schuur Hospital. For most of its length it is bordered by scrubby *fynbos* and pines.

I knew the spot in question. If one wanted to hike up the northern flanks of Devil's Peak, it was the most convenient place to leave the car.

'Well, there are those big pine trees there, on the right, you know?'

'Uh huh.'

'So, this old couple and their dog are about to start their morning constitutional, when the dog suddenly goes bananas, growling at something on the ground.

'The old *toppie* goes down on his knees to take a look, and fok me if it's not some guy's *piel*! They grab the dog to stop him eating the fokken thing, and then they see some blood and some more meat. This time it's the guy's balls. Only then does the old lady look upwards!'

Christo paused for effect. '*Ja...* there, two metres above their heads is the corpse hanging on some wire. *Kaalgat* naked with a fokken gaping hole where his tackle ought to be.'

Christo looked at me. 'Come, finish your beer and I'll show you.'

In the early eighties, while Christo and I were at Stellenbosch together, Christo studying criminology and I law, there had been a catastrophic derailment of a passenger train near Atlantis. Seventy-three people, all coloured commuters, lost their lives. I remembered that Christo attended every post-mortem, all seventy-three of them.

As a student of forensics, he had access to the pathology lab at Tygerberg Hospital where the corpses were dissected to discern the cause of death. He would return in the evenings filled with awe at the amazing variety of curious traumas that occasioned the victims' demise.

He seemed genuinely enthralled - not in any way perversely fascinated by the gruesomeness of it - but dispassionately, scientifically, mesmerised by the human body and its mechanical limitations. I had been amazed that Christo seemed emotionally untouched by attending all those autopsies.

As we pulled up in the car park of the police mortuary in Wynberg, I had a queasy feeling. Unlike Christo, I found corpses totally unfascinating. Whenever I passed the scene of a motor accident I would close my eyes or look away if there was a casualty lying on the tarmac. I had no desire to look at dead bodies. I secretly hoped that one of the policemen at the desk would challenge me and ask me for my ID and tell me I wasn't authorised.

With a sinking heart, I followed Christo as he breezed past the desk, greeting the cops on duty by their first names, through some swing doors and down a series of white-tiled corridors, through some more swing doors and into a large pathology lab with half-a-dozen autopsy tables and a wall full of stainless steel refrigerated drawers.

Christo handed me a green apron and surgical mask from a rack and approached one of the tables.

'Hey Pieter! *Yebo* Ndaba. How's it going? This is Anton Venter... Pieter van der Walt... Ndabaningi Sisulu.'

The two pathology technicians offered their forearms for me to shake - their gloved hands were smeared with blood and viscera. To my disappointment no one asked me why I was there or where my authorisation pass was.

I steeled myself and turned to look at what was on the stainless steel table.

Fourteen

The corpse was very white. The eyes were open and stared blankly at the bright operating lights and the microphone hanging above the table. The mouth still had a broad strip of red gaffer tape or duct tape across it. The neck was severed by a wire noose that had cut through the throat and soft tissue right down to the vertebrae.

A fresh incision - obviously made by the pathologists - down the full length of the chest and belly revealed the internal organs. Our arrival interrupted Ndaba Sisulu in the act of removing the liver. He now completed this operation, placing the dark red organ in a large stainless steel bowl.

I looked at the corpse's groin. Remnants of pubic hair surrounded a jagged wound as big as a fist. Even my untrained eye could see that the penis and scrotum had been torn, not cut off. There was a dark swathe of dried blood from the groin wound to the right armpit - as if the body had been hanging upside down as it bled.

There was another wire noose around the left ankle. Like the noose around the neck, it appeared to have cut through the flesh to the bone.

At the foot of the table were various dishes and bowls. I could see the severed penis, still covered in blood, sand and pine needles in a kidney bowl, and in another, the scrotum - or what was left of it - one testicle lying loose beside it. A rectangular tray held a bloody pair of handcuffs and more coils of what looked like bloodstained piano wire or guitar strings.

At that moment a young woman wheeling a trolley laden with surgical implements and evidence kits joined us at the table. She wore a white *charwal-chemise* under her green surgical gown. She noticed Christo and me, and mumbled a greeting through her mask.

Christo made the introductions: 'Anton Venter... Dr Rashida Asvat... forensic pathologist.'

Her eyes under the modest headscarf were dark and attractive, and seemed out of place in these grisly surroundings. Using her gloved hand, with her little finger she pulled the mask down under her chin so that she could talk more intelligibly. She had a very pretty mouth, I noticed.

'Okay, this is what we've got so far…' While she spoke she took a forceps from the trolley and carefully began removing the strip of gaffer tape from the corpse's mouth.

'Subject: white male, about forty years of age…'

'Johannes Jacobus van der Spuy, thirty-nine,' chipped in Christo.

Dr Asvat smiled and continued. 'Good. So we have an ID…Probable cause of death: multiple organ failure due to blood loss and or asphyxiation…'

She nodded at Christo. 'We'll confirm exactly which for you within the hour, but I doubt it has any real material bearing on the case.'

She had finished peeling the gag off the corpse's mouth. There was blood on the lips and teeth, and the mouth was frozen in a hideous, contorted grimace. She carefully dropped the red gaffer tape into an evidence envelope, and sealed it.

She then lifted the tail of the wire noose that was around the neck. To me the wire looked to be about a millimetre thick, and shiny, silver-nickel steel, or something like that, like a guitar string, but a bit thicker.

Dr Asvat parted the gash in the throat with her gloved fingertips. The wire had cut through to the bone; all vessels and muscles had been neatly sliced through.

'Severe ligature injuries to the neck … wire lariat still attached… Note how the ligature completely severed the thyroid cartilage, and separated the hyoid and mastoid muscles, in a cutting motion from the anterior to the posterior as the noose tightened… The trachea and oesaphagus are similarly dissected… also the external jugular veins and the carotid arteries.

'Here, on the posterior, the trapezius and splenius muscles are completely severed.' Dr Asvat looked Christo in the eye. 'The only neck structures not completely severed or terminally compromised are the occipito- and alto-axoid ligaments - here - which articulate the cervical vertebrae and the occipital bone... else the subject would have been decapitated.

'All soft tissue structures have been parted. These injuries indicate that at some point the full weight of the subject was brought to bear on this one wire lariat with considerable momentum. At a guess, I'd say he dropped at least one and a half to two metres before this wire arrested his fall, but don't quote me on that till we do some proper calculations...'

She indicated the side of the head. 'Haematoma just below the left temple: blunt instrument, maybe even a fist. At first examination it would appear to have been a single impact.'

I looked and could clearly make out the bruising just below the ear, but I hadn't noticed it until it was pointed out to me.

She continued, 'Note that the blow was directed precisely at the junction of the infra-orbital and temporal nerves... This probably would have resulted in an immediate, brief loss of consciousness... Could have been a lucky accident, but then again, your perpetrator might have known exactly where to hit him!'

She moved round to the side of the corpse. 'Contusions to both wrists...' She gently raised one of the corpse's arms to illustrate her point. There were deep abrasions on the wrist, and some dissection had already been undertaken.

She pulled aside the loose flap of skin, exposing the damaged tendons underneath. 'Severe compression of the ligaments of the external primi and secundi pollicis, and here... the extensor carpi ulnaris. Dislocation of the carpal and inferior radio-ulnar articulations...' she lowered the dead man's arm, '... consistent with the body having been suspended by handcuffs. We have already removed them.'

She pointed to the cuffs in the tray. There was a piece of piano wire attached to them. 'Incidentally, he was handcuffed with his hands *behind* his back. Having his entire weight suspended from his wrists would have resulted in acute discomfort to the shoulders, as I'm sure you can imagine.'

Dr Asvat moved down the table and indicated the left ankle. The wire noose was still attached, but completely buried in the flesh. 'Note how the lariat has severed the dermis around the entire circumference. Here, on the anterior, the extensor longus, and tibialis anticus have completely parted.'

She lifted the leg and pointed to the rear of the ankle. 'The Achilles tendon is still intact, but the tendons of the flexor longus and posticus have been partially severed. This would indicate prolonged suspension of the subject's full weight upon this one noose.'

She turned to Pieter. 'By the way, did the lab come back to us with an alcohol count?'

'*Ja*, zero point two seven… He was pretty drunk last night.'

Christo nodded. 'He was last seen leaving the Pink Pussycat, in Sea Point, at around one forty-five this morning.' His squad had been scouring Cape Town for evidence all day.

'The barman says he served him at least six or seven double vodkas. Last person to see him alive seems to have been the bouncer. He says he thought the guy must have parked in the main car park, because that's the direction he headed.

'My guys found a *VW Golf*, registered to one J J van der Spuy parked in the empty lot behind the Pussycat. We found a set of *VW* keys with his wallet, ID, cell phone, shoes and clothes at the scene on De Waal. The killer wasn't after his cash or valuables, that's for sure,' Christo concluded.

Dr Asvat walked around the table till she stood opposite me, level with the corpse's groin. The men edged forward to hear her explanation.

'Now, Detective Januarie, here is where this all gets very complicated. We have had a close look at the injuries and it would appear that the subject was suspended by these different wires sequentially,' she pointed to the ankle noose, the handcuffs and the coils of piano wire in the tray. 'Specifically these two areas' she indicated the points where the scrotum and penis had once been.

'It seems that he was suspended first on the one wire and then on the other. However, both the scrotum and the penis are too insubstantial to support the full weight of the body on such a small diameter line. The wire would have cut right through the tissue, which was not the case. Consequently, it is our opinion is that the subject was supported by a combination of wires... at least for a period.'

'Observe the scrotum...' She took a small forceps and a needle-like probe from the trolley. She indicated the kidney bowl, and Ndaba lifted it and held it at a convenient height in front of her. 'Thank you, Mr Sisulu... Note that the dermis, the dartos... here, the cremaster muscles... the tunica vaginalis are all insubstantial structures.

'These would have parted almost immediately, as would these vessels, the vas deferens and the spermatic artery, had the full body weight been applied.'

She nodded at Ndaba, who replaced bowl with the scrotum and testicles on the table. 'If you look closely,' she bent over the corpse's groin and pulled at a loose flap of mangled skin of the perineum near the anus, 'you can clearly see the different layers that make up the cutaneous pouch that is the scrotum.

'Here, where the outer layer, the integument, has parted, you can see that the inner layer, the dartos has not... the dartos has in fact parted...' she pointed with the needle, '...here, five or six millimetres lower down.'

She straightened up and looked Christo in the eyes. 'Detective Sergeant, what we see is that the skin is torn rather than cut. Had it been cut, with a blade or a scalpel, for example, or by the abrupt tightening of the wire noose, the two layers would be of equal length... here, the one layer has parted before the other, as tension was applied progressively.

'I would postulate that the subject was initially suspended by both the scrotum and the ankle.' She pointed at the wire attached to the lower leg. 'Had the full body weight been applied to the scrotum, the wire would have sliced through both layers of the scrotal sac, leaving a much cleaner separation.'

'Like a cheese cutter?' Ndaba ventured.

'Exactly,' Dr Asvat took a deep breath. 'So it would appear that the scrotum was wrenched from the body relatively slowly. This is possible in view of the fact that a substantial proportion of the victim's body weight was taken by the ankle wire.

'By flexing the leg - bending his knee - the victim would have been able to reduce the tension of the scrotum wire, and hence ease the pain, at least temporarily. As his muscle strength gave out, and his leg straightened, more and more weight would have progressively been taken up by this wire until the scrotal tissues parted.

The four men were each suddenly acutely aware of their own genitals, each of us experiencing a very private, shrinking vulnerability. The perceptive young woman pretended not to notice our discomfort.

'The second ligature,' she lifted a coil of piano wire from the tray and then replaced it, 'was attached to the base of the penis.'

She took the jagged edge of ripped skin between the thumb and forefinger of her gloved hand, and then, using a forceps, picked up the severed organ from its kidney bowl and held it against the pubis to show where the flesh had torn apart. 'When the scrotum parted, the lariat around the base of the penis would have then taken the weight…'

I swallowed hard.

'As you can see, the penile tissue, the pubis, the crus penis here… the corpus spongiosum, the two corpora cavernosa and the urethra are, when taken as a whole, considerably more substantial than are the tissues of the scrotal sac. Consequently, the separation of the penis, the tearing, if you will, would have taken longer than was the case for the scrotum.

'Obviously, the victim would have attempted to delay this process as long as possible by once again bending his knee, taking his weight on the ankle wire, but as his strength gave out...'

She looked at Christo, then at me. 'Note that the point of separation for the different tissues varies. As was the case of the scrotum, the different lengths of the integument... here... and the urethra, and this vein here... indicate that the wire did not slice through the tissues, but gradually pulled them apart, one layer, or one structure, at a time as the noose tightened progressively.'

Dr Asvat picked up a magnifying glass from her trolley, and using the small forceps she extracted the severed end of an artery from the wound where the scrotum had once been. She peered through the glass, and when she was satisfied, passed the magnifier to Christo, and picked up the small needle probe.

'If you look closely, you should be able to see the spermatic artery... this one...' she picked it out of the gory mess of the mangled vas deferens with the probe. I positioned myself behind Christo so that I could also see the whitish tubular structure through the magnifying glass. Dr Asvat's probe skilfully teased the torn artery open.

'It is clear that there was considerable haemorrhaging of the wound. Had the injury been inflicted post-mortem - after death - with no blood pressure, this aperture wouldn't be as dilated. Did you find a lot of blood on the scene? I'd expect you did.'

'*Ja* no, the place below where the corpse was hanging was soaked.'

'That figures. The subject had lost over seventy per cent of his blood. Looks like these injuries were inflicted quite a while before he died.'

Christo wanted it spelled out. 'Okay, Rashida... er Dr Asvat. Tell me. How long did this guy take to die? I mean, from the moment that this first wire started to pull off his ba... er, scrotum... 'til he lost consciousness. How long?'

'I'd say a good thirty-five to forty minutes… at least. Maybe an hour… it's difficult to know exactly… it would depend on a number of factors.'

'Hey, Pieter!' A voice called from the door to the labs. Van der Walt left us and went over to see what it was. He came back almost immediately with a clipboard holding the pharmacological report.

'Looks like our man must have been asleep at some stage last night. A cocktail of pethedeine and hexabarbitol. Knockout concentration. Pharmacology also found elevated levels of ephedrine metabolites and histamine. Apparently these act as antidotes for the sedatives.'

Dr Asvat nodded.

There was a hint of surprise in van der Walt's voice as he continued: '…also, metabolites of …what's this? …Lysergic acid dithylamide-25…?'

'That's LSD! Phew!' Dr Asvat frowned. 'Okay, well that explains these…' She pointed at the cluster of hypodermic punctures in the upper forearm. 'It seems the subject was first sedated… and then very, very rudely reawakened.'

The pathologist was deep in thought for a moment. 'This combination of sedative reversal drugs, ephedrine and histamine, would have the added effect of neural over-sensitisation. In other words, the ephedrine would have woken him from the sedation; but thanks to the histamine his nervous system would have been excessively sensitive, on edge, as it were.

'To put it bluntly, after the administration of the ephedrine-histamine cocktail, he would have been wide awake and his pain threshold would have been significantly lowered.'

She raised an eyebrow in Christo's direction. 'You know… like when you're coming down with 'flu, even stroking the hairs on your arm the wrong way is painful. In this condition, any pain he experienced would have been appreciably amplified.'

Dr Asvat paused. 'On top of the physical agony, the victim would have been hallucinating from the lysergic acid... tripping on LSD! He would probably have been experiencing unimaginable distress and panic! Your perpetrator sure knows how to make his victim suffer!'

She went on, 'You say he left the nightclub at quarter to two and failed to reach his car in the car park. One could suppose he was attacked before two a.m. and injected with the tranquillizer cocktail of pethedeine and hexabarbitol at around that time.

'The LSD, which takes a few hours to attain its maximum effect, was probably administered then too.' Dr Asvat did the mental arithmetic. 'When was the body discovered?

'At six forty-five,' Christo reminded her.

'And Pathology got to the scene at seven twenty... and the body was still warm...' She frowned. 'What did we say? The time of death around six fifteen, six twenty?'

'*Ja*, this morning you guys put it at six twenty.'

'So, it would look to me as if the killer had from two a.m. till five twenty to get his sedated victim from the nightclub to the lay-by and to set up. At around five fifteen or five thirty he administered the ephedrine-histamine combination, and the subject regained consciousness in minutes.

'By then, of course, he would also have been experiencing the full psychotropic effects of the LSD. He was likely in full panic mode. Utterly terrified!'

Briefly, Dr Asvat's eyes involuntarily looked to the ceiling. 'Allah!' she whispered to herself. Then she looked squarely at Christo. There was a hint of moisture in her eyes. 'Then the pre-programmed torture began.'

'He woke up just in time to enjoy the show,' Christo mused softly, almost to himself.

They were winding up, at least for now.

'Hang on, Detective Januarie.' Dr Asvat followed the ankle wire that hung over the edge of the table to where it ended on the floor. She lifted it up. The end of the wire had been threaded through the barrel of a small syringe, which was still attached. She held the syringe vertically, the orientation it would have had when the victim was dangling on the wire.

'Look inside the syringe.' She tilted it for Christo and me to see. 'The wire is corroded, see? The wire broke because it was corroded by sulphuric acid. The syringe is an acid reservoir! If you know what concentration of sulphuric acid to use - and you can determine that by simple trial and error - you can get the wire to break after five, ten... fifteen minutes... whatever you want... it's up to you.

'Remember, this piano wire is manufactured to pretty high tolerances, so it will corrode at a very regular, predictable rate. Look here.'

She lifted the wire that was connected to the handcuffs, and selected the loose end. She handed Christo the magnifying glass again. He peered through it and then gave me a look: the end of the wire was blackened, and seemed to taper to a point.

'The end of this wire is similarly corroded, and I can only assume that there was another similar syringe barrel on this wire. The killer could get his timings very exact if he so wished.' She raised an eyebrow meaningfully.

Christo smacked his big meaty fist into the palm of his other hand. 'Okay! So now I know what the other syringe we found at the scene was for! We were wondering.' He had just had an 'aha!' experience. 'Thank you, Dr Asvat!'

When we got back to the car I lit a cigarette and dragged on it heavily. I opened a beer and drained it in one gulp. I was sweating, but was secretly proud of myself that I hadn't vomited or fainted or done anything childish like that.

'I'm fokken off duty now, even if only for blerrie fifteen minutes. You can pass me a beer.' Sitting in the buggered Cressida in the Wynberg police car park, open beer in hand, Christo made a verbal checklist,

'Okay. So what have we got? One: Van der Spuy drives to Sea Point. He parks in the Pussycat's allegedly secure car park, and goes inside. That's at about eleven fifteen, according to the bouncer.

'Two: He drinks quite a lot of vodka. We don't know how drunk he is when he arrives, but when he dies five hours later his blood alcohol is more than three times the legal limit.

'No one in the Pussycat can remember anything about him, except that he arrived alone and left alone, and that he drank vodka. We're trying to find someone who may have noticed something; perhaps one of the strippers remembers something. We're still working on them; maybe we'll get lucky.

'Three: At one forty-five he leaves the Pussycat. Alone. He walks towards the car park. Apart from the bouncer, no one sees him. The so-called fokken security guard at the car park must have fallen asleep. He says he saw nothing.

'Four: Someone hits him on the side of the head, and knocks him out, puts on the handcuffs, gags him, then injects him in a vein with the pethedeine-hexabarbitol tranquillizer and probably also the LSD. Where does this happen? Well it has to have been somewhere there, in or near the car park. *Nê*? Anyway, van der Spuy is fast asleep by now.'

Christo took a long suck from his can. I was already on my next one, and had lit myself another Marlboro.

'You know, I fokken hate it when someone smokes in my blerrie car!'

'Fuck you! I hate it when someone drags me into a bloody fucking butcher shop.'

'Okay…okay!

'Five: Then, fokken magic takes over, because no blerrie living soul sees or hears anything till the poor old folks find him at six forty-five, six kilometres away, hanging from a fokken thirty metre pine tree! The branch of the pine tree has marks of a cable having been hauled over it under load.

'You got any idea how much fokken force it takes to haul a deadweight of… what was that guy, seventy, seventy-five kilos?' He shook his head. 'You try pulling a cable over a branch with seventy-five kilos on the end of it. The friction will make it feel like half a fokken ton. The guy must have pulled the cable with the vehicle.'

'Surely a passer-by would have seen something suspicious if the guy used a vehicle to haul up his victim. That lay-by is pretty small; he would have had to reverse right out into De Waal in order to pull the guy high enough.'

I felt I might as well throw in my ideas while I was at it. 'The chances are that a car passes there every couple of minutes at that time of the morning. Too risky! His whole plan - and it looks like the killer had a fucking complicated, well thought out plan - would fall apart if someone stopped to ask him what he was doing, wouldn't it? More likely he used a winch.'

'Maybe you have a point there. It must have been a winch, a winch on the vehicle. Good thinking, Anton. That way he could park the vehicle in the lay-by, under the trees, pretty much out of sight. You're right. Otherwise someone would have seen him reversing out of the lay-by, hauling the cable.

'Anyway, the cable that left the marks on the branch was what he used to haul his victim up into the air. But there was also a rope involved. When we found him, the stiff was hanging from one wire connected to a rope with a snap-link, a karabiner. You're a climber, so you know what I'm talking about.

'Once our man had hauled him up to the correct height, he tied the end of the rope to the steel frame of the rubbish bin. You *mos* know those refuse bins they use around here - the ones the baboons allegedly can't get into? Well, when the weight of the victim was suspended by the rope, over the branch and on to the rubbish bin frame, our man must have slackened the winch cable which unhooked itself from the karabiner, and he rewound it, leaving just the rope. You still with me?'

'Uh-huh.' Christo was still making sense.

'Six: Right! So now the victim is hanging from the tree. Okay. So, let me describe to you the way the fokken piano wires were strung. The rope ended in a loop through the karabiner. The five separate pieces of piano wire - I'm getting it checked out, but we think it is genuine piano wire - are each also looped through the karabiner.

'Piece one is the shortest, and is tied to his handcuffs. This is the piece of wire that hauls him up into the air. It is also the piece with the strongest sulphuric acid in the little reservoir, the little syringe thing Rashida was showing us in there.

'So, he's hanging from the handcuffs with his arms up in the air. He's wide awake by now, tripping to hell and back on the blerrie LSD *nê*? The sulphuric acid burns through the wire. The wire breaks. Now his weight falls on to the next two lengths of wire, piece two, which is tied to his ankle, and piece three, which is round his ball-bag. It is just short enough to make him hang at an angle.

'Imagine him…' Christo tried to make a stick figure with his hand, 'imagine he is suspended, forty per cent of his weight from his balls, and sixty per cent from his ankle, which is right up here, and his head is way down here, *nê*?

'So, if he bends his knee, the weight on his balls gets less… the more he straightens his leg, the more it pulls on his balls. Remember the histamine makes everything fokken twice as sore.

'Okay, so after a few minutes, the strength in his leg gives out and the balls slowly get pulled off. *Eina*! His weight shifts to the next wire, piece number four, round his *piel*. Now it takes, maybe fifty per cent of his weight, the other fifty per cent is still on wire number two, the ankle. He tries his best to take the weight off his *piel* by bending his leg, but he's fokken tired by now, and slowly his *piel* also gets ripped off. *Nê*?

'Now the whole weight is on the ankle and by this stage the wire has cut him to the bone. …Okay?' Now Christo was getting excited. It was all falling into place. 'Then, after a long enough wait for the *ou* to appreciate the true meaning of pain, the sulphuric acid - diluted to the exact concentration - in the second syringe reservoir thingy finally burns through wire number two, the ankle wire.

'All that's left is number five, the wire round his neck. It's *lekker* slack, so that he falls a couple of metres before it pulls tight.' Christo loudly clicked his fingers. 'It garrottes him and he dies. That's if he isn't dead from pain and shock already!'

'Makes sense to me!' I thought it was as good a scenario as any we could have come up with, given the information to hand.

Christo took out his cell phone and pushed some buttons. 'Hey, Songo! We took a lot of blerrie photos of footprints and tyre tracks and stuff this morning. I want you to meet me at the scene with a laptop with all those images. *Ja*. Also, bring a couple of extra floodlights. We're going to need them. Cheers.'

He turned to me. 'Come, let me drop you home; then I'm going back to the lay-by on De Waal. I want to check out this vehicle-with-the-winch theory.'

The thought of an evening alone with Charmaine didn't sound too inviting. 'I'll come with you,' I said.

As we drove along De Waal Drive towards the lay-by I could make out Christo's expression in the gathering twilight. It was grim. 'D'you realise, *Boet*, van der Spuy wasn't blindfolded. This might be a minor fokken detail, but it has three chilling implications.

'One: The killer trusted his engineering... he believed in his blerrie plan.

'Two: He wasn't afraid of being seen by the victim... he was fokken cocksure that his victim wasn't going to survive to identify him.

'Three: In the dawn light, naked, hanging from the handcuffs, with the other wires attached to his bits, strung out on the histamine and LSD, as he waited for the first wire to burn through, van der Spuy would have been able to work out what was going to happen to him. To see what was coming. *doos*!'

* * * * *

177

All that had been more than two years ago, but it was still fresh in my mind. I reminded myself that the murderer had killed five more times since then. At least five more times!

It was well after midnight and Kelly was snoring gently. I was still wide awake. I got off the bed, careful not to wake her, and covered her with a sheet, though the Mauritian night was barely cool. I switched on the light least likely to disturb her, picked up Solly's hundred pages of notes, lit a cigarette, and settled down in an armchair to read.

Kelly found me in the morning, fast asleep in the armchair with my head at what felt like a ridiculously uncomfortable angle. She went round behind the chair and began to massage my neck and shoulders. I awoke to her kiss and the firm, gentle touch of her strong fingers and slowly opened my eyes.

'I know you must be sexually frustrated, but there's no need to go sleeping in the fuckin' chair!' Her tone was gently teasing.

I pulled her around the chair and she collapsed on to my lap. I wrapped my big arms around her. She stroked my chest, and I nuzzled her ear.

'Somehow, that doesn't hurt so much anymore! Come on, get off! My bladder's bursting!'

'Okay! Time for my exercises, anyway.'

Solly's notes lay scattered on the tiled floor in front of me where they had fallen when I nodded off. *Oh well*, I thought, at least I had read most of them. I knew the case well enough, and there seemed to be nothing new in these pages. I was confident that I was ready to walk into the Botswana Court of Appeal and to save Benjamin Tsotsetsi from the hangman's noose.

When I came out of the shower she was in the middle of her exercises. Today she was doing kata - whether Gung Fu or Karate I couldn't tell. I marvelled at the precise, compact action and her rock-steady posture. She was clearly very accomplished, and took her art very seriously. The kata finished with a flourish of spinning kicks and thrusts, accompanied by the traditional vocalisations as the blows found their imaginary targets.

Wouldn't pick a fight with her... I'd be picking up my teeth with a broken arm, I thought to myself. In fact, I wouldn't fancy the chances of most men I knew. I pitied the guy, or guys, who tried to attack Kelly in a dark alley. They would clearly wake up in intensive care.

Fifteen

What I remember most acutely is the smell. The darkness and the smell. The darkness, the smell and the pain.

We were in a strange place. I had fallen asleep during the later part of a long, tiring journey and had no way of knowing where we were. We arrived at night and I was asleep.

When I awoke it was pitch dark in the house where I lay. I couldn't breathe because I awoke with a big strong hand over my mouth. A giant heavy monster lay on me, squashing the air out of me. When I struggled and stole a breath it was filled with an incredibly sharp reek of rottenness. A sour, prickly rottenness. A stench like the taste of vomit.

The monster whose firm, rough hand held my mouth breathed its stench hard in my ear. Its voice was deep and gruff. It gurgled and hissed, scraped like stones. It spoke slowly, in a deadly whisper: 'Fa o ka kua, ke tla go bolaya!'

'Scream, and I'll kill you!'

Then I became aware that my body was strange. My legs were bent up and wide. Held so they couldn't move. It hurt where something pressed me. In that part of me.

Then the monster was clawing at me. At that part of me. Poking me. I nearly screamed, but the growl of the monster reminded me. It would kill me!

Then it belched. The rotten smell made me retch, and the hand on my mouth gripped tighter so that I thought my face would break off. Then I heard the monster clear its throat, like something heavy dragged through gravel, right next to my ear. It spat, and the hand that had been poking me now smeared slimy spit on me. Into that part of me.

It was completely dark. The pain came so sudden and so huge that as it got bigger I thought I would burst with pain. Something like a burning stick went into me. Into that part of me. The pain wouldn't stop. It went on and on. The monster's hand still held my mouth and I couldn't scream.

I couldn't scream, though even if it would have killed me, I tried.

Then I remember nothing.

There was a hullabaloo in the morning. There was blood everywhere, and I was hot and feverish and delirious while Mama and some other women yelled and panicked. Mama kept asking me, 'Who was it? Who was it?'

She kept shaking me as if to pull me from the delirium. 'Who was it? Oh, my child, who was it?'

But the monster had no name. Only a smell. And a hard hand like a claw. And a burning stick that tore me apart, so that I bled all over the blankets, and the children who had been sleeping on the floor near me were all wide-eyed and shocked, and spattered with blood on their clothes and on their faces.

Then I must have passed out again, for I remember nothing until I woke in the hospital.

That was my first rape. I was just four years old.

I swallowed hard and looked up from the neat script. Kelly had paused in her writing, and was looking out to sea, her pen poised above the page, her left forefinger worrying the scar on her neck. Her eyes were wet, and as I watched, a tear dribbled over the eyelid and ran down her cheek. Although I was reading a different part of her story to that which she was writing - she was using another exercise book so that she could continue writing while I read yesterday's copy - by some means, our melancholy moods were in concert.

Somehow, reading the detail of the rape made me more sad than mad. The anger I experienced last night seemed so futile and inappropriate now. Here was the victim - right in front of me. Here was the very same little girl who had suffered this thing. There was no place for my self-righteous rage here, just room for compassion.

That was her first rape. That meant there was another? My God!

She noticed me watching her, and quickly wiped away the tear but didn't look away. I held her eye for a long moment. I was overwhelmed with emotion.

'I love you, Kelebonye.'

She looked down. She was rigid, and seemed to have stopped breathing. There was a long moment where neither of us moved. Then she looked up, took a deep breath and met my gaze.

'...Too!' She was crying now. I crawled over the books on the beach towel and took her in my arms. Her little body shook with sobs. After a long, close moment, she suddenly got up.

'Going for a walk. If you're not here when I get back I'll find you at the apartment. Okay? See you!'

I watched her head off along the beach. For a moment I forgot my overwrought emotions and just drank in her wondrous beauty. She walked with such natural grace, the swing of her hips - the flawless figure – I was overwhelmed. What a doll! What a perfect little woman! God, I was lucky to have found her!

But oh! It was so bitter-sweet.

And then, there was still Zeerust!

We had been on the beach for less than half an hour. The morning had been busy, starting with a bus ride into Grand Baie, a visit to a bank and a travel agent to confirm our flights for tomorrow.

We had talked about hiring a car and doing the tourist trip to the renowned botanical gardens at Pamplemousses, or the famous market in Port Louis, or going up into the mountains or to Flic en Flac on the west coast, but quickly agreed that we both wanted nothing more than to chill out on the beach.

We did a quick bit of necessary shopping and as soon as we were through with business we were back on the bus to Mont Choisy. We dropped off our bags at the apartment, walked straight to the beach and found a lovely spot just before the hotels at Trou aux Biches - we were determined to make the most of it before we went back to smog-ridden Jo'burg, miles from the sea.

On the bus, we had held hands like teenage lovers, while I tried temporarily to suspend my holiday mood and sort out my programme for the next few days. 'If I leave Jo'burg early on Wednesday morning I can be in Zeerust well before lunch. Then I can spend the afternoon with my folks before heading for the border.

'Thursday and Friday I'll be in Botswana. The appeal should be over by Friday afternoon, and I can be back in Jo'burg by eight, latest nine.' I gave the strong little hand a squeeze. 'Can I make a date with you for Friday night?'

She squeezed back. 'Why not?'

Before I could forget I grabbed my phone and quickly sent Antjie a text message:

'Tell Mammie I'll be there lunch Wednesday. Love.'

God, I smoke too much! As I reached for yet another Marlboro, the sight of the cell phone on the beach towel made me suddenly think of Christo.

I had been procrastinating for far too long and knew I should have phoned him. I had to admit to myself that the real reason I hadn't was Kelly's presence with me in Mauritius. I knew I would have to own up to Christo. After all, we went back far too long to hide something that was turning out to be as significant as this! I knew that the more I put off verbalising it, the longer I could indulge myself in blissful denial.

Telling Christo would mean I would have to begin a process of evaluating the relationship, and of admitting to myself that the die was now cast - that there was no way I was not going to be forced to tell my parents about her.

I switched on the cell phone. Immediately there was the beep-beep of a message, and inevitably it was from Christo. 'Poepol! Where the fuck are you? Have you disappeared off the face of the earth, or what? I said bloody well phone me!!!'

Christo appeared to be really excited. This was the third text message in less than two days, and the tone of this one was even more strident than the previous two. I called Christo's number, mentally preparing myself for the ribbing I was bound to get when I told Christo where I was, and more specifically, with whom I was.

Almost immediately, I cancelled the call and looked up and down the beach. I knew I was going to become all self-conscious and awkward if I had to tell Christo about Kelly and she showed up in the middle of it. There was no sign of her, though, and I hit the redial button.

The wonders of GSM networks! As I waited for the connection to go through, I reflected how much we take them for granted. Here I was on a beach in Mauritius, calling someone who could be in Jo'burg, Cape Town or anywhere in between, or in Vladivostok or Vancouver for that matter, without so much as a second thought.

Fifteen or twenty years ago it would have been the stuff of science fiction, yet now it was so commonplace that my annoyance and impatience at the 'Network busy' signal was entirely genuine. And we think of evolution as a slow, gradual process! Wrong! It happens in leaps and bounds!

After a few more tries, I made a conscious effort to stop getting frustrated and to relax and enjoy my surroundings instead. I switched off the cell phone. I would try later.

The sun was hot and the water looked cool. I used an old trick from my surfing days. I put the cell phone, apartment keys, wallet, Kelly's exercise book, cigarettes and *Zippo* into a plastic bag, and tied it securely. Then, careful that no one was watching, I surreptitiously buried the bag in the soft white sand, and casually left my towel, shirt and sandals on the beach in full view.

The ruse had always worked in the Cape. Pickpockets were on the lookout for a quick valuable grab, and a shirt and a towel were hardly worth the effort. My valuables secure, I sprinted to the sea, running flat out till the deepening water tripped me up and I dived in.

I was intrigued about Christo's news. As I swam, I puzzled over what the breakthrough could be. The DNA profile? Had they found a positive match? Somehow I doubted it. I was still convinced that this Sylvester Cupido, the suspect Christo's unit had arrested, couldn't possibly be the Castration Murderer.

Poor Christo! He'd had a frustrating two years. I wished that my friend could finally have something to celebrate. The lack of job satisfaction must be getting to him, and the eager enthusiasm that characterized Christo's approach to the investigation of the first murder two years ago must surely be wearing thin by now.

I remembered how keen Christo was that evening after we left the Wynberg police mortuary and drove up to the murder scene at the lay-by on De Waal Drive. Despite the long day, and the long evening that loomed ahead, he exuded enthusiasm.

He was visibly excited and eager to check out the feasibility of my theory that the murderer must have used a vehicle-mounted winch to haul his victim up into the pine tree. I had tagged along merely by chance. The alternative would have been to go and keep Charmaine company, and that certainly didn't appeal to me.

Detective Constable Vuyo Songo, a bright-eyed, keen young officer was already at the scene when we got there, busy with a laptop in his parked car.

He jumped out of the vehicle and shook hands with me. He had a very youthful demeanour, and hardly looked old enough to be a policeman. The three of us walked to the edge of the search area. The place was lit up like a movie set, and the floodlights shimmered on Songo's shaven head.

Eight or ten other detectives dressed in white overalls were on their hands and knees in a line, moving at a snail's pace through the tussocky grass and fallen pine needles on the verges of the parking area, still combing the locale for evidence.

Here and there I could see little numbered plastic pegs stuck in the ground, like the ones used by gardeners to identify the cauliflower seedlings or the carrot patch.

Introductions were made over the hum of the generator that powered the floodlights and the four lanes of evening rush-hour traffic that rumbled past just a few metres away. The search team had nothing new to report, and Christo let them get on with it.

Christo was eager to get to work. 'Did you bring the images of the tyre tracks?'

'Hey, Sarge!' Songo was excited. 'Wait with the tyre tracks! Check this out!' He sounded almost breathless. 'This arrived this afternoon while you were at the mortuary.' Christo and I flanked Songo as he took out the laptop and set it on the roof of the car.

'It's some footage from a CCTV security camera. Belongs to First National Bank, in Sea Point. The camera that covers the bank's rear entrance also has a partial view of the Pink Pussycat's car park! Check this!'

Christo huddled closer to get a good view of the screen, as Songo clicked the 'play' button.

The video footage was grainy and grey, typical of a low-grade security camera. Nevertheless, there was sufficient definition to make out the scene.

That part of Sea Point is filled mostly with six- to eight-storey buildings, by and large business premises. The area is pretty quiet at night, unlike a few blocks away on Main Road where the bulk of the clubs and restaurants are and where the real nightlife happens.

The scene showed the deserted backyard of the bank, and in the background, past the security fence, the street. Beyond that we could see the entrance to the nightclub car park, the little security hut clearly visible under an illuminated sign: 'The

Pink Pussycat – Secure Customer Parking'. The date and time were recorded in the lower left corner of the frame.

'Okay, this is the first bit: Van Der Spuy arriving.' Songo had clearly already been through the footage, and knew his stuff. A white *VW Golf* appeared from the left of screen and turned into the car park. The motion was jerky: to save tape the camera operated at only a couple of frames per second. Though the action was happening in the extreme background, near the limit of the camera's night-time range, the silhouette of the security guard raising a hand in greeting, as the *Golf* turned in past the sentry box, was clearly visible. The time in the frame read 23:12.

'Watch now!' A four-by-four, pale grey in the black and white footage, drove across the screen from left to right. It slowed down as it passed the car park entrance, then moved on. It was too dark to see any details, or to make out the driver. The fact that it was at right angles to the camera meant that the number plate never came into view. Songo pointed at the four-by-four with the mouse. 'That's the vehicle!'

Christo frowned, clearly sceptical.

Songo leant forward and selected the next clip. A shadowy figure came out through the car park entrance on foot and turned towards the nightclub, disappearing to the right of screen. Time code: 23:14.

Songo kept up the commentary. 'That's van der Spuy. He's parked the car and is on his way to the Pussycat!'

There was no movement on the screen for perhaps thirty seconds. Christo was about to say something but Songo held him in check with a stern look and pointed to the monitor.

'Watch, here it comes again…'

Time code 23:15: There was the sheen of headlights reflected on a pole and a parked van. A vehicle approached slowly from the right. For a few seconds it seemed as if it was stationary, just out of picture, but then, at the very edge of the screen, the right-hand headlight of a vehicle crept into view, as it parked against the kerb. Only the extreme front of the vehicle - one front corner - was in the frame. The light went out and there was no further movement.

The number plate remained tantalisingly out of view, but in any case the angle was too oblique, and the light too bad. Even I could tell that there was no chance of getting a positive vehicle ID from that shot, irrespective of any computer enhancements.

Songo continued, 'Toyota Hilux four-by-four double-cab two point seven, petrol, 2005 model with standard-issue canopy. Judging by the shade of grey the chaps down at Imaging said that at first glance it looked like the Kalahari Sand paint option. That's beige to you and me!

'Toyota say that after white, it is their most common colour for that model, by the way. The guys at Imaging say they'll confirm as soon as they can that it is beige. Could be light blue though.'

Christo was clearly impressed with Songo's presentation. 'You've been fokken busy this evening, hey Kaaskop!' He pummelled him affectionately on his shiny head, rubbing in the nickname. 'Anything else?'

'Oh, yes!' Songo selected the next clip. 'By the way, the security guard wasn't lying… he really was asleep. The next we see of him is at about four thirty in the morning. He comes out of his little hut and goes for a piss. But forget him, Sarge, take a look at this.'

The scene was almost identical to the previous, except that there were a few new cars in the Pussycat's car park, and some that had been there earlier had gone.

The time code was 01:47. The headlight of the Toyota was still just visible in the right-hand corner of the screen. It hadn't moved for two and a half hours. Then the headlight suddenly came on. I blinked, and looked again. It sped across the frame, disappearing to the left of screen.

'Fok me! You're blerrie right! It is the fokken vehicle! Check the time! That's when he fokken left the club!' Christo was jubilant. 'The killer followed him to the club. He was waiting for him and he must have jumped him right there, on the pavement, just out of picture. That's the breakthrough we need! Let's check out the tyre tracks. I bet you they'll be a match for a Hilux!'

Songo had a broad smile. 'Sarge, I already had Lynette get on to the Toyota people. Those models were issued with Goodyear Wrangler one-nine-five-seventy R-fifteen radials as standard. Look!'

He busied himself with the mouse and selected a JPEG file from a list of hundreds. 'Here's one of the shots we took this morning under the trees over there.' He pointed across the lay-by to the tall pine trees. The shot of a faint tyre print in a patch of bare, muddy earth with its numbered plastic peg was on the screen. 'Lynette checked it out. It's a Goodyear Wrangler one-nine-five!'

'Fok me! You have been busy!' Christo had to raise his voice over the noise of a truck engaging its exhaust brake as it rumbled past the lay-by. 'Blerrie well done, Kaaskop! I'm fokken impressed!'

Christo had a brainwave. 'Just go back to that last clip, the one where we see the Toyota driving off.' Songo selected the file.

The headlight came on and it came into view. The light was so bad and reflections rendered the windows so opaque, that there was absolutely no indication of the number of occupants, or any other useful details.

Christo waited till it cleared the parked vehicles in the street and a few other obstructions, '*Ja*... okay... freeze the frame... wait... now!' Christo stabbed the screen with a big stubby finger. 'Look! You see, Anton? You were fokken right!'

The finger was pointing at the front fender of the Toyota. Despite the grainy quality and the poor light, the utility winch was clear to see.

* * * * *

I smiled to myself when I remembered that moment. Christo complimenting *me* on my detective work! Well, there is a first time for everything, they say!

I stood up in the lukewarm, crystal-clear water, and carefully scanned the beach. Still no sign of her. I hoped she was okay.

I turned around and faced the ocean. Nothing and no one obscured my view of the horizon. Tomorrow was going to be smog and traffic and hijackers and millions of people and all that urban banality.

I tried to imagine how Kelly was going to fit into my life back home... was I dreaming? Was it going to be possible? And what about Mammie? What had I got myself into?

But there was no going back now. In a few short days she had made a space for herself in my heart. I could not imagine that space being filled by anything or anyone else.

The water closed in over my head as I lazily glided over the white sand. The memories of the events that evening in Cape Town two years ago were still clear in my head.

Sixteen

Songo's revelations hadn't ended there. He had indeed had a busy, productive day. 'Hey, Sarge, look at this. You remember the shoe print we looked at this morning?' He was fiddling on the computer again. A picture appeared. 'Well, the boys in the office came up with this.'

He clicked a few more times and the faint shoe print in the photo had a computer-generated pattern superimposed on it, matching and filling out the partial print in the mud.

'That is a Hi-Tec North Ridge boot. Size eleven.' Songo and Christo looked at one another.

Christo raised an eyebrow. 'He's not a small guy!'

'No, Sarge, he's not!'

Christo's cell phone rang.

'Hello Januarie! ...*Ja*?' Christo listened intently for a few moments. His face showed renewed excitement. '*Ja*, I'm still at the scene. What... you're bringing him here? ...Okay ...okay ...see you!'

He turned to me. 'Sorry *Boet*! This is going to be a long night! Sure you don't want to go home?'

I smiled and shook my head. 'No... don't worry about me. As long as I'm not getting in your way.'

'Of course you're not! Songo. That was Bellville police station on the line. The guys are bringing a possible witness here to talk to us. Apparently he walked into the station and told them that he saw something here early this morning.'

Christo was walking towards the pine trees. He looked over his shoulder at Songo and me. 'Careful! Make sure you stay on the clean tarmac! I'm not having you guys contaminating my fokken crime scene!'

We carefully followed him, ducking under the yellow plastic tape - *POLICE LINE - DO NOT CROSS* - that demarcated the search area, and entered the brightly lit arena. The hum of traffic continued behind us.

Christo stood at the point where the paved area of the lay-by gave way to the muddy earth. Songo and I stood behind him, careful not to stray off the bare asphalt.

The pine trees were a few metres ahead of us. The stained earth, which pinpointed the spot where van der Spuy had bled to death, was directly in front of us, vertically below a bough of the nearest pine tree.

A metre to Christo's left, and slightly ahead of him, I could make out a faint tyre print on the muddy earth at the edge of the asphalt, a numbered plastic marker peg stuck into the ground beside it.

'*Ja*. You see, the vehicle stopped here... with the winch about...' he illustrated with his outstretched hand just ahead of his knees, '...here.'

He looked up. '*Ja*, that fits, because the cable marks on that branch point exactly in this direction, and those drag marks,' he pointed to some scrapes in the mud and flattened grass between where he stood and the bloodstained patch straight ahead, 'show how the victim was dragged on the ground for a metre or two until the cable lifted him into the air.' He paused, scratching his chin.

'Hey, Songo! Where did we find that boot print?'

'There, next to the rubbish bin. You see, number C twenty-seven.' Songo pointed to a plastic peg ahead and to our right. 'There, just where he would have stood while he tied the rope to the refuse bin frame.'

Christo looked satisfied.

'Okay. The angles seem to check out. A winch it definitely was!' He turned to Songo. 'Let's ask the office to start checking out beige Toyota Hiluxes.'

'Lynette's already on to it.' Songo had been excelling himself.

'Fok me, *Kaaskop*! You looking for a promotion or what?'

As we walked back to where we had parked, Christo put a hand on Songo's shoulder. 'Why don't you ask the office to send us out some coffee and maybe some chicken and chips or pizza or something? Ask those guys what they want.'

Christo and I went and sat in the car. I amused myself by clicking through the many photos on the laptop - countless images of carefully numbered items, some obviously relevant, many probably not; flattened grass and scrape marks, bits of paper, tyre treads, used condoms, cigarette butts, gruesome shots of van der Spuy's body parts lying on the earth and studies of the naked corpse hanging from the pine tree in the cold morning light.

There were close ups of the rope - what looked like ordinary ten-millimetre kernmantle rope - tied to the steel pipe frame of the rubbish bin and the climber in me couldn't help noticing that the killer had used a double-overhand knot.

There were aerial views of the cable and rope marks high on the overhanging branch, for which I presumed the police photographer must have used a long extension ladder.

Christo was back on the phone, talking to Lynette at the office. When he hung up he turned to me.

'Lynette has been checking out the vehicle registry. There are seven hundred and eighty-fokken-something beige 2005 model Toyota Hiluxes in the Western Cape, over three hundred in Cape Town alone. Then again, it could have been a Kwa-Zulu vehicle, or from the Free State or Gauteng.

'She's already checked with the car hire places. *Avis* have seventeen registered here, *Budget* another twelve. Apparently *Avis* say they have a total of fifty-six beige ones countrywide, most with a winch fitted. Fok! Why do they all buy blerrie beige ones?'

The enormity of the task of trying to isolate the vehicle without a registration number was clear. 'I've asked her to get back to the car hire firms and check which ones have a winch.' He frowned. 'And we're not even a hundred per cent sure it was fokken beige, you know. As Songo said, the light blue one looks pretty much the same on a black and white security camera...

'At least the winch narrows down our field a bit, though our guy could easily remove the fokken thing in five minutes if he is clever... and we know he is!

'I've put out an APB for beige and light blue 2005 Hiluxes, with or without canopy, with or without a winch. The cops have all been told to look out for signs of a canopy or a winch having been recently removed. Clean bolt holes, fresh scratches, that sort of thing.

'Also, to keep an eye out for Hilux drivers wearing Hi-Tec North Ridge size elevens while they're it! Hey!' Christo scowled at my raised eyebrow. 'I know it's fokken little to go on, but we've *mos* got to try everything!'

Songo rejoined us. 'Hey, Sarge, you know, I just thought of something...'

'*Ja?*'

'Aren't there any other CCTV cameras in that part of Sea Point? Maybe one of those would have recorded the vehicle passing on its way to or from the nightclub. Maybe you'll get a registration from one of them.'

'Fok me! *All* your blerrie lights are switched on today, hey *Kaaskop*! Good fokken thinking!' Christo grabbed his cell phone and dialled a number. He strolled around the cars as he spoke intently into the phone. I could pick up snippets. '*Ja*, moving towards the Pussycat in the minutes leading up to eleven fourteen... *Ja*... after one forty-five this morning, heading towards Devil's Peak... *Ja*... No, on the westbound carriageway... Okay! Hey thanks, man!'

Christo came back towards us. '*Ja*... the Sea Point cops are going to check it out and get back to us. *Kaaskop*! Get on to your mate at Metro Police and ask them to check their speed-trap cameras too - between Sea Point and here.'

'Sure thing, Sarge!' Songo immediately put through a call to Metro.

Just then a squad car pulled up. There was a bit of traffic chaos as it blocked the left-hand lane of De Waal, while Songo moved his car to make space on the verge so that the newcomers could find a parking spot.

It was the two policemen from Bellville police station. With them was a frightened, Slavic-looking little man of about thirty-five. They came over to where Christo and I were sitting on the bonnet of the Cressida.

After handshakes and introductions all round, one of the Bellville cops delivered a little preamble. '*Ja*, Christo! This is Slobodan Mandic, the guy I was telling you about on the phone. He's got a little story I think you will find interesting. Go on, Slobodan. Don't be scared of him!' He indicated Christo. 'He may be big and ugly, but he doesn't bite!'

Everyone laughed except Mandic. The little man looked as if he was about to burst into tears. He put a cigarette into his mouth with shaky fingers and started patting his pockets, looking for matches. Ever ready for an excuse to smoke, I lit it for him and then lit my own. Christo tried to suppress his impatience. 'So, Slobodan, what is it you want to tell me?'

Songo joined us. He nodded at the newcomers. 'Metro say they'll do their best, Sarge. Said we should check them again in the morning.'

'Thanks, Constable.' Then to Mandic, 'You were saying…?'

'Er… ' Mandic looked at his feet. His eyes darted around and settled on Songo. Perhaps he looked the least threatening. 'You see, boss, I hear him in the TV today about a dead man they find him here. This place.' He pointed towards the brightly lit lay-by. 'Well… las' night... I mean this morning… I not sure… maybe around half three, to four…'

'Go on,' Christo was doing his best to look friendly and approachable. 'You can speak up a bit.' The rumble of traffic just metres away all but swamped Mandic's timid voice.

He raised it. 'I have pick up girl… you know…' he took a drag on the cigarette. '…Prostitute.' His eyes flitted furtively around the group, and settled back on Songo. 'I picking her up in Rondebosch… yes? We driving in my car, I looking… you know… for a place… a place to fucking her… no?'

Christo nodded enthusiastic understanding. 'Go on!'

'I driving here… in this... parking place. Me, I thinking maybe I fucking her here… yes? When I am turning…' Mandic indicated with his hand, 'I see there another car already here. So I no wanting to share…no? I going look for another place.'

'What kind of car was it… did you see it clearly?'

Mandic hastily expelled some smoke. 'I no looking very close… maybe some bad guy, no? These days… many bad guy, no? He can just shooting you for nothing… yes? But I think it… er, brownish… light brown colour… *Nissan* maybe Toyota, you know… four-by-four. He got canopy… He parking there,' he pointed towards the area where we had been standing shortly before.

'Anything else you remember? Did it have Cape Town plates? Anything?'

'No… er… I no remember…' He sucked hard on the cigarette.

'Did you see anyone?'

'No… you know I afraid I disturb them… so I turning off my lights… you know, I not want to making him angry… so I reversing… like this… then I going… yes?'

Christo looked at Songo. 'Well, at least we can tell Lynette to ignore the light blue option, sounds like it was beige after all.'

'Sure, Sarge…'

Christo turned back to Mandic who looked slightly less terrified. 'Is that all? Did you see anything else? Anything at all?'

Mandic looked at the two Bellville cops, then at Christo. 'After I leaving this place… you know…' he took a quick drag, 'I going to next parking…' he pointed down De Waal towards town. 'I find good place there… I… er… you know, I finish… er… we fucking. Finish.' He looked embarrassed and guilty, and puffed hard.

All the listeners were doing their best not to intimidate him, to let him carry on. For a few moments the hum of rush-hour traffic was all that could be heard. 'When I am finish, I coming back this way, to go to Rondebosch.' Mandic pointed, indicating the eastbound lane of De Waal, across the divide of the dual carriageway. 'You know… now I have to taking the girl back to Rondebosch… no?'

Christo nodded. 'Yes?'

'When I driving past here, I look… no? I don't know why I looking, but I look. I see the van he gone.'

'And do you remember the time? What time did you pass here?'

'Yes… you see I arguing with the girl… she say I must paying her three hour… but I say no, he's only two hour… you know. So I remember the time is exactly half five. This I sure!' Mandic could see that this was good information, and that Christo looked pleased. He flicked the cigarette butt away with an air of achievement.

* * * * *

As I waded out of the water towards my towel on the beach, I reminded myself of the chilling significance of Mr Mandic's clear recollection of the exact time that morning. Dr Rashida Asvat had put the time of death at six-twenty. Yet, at five-thirty, fifty minutes earlier, the vehicle was already gone.

That meant that by five-thirty van der Spuy had already been injected with the ephedrine-histamine cocktail. The sulphuric acid - two different concentrations of sulphuric acid - had already been poured into the two syringe barrels on the piano wires. The victim had already been hoisted up into the tree and the killer had set up his contraption, and had gone.

Van der Spuy's fate had been sealed, the machinery that would torture and kill him had been inexorably set in motion, and the killer had left. He had not even stayed to observe his handiwork. *Weird*! *A squeamish serial killer*? I couldn't get my head around it. I knew that Christo also found it baffling.

I dried myself off and sat down on the towel. I retrieved my plastic bag of valuables from the sand, opened it and lit a cigarette. It had been bizarre. That evening on De Waal Drive, with Mandic's evidence, the vehicle search well underway and the other encouraging leads, Christo and his team had been on a high. They exuded self-belief, and one would have sworn that an arrest was only a matter of days away. But that evening had in fact marked the end of forward progress.

There hadn't been any more breakthroughs. The Sea Point CCTV search drew a blank. A painstaking hunt for the vehicle, through registration data, roadblocks, winch sales records, and every other possible source drew a blank. The car hire company records too showed that all the beige Hiluxes that were out on hire at the time were in the hands of *bona fide* tourists, or could be traced as having been out of town that night.

A separate, more detailed examination of the hire records for Hiluxes with a fitted winch similarly revealed nothing. The Metro police traffic cameras also drew a blank. The piano wire, it turned out, may have been stolen in a robbery on a music store: Johnnies Music, in Rosebank, months before - a case that also remained unsolved.

The duct tape on the corpse, the karabiner, the victim's personal effects, shoes, clothes, wallet and car keys had between them not yielded even a partial fingerprint. No more witnesses had come forward. No new forensic evidence had been uncovered. As the weeks passed, the trail had grown colder and colder.

When Christo was called to Nelspruit in Mpumalanga to advise the police there on a castration and murder that had happened near the Mozambique border town of Komatipoort seven months after the van der Spuy killing, there was excitement that maybe the murders were linked. No real evidence supported this hunch, except that both crimes involved torture and genital mutilation.

At first the police suspected that it was a copycat killing. But when Christo and the Mpumalanga Serious Crimes Unit pieced the sequence of events together, the chilling fact became apparent: like van der Spuy, this victim's grisly death had taken place in the murderer's absence. The apparatus that had tortured him and taken his life had been set in motion, and by the time he died, the killer was already far away.

Information on this bizarre quirk of the van der Spuy case had never been released to the public. The press had never been told that van der Spuy's killer was not present for the entire painful process; that he had left before the show. How could a copycat killer have known?

However, the Komatipoort case yielded even fewer leads than had the Cape Town killing. To be precise, it gave the police nothing.

Six months later, when there was a third killing, and within days, a fourth, both in the Jo'burg area, the bigwigs decided to create a task force to work exclusively on the Castration Murders. Detective Sergeant Christo Januarie was promoted to Detective Inspector and appointed to head the team. The next killing was in Ermelo, and the sixth, just five months ago, was in Amanzimtoti, near Durban.

Only four pieces of apparently hard evidence linked any of the six killings, and all of those were only circumstantial. Most significantly - at least to Christo - was the fact that all six victims had been gagged with gaffer tape. The same brand, size and colour had been used in every murder: 3-M, fifty-millimetre red.

The boffins at forensics couldn't swear it was off the same roll, but it had been established that all six pieces came from the same batch, from the same production run. There was every likelihood, but no proof, that they all came off the same roll. This was by far the strongest physical evidence linking the six killings.

At the Ermelo murder scene, Christo's team had found a footprint, a Hi-Tec North Ridge size eleven footprint identical to the one found on De Waal. Coincidence maybe, but then again, maybe not.

All six victims had been drugged: first with sedatives to allow the murderer to set up his killing apparatus, and then with stimulants and hallucinogens to maximise the agony and terror. The cocktail of drugs varied from case to case. Although pethedeine, hexabarbitol and histamine had been used in all six murders, ephedrine had been replaced by Methedrine in some instances. To enhance the victims' panic, LSD had been used in four of the murders and PCP, or Angel Dust, in the other two.

The Amanzimtoti killing yielded another significant link. The killing there had also involved piano wire. The microscopic, metallurgical and chemical analyses of the wire suggested that it was of the same manufacture as the van der Spuy wire - Yamaha, made in Japan. Although he had no incontrovertible proof, Christo was sure it was off the same roll that had been stolen from Johnnies Music.

Everything else that hypothetically connected the six murders was just that: hypothetical. This killer did not leave a signature, as serial killers often do. The closest he got to a signature were the drugs and the red gaffer tape. And those connections, Christo had to remind himself, were still only circumstantial.

Each killing had a different technique, but in all of the cases the conscious, spaced-out victim watched his own castration and emasculation, and then after an interval, during which he endured unspeakable agony and distress, he died. Whoever was committing these murders wanted his victims to suffer. That at least, was incontestable.

If there were different killers on the loose, they must all be having the same evil, sadistic dreams. Too much to swallow, I told myself. I knew that Christo also refused to believe that there was more than one murderer. He was so convinced of the single killer theory that he had staked his whole career on it. His head would surely roll if he was wrong. But, I reflected,

Christo's head was likely to roll anyway if the murders remained unsolved and progress continued to be so minimal.

Now there was a suspect in custody, and everyone was excited, but I was unconvinced. If it was the wrong man, where would that leave my friend's credibility?

But, I conceded, I could be mistaken. I hoped I was.

I switched on the phone, and dialled Christo again. This time the call went through immediately.

'*Waar die fok kruip jy weg*? Where are you hiding?'

'No, I'm not in hiding! I've been meaning to phone! It's just... I tried a couple of times, but couldn't get through.'

'Don't talk *kak*! I *mos* know you well enough! Don't *praat* shit! The only thing that could make you hide away like this is a woman, *nê*? Where are you? Huh? Who is she?'

I had prepared myself for this interrogation. I wasn't going to resist. 'Mauritius.'

'I fokken knew it! So what's her name, hey? Is she *lekker*?'

'Her name's Kelly... yes, very nice. No, honestly, Chris, she's bloody gorgeous! Utterly sexy! Really lovely person, too.'

'You blerrie falling in love, or what? Don't fokken tell me that Mr Iceman, Mr Fokken Confirmed Bachelor has finally cracked! So, tell me about her. Where d'you find her?'

'Well, she sort of found me, I suppose. I guess we bumped into one another... at court last week. She's...'

'What kind, heh? Afrikaans? English? Just don't tell me she's blerrie Jewish... remember what happened last time!' Christo was laughing.

'No, she's a Motswana, a South African who lived in England for about fifteen years.'

There was incredulity in Christo's voice. 'A Tswana? You mean she's a black chick? Fok me!'

'No thanks. Not while there are still dogs in the street!'

'No really, you're not having me on? A black chick?'

'*Ja*, really really!'

'You must be fokken kidding me! Anton Gerhardus Venter falling in love with a black woman! Jesus Christ! The blerrie sky's going to fall on our fokken heads!'

'Come on, don't make it sound like it's some newfound wonder of the world. It's not the first time people from different backgrounds fall.'

'No, not the first time, but the first time for a blerrie Venter, that's for sure. Have you considered what your pa is going to say? Hey? Have you thought of that? Your ma?'

'*Ja*, of course I have. I'm shitting myself! But what can one do? One doesn't choose these things! Anyway, enough of that. This call's costing me bucks. What's up?'

Christo was still clearly bowled over. 'Fok me! Anton and a darkie! What next?' He paused. 'Fokken well done, Boet! I hope it turns out good for you! Anyway, now, instead of hating fokken coloureds you can start making them…Hey?'

'Fuck off. Not so fast, Chris!'

'Okay, okay.' Christo was chortling at his own joke. 'Anyway, the reason I've been trying to get hold of you…There's been a bit of a breakthrough.'

'You mean with the DNA?'

'No, well, not exactly. The DNA thing turned out to be a fokken big disappointment. You remember I told you we were working on that miniscule skin sample that was off the Mpumalanga murder victim's fingernail?'

'*Ja*, I remember. Have you got a match with your suspect... whassisname?'

'Sylvester Cupido. No, no such luck. No match. Some of the other evidence we had on him is also looking weak. His alibis all seem to be checking out, too. Fok it, Anton, I think we're going to have to let the blerrie moffie go!'

'Pity! I was really hoping you had the thing wrapped up.'

'*Ja* no, Anton. But I was telling you about a new breakthrough.'

I looked up and down the beach. Way off in the distance I saw her, strolling casually towards me. God, I love you, I thought.

'You know, when we profiled the victims we also checked out their police records; criminal convictions and that sort of thing. Well, at the time, nothing significant showed up. But we were wrong, you know, the national police computer database only records convictions, not arrests.

'Arrests are recorded by the different local police authorities, but if there's not a conviction, the information isn't put onto the national register. It's all this blerrie political correctness kak. You know, we're not allowed to hold potentially compromising information on innocent members of the public and all that crap.'

Christo paused for breath. 'Anyway, all this time we've been overlooking a fokken vitally important fact: all six victims have had a complaint of rape or sexual assault against them at one time or another. Van der Spuy in Cape Town was arrested for rape of a thirteen-year-old. The charges were dropped. There was some suspicion that the girl's family had been paid off.

'Then, there was Dlamini in Komatipoort. He'd been found not guilty of three counts of rape after the prosecution lost a vital dossier and the case was thrown out. Mandla Dube had charges of child rape dropped after the complainant was murdered before she could testify. You remember the case, *nê*? It was big in all the newspapers.

'Fokken stupid thing, no one remembered the name in the newspaper stories three months later when the *ou* was killed. The rape and murder had happened in Newcastle, down in KwaZulu-Natal, and he was killed here, in Orlando, Soweto, so not even the journalists realised it was the same Mandla Dube.'

'*Ja.*'

I was taking this all in. The Castration Murderer was beginning to take on a new persona in my mind. All this time I had visualised a twisted, depraved pervert. I hadn't imagined that the killer might be some sort of crusading vigilante.

Christo was on song. 'Then, Mackenzie in the Booysens murder, you remember, the guy whose goolies were burnt off with the blowtorch?'

'*Ja*, I remember! Could I forget?!'

'Well, he had also been arrested for molesting young girls but his case had also been dropped. There was a suspicion that the investigating cops had been paid off. Never proven, of course!'

'Of course.' Kelly was much closer now, walking on the water line, looking towards me. Even at this distance I could see from her wistful look that she was in love… in love with me!

'Well, of course as a result even Mackenzie had no fokken criminal record either! Nothing showed up on the database. Then there was that guy at Amanzimtoti - Vusi Mnkandla. It turns out that he had been arrested for raping a kid - a ten-year-old. She also was murdered while he was out on bail, before she could testify against him.

'The police never managed to find the killer, and his rape case was dropped. So, of course, it also never appeared on the fokken database!'

She was quite close now. I waved. 'So, Chris, looks like you've got yourself a whole new line of enquiry, hey!'

'Too true, Boet! It's all a bit embarrassing though, you know. We should have fokken realised sooner. But now that we've finally made the connection, I'm fokken excited! I… after… fokken … long …I …' the line was breaking up. Typical bloody cell phone networks! I thought.

'Hello! Hello! Can you hear me? Hello…' The line was dead.

I looked up. 'You are so damned beautiful!'

She smiled.

Seventeen

It was our last evening in Mauritius. I could well have been disappointed. As a sex holiday, which had been the original intention, it had been a complete failure. However, something much, much more profound had occurred, and the bonding I had experienced with this amazing little woman was far more than mere carnal coupling.

Anyway, the sex part will work itself out. Just don't push it, I told myself for the umpteenth time. It was difficult, though. Kelly was as relaxed and as natural as ever and, as I sat on the edge of the bath, a Phoenix in my hand, watching her in the shower while she blithely chatted about this and that, I marvelled at my patience.

She was as beautiful and as sexy as I believed I could ever have imagined a woman could be… and it seemed she was mine. Strange though, I confessed to myself, she was mine despite the absence of a proper physical consummation.

Somehow the way she had exposed her innermost soul to me was more intimate than any giving of her body could have been.

We were talking about our favourite leisure pursuits.

'Most of my climbing was in Cheddar Gorge, and up in Skye; the Black Cuillins, also on Nevis, of course. That's when I still belonged to a climbing club at SOAS, you know, the School of Oriental and African Studies at London Uni. We had a great climbing club, and we did tons of climbing weekends. Oh, they were wicked! But you know British rock. I think greasy is the technical term. I'll just call it fuckin' wet! I far prefer the dry. You can push yourself much further.'

We had wandered on to the subject of climbing. We were getting along so well, but the limited time we had had together thus far meant that we were still finding out pretty fundamental things about each other. I was chuffed. What a bonus, I thought. Not only is she gorgeous, and sexy, and wonderful, and in love with me, but she climbs too!

'Have you climbed much in the Cape?'

'Not that much. Of course, I've done the tourist routes on Table Mountain; you know Africa Face Direct, Bakoven, Skyhook, that sort of thing…'

'Tourist routes, my foot! Those are serious climbs!'

'Also did a few routes on Du Toit's Peak. Full Frontal. Know it?'

'Know it? Fucking sure I know it! I've climbed it. Rather, I've been hauled up it. That's a pretty rigorous climb, twenty-five South African, E4 in the British grading, 5.11c they'd call it in the US. Don't tell me you've led it.'

'I don't lead, and I don't belay. I've long since given up all that rope and ironmongery shit. Only climb free-solo these days - or did when I still climbed - haven't been out in more than a year.'

I looked at her open-mouthed.

'Yeah, been climbing free-solo for about six years. Can't be bothered with all that competitive shit you get in a group. Prefer it on my own. More spiritual, like, just you and the mountain, know what I mean?'

I was aghast. 'What? You've climbed Full Frontal? Solo… free-solo?'

Full Frontal is a breathtaking, uncompromising three hundred metre plus vertical line up the face of Du Toit's Peak, in the Hottentots Holland Mountains, up a series of long, narrow cracks barely wide enough to fit your hand into, and through a succession of vicious overhangs.

I took seven hours for my ascent - though the best climbers do it in half that - and needed a tight top-rope, and lots of shouted encouragement to get up most of its pitches.

Traversing the overhangs was like crossing the ceilings of a few average-sized rooms, and I had only managed to do it by standing in slings hanging from wedges lodged in fissures in the underside of the inverted projecting ledges.

Climbing Full Frontal solo had only ever been achieved by a handful of climbers. Five years ago, Max Courtney, one of

South Africa's most brilliant and colourful climbing personalities had fallen to his death from the final overhang.

It was one of the toughest, most committing free-climbs anywhere in South Africa. The overhangs particularly, required enormous finger and upper-body strength, as the free climber had to swing hand-over-hand from tiny finger-jams in the ceiling cracks, legs kicking free in a thousand feet of empty air with no rope, no slings to stand in, no climbing partner, no margin for error.

I looked at the tiny, naked figure in front of me in utter wonder and disbelief.

'Jesus! And Africa Face Direct! Bakoven! Solo? Don't tell me you've solo-ed Skyhook! That's a fucking twenty-six, 5.11d American!'

Her tone was almost dismissive. 'Yeah. So I can climb, so what? It's all relative, innit?'

'*Ja*, it may be fucking relative, but those are awesome climbs! Fuck, I consider myself a fair climber and I've only managed to lead eighteen's and nineteen's - 5.9's - I think I can claim to have led a 5.10a pitch once… and that was with a double rope too!'

I was totally gobsmacked. 'Twenty-six! Free-solo! I'm impressed… I really am!'

She shrugged it off. 'My recent climbing has all been in Tonquani Gorge in the Magaliesberg. D'you climb there? You know: Lightning Strikes Twice, Cardiac Arrest?'

'*Ja*, of course. It's the best climbing anywhere near Jo'burg, after all, but I haven't climbed at all for almost two years. Hey! As soon as we get back and we get a chance I'm taking you to Tonquani for a weekend. D'you hear?'

She smiled as she got out of the shower and began to towel herself dry. 'Yeah, okay. Though, I'd really like to try the Waterberg, you know. Much longer routes than Tonquani.'

It was the first real admission that we were going to continue being together after this holiday. My heart leaped with joy.

'Anywhere you want! If you're so bloody allergic to ropes and stuff, you can solo the routes with a coiled rope in your backpack. When you're at the top you can chuck down an end and top-rope the poor old geriatric. Okay? Tight rope up the difficult bits!'

'You're on!'

We decided to have our farewell supper at the non-touristy restaurant in the backstreets of Mont Choisy, where I had related the story of my birth in Dr van der Merwe's spare room.

That evening seemed so long ago! There was already an air of nostalgia about us as we realised that tomorrow the holiday was over and the rat race would begin anew.

I was still speechless. Over the last few minutes I had reclimbed some of those routes in my head, especially Full Frontal, Skyhook, Bakoven and Cardiac Arrest in Tonquani. Climbs on which I had spent many arduous hours, fully protected by the whole gamut of ropes and karabiners, and slings, and belays, and supporting climbers.

I tried to imagine the inner steel one would require to attempt those climbs alone, with no moral support, with nothing but fingernails, lightweight EB's on your feet, and a chalk bag to absorb the sweat off the fingers. *Fuck! Would I have sweaty fingers, or what?*

Kelly seemed to take it all in her stride. While she was putting on her body lotion before getting dressed, I had asked her if she knew whether she was the first woman to solo any of her incredible ascents. Was she in the record books? She dismissed the notion with disdain and bored nonchalance.

'Couldn't give a fuck, mate. Just enjoy climbing, that's all.' She looked me in the eye as with equal nonchalance she spread her gorgeous naked legs and slipped in a tampon.

Wow! What a woman! One of a kind, I thought, swallowing hard. One of a bloody kind!

Over another delicious Indo-Chinese meal, we planned our last Mauritian morning.

'Our flight's at three, check in at two. That means we need to leave for the airport at what, twelve forty-five.' As ever, I was being my methodical, organised self. 'Herr Ober Organisator' as Hannah's German grandmother used to teasingly call me.

'That means we can go to the beach in the morning!' Kelly was as enthusiastic as a small child. 'I'd love to do a bit of snorkelling. I've been meaning to suggest it, and now we're out of time.'

'I'm sure we can arrange a quick trip tomorrow.'

We were up early the next morning. After a short search we found a place nearby that did boat trips to the reef, and by eight-thirty we were in the water, diving over the spectacular coral.

As we dived from the little glass-bottomed boat, our Mauritian boatman plainly ogling Kelly's tiny bikini and scrumptious curves, I marvelled at her prowess.

We would dive together, kicking down the three or four metres to the coral, amid an explosion of brightly coloured fish. Forty-five or so seconds later, I would be running out of oxygen and heading for the surface.

After a couple of good breaths I dived again, only to see Kelly far beneath me, fifteen or twenty metres further along the reef, lazily chasing a school of fish. I barely caught up with her when I had to head for the surface again, gasping.

After my third dive, Kelly casually drifted to the surface, a good two to three minutes after submerging, and instead of gasping, as she spat out the snorkel, she said something like 'Hey did you see that little silver one with the blue tips to its fins?' without the slightest shortness of breath.

After the third or fourth time, when I had submerged fifteen times to her four, when we briefly met on the surface, I said, 'Shit, I know I smoke and all that, but are you sure you don't have gills or something!'

'It's just that I know how to conserve my energy!' She mimicked me. 'Ooh…aah! Kelly… ooh!' She winked mischievously through her mask and dived again.

I knew what she was referring to. In the middle of the night I had awoken to the heavenly sensation of Kelly giving me an unsolicited blow job, and with all the pent-up sexual energy within me, when I had come I had groaned and moaned so expansively, and so noisily, that Kelly had burst into delicious laughter, mouth full and all! She had been teasing me about it, one way or the other, all morning.

Significantly, she had whispered a confession into my ear as we rode the boat out to the reef: 'Believe it or not, as you like, I've never done that before. That was my first time, I mean ever!'

She giggled. 'You know, apart from the other night when we didn't...' She gave me a squeeze. 'Sorry about that...' I squeezed back as she whispered, 'Do you always make so much fuckin' noise?' Then, as an afterthought through the stifled giggles, 'My God, it's salty!'

Kelly and I both fell silent in the taxi to Plaisance Airport, holding hands in the back seat like teenagers being driven home after a dance, soon to be dropped off at their respective doors. The few short days had been momentous for us both, and now we each had a lot to reflect upon.

Johannesburg was going to be very different. I knew that the pressures of life - work, my daughters and my domestic arrangements - would no doubt cast the new relationship into a very different light, and subject it to stresses and demands that neither of us could yet conceive of.

And then there was still Zeerust.

I had to admit to myself that my paranoia *à propos* my parents finding out about Kelly and me was not the same as it had been before the relationship began.

When I had looked up from my chair in the courtroom six short days ago, the prospect of having a relationship with a black woman, and my parents' probable reaction to that possibility, had been purely academic, hypothetical conjecture.

Now, I couldn't see it the same way. I was not involved with a black woman. I was involved with Kelly. She was no longer an objective thing, a category, a demographic. She was my lover, a dear friend, a deeply hurt and remarkably recovered heroine, a quirky comedienne, a superb athlete, a sensitive soulmate.

Although I knew how set in their ways my parents were, I could no longer see Kelly through the eyes I had previously presumed for them. They would just have to get to know her as a person, as I was doing, and despite their prejudices, they would come right. At least I hoped they would.

Maybe I should enlist Antjie's help. She was from a different generation, a New South African. She'd see it differently. Perhaps I could get her to help me ease the old folks into the reality of my new life - like a shuttle diplomat, as it were.

The taxi was passing through Curepipe, where we spent our first night together in less than romantic circumstances. I caught Kelly's eye, and she squeezed my hand harder.

There was an intense look in her eyes. I held her gaze for a long moment. She leant her head against my shoulder, and in a low voice, so that the taxi driver couldn't hear, began a sort of declaration.

'Anton... I...' her voice was husky, full of pent-up emotion. 'I know we only met last week. Sure. I know any sane person would tell me... us... that what I am about to tell you is bullshit... that it can't be true... but fuck it! ...Yes, it is less than a week, but that's not the point. I admit you had sort of entered my life a bit before that, in the sense that I was fascinated by you. I mean, I was wildly attracted to you, for a couple of weeks, maybe three, before you finally noticed me!'

'No, I ...' she put her hand to my lips.

'My turn.' I realised that she was trying to say something important, to express something difficult and heavy, and resolved to hear her out without any of my usual impulsive interruptions.

'The thing is... and I don't want you to misunderstand me or to let your big head swell any more than it already fuckin' has... the thing is that you are the first... I mean... you are the only...'

She was having trouble finding the words. She took a deep breath. 'Anton, I've told you a bit about myself now... and I think you're beginning to understand where I'm coming from... What I'm trying to tell you is that I have never, in all my thirty years, loved a man. Any man! I have never made love to a man... ever. I have never fallen for a man... ever.'

She looked up at me and stared intensely into my eyes. 'But I am falling in love... No! Let me be brutally fuckin' candid. I have fallen in love with you, and I am terrified, I am helpless... I...'

Suddenly, she lost it and smothered her face into my chest and sobbed and sobbed uncontrollably, while I held her as tight as I could, oblivious of the driver, and of the entire world beyond that intense, vibrating space. But she hadn't finished having her say, and continued, choking through the tears. 'Please God, don't you ever leave me, Anton. Don't you ever leave me... no matter what... what ... tell me you won't... no matter what... Oh, Anton! ...Love...'

I heard the words coming out of my mouth, and they did so without the slightest resistance, without doubt or hesitation. 'I'll never leave you, Kelly. Never! I love you... I love you... I love you!'

The mood of profound intimacy stayed with us all the way to Jo'burg International. Gradually the *gravitas* that pervaded our interactions had lifted, and by the time our flight landed at a little after eight, we were back to something resembling our bubbly selves, making the most of our last minutes of carefree togetherness. Both of us knew that things were about to change. Mauritius and the blithe holiday mood were behind us now.

As we cleared customs and walked through the concourse, I couldn't help making the comparison with the naïve, tentative couple that had passed through the same airport on Thursday evening. Here they were again, but their body language spoke eloquently of a familiar closeness that appeared natural and uncontrived. An observant onlooker, noticing their easy familiarity would have suggested that they had been intimate for years, not mere days.

The Audi was still there in the covered parking where I had left it. We chucked in our bags and headed towards the freeway into town. Under the yellow glare of the sodium lights, her face suddenly looked tired. She looked all of her thirty years for the first time since I had met her.

'When am I going to see you?' She sounded sad and drained.

'I thought we had a date. Friday night, around nine, remember? As soon as I get back from Botswana.'

'Friday? What's today? Tuesday! Shit, Friday sounds ages away.'

I stretched out a hand. 'Don't worry, I'll phone you every day.'

'Hmm…' she sounded unconvinced.

We left the freeway and entered the city, edging up towards the towers of Hillbrow - some of the most densely populated square kilometres on the planet. Hillbrow is the epitome of inner-city urban decay, even though many locals seem to find it perfectly okay.

The place has a desperate reputation for crime and violence, much of it richly deserved. But there are even still a few of the pre-liberation residents, old white pensioners and the like, who seemed to get along fine alongside the murder and mayhem, the Nigerian cocaine dealers, the gangsters, rapists, bent cops, whores, hustlers and pimps.

But much of Hillbrow is far less glamorous that it is reputed to be. Just thousands of struggling poor people living ten to a one-roomed flat with non-functional toilets and broken windows, surrounded by countless informal street traders, desperate illegal aliens, street children, crackheads and drunks.

Kelly squeezed my hand tighter the closer we got to her building, one of the ubiquitous twenty-storey blocks just off Kotze Street.

'You can stop here. I'll get my bag... it's probably better if you just stay in the car, luv. Rich-looking white folk draw too much attention around here.'

I pulled her across the seat towards me. With one eye on the rear-view mirror and the other scanning the pavement, I kissed her, trying to convey in a few short seconds all the intensity of the emotion I was feeling. Suddenly, I had an idea. 'Hey, why don't you come with me?'

'Where?'

'To Botswana. Tomorrow!'

'But hey, Anton, I don't want to impose, you know. You're going to be busy and...'

'Well, bring a good book! I'll only be busy for a few hours each day. We'll have the evenings together, and the drive there and back,' I paused, and tried to introduce a light-hearted flirtatiousness into my voice, 'and the nights!'

She pulled away, leaning against the door, one hand on the handle, ready to get out. She looked at me quizzically. 'You sure?'

'Dead sure'

'Okay then.'

I was excited. 'I'll pick you up at six... here... tomorrow. You'll be here?'

'I'll be here. Six.' A quick peck and a last squeeze, and she was gone. I smiled to myself. The boot opened and closed and then she came back to the passenger door, opened it and tossed a blue exercise book on to the seat. A moment later she was darting up the steps past the drunks and the weirdos, into her building, her dreads bobbing about her head, her pert butt wiggling delightfully.

No sooner had I pulled away from the kerb than I smacked myself forcefully on the forehead with the palm of my hand. *Zeerust! You forgot Zeerust, you stupid cunt*! I had put my foot right into it!

How was I going to wing it? Taking Kelly to Botswana and going via Zeerust? Sometimes my impulsiveness really gets in my way. *Stupid fool*!

I'd had a perfectly good plan: drive to Botswana, visit my sick father on the way, and come home to resume the thing with Kelly. Now I had gone and unthinkingly, stupidly, fucked up the whole arrangement by giving in to my emotions, my stupid impulses. *Idiot*!

Oh well…

The phone rang. It was Solly. '*Heyta*, bro! Howzit?'

'Where are you? You back from gorging yourself on Creole pussy yet?'

'Yeah, just barely back. Still on my way home from the airport. Where are you?'

'Just getting into ThabaNchu, you know, all the hoo-ha with the *bogadi* is tomorrow. I've got to be up and at my best at bloody five a.m. Receiving the bride price is a serious affair, and we'll fine the groom's party if they're late, so we have to be there first, waiting for them! I *am* the chief uncle, after all.'

'When is the wedding?'

'Well, it all starts tomorrow… we'll talk about that. The real reason I'm phoning is that I just heard that your friend Jabu Zulu has been kidnapped!'

'What? Say again! When?'

'Sometime this afternoon, I'm told. It appears that some guy jumped him in the underground car park at African Diamond Corporation. His goons must have been looking the other way. Apparently he's disappeared. Everyone, his security, African Diamond's security, the cops; everyone all running around like chickens with their heads cut off. No one seems to know what the fuck is going on!'

'Jesus! I can't say that I give a shit. The kidnappers can bloody impale the son of a bitch as far as I'm concerned. But what about my case? Poor Nozipo deserves to have this thing brought to a conclusion, you know. If he's not found soon, alive, I mean, it's bound to lead to another bloody postponement!'

'Well, maybe they will find him soon. He's worth a few bob, after all. There are probably ransom negotiations happening as we speak.'

'Whew!' I was stunned. What an unexpected turn of events. 'Anyway, where were we? The wedding; you were saying…?

'Well, the whole process starts tomorrow, but the church wedding… you know, the bloody white wedding thing that is really impoverishing me, is on Saturday, you know, colossal marquee, four hundred guests, sit-down luncheon, bar. The full catastrophe! Going to cost over fifty big ones.'

'Well, good luck. At least you're receiving the cattle, not delivering them. How many cows are you guys selling her for?'

Solly was quick to correct me. 'You damn honkies! Always misunderstanding our African customs! Paying *bogadi* is not buying the bride. You make it sound so crass. It's more like an insurance. You know, if he mistreats her or fails to look after her and the children, and she has to return to us - to her parents - then they have got a little something to support her and her kids. It's not a bloody commercial transaction.'

'Yeah, yeah, I know… I was just winding you up!'

'Well, the answer is twelve, since you ask. Ten is the actual *bogadi*, one is to open the negotiations - *pulamolomo* we call it - literally the opening of the mouth. And the twelfth is like a fine, because they already have a baby. We are charging the groom for having come and, you know, unceremoniously plundered our *kraal* in the night.'

He changed the subject. 'Anyway, originally I was going to phone to ask if you were ready for the Tsotsetsi appeal. I mean, I know it was a bit unfair of me to chuck it at you like that, I didn't really have a choice.'

'No problem, Solly. I'm on top of it. Don't worry, my fee note is in the post!'

'Oh yeah, also, I popped in to pay my respects at your judge's home yesterday. Poor fellow seems to be taking it rather badly. Passed on your condolences, mind. Mrs Mazibuko's funeral is on Saturday. I won't be able to make it, of course, and you'll probably be on your way back from Botswana, so I've asked Abby to go and represent the firm. She'll do a wreath, and all that.'

By the time Solly finally hung up it was already nearly ten o'clock. *Much too late to phone the girls*, I thought. I should have phoned as soon as I got off the plane. *Tomorrow morning, before they leave for school, then.*

I set a reminder on my cell phone.

Eighteen

The dogs were happy to see me. Esther seemed relieved that I was back, and immediately prepared me a quick supper: soft-boiled eggs, toast and tea. I was glad to be home, and when I passed the fridge and caught sight of the Mauritius postcard that had started the whole mad, exciting escapade, I felt flushed with the success of my adventure.

Back home in my familiar solitary surroundings I was astounded at my newfound status. I may well not have slept with her yet, but there was no denying that we were now a couple.

The sex bit was going to take some working out, but the emotions were undeniable, and to me at least, they were totally authentic. There had been a fundamental inner change. I was no longer a single man.

'I'm off to Botswana tomorrow morning, Esther.' The matronly housekeeper looked around from the sink. 'I want to leave early so that I can visit my parents on the way, so I need to be out of here by five thirty. You'll make me some coffee, won't you? Should be back on Friday night.'

'All right, Mr Anton, I'll wake you myself at half past four, with coffee.' Her face was full of maternal concern. 'Ooh, but you are travelling too much, Mr Anton. You are going to become very tired! You should rest a few days.'

'I have been doing just that for the last few days, Esther, but it's a very important case I've got to do in Botswana. Some poor fellow is facing the death penalty! This is his final appeal. Maybe I'll get some more rest when I get back. By the way, the girls will be here for the weekend. They'll be coming on Saturday.'

'That's okay, Mr Anton. Their room is already prepared.'

After my supper I settled down in the study with another mug of tea to pore over the Tsotsetsi case. Before I started I couldn't resist grabbing the cell phone and giving Kelly a goodnight call, while I downloaded a week's worth of emails.

She sounded genuinely happy to hear from me. 'You haven't changed your mind, have ya?'

'About what? About taking you to Botswana with me?'

'No, silly! About loving me for ever and ever.'

'Of course not! That's as long as you'll love me for ever and ever too!'

'I will! ...I do.'

'Me too... night, love!'

'Night, Anton!'

'Hey, by the way, I just heard that that bastard Jabu Zulu has been kidnapped.'

There was a sharp intake of breath. 'What?' She sounded incredulous.

'Yep, Solly just told me. So far, no details, only that he was abducted from the underground car park, at his office this afternoon. Well, we'll see if we've still got a case to continue on Monday. I'm sure Judge Mazibuko will suspend the trial if the main prosecution witness has been abducted.'

'Fuckin' hell. This crazy country! It's just like the Wild West!'

After speaking to Kelly, I called Nozipo to tell her, but she had already heard the news. She was asleep when I called, and I apologised for waking her, only then realising that it was already past eleven. We agreed to keep in touch, in case the court schedule was going to be altered. I finished the call and returned to the task at hand.

On impulse, I decided to download on to the computer all the pictures I took on my phone camera while we were in Mauritius. For five minutes I browsed through them. The first one - which I had taken in the bar at Jo'burg International airport before we left - showed an almost shy Kelly, tentative and a little unsure, the glass of beer on the table appearing almost too big for the tiny, youthful lass.

The last had been taken yesterday on the boat when we had gone snorkelling. The sun sparkled off the water droplets on her lustrous skin. She smiled confidently, her diving mask jauntily on her head, the love plain behind the smile. Clearly *my* girl!

What a magic time it had been! I marvelled again at the massive change that had come over my life. What a week!

Before I started work on the case papers, I gave in to yet another impulse and Googled for Full Frontal - first ascents. I felt guilty for it was as if I doubted her claims. Anyway, I thought, if there was any truth in her ostensible disdain for records and the like, then in all probability her ascents wouldn't be registered anyway. No sooner had that thought entered my head than the page appeared.

I was looking at the records for solo ascents of Full Frontal. The Mountain Club of South Africa: Official Confirmed Ascents. Only two woman climbers had ever conquered Full Frontal solo, and neither was Kelly Modise.

When I checked Africa Face Direct, Bakoven and Cardiac Arrest, it was the same. Only a few women had ever solo-ed those climbs and none was K Modise. I had a quick look at Skyhook. No K Modise there either.

I thought about it for a minute. I could taste my disappointment, and for a moment the notion that she had lied to me was a bitter, painful thought. But then, I reminded myself that she despised records. Of course she wouldn't be on the official lists.

But the taste wouldn't go away. A small worm of doubt began to wriggle and nibble inside me.

The Botswana Court Roll was one of the emails Solly had sent me. I saw that the Tsotsetsi case was to be heard by the full bench of the Botswana Court of Appeals. The names of the judges read like a Who's Who of the legal world: Sir Eban Appiah, from Ghana, Gustav Ackerman, South Africa, Sir Hubert Obougu-Obougu, Nigeria, Charles Selolwane,

Botswana, Sir Virendra Naipaul, India, Lord Cole of Bury, and Lord Douglas-Smith of Scarborough, both from England.

In thirty-six hours I would be facing these learned gentlemen in a matter of literal life and death. Even after fifteen years at the bar, the thought of arguing a capital case in front of some of the most senior and most highly respected members of the profession was a daunting prospect.

There was also an email from Mathatha 'Matt' Mmino, one of the Botswana-based attorneys who would be joining me for the appeal. I had never met Matt but had heard glowing reports from Solly about the eager young lawyer from Kang in the Kgalagadi.

The message was brief, 'Hi Mr Venter. See you at Lobatse Thursday morning. I'll come to your hotel at seven so we can go over a few points. Cheers, Matt.' Attached were a number of bulky documents, and I knew I was in for a long night.

I printed out Matt's documents. Most of the points were already summarised in Solly's material, and for a couple of hours I re-read the arguments, pencilling notes in the margins and occasionally speaking out loud, rehearsing the rhetoric.

I caught sight of the blue exercise book that she had slipped to me in the car in Hillbrow. Instantaneously I lost my train of thought. My enthusiasm for the appeal abruptly dissolved and I pushed the papers aside, reached for the exercise book, lit a cigarette, put my feet up on the desk and began to read.

My physical wounds healed quickly enough. The pain dissipated swiftly, turned to itchiness and then disappeared completely until even the memory of the pain was spent. The torn flesh knitted itself back together, the stitches came out, and that was that – although, of course, I have some scar tissue that other women don't have.

But the fright didn't dissolve at all.

The days in the hospital were strange and alien. My world till then, in the village and on the farm in the labourers' shacks, had been delimited by the familiar, soft margins of earth and thatch, sand and grass, goat and hen.

The hospital ward, that aseptic, rectangular, painted and tiled environment – Cartesian space – was foreign to me, and merged with the dreamlike delirium into which I had retreated to fashion an otherworldly cavern that my forlorn, terrified little spirit inhabited like a wraith.

Into these surreal surroundings, like figures on some kind of slowly revolving merry-go-round, came Mama, and nurses, and a doctor, and others whom I later supposed were social workers and police.

Each face appeared in turn as if emerging from a mist and then dissolved again, to be replaced by another. All wore solemn frowns and treated me with exaggerated care.

Much attention was focused upon my injured vagina, which all felt they needed to examine again and again. Hushed conversations in grave tones accompanied the raising up of my nightie and the peering, prodding and palpating that I endured.

None looked me in the eye, as if I was somehow too soiled to be part of the normal, regular world.

Even after I left the hospital and went back to stay with Mama, no one really looked me in the eye. I felt somehow to blame for being dirty, evil, bad, naughty.

The thing that had happened to me had happened to my vagina, and that is a bad thing. A bad girl is a girl whose vagina becomes a thing of public knowledge, and my vagina had been seen and touched by all those people, and had been spoken about openly, and that was unclean. That was shameful, bad.

Relief of a kind came when Mama my grandmother took me to stay with Mmane, my mother, Phatsimo.

At that time Mmane lived on a farm near Rustenberg, on the slopes of the Magaliesberg. The farmer turned a blind eye to one of his labourers bringing her retarded relative to stay on the farm, as long, of course, as she kept out of the way and didn't cause any trouble.

In those days people needed a pass to live on a white farmer's land, but in the country districts no one paid the law any notice as long as one kept a low profile. Anyway, as a handicapped person, Mmane seemed to be exempt from most rules. The farm labourer in question was Mmamoratwa, my grandmother's elder sister and Mmane's aunt whom I called Nkoko, or 'Granny'.

Mmane and I had not lived together at all since I was very young and I had all but forgotten her. Had I remembered the silent, withdrawn creature that had given birth to me in secret on the back seat of a moving car, I would have been amazed at the transformation, for here was an alert, communicative, wisp of a young woman who bore little resemblance to the feeble, autistic child who had been enveloped by the Bishop's flaming coat.

A dispassionate observer would have seen a grossly underweight, bony girl who looked much younger than her seventeen years. She had overcome her deafness to the extent that she had taught herself to lip-read to some degree. Her speech was childlike and monotonous, and few could understand what she said.

Her sparse, orange-tinged hair and swollen knees, her blackened and broken teeth, and the whining, humming sound she inadvertently generated, all combined to lend her an almost non-human air. Young children who visited the compound sent there on some errand or other were terrified of her.

Most adults, at least those who didn't know her, simply ignored her – sidestepped her with varying degrees of distaste. Nevertheless, her eyes conveyed a bright awareness, something that had been totally lacking in her before my birth.

In my four-year-old eyes she was a magical being, a supernatural playmate. She was a big person who behaved like, and understood, a little one. She loved me in a special way that I felt only I could understand. Unlike the rest of the world, she seemed to have no fixation about my vagina. She didn't blame me for what had happened, and she made me feel clean and wholesome again.

The time I spent on the farm with my mother was a brief respite from a harsher world. But by the time I was seven I was back in Pretoria with Mama, who now worked as a domestic servant. Then, for a few years I lived in Botswana, with my great-great-aunt at the lands near Mochudi where I was born.

I was always a burden to someone or other, a piece of baggage that was shuttled between unwilling relatives. School was a rare thing for me. I would be enrolled at one school, and after a few months my domestic arrangements would be disturbed and I would find myself somewhere else and out of school.

Eventually, when I was twelve, I moved to stay with my great-aunt Florence in Atterigeville, a great big sprawling township or 'location' outside Pretoria. Though she was my grandmother's younger sister, whom I should have called 'Mmangwane', or 'Auntie', it was probably due to the somewhat eccentric and unconventional nature of my family, with two successive generations of husbandless mothers, that I called her 'Ausi' – elder sister.

Florence was older and plumper than in the days when she and the Bishop had shared secret moments behind his wife's back. She now worked as a shift worker at a poultry battery farm on the far side of the city, plucking and gutting birds every day from eleven in the morning till eight at night.

Her daily commute across Pretoria, from Atterigeville to Silverton took another two hours each way, which meant that she was out of the house from eight-thirty in the morning till after ten every night.

I was already quite sharp for my age. Although my formal schooling had been interrupted so often in my young life, I had managed to pick up a fair bit just by being alert and eager. Whenever I arrived at a new school, Mama would exaggerate my age a bit and I would put on my best school manners, and I always ended up in a standard where I was the youngest, by far the brightest, and I always came first in class.

My body too had developed rapidly. Although I was still a child and small for my age, I was just a few months from my first menstruation and a pubescent femininity had begun to make itself apparent in the shape of my hips and buttocks. My thighs, too, had begun to acquire those particular curves and my little breasts were just beginning to look like breasts rather than like oversized mosquito bites.

Maybe it was this coming into bud that caused some of the boys at school to pass silly remarks, like 'Hey, Cookie, come wrap up my lollipop,' 'I've got a big spoon to stir your pot,' or 'Come, Sister, let me bury my head!'

I found the remarks annoying but had no idea what they meant, for despite the ordeal I had been through, I had no inkling at all of regular, normal sex.

In fact, I was unable to relate the experience of my rape with anything else in my life or in the world around me. It was as if the memory had been packaged and stored away in a dark corner. Anything that even vaguely approached the point where the package would be re-opened was off limits to my conscious mind.

When I saw magazine pictures of film stars kissing, or watched young people around me exchange intimate embraces, I had no mechanism to connect what I saw with the process of intercourse. I suppose I was as much in the dark as my dear grandmother had been before she met my grandfather, the boy under the morula tree.

Unlike her, however, my ignorance was not innate. It had been driven into me like a stake with a sledgehammer.

My classmates were all older than me, and I am sure they - particularly the girls – thought me a silly, ignorant, immature little child. I remember a lot of giggling and a certain tone of voice, which I'm sure must have been reserved for sex talk, but it all wafted unintelligibly over my head as intangible and as out of reach as the clouds.

Despite my ignorance, I suppose as a twelve-year-old I must have had the naïve beginnings of a suspicion about intimate relations. I had a sort of awareness of physical tokens of affection as a part of romantic love; a Mills and Boon sentimentality that I presumed vaguely included kissing and embracing and maybe something more, but it was precisely that 'something more' that my mind refused to explore.

Had I been asked, I guess, I would merely have said that people who fall in love get married, and left it at that. The physical consequences or manifestations of marriage would not have entered my head.

The thing I had experienced was an alien aberration – a painful, dark, nameless, mysterious terror. I had not managed to envisage the process by which I had been injured, nor had I ever identified the nature of the 'burning stick' that had torn me apart in the dark. The event had been so deeply shrouded in horror and secrecy that I had not managed to piece together the evidence in order to grasp the obvious.

I had never conceived of the act of sex. More importantly, I had certainly never conceived of it as an act of gratuitous vulgarity, or of recreational violence.

That is, until one unforgettable afternoon in Atterigeville.

I had just arrived back from school and was alone in the little matchbox of a house. It had one tiny bedroom, a minute kitchen, a living room and a little shower and toilet as big as the average wardrobe.

I was sitting on the toilet, my black school tights and knickers around my ankles, my black school gymslip up around my waist, when I heard the pressed-steel front door open with the characteristic screech of its unlubricated hinges.

In our African society there are very strict rules of etiquette governing one's entry into another's house. A visitor – particularly a stranger, but even a regular, familiar visitor –

would usually stand at the gate or at the entrance to the yard and call out 'Ko-ko!' and wait to be invited in.

At the very least, there would be a polite knocking at the door. So when the door opened peremptorily as it did on that afternoon I immediately assumed that it was Ausi back early from work, as, at that time, she and I were the only residents of the little house. Out of politeness I leant forward on my perch to close the toilet door that I had innocently left open, seeing that I had expected to be in the house alone.

As I did so, there was a sudden movement, the door rebounded to its open position, and a man, a very large, strange man, filled the doorway. My first thought was for my modesty, being as I was, in the act of defecating. I was a well brought up little girl, and I had been taught to make every effort to perform my private bodily functions in secret, or at least out of sight of adults and strangers.

I was about to apologise to this stranger for my carelessness when I noticed that at least two more men had entered the house behind him, and I was seized by a sudden sense of alarm.

I grabbed my knickers to pull them up, sliding off the seat as I did so.

The big man smiled a grotesque, sneering smile. The smallness of the room meant that he was very close to me.

'Hello, my Tjerri!' and with a look over his shoulder at the others, 'Hey, look what we've got here, boys!'

There was an unambiguous inference in his calling me his Cherry.

The other two were younger. One looked to be almost a teenager. All three were ugly and menacing. I knew that I was in big trouble. I think I expected to die. Strange – in retrospect my fear of being murdered was a cold, calm fear. I don't remember panicking as such. However, had I known what was going to happen I would probably have passed out through sheer terror.

Housebreaking was a common enough crime in South Africa in those times, even if it was not yet the epidemic it is today. Often, people got murdered. Life in the townships was pretty cheap. I had heard of women being raped, but had never stopped to ask myself what exactly that meant. I was about to find out.

'Tjo! Tjo! Tjo!' It was the middle one, the ugliest of the three. 'Au Madoda! Hey gents! We are going to eat very, very sweet meat! Look!'

He pushed past the big one, and stretched out a hand to grab me. The big one shoved him out of the way. 'Wait... wait, you animal! Fresh food needs to be cooked slowly... slowly. What's your hurry, hey? Anyway, you'll wait your turn.'

He saw me struggling with my tights, trying to pull them up. They had become tangled in the buckles of my shoes.

'Don't worry about those, Tjerri... you can start by taking them off. Let me help you.'

It was the ugly one again. He bent down, grabbed the tights between my ankles and pulled so violently that I fell on to my back.

My head hit the toilet as I fell. He dragged me along the polished cement floor of the little hallway into the living room, and yanked at the tights so that I was almost upside-down, with my feet straight up in the air. The tights came off with both my shoes and I collapsed into a terrified heap in the middle of the floor.

There was a crash as the big one pushed the ugly one violently out of the way into Ausi's display cabinet. I saw that some of her favourite cups, little white ones with roses and a gold rim, smashed. The glass door was shattered.

'I told you to wait your damn turn!' He was holding an Okapi knife that had materialised in his hand. 'What's the matter with you?'

The big one pointed the knife at me. 'Now, Tjerri, you can help me. Why don't you take off the rest of your clothes, hey?' In my state of terror I had no idea what he was going to do, or why he wanted me to undress. I huddled, frozen in fear.

Then, to my complete bewilderment, he began to unbutton the overalls he was wearing. He stuck in his hand and withdrew his penis. It was erect and enormous. I had never seen a grown man's penis before, and I was utterly horrified. He stroked it and pulled back the foreskin. Underneath it was shiny purple.

His sneer showed the inside of his lip was the same shiny purple. 'I said, get undressed!' He knelt down next to me and almost gently held the point of the Okapi to my throat. 'Now!'

I was too terrified to move. He looked at the young one. 'Come, hold her.' The young one knelt down behind my head and violently grabbed my arms, pulling me into a prone position.

The big one hooked the blade under my collar, and in one swift movement from my neck to my waist, sliced through my vest, my shirt and the bodice of my gymslip. They fell aside, and with a second stroke, he cut through the skirt, leaving me bare except for my knickers.

When I opened my eyes, I could see him smirking, ogling me, and stroking his enormous penis. Then he inserted the knife into my knickers and cut them off me. Perhaps he was expecting me to have real pubic hair, because the sight of my pre-pubescent nakedness with its feint downy fuzz seemed to fascinate him.

He made a few stroking motions over my genitals with the knife, pretending to shave or scrape me with the blade. His tongue mimicked the movements of the blade, like someone unfamiliar with writing, trying to sign his name. Then his lust overcame him, and he began.

He struggled to enter me, even though I didn't resist. Such was my ignorance and confusion that initially I didn't even fathom what it was I should resist, had I wanted to. He was so big, and I was so small, that he needed substantial force to prize open my vagina, and to thrust into me to the hilt.

The pain was terrible, but the re-awakening of the memory, and the sudden, clear comprehension of the nature of the 'burning stick' that had torn me apart when I was four, was much more excruciating.

What followed was, in retrospect, utterly predictable. The big one with the enormous penis took an eternity. The ugly one made up for his lesser endowment by thumping as violently as he could. The young one was embarrassed and didn't want the others to see his manhood. He couldn't bear to meet my eye, and he ejaculated almost as soon as he started.

No sooner had he done so than the big one was back, rampant and ready for another go. This time he took even longer, and the ugly one started jeering him and telling him to get a move on. Then it was the ugly one's turn again.

'This hole is full! It's all used up!' He violently pushed my knees up past my ears and forced his penis into my anus. I could feel the flesh tearing and the awakening of a new source of pain. All along I had tried not to cry out, sure that they would kill me if I did. Now I couldn't control myself, and I whimpered and moaned continuously.

The big one laughed. 'Hey, Jakes, you filthy bastard! Is that what they teach you in jail?'

He may well have feigned disgust but when it was his next turn he also sodomised me, his massive penis almost splitting me in two.

My memory is vague about how many times they each raped and sodomised me. I was pushed and pulled, draped over the arm of the small sofa like a piece of meat. I was raped from behind and from in front, from above and from below, on the floor and on the chairs.

For a while it seemed to give them great amusement to lay me across the table, face down and with my legs hanging over the edge, so they could do it to me standing up.

Then the one called Jakes, the ugly one, wanted to sodomise me while the big one was already pumping me in the vagina.

They tried it, the big one lying on his back on the floor, holding me on top of him, while Jakes knelt behind me, between the other's legs. But they kept getting in each other's way, and for a while I was shoved and stretched and pummelled, as they tried to get my orifices lined up to their liking.

Eventually, they mercifully gave up trying to enter me simultaneously, and just reverted to taking turns, each trying to outdo the other with the ingenuity of his position and the creative originality of his technique, guffawing with crude, decadent, malevolent glee.

The young one seemed to be unable to regain his erection after the first time, and concentrated instead on ransacking the house and selecting anything of Ausi's that had any value, between rolling interminable joints from the large plastic bag of cannabis he had with him.

I don't remember him raping me again, but the other two seemed to have inexhaustible libidos and even took breaks during their go, had a smoke, and came back to finish their turn. They had a bottle of brandy with them and took pulls on it from time to time. They smoked cigarettes and the joints that the young one continuously rolled, and had a long lazy orgy, probably for about four or five hours.

They laughed and made filthy jokes about me and my private parts, and were seemingly totally undisturbed by my agony, by my moaning, wailing cries, or by the pool of blood that gradually spread from my groin to all parts of the little room.

I swallowed hard, grabbed a cigarette from the pack and stuck it into my mouth. I was breathing in shallow gasps, and my shaking hands were sweating. When I reached for the lighter, I realised that there were already two cigarettes of different lengths burning in the ashtray.

I looked uncomprehendingly around me. The wall, the furniture, the legal files and papers, the computer, everything, seemed unreal - like a mirage. I was in a little darkening room in Atteridgeville, and there was pain in the air and blood on the floor. In the centre of the room was a dying child.

I shook myself and despite the bright lights and the warm evening air, I shivered involuntarily. With an effort of will I lowered my eyes to the page.

I must have passed out towards the end, but as they left I regained consciousness. The pain had become like a monotonous scream - so loud nobody hears it.

The big one came to where I lay. He kicked my legs apart, and stood between them. He cleared his throat and spat on my body with an expression of acute repulsion. He pulled out his now limp penis and urinated on to my belly, and on to my bleeding crotch. He saved the last few squirts for my face.

He took the knife out of his pocket and opened it. When he squatted down beside me and raised the blade in his fist, I knew it was over.

'So long, Tjerri.'

I don't think I felt any fear. I was past fear. Our eyes met.

I held his gaze for a long time. Something in his expression changed, and with a sigh he stood up, closed the Okapi and returned it to his pocket. Then they were gone.

Or so I thought. There was the sound of an argument outside, and after a time the door opened and the ugly one, Jakes, was back. He had a knife. He came straight to where I lay, and with one sudden movement, he stabbed me in the neck. He jerked the blade out and stabbed me again, in the chest, right through my left nipple. When he went outside I could hear the bravado in his voice.

'Well, now she won't be telling anybody about the party... that's for sure!'

As I passed out I could hear their laughter.

Hospital was very different from the first time. There was no delirium, no escape into a dream world, just harsh lights and crude, raw, unrelenting sensation.

I suppose some of the medical staff were caring and concerned, but the police, the social worker, and the people at the District Surgeon's offices who examined me to establish whether I had in fact been sexually assaulted, were each as rough, as hardhearted and callous as the other.

Kalafong Hospital in Atterigeville was typical of apartheid-era black hospitals and other government institutions in that the vast majority of whites who worked in them were Afrikaners.

The lingua franca of such places was Afrikaans, and the African vernacular was used only in informal situations when there were no bosses about.

Dr Blair, however, was Scottish, and hardly spoke any Afrikaans at all. Unlike almost all the other white hospital staff, he was quite fluent in Setswana, which he spoke with an atrocious Scottish accent.

He had worked in Botswana for many years prior to moving to South Africa to be near his children's schools, and had lived in a remote village where few people spoke English.

He was patient with me, and seemed to understand better than anyone else what I had been through. He had a knack of getting me to deal with my physical injuries in a dispassionate and objective way, while at the same time never undermining or trivialising the gravity of the psychic trauma I had experienced.

He also helped me to discover that I was very fluent in English. My schooling till then had been in Afrikaans, Sesotho and Setswana, and although I had learnt to read and write English, he was the first person I ever had the opportunity to properly converse with in that language, and I surprised myself with my articulacy.

I remained in hospital for about eleven weeks. My injuries were quite serious. The knife in my neck and my chest had miraculously missed all the vital organs and the stabbings turned out to be the least serious of my wounds.

My bowel had been perforated, and my cervix and vagina were so badly damaged that their reconstruction eventually required a total of three separate operations.

From a state of blissful ignorance about the reproductive process, I suddenly found myself inadvertently becoming an expert in gynaecological details. Dr Blair was patient in his explanations, showed me wall charts and diagrams, and even drew sketches for me, depicting the damage and showing the way in which he was about to repair it. He made it clear that it had been touch-and-go whether I was going to have to have a hysterectomy, and to lose my womb.

Of course, I had to be treated for both gonorrhoea and syphilis, but that was by the by.

Despite the unsympathetic and painful examinations by the district surgeon and the seemingly endless, insensitive interrogations I endured so that the police could complete the requisite volume of paperwork, no arrests were ever made, and my assailants were never required to answer for their iniquitous revelry. The case docket joined thousands of others on dusty shelves throughout the country, never to be re-opened.

It was while I was recuperating in Kalafong Hospital that an event occurred that was to change my life. One morning when Dr Blair came to examine me on his daily rounds he was accompanied by a middle-aged couple whom he introduced as Dr and Mrs Applebury, old friends from his Botswana days.

They were on their way home after decades of missionary work in that country, and were visiting Dr and Mrs Blair for a few weeks before leaving for the UK. Dr and Mrs Applebury, or Uncle Chester and Aunt Muriel as I soon came to call them, were members of the Congregational Church, the U.C.C.S.A, formerly the London Missionary Society, the legendary institution of David Livingstone, the nineteenth century explorer of Victoria Falls fame, and of Robert Moffat, his missionary father-in-law.

Aunt Muriel was an angel. She visited me every day and seemed to know what I needed to feel whole again. She was gentle and kind, and though I was supported by regular visits from Mama and Ausi, Aunt Muriel was not bound by the taboos and constipated sexual mores of my culture, and could counsel me with straight talk and understanding in a way that my blood relatives could not. She achieved this despite her prim, Victorian, missionary upbringing.

I say that I soon came to call the good doctor and his wife Uncle Chester and Aunt Muriel. Truth be told, that was only an interim measure. Within a few short months it was to change, and they became my mum and dad.

It all happened very suddenly and most of it occurred in my absence. There were a number of meetings between the Appleburys and Mama and other family members. Various legal processes were undertaken and permissions obtained. I was consulted only once. Mama, Ausi, Uncle Chester and Aunt Muriel sat around my bed with Dr Blair at my side and asked me if I would like to go to England with the Appleburys and live there as their daughter.

I could think of nothing I wanted more.

It was barely three months after the gang rape that I found myself in a bright, airy, first-floor bedroom overlooking Brockwell Park, in Herne Hill, London SE24, with Paddington Bear seated on my pink and white plaid duvet, and my new mum and dad across the landing. I was enrolled in Dulwich Girls' School and settled in very quickly. I was now the ward of my legal guardians, Dr and Mrs Chester Applebury, and I became the adoptive daughter of the most wonderfully loving and caring people I had ever known.

I had reached the end of the exercise book. So that explains the South London accent! But what a fucking gruelling road to get there!

I was exhausted. The long day, the intense, soul-baring declarations of undying love, the flight, and the harsh emotions of what I had just read were suddenly too much for me. I knew I needed to get some sleep before another long day tomorrow. It was already after two. Esther would be waking me in a couple of hours.

But somehow I couldn't move. I sat in the chair, staring blankly at the ceiling, smoking one cigarette after another. I could only think of one thing: that poor, sensitive, beautiful girl who had been given such a raw deal and who now seemed to find some comfort in me.

I wished she were here, now, in my arms and under all the protection I could possibly offer. I felt I wanted to repay her on behalf of all of mankind. The burden of responsibility and the sheer empathy were suddenly too much for me, and as I sat, the tears began to roll down my cheeks, I gradually dissolved into sobs that racked my body and I wept like a child.

Nineteen

Esther woke me at four thirty with coffee, as promised. She hadn't expected to find me asleep in my chair in the study though. I felt like death warmed up.

My first memory of yesterday was of the horrendous story I had read of the gang rape. The more I tried to think of something else, the more the images of Kelly's ordeal forced themselves into my consciousness. I screwed my eyes shut, but all I could see was a naked child lying on a cold cement floor in a pool of blood.

In the shower, I started to wake up. I remembered, with a pang of mixed emotions, that I was to collect Kelly in just over an hour, and that I would be in Zeerust in less than five.

What was I going to do? The immediate future seemed fraught with potential hazards. Someone was likely to get hurt or be affronted. I would probably make a fool of myself, one way or the other. If only I could wangle it so that Mammie didn't have a shock, Pappie was subjected to no further aggravation of his condition, and Kelly didn't feel slighted or patronised.

Despite my proficiency at the bar, and my unerring ability to trap an adversary adroitly in court, when it came to real-life situations I was woefully unsophisticated.

I knew that any attempt I made to hide the truth from my parents was doomed. I was bound to offend them, or upset Kelly, or both. One thing was certain: playing it straight and just introducing Kelly as my girlfriend was out of the question!

The thought of phoning Kelly and somehow putting her off with an excuse crossed my mind, but I wasn't up to conjuring up the necessary deceit. And anyway, I wanted to be with her.

It hit me as I got out of the shower. Somehow, last night, with all the emotions, I had missed it. Yet, something had been prickling my subconscious and I hadn't been able to put my finger on it.

I had to make sure. *Now*! I rushed into the study with the towel around my waist, water dripping on the floor, and impatiently waited for the computer to boot up. I selected my Internet connection and waited for the whirring squeal of the modem.

'*Come on! Hurry up!*' I promised myself I would get a broadband connection soon. This dial-up stuff was archaic! I was shivering, but it wasn't only the chill morning air.

Finally, the Mountain Club of South Africa web page I had looked at last night downloaded and I was looking at the name of the first woman ever to free-climb Full Frontal solo: K Applebury.

So it is true! So it is you!

I checked Africa Face Direct, Bakoven, Skyhook and Cardiac Arrest, the same name appeared. In all cases she had been one of the first women to free-solo the route. For Skyhook and Cardiac Arrest, like Full Frontal, she had been the very first. First female free-solo ascent - MCSA certified.

Sorry for doubting you, Kelebonye Applebury!

So, not only did she use two passports, but two surnames as well!

In the cold morning light, Hillbrow was a bleak and forbidding place, windblown jetsam, and booze bottles smashed in the gutters. None of the street vendors were out yet. Their deserted makeshift stalls, with their tattered awnings and yesterday's detritus, made the scene look very forlorn.

At a street corner a block from Kelly's I passed a parked police car, its blue lights flashing, with a small crowd of onlookers standing in a tight knot, looking down at something in their midst. Probably a corpse, I thought, and looked the other way.

Despite the presence of some shadowy street people, many of the folk up and about at this time of the morning were well presented and heading to work in the city, slightly incongruous figures in the grey desolation, their stylish silhouettes in stark contrast to the boarded-up shop fronts, broken windows and peeling facades.

Kelly was there, standing on the kerb outside her building, just as she said she would be. Dressed in her customary tight jeans and sandals, with a denim jacket, and a bag slung over her shoulder, her eyes bright and her smile stunning, she stood out against the wretchedness of her surroundings like a blossom in the desert.

My heart skipped a beat at the sight of her. All the intensity of what I had read last night leapt into the forefront of my mind, but her bright presence amid the grey was suddenly very far removed from Atterigeville, and from the gang rape.

Her face was so serene and gorgeous, her kiss so warm, her smile so reassuring that, within seconds, we were back in our familiar emotional space, as if the brief separation of last night and the horrific tale had merely been a dream.

I knew from experience that I was not to mention it.

The sun was a dull dark-red ball caught in the smog behind us, as we cleared the high-rises of Hillbrow and set off towards the west. The morning traffic was mostly inbound and moving in the opposite direction, as millions undertook their daily commute. The Audi made quick progress out of the city and soon we were through Fourways and winding down towards the Hennops River valley.

My phone beeped a reminder. I had promised myself I would phone the girls before they left for school. I felt self-conscious and awkward. I was determined not to give Kelly any more ammunition to tease me about 'jumping' whenever I spoke to Hannah, and steeled myself to keep my voice thoroughly level and relaxed throughout.

I was not brave enough to use the hands-free set-up through the car speakers, and preferred the partial privacy of illegally holding the phone to my ear while I drove. In the event, Hannah's home phone was answered by Angelica, the maid.

The family had already left for school. And predictably, Hannah's cell phone was off - she hated the thing and refused to drive with it switched on. I waited for the voicemail prompts, sheepishly aware that my panic had been for nothing.

'Hi. It's me. I'll collect the girls on Saturday morning, about eight thirty, okay? Say hi to them.' Kelly sensed my awkwardness and gave my thigh a squeeze.

I had devised my own favourite route out of the city towards the west. Years of visiting my parents in Zeerust had allowed me to refine my course, so that I avoided the worst of the traffic and enjoyed the best of the scenery.

I steered clear of the main trunk road through Roodepoort and Krugersdorp and preferred to swing northwards, towards Hartebeestpoort dam.

The stretch to Pelindaba was my favourite. The road was hilly and windy, threading its way through the foothills of the Magaliesberg, crossing the Hennops six or seven times in as many kilometres. After all, that's why I drove an Audi instead of some utilitarian Hyundai or Toyota.

I loved to push it a bit, to get the adrenalin pumping and the concentration sharpened. Out of the corner of my eye I could see that Kelly was enjoying herself too, smiling each time the turbo kicked in. Clearly a bit of a speed freak too, I thought.

The radio had been on all morning but the volume was very low and we hadn't been concentrating. Suddenly, I heard the name Jabu Zulu and turned up the volume.

'...spokesman said that Mr Zulu escaped by climbing out of a bathroom window at the farmhouse where his kidnappers had been holding him. No further details are available at this time, although it is understood that Mr Zulu is currently undergoing a medical examination at an exclusive clinic in the city.

'A spokesperson for African Diamond Corporation, of which Mr Zulu is a director, and from whose premises Mr Zulu was allegedly abducted yesterday afternoon said that Mr Zulu was "as well as could be expected" after his ordeal, and added that no further statements would be issued at this stage as this could hamper police enquiries.

'When asked if a ransom demand had been received while Mr Zulu had been in the hands of his abductors, the spokesperson declined to comment.

'Mr Kofi Annan is to fly to Tehran later today to hold talks with…'

Kelly killed the radio, and looked at me. Her expression was intense. She was about to say something, but in my usual fashion, I beat her to it.

'Piece of shit! I'm sorry they didn't cut off his bloody ear and put it in the envelope with the ransom demand!'

'His ear!' she snorted, 'stuff his 'kin' ear! They should have cut off his 'kin' dick, an' all!'

I laughed. 'Ooh, I love it when you're angry; your Sahf Lunnun really comes out!'

''Kin' slime ball! The world doesn't need shite like that! Just watch, you'll see, the arsehole will get his fuckin' comeuppance!' She looked stern. 'Sooner than fuckin' later! Mark my fuckin' words!' Clearly few things made Kelly angrier than Jabulani Benedict Zulu.

It was just past seven o'clock as we drove into the designer-village of Schoemansville along the banks of the Hartebeestpoort dam, the stockbroker belt traffic of Jaguars, BMW M5s and Mercedes CLKs mixing with farmers' *bakkies* and overloaded minibus taxis.

I couldn't take my mind off the fact that every kilometre was taking me closer to Zeerust and to the embarrassing situation I had created for myself.

Fact: my mother was definitely not yet ready to be presented to my black girlfriend. That was out of the question. I could still hear the strident tone in her voice, thirty years ago: '*If you or Willem or God forbid, Anton, could ever do such a thing, I would die!*'

Then again, I acknowledged, it was not my mother who was going to change.

Fact: the only person who could possibly change was me. I had to stand up for what I believed, I had to stand up for whom I loved, and just accept the consequences. There was nothing else to be done!

No sooner had this thought entered my head than I opposed it with a torrent of counter-arguments, all trying to find myself an out. I knew that I was being weak, but felt I had to buy myself some time. Maybe Antjie would somehow come to my rescue. But not now! Not today! Today was far too soon.

Fact: then again, there was my father. The poor old man had just had a stroke. It would be totally selfish to confront him with something like this.

It was completely beyond the realm of his experience. He came from another era, when things were different. He too could probably be gradually and graciously eased into the idea of his son having a black girlfriend, with excessive emphasis on the 'gradual'! It was not something that was going to work if it was rushed.

Fact: then there was Kelly herself. I would feel really bad if I tried to suggest some patronising reason for her not to meet my parents. If I were to suggest it was too early in the relationship, or make any other feeble, dishonest excuse, she would see it for what it was: racist crap. More than anything, I didn't want to be tarred with that brush.

Damn and blast! Why the fuck did I invite her along?

The Audi pulled up at the traffic lights that regulate the flow of traffic through the little tunnel that gives on to the narrow one-way roadway across the dam wall itself. At that point the pass, the *poort,* through the Magaliesberg is at its steepest and most spectacular.

I looked across at her. She was craned forward in her seat, looking up and to her right, clearly mentally climbing the vertical rock that rises abruptly from the roadside. She looked so full of life, so energetic, the perfect companion. I knew I wanted her there always. In the seat next to me. I felt a complete heel for the implicitly racist nature of the mental gymnastics in which I was embroiled.

The lights had just changed for us to proceed across the dam wall when my phone rang. It was Hannah. Kelly instinctively looked at the phone in its cradle as it rang, and I knew she could see Hannah's name on the screen.

There was no way I could pull off the road to take the call privately. The roadway across the dam wall is barely wider than a car and the sidewalk is a mere catwalk, less than a metre wide. The road immediately after the dam wall is narrow and twisty with no-stopping signs for the next three kilometres.

One look in my rear-view mirror confirmed that Sod's Law was in full effect: there were at least twenty vehicles in the queue behind us and the car immediately behind us was the traffic police. In South Africa it is illegal to hold a phone while driving.

I realised that, right on cue, I had indeed jumped.

Kelly wasn't able to disguise the chortle that forced its way through her nose. I had tried not to jump, but the combination of the unexpected call at the totally inappropriate moment, with the police right behind me, was all just too much. I was acutely aware that my anxiety was discernible.

Kelly was contorted in silent hysterics and only the seat belt stopped her from rolling on to the floor. I was red to the tips of my ears, and did my woeful best. For an instant, I considered rejecting the call, but that would inevitably bring its own, unpalatable consequences. With severe trepidation I pressed the green button on the phone.

'Hi!'

Her voice was at its bipolar worst: strident and confrontational. She was having a bad day. 'Anton! I got your message. Why are you only picking up the kids on Saturday? Why not Friday afternoon? Hey? Remember, you're a whole bladdie week late as it is. Ivan and I had to take them to bladdie Sun City after you disappointed them!' Her voice boomed out of the Audi's quadraphonic speaker system.

'Yes, sorry about last weekend, Hannah.' Kelly was having a fit, and I struggled to keep my voice level. 'I can only fetch them on Saturday because I'm on my way to Botswana to do an appeal. I only expect to get back late on Friday evening.'

Another noise, a mixture between a groan and a suppressed sneeze escaped Kelly. She glanced at me. She looked as if she was about to be seriously ill, hugging her sides and rocking back and forth violently in her seat.

'Bladdie Botswana now, is it? And who is she this time, hey? I'm sick of your bullshit stories about work. Now, it's a bladdie appeal in Botswana. Last week it was some cock and bull story about Mauritius. I'm telling you, Anton, I'm bladdie sick and tired of your damn fairy tales! When are you going to bladdie spend some time with your children, instead of rushing all over the place with that bladdie fat bitch of yours?'

Kelly looked as if she was going to have a seizure. A high-pitched squeak escaped from some part of her.

Hannah went on, 'What was that? D'you say something?' There was an awkward pause. '…Or is it a different little tart this week? You make me bladdie puke, Anton!'

I did my best to stay in control, and struggled to stay on the road. We had made it across the dam wall and were in a long line of vehicles on the narrow, twisty section of road. 'Look, Hannah, you can check with the registrar of the Botswana Appeal Court for all I care. I have to be in Botswana for this appeal. It's some bloke facing the death penalty.'

There was a moment's silence on the line, and I took full advantage. I knew that Hannah was passionately against capital punishment. It was one of the issues that had thrown us together in the first place.

'The death penalty, Hannah! Yes, they still have it over there. Surely you don't want me to rush back early and let the poor bugger hang, do you?'

Silence.

Kelly's eyes were wide, and she continued to rock back and forth. She dared not breathe, lest another snigger escape her lips. She looked as if she was about to suffocate. Then she farted loudly, like a blast on a trumpet, and her contortions were instantly multiplied.

'What's that? What d'you say?'

I was barely able to hold my voice steady. 'Look, Hannah, I'm in heavy traffic right now. I'll pick up the girls on Saturday, eight thirty. Okay? Bye, Hannah!'

More silence.

I barely waited one second before hitting the button to end the call, and Kelly exploded. I couldn't help myself either, and only just managed to swing out of the traffic into someone's driveway and slam on the brakes before I too lost it, and we cried in each other's arms, shrieking uncontrollably.

Panic lit Kelly's eyes. She was struggling with the door handle. At the second attempt it overrode the security lock and opened. For a moment, I didn't know what was going on.

Kelly released her seat belt with frantic, scrabbling fingers, dived out of the car, ripping open her jeans and pulling them and her knickers to her knees. She squatted down, right next to the car, only partly obscured from the passing traffic by the open door.

The pee whooshed and whistled out of her, and gurgled and splashed on the ground, as we continued to shriek and scream till we ran out of breath.

Kelly had tears streaming down her cheeks, when she finally stopped laughing. She settled back in her seat, doing up her zip, breathless and exhausted. I had not laughed so much in years. My pulse was still thumping in my ears in response to the effort. I too was out of breath.

'Oh you are naughty, you wicked, wicked woman, you!'

'*You jumped*! You did!' She had started laughing again. 'I saw you! You jumped!' She shrieked. '*You jumped*!'

She was back in full flow. I soon joined in, and for a couple of minutes we were as helpless again as fish on a beach.

Eventually, I calmed down. 'Yeah, but I don't mind making an idiot of myself if you show me your sexy little arse every time!' We guffawed again, the giggles unrelenting.

'What? You saw my arse?'

'Not just your arse, love. As you bent down, I could see right up to the middle of next week!'

Soon, we were on the toll road, rapidly nearing Zeerust. I looked at the clock. It was nine thirty. We would be in Zeerust before ten. The problem I faced was going to come to a head very soon.

* * * * *

The drive had been great fun, though. After the giggling fit that so nearly resulted in a bent Audi for me, and wet pants for her, the mood was as light and as comfortable as I could ever have hoped.

I felt so damn good in her company! She seemed to respond well to my companionship, too, and kept up a stream of witty observations and affectionate, loving gestures that buoyed me and made me feel really good inside. I hardly even felt the lack of sleep.

At one point shortly after eight, Kelly had taken out her cell phone and made a couple of business calls. Her assistant at SAWAA, Maggie, seemed to have everything under control.

'Everything quiet on the Western Front?' I asked when she had finished.

'Yeah, everything seems okay. No big crises recently. It's a wicked job. At least when one's not pickin' up the bleedin' pieces of some woman's destroyed life, that is.'

When we were halfway between the dam and Rustenberg where the toll road passed within a couple of kilometres of Mooinooi, I had a sudden flashback to the incident with Eileena under the mulberry tree.

I smiled to myself when I remembered my first encounter with the bare skin of a woman, my first touch of pubic hair - my first close encounter. Then I remembered hearing Sergeant

Nievoudt describing *Oom* Sakkie van Zyl hanging from a tree on his farm: the prohibitive price of interracial sex. I could still hear the sound of my mother's voice: '*If you or Willem or God forbid, Anton, could ever do such a thing, I would die*!'

I had a lump in my throat that refused to go away.

Shortly after Mooinooi we passed the turnoff to Buffelspoort, the road through Barnardsvlei and to the farm where mountain club members park when they go climbing in Tonquani. We looked at one another. Clearly, both of us had been there many times before.

'We still on for a climb then?' she asked.

'No.'

She looked disappointed. 'But I thought you said…'

'Not for *a* climb… for many, many climbs!'

'You mean that?'

'Absolutely!'

''Kin' wally!' She leant across and unceremoniously squeezed my dick. The Audi changed lanes abruptly.

I wondered if I should pursue the subject of her incredible climbing record and her notable first ascents. I hesitated, not sure whether I should own up to my research about her climbing claims. No matter how I presented it, it was going to appear as if I had doubted her story and had been checking up on her. I let it go.

The Audi was sweeping through the final series of bends before the eighty speed limit and the beginning of the Zeerust municipal district. We would be at Mammie and Pappie's in less than ten minutes, and I still didn't have a plan. How was I going to introduce her?

'Hi, Mammie, Pappie, this is a friend of mine? Or, Ma, Pa, this is Kelly who is getting a lift to Botswana with me? Or, she works at court in Jo'burg with me. Or, she is involved in the case I'm busy with'?

If only I had the guts… I knew exactly how my heart would want me to put it:

'Hi, Mammie, Pappie. This is Kelly, the woman I love, the woman who I hope will bear any grandchildren I may still produce for you. The woman who will probably one day carry your surname, the woman I hope will one day lay me to rest.'

God! You sentimental fool! You've only known her a bloody week!

'Slow down! There's a speed trap. Look!'

I slammed on the brakes. Too late. We were already in the sixty zone. Luckily, the cop was busy writing out a ticket for some Indian guy in a flashy Mercedes, and we escaped detection.

'Ta! I was daydreaming. Didn't notice the sign.'

'Well, daydreamer, I'm not ready to be introduced to your parents today.' Kelly sounded serious. 'It's just too soon! I'm not quite prepared for it. Please drop me off somewhere.

'It must be twenty years since I passed through this one-horse town. Isn't there, maybe, a shopping mall around here? I'll amuse myself for a couple of hours while you go and be a dutiful son. Okay?'

I couldn't believe what I was hearing. I was being let off the hook! It was too good to be true!

'No, you should.' I knew I was being dishonest, and changed tack. 'Are you sure, love? Won't you get bored?'

We were in the centre of town now. The one and only shopping centre worthy of the name was coming up on the left.

'See, there's even a *Wimpy*. I'll have a lazy, grubby, high-cholesterol brunch, and walk around the shops. Look, there's even a bookshop. I'll buy myself something to read. No, fuck it, I'll write. I've got a bit to do yet.'

I looked at her sharply, anxious for a moment. I didn't know if I could manage to read through another rape.

'Don't worry, the hard part's all finished.'

I was slowing down. I felt like a real coward, and Kelly was letting me off. She had probably been reading my mind all the way, female intuition and all that. I squirmed with awkward discomfiture. *Spineless ass!*

'You sure, love? I mean…'

'Sure I'm sure!' She smiled her gorgeous smile. 'Drop me off. Here is fine.'

It was with mixed emotions that I turned into the car park. On the one hand, I was immeasurably relieved that my dilemma had been resolved. On the other hand, I felt like a pathetic, gutless, timid fool, allowing Kelly to bail me out like that.

'I'll be fine. You take your time, luv. You'll find me around here somewhere. Anyway, I've got my mobile. Give me a buzz when you're on your way, and I'll meet you here.'

I pulled into a vacant parking space. I tugged her across the seat and kissed her. 'Thanks, love. It's very considerate of you. I'm sure you'll meet them next time. Right now, with the old man sick and all, it's probably for the best.'

I didn't know how I sounded to Kelly, but to myself I sounded as sincere as a second-hand car dealer. Anton Venter, hero of the struggle against *apartheid*, human rights lawyer. Man of unwavering principle! What a load of crap! At the first opportunity, here I was pandering to the basest, meanest, racist impulses.

Kelly began to get out of the car.

'Here, let me help you get your book.' I jumped out and went around to the boot and opened it for her to retrieve her writing things from her bag.

As we stood side by side at the back of the Audi, I heard a very familiar voice behind me. Instantly, the hair on the back of my neck was on end.

'*My liewe hemel! Is dit jy,* Anton? Dear heaven, is it really you?'

I spun around. Mammie, with Antjie close behind, was crossing the car park, arms extended.

My heart was in my mouth. 'Hello, Mammie!' I leaned forward to hug the diminutive figure. She stretched her old neck and puckered her lips for a kiss.

I turned to my sister. 'Hey, Antjie! Hello, sis!' I hugged her too. She didn't seem to be looking at me. Her concentration was somewhere over my shoulder. As I kissed her cheek, I heard my mother. 'And who is this pretty lady? *Wie is hierdie pragtige jong dametjie?*'

I turned to stare in utter disbelief as Mammie approached Kelly with her arms outstretched. Kelly responded and the two women embraced, and Mammie planted a kiss on Kelly's black cheek. I stood open-mouthed. It never even occurred to me that I ought to make the introductions.

'Hi, Mrs Venter…I'm Kelly.'

'Well, Kelly,' Mammie's English was heavily accented. 'I'm so happy to meet you... Anton!' She turned to face her son. Her tone was playfully stern. 'Why didn't you tell me you were bringing a lady? I haven't prepared for visitors!'

Twenty

Not only was Pappie looking well, he was in the best form I had seen him in for years. Most significantly, it seemed clear to me that Kelly's presence was the chief reason he was excelling himself.

In fact, at a glance, he reminded me of TV footage I had seen of Nelson Mandela when he was visited by Naomi Campbell, or the time he hosted the Miss World finalists - gushing with testosterone and olde-worlde gentlemanly charm, a broad grin stuck on his face, a flirtatious wink permanently in his eye.

We were sitting having tea in the garden of the old vicarage - *die Ou Pastorie* - under the twin ornamental palm trees that were more than a hundred years old. Mammie and Antjie were fussing about in the kitchen and Kelly, like a guest of honour, was seated on an old thong-strung *riempie* bench, flanked by Pappie and me.

I was in a state of shock. Not only had my mother taken me totally by surprise in the car park by welcoming Kelly without betraying the slightest hint of her seven-odd decades of racial stereotyping, but Pappie, far from aggravating his condition, had apparently reacted to the arrival of the unexpected guest by simply falling in love with her. It just didn't make any sense.

Years ago we resolved, as a family, to stop discussing the race issue. When I announced my leftist political views in the late seventies, my parents were flabbergasted. Their initial hostility was intense.

Very few Afrikaners had 'gone over to the enemy'. They could be counted on the fingers of one hand. None was more famous, or infamous, than Braam Fischer, or Rev. Beyers Naudé.

Fischer, an Afrikaner aristocrat from the heart of the Orange Free State, home of rabid segregationism, was a communist and therefore an out-and-out traitor. He was eventually to end his life as a prisoner, released 'on humanitarian grounds' three months before the cancer claimed him.

But the treachery of Beyers Naudé, a Dutch Reformed minister like Pappie, was even more difficult for the *volk* to endure. He had been a member of their inner circle, one of their own. A founder of the Freemason-like *Broederbond*, the secret society that came to embody Afrikaner political power and intrigue, he was one of the custodians of the *apartheid* standard - a torchbearer for the master race.

When he began preaching equality and integration and compassion to unsegregated congregations the nation was aghast. In the eighties, when he became a very public member of the leadership of the United Democratic Front - the ANC's 'internal wing' - he was confirmed as the nation's number one traitor. The principal *volksveraaier*!

When at age eighteen I declared my opposition to *apartheid* I was cast in this same light. *Volksveraaier*! There were some monumental family fights, with Antjie, Willem, Mammie and Pappie united in their condemnation of my position.

It turned very ugly. Mammie wanted to banish me from the house but, mercifully, Pappie stepped in and brokered a peace deal that endured until today. The Venters never discussed politics if Anton was home. The subject was banned.

Now, all of a sudden, it seemed that Pappie and Mammie had come round! I was mystified. Stunned.

And Pappie was gushing, charm oozing from every pore. 'So, Kelly, tell me. Is Kelly your full name, or is it a... an abbreviation?' His English was measured and precise.

'No, Reverend, my real name is Kelebonye. Kelebonye Modise.'

Pappie sat up. His face registered total surprise. A smile slowly spread across his wrinkled features. '*O a reng*? What's that you say? Kelebonye Modise! *A o Motswana*?' The naughty twinkle flickered in his eye.

'*Ee Rra, ke Motswana... ke Mokgatla kwa Mochudi.*'

I was stunned. I hadn't expected this, but in retrospect it was completely predictable. After all, Pappie spoke flawless Setswana. I should have known.

'Anton, this young lady's telling me she's a Motswana, a Mokgatla from Mochudi. All this time I thought she was a damned Englishwoman - you know - no disrespect, Kelebonye, no disrespect, my dear – but you know your accent, you sound just like one of *Mmamosadinyana's* people, you know, one of Queen Elizabeth's folk!'

'Yes, I know. I lived there for nearly fifteen years, Mr Venter... er... Reverend.'

'Hey! None of this Mister Venter stuff, you call me *Rraago* Anton, Anton's dad, d'you hear, my dear, *Rraago* Anton!'

'*Ee Rra*!'

Pappie and Kelly started a long conversation in Setswana, laughing and joking with comfortable familiarity. I was completely lost. I understood barely a word, and soon I had absolutely no idea what they were talking about.

All I could tell was that my dad was doing his best to charm the pants off her, and she was revelling in the attention. I watched them for a few minutes.

What was immediately noticeable was that as soon as they began speaking Setswana, their body language and gestures changed. While they had been speaking English, Kelly had treated Pappie almost as an equal; politely, but with almost no overt signs of deference or more than common, everyday courtesy.

She sat comfortably, leaning back, knees apart, one leg crossed over the other, her gestures wide and expansive. At a glance, their bearing could be summarised as being adult to adult.

But, as soon as they started speaking in the vernacular, despite the relaxed, familiar tone, I could discern a much more exaggerated, distinct respect on her part, as if the language and its norms immediately brought out a different cultural standard in her.

She sat up straight, her knees together. Her gestures were much more contained, elbows by her sides. Often she would clasp her hands together, particularly as she agreed with something Pappie said, almost bowing her head slightly as she uttered, '*ee Rra, ee!* Yes, my father!'

Pappie too showed a more formal, avuncular manner when they spoke in Setswana. When he teased her in English, the naughty sparkle, the flirtatious twinkle, was much more pronounced. As soon as the language changed, so did his manner.

Speaking English, they were just two people, two indeterminate adults, and any respect and courtesy they chose to show one another seemed almost optional. As Africans, however, their roles were much more clearly defined - parent and child, adult and youth, elder and youngster - the terms of their interaction more precisely identified. The element of respect much more to the fore.

Despite making this educative observation, after a few more minutes of watching a conversation that I couldn't follow, I found myself becoming bored, and wandered to the house to chat with Mammie and Antjie. I found them in the kitchen with old Agnes, the same housekeeper from our Mooinooi days, preparing lunch.

'*Dumela* Agnès!'

'*Ahee.*' Her greeting was the barest minimum, a mere acknowledgement of my existence. No 'How are you?' She didn't meet my eye.

Mammie seemed still to be in high spirits, but Antjie's mouth was tight and she appeared to be struggling with something. Whatever was bothering her was clearly not for discussion in front of the domestic servant, and it was obvious that Mammie wanted us to pretend to be as normal as possible, and she tried to make light conversation with me, asking after Margot and Rachel, their school, and the like.

Antjie's sullenness was just too overt, however, and eventually Mammie had had enough.

'Antjie, take Anton into the sitting room and speak to him yourself then. I'm not having you banging around my kitchen, turning the milk sour with that frown! Go and talk, you two. Go!'

For a moment, I was in the dark as to what Antjie's problem might be. The unplanned introduction of Kelly into the household had passed off so unexpectedly well that I was on a high and had clearly missed whatever signals my sister may have been sending. No sooner had we gone into the sitting room and she had firmly shut the door behind us, than it immediately became plain.

'What do you think you are doing? Hey? Anton!'

'What d'you mean?' I could see what was coming, and decided to play dumb. If she was going to be so damn confrontational she could at least spell out her problem. I wasn't going to make it easy for her by making suggestions for her.

'How can you come here with that woman?'

'I don't know what you mean. Anyway, she's not *that woman*. She's my friend. We're on our way to Botswana together.'

'Oh! How could you, Anton? Don't you have any respect?'

'I still don't know what you mean.' I knew I had the high ground, and was going to force her to say it out loud, just so she would be able to hear for herself how ridiculous she sounded.

'Pappie's just had a damn stroke! How could you?'

'How could I what?'

'You damn well know what I mean! Have you no respect for our traditions, for their beliefs? I'm not asking you to agree with them, I know you've always been embarrassed to be an Afrikaner; you've always been ashamed of your nation.'

'That's nonsense, and you know it! I have never been ashamed to be an Afrikaner. Only ashamed of the way the majority of Afrikaners treated their fellow South Africans for the last three hundred years! We've been through this a thousand times, Antjie! I don't understand your problem.'

Antjie was flushed with emotion. 'How can you expect them - our dear old parents - to change so quickly, hey? Have you no respect for their age, Anton? For their way of life? How can you just come here and *force* them to accept your way, hey?'

I was getting impatient with her. She wasn't being honest. 'Force them? Force them? Force whom, please? My dear sister, it seems to me that you are the one with the problem.'

'Me?' She was flushed with anger, now. Her dark eyes flashed. 'How dare you?! *I* don't have a problem! As far as I am concerned, you can go out with any damn woman, black, white, pink, green with yellow spots, for all I care! I don't have a problem!'

She couldn't hide the self-righteousness in her voice. '*I'm* not a racialist!' She tried to calm down, and lowered her voice. 'Anton, it's just not right that you force our parents into accepting it!'

'That's bullshit, and you know it! Just look how Mammie greeted Kelly at the car park! No one was forcing her.' I went to the window. 'Come. Look.'

Antjie reluctantly followed me. Pappie and Kelly had got up from their seats and were making a slow perambulation of the garden. Pappie had his walking stick in one hand, and the other was held, a bit ostentatiously, in that old-fashioned way gentlemen used, when they offered a lady their arm.

Kelly had her arm through his, and as we watched, she gave Pappie a squeeze and snuggled her head against his shoulder in response to something he had said. They both wore radiant smiles and were talking animatedly.

'Tell me, who's forcing Pappie to do what?'

Antjie was silent.

'Look, sis, we didn't plan it like this, okay? When you found us stopped at *Wimpy* I was actually in the process of dropping her off, precisely so that we *wouldn't* upset anyone. It was you and Mammie appearing out of nowhere that wasn't planned. That was totally unexpected.'

Antjie looked at me. She seemed to realise now that it was her own racial inflexibility not our parents' that was upsetting her.

I put an arm around her. 'I was scared of upsetting Mammie and Pappie. I never thought I was going to upset my *sussie*!'

She looked at me. Her expression was a bit sheepish. She lowered her eyes.

I smiled indulgently. 'It's not as if one chooses who to fall in love with.'

'*Ag. Ja*!'

We stood in silence, watching our old father basking in Kelly's attention. Time stood still.

Suddenly, Mammie was calling. Lunch was ready. Antjie pointed at the pair through the window. 'Well, you'd better go and separate them, before he steals her away from you!'

By the time we all sat down together at the table, the issue was pretty much resolved - at least as far as Antjie was concerned. Her expression still betrayed remnants of her illogical outburst, but her mood had improved and she was no longer being hostile.

I was still at a loss to explain why Mammie and Pappie seemed to have taken it all so in their stride. It just didn't make any sense - but I wasn't complaining. Kelly looked radiant and completely at home.

The one person in the house who was very ill at ease was Agnes. I could read her mind. In all her thirty-something years of caring for the Venters she had never been so insulted, never been made to feel so uncomfortable. How could she be expected to serve a Motswana, a mere black - and a young girl at that - at the table! With the *Baas* and *Miesies*! Eating from the same plates, using the same cutlery! It was outrageous!

Not to mention her using the guest toilet, too! She didn't even have the decency to ask for the servants' ablutions. When she arrived she just waltzed in through the *front* door and went straight into the *guest* toilet as if she had a *right*!

If she got the chance she was going to tell this young strumpet a thing or two! Who did she think she was? And *Kleinbaas* Anton! What was he thinking? It was one thing for a man to have need of that sort of diversion, in private.

She had heard of it happening in faraway places like Johannesburg. But it was a completely different matter to arrive at his parents' door with his little black slut in tow! What was the world coming to?

Agnes positioned the last dish with an unnecessarily hefty thump and withdrew. I could visualise her expressing her bitter disillusionment in a lecture to the kitchen sink.

Pappie said grace in English for Kelly's benefit, although her Afrikaans wasn't all that bad, just woefully rusty. The family held hands around the table - Kelly once again flanked by the two men - and bowed their heads. Pappie was an old hand at bending the Lord's ear for a particular purpose, and he closed the grace with a little extra prayer.

'…And, dear Lord, we pray that you guide and protect us as we seek out our partner for this long road of life, that we may be comforted and give comfort. We thank you for the gift of love, and for your guidance that we may each find our own true, faithful companion. Dear God, bless these young people, in Jesus' name. Amen.'

As we ate Mammie's delicious traditional Malay-style *bobooti* and fresh green salad from the *Ou Pastorie* garden, I marvelled at my good fortune. I had taken the plunge. I had fallen in love with Kelly. And the one major obstacle I had so terribly feared seemed to have vaporised like a dandelion in a gust of wind.

I looked across at my mother. She was studying Kelly intently as she regaled the Venters with an account of my brilliant court performance in defence of Nozipo Nxumalo. Mammie's face betrayed no hint of that which I had so feared. She smiled involuntarily, as Kelly praised her son, beaming with maternal pride. When she sensed my eyes on her, she glanced at me and gave me a meaningful wink. *She approved! How I had underestimated her*!

After the sullen Agnes had cleared away the plates and brought in the coffee and Mammie's renowned homemade *melktert,* Pappie leant back in his chair.

'You know, my dear,' he looked affectionately at Kelly, 'I have been to Mochudi many, many times in my life. Of course, you know that our church, the *Nederduitse Gereformeerde Kerk*, has a mission there, *nê*?

'The big old church and the hospital have been there for years and years. Well, way back in the sixties, when Anton here was just a little thing in nappies, I was appointed to the Board of Trustees of the Deborah Retief Memorial Hospital Trust.'

'*Ag* Pappie, man!' Antjie was back to her usual light-hearted, teasing self. 'I'm sure Kelly isn't interested in all that ancient history! You *mos* know you just want to impress her with all your high office appointments!'

Pappie was not to be diverted. 'No, Antjie. You're right. I don't expect Kelebonye to be interested in my important executive past!' He winked at Kelly and patted the back of her hand. 'I was just setting the scene for a story I wanted to tell her. Something extraordinary that occurred many years ago. You know, I had forgotten all about it, and meeting her has suddenly reminded me.'

He accepted a slice of *melktert* from Mammie. '*Dankie* Mammie.' He turned to Kelly. 'Come, eat up! *Mmaago* Anton bakes the best cheesecake in the whole of South Africa. You taste that. Not too sweet, just perfect, isn't it?'

'Delicious!'

'Well, as I was saying, I was a member of the board of trustees at your hospital, and so I had to travel to Mochudi every three months, or so, for our meetings.'

He paused, eyes closed, as he savoured another mouthful of tart. 'Yes, let me tell you, in those days the roads were terrible. Terrible!'

He looked at Mammie for corroboration. 'You remember, *Skattie*, sometimes from Pretoria it would take almost a full day! I would drive to Swartruggens, and then over Lindleyspoort to Dwarsberg, past Abjaterskop and through Dwaalboom, then across the border at Derdepoort. That's Sikwane on the Botswana side.

'Oh man! The stretch from Dwarsberg all the way through to Mochudi, the road was awful!' He took a sip of coffee. 'Especially on the other side of the border. That was before they discovered diamonds up in Botswana, and the country was still dirt-poor. The roads were atrocious!

'Well, for years I undertook the journey to Mochudi. I used to stay with Doctor Rautenbach and his wife at the hospital. You must have heard of him?'

Kelly nodded. She was looking at Pappie with her beautiful big eyes, hanging on his every word.

'So, let me come to the point. One year, in the mid-seventies I think it was, while we were staying in Mooinooi, near Rustenberg, Anton, you *mos* remember, we still had the old '57 *Chev Impala*, the blue one with the fishtail fins.'

'Oh yes, I remember it. I also remember the hiding you gave me when I crashed it into *Oom* Stoffel Janse van Rensburg's gate post!'

'Yes, well that was richly deserved, richly deserved! But you mustn't distract me, Anton. I am telling your delightful little ladyfriend a story. Where was I?' Pappie smiled his charming smile. 'Oh yes, one year, it must have been seventy-one or seventy-two when I was making the trip to Mochudi for the quarterly board meeting, I remember I had a breakdown somewhere near Skuinsdrift. I think it was the alternator, yes, the alternator.'

Pappie paused while Mammie poured us all some more coffee, and handed out more *melktert*.

'Anyway, the long and the short of it was that I had to spend the night at old Fritz Kempelmann's place, the German fellow who had the little garage in Skuinsdrift, while he fixed it.

'In the morning I was in a devil of a rush, because the meeting in Mochudi was at nine, and I still had a long way to go. The border only opened at seven, if my memory serves me well, and I think I arrived there before six.

'Of course, the policeman on the South African side knew me well, and he unlocked for me and then very kindly climbed the Botswana gate to go and look for the Botswana immigration fellow, who was persuaded to come and open for me, so that I could be on my way. Of course, they all knew me quite well over there, but it was still very kind of them.'

He looked at Kelly. 'I'm not boring you, am I?'

'No, not at all! Do go on.'

'Well, there I was, hurrying to my meeting in Mochudi along this red, dusty road when I saw an old woman frantically waving me down. I came to a halt and she hobbled up to the car.

'She greeted me nervously, but I could see she was relieved when I replied in Setswana. At least I would be able to understand her request. You know, that's what I love so much about the Batswana; if you make the effort to speak their language, you know, they treat you with such demonstrative respect!

'Anyway, she told me she was very worried. Her child was very sick, and needed to go to the hospital. It was very urgent.'

Pappie took another mouthful of *melktert*. 'Of course, although I was in a terrible hurry, there was nothing for it but to help this old lady. She climbed in and pointed out a narrow path, more a ditch or a *donga* than a road, winding through the thorn bushes. I hate that screeching sound you hear when you know the paint is being ripped off your car, you know?

'Anyway, after a few torturous miles, we came to a small *mokgoro* out in the fields - just a simple hut beside an old morula tree. These people were so poor, the little red mud hut had holes in the thatched roof, and the courtyard was in ruins.

'Well, out of the hut came another, much older woman helping a little child of about ten or eleven whom I didn't see very well as she was all wrapped up in a blanket. They helped the child into the car, very nervous and extremely grateful, and with all three of them in the back seat, I turned the *Chev* around and headed back along the track through the thorny Acacias - the *haak-en-steek* and the *wag-'n-bietjies* - to the main road.

'I was running late, and so once I got back on to the road I drove a bit faster so that I might still get to my meeting on time. The three passengers sat quietly at the back. But just when the hills of Mochudi were visible ahead, and my journey was almost at an end, the first old lady tapped me on the shoulder.

"Rra we must go back!"

"But Mma, we are almost there. Look, the hospital is there, at those hills."

"I'm begging you, Rra. We must go back. Now!"

"Has the child recovered? Has the sickness passed?"

"We must go back! Now!"

'Well, there was nothing for it but for me to turn around. I was a bit annoyed because after all the effort of getting up at three in the morning and organising for the border to be opened specially for me, it looked as if I was going to be late for the meeting after all.' He looked at Kelly. 'You can ask Anton. I hate being late for an appointment!'

'I can vouch for that!' It was Mammie.

'Anyway, when I finally reached the little broken hut in the middle of nowhere, they all got out and the old women thanked me profusely. I admit I was a bit irritated at having been made to drive through the thorn bushes for nothing and because I was now late for my meeting, and I raced away in a cloud of dust.

'My last sight of them in my mirror was of the women helping the child towards the hut. One of them was walking sort of bent double, carefully holding the blanket off the ground between the child's legs.

'Well, I got to my meeting late of course, but the interesting part of my story is what I heard the following day. Just before I left Mochudi in the morning, I was chatting to the matron, and she told me some startling news.'

Kelly suddenly looked very ill. She croaked and shuddered.

'You okay, love?' I leant forward to support her. She looked as if she was about to faint.

Mammie jumped up out of her chair and came around the table to Kelly's side. 'Quick, Antjie, fetch her a glass of water.'

'Kelly! Kelly! You okay? Speak to me!' I was beginning to panic.

'Oh my God! Oh my God!' She was panting, her eyes wild.

'What, love? What's the matter?'

Pappie was deeply concerned. 'What is it?'

Kelly finally seemed to focus. She looked at Pappie, her eyes were wide. 'That was *you*?'

Pappie was confused. 'What? What was me?'

'The driver of the car, don't tell me it was you!'

'Yes, my dear, I'm telling you the story of when I...'

'Oh my God! ...My *God*!'

'What is it?'

'What did the matron say? Did she tell you the child had given birth to a baby? In your car? On the back seat of your car?'

Now it was Pappie's turn to look amazed. 'Yes... exactly!' He frowned at me, then looked at her, confused. 'But how do you know?'

'My God!' Kelly was almost hysterical. 'My *God*!'

Pappie was alarmed. 'What is it? Kelebonye, what's the matter?'

Kelly looked at me, then at Pappie. Her eyes were full of shock and disbelief. 'That was *me*! The bundle in the blanket, between my mother's legs! That was me! My God! ...Oh my God! *In your car*! I was born in your car!'

Twenty-One

The Cumberland Hotel in Lobatse is from another era. Recent refurbishments have failed to disguise the fact that it was built when a more gracious ethos ruled. Although the building itself is not very old, probably only forty-odd years, the colonial ambience dates from when newly independent Botswana still only had five kilometres of tarred road. Five kilometres of tarred road in a country the size of France.

It ran from the railway station and the District Commissioner's residence, northwards past the entrance of the Cumberland, and ended at the gate of the High Court of Botswana.

At the time of independence, the High Court was just a collection of modest buildings, but like the road that grew from five kilometres of narrow, uneven tar to thousands of kilometres of superior highway, the court was transformed by the diamond-fuelled development budget that modernised every aspect of the nation.

In forty years the country, once ranked the world's seventeenth poorest, was now emerging as the financial services hub of the sub-Saharan region. A budding Switzerland, though it must be said, drier and hotter. And flatter!

The High Court of Botswana was housed in a pretentious new building: a grisly concoction of marble, structural steel, glass, copper and Tuscan terracotta roof tiles - an architect's worst hangover brought to life.

In the grounds were a few of the original buildings, simple white-painted structures of cement block with granolith floors

265

and corrugated steel roofs that still gave the visitor a hint of how it once was.

As Kelly and I drove into Lobatse the huge scale of new development in the little town confused me. In the deepening twilight we inadvertently took an unguided tour of the new suburb of Woodhall, made a vast looping detour, and consequently entered old Lobatse not from the east, but from the north, driving past the High Court on our way to the Cumberland.

'There it is. Where I have to be at nine tomorrow.' The floodlights dazzled off the marble. 'Wish me luck!'

The drive from Zeerust had been uneventful, in the sense that we encountered nothing out of the ordinary of the objective connotation. But internally our psyches raged in hot confusion. Ever since the unnerving event at the lunch table, where coincidence had become a tangible, corporeal entity, Kelly and I were both wrestling with the probabilities, the implications, and the significance of what had been revealed.

Pappie had taken me aside for a few parting words as we wandered towards the car.

'You are blessed, my son! The Lord has spoken very clearly to you, Anton, very clearly. Take this woman and care for her with all your heart. That's all I can say to you, as a father and as a pastor. She has been pointed out for you, of this I have no doubt. Treat her well, and never take this relationship lightly!'

'Yes, Pappie, I will.'

As we sat in the car, engine running, putting on our seat belts, Mammie came up to Kelly's window and motioned for her to open it. When the glass slid down, Mammie leant in through the window and in a very deliberate, almost ritualistic - and certainly very un-Calvinist gesture - kissed Kelly on the forehead, and then with her finger drew a small cross over the kiss. 'Bless you, my child, bless you!'

As we reversed out of the driveway, Mammie and Pappie stood arm in arm, waving and blowing kisses. Even Antjie was warm and affectionate, and waved too. The waving continued until we turned the corner at the bottom of the street.

The unexpected connection between the Venter and Modise families - this seemingly pre-ordained blessing of our relationship - wasn't the only thing that I was having trouble comprehending. My parents' amazing political coming of age knocked me out. When had it happened? Why did I have to wait till now to discover it? All that panic about bringing a black girl home! All for nothing!

My confusion was only partly resolved by the discussion Mammie and I had after lunch, while Pappie was having his siesta. Antjie had gone to drop Agnes at the nearby black township of Lehurutse, and Kelly had settled down on the stoep with one of Herman Charles Bosman's books of short stories, all set in the Marico, the Zeerust area, leaving me to be with Mammie in her little sewing room. She could never just sit without doing something useful with her hands and she immediately opened her sewing basket and began to do some mending.

'Antjie told me you've got a girl,' she ventured as an introduction.

'Yes, Mammie.'

'You know, your *sussie* is quite fey. When she arrived here the other night, you know, that first night your father was in hospital. When was it?'

'*Ja*, Saturday, I think.'

'Yes, that's right. Anyway, Antjie told me she had spoken to you, in the Seychelles, was it?'

'Mauritius.'

'Yes, yes, of course. She told me that you were very cagey, you know, on the phone.' Mammie looked me in the eye over the rim of her thick sewing glasses, the blue of her eyes fainter and paler than I remembered. 'Antjie said… she said, "Anton's got a new girlfriend, Mammie."'

'I was so happy for you when I heard that, you know. You've had a hard, lonely time, my son. Ever since you and that

Hannah Zuckerman parted. So I asked Antjie to tell me more, and she said, "He didn't tell me much. He just told me her name's Kelly, but the way he was talking, you know, he was being all guarded and secretive. I *mos* know my little brother, Ma. I'm sure she's a coloured, or something. You know Anton. I wouldn't put it past him! Maybe even a black!"'

Sheepishly, I looked down at my feet. Was I really so transparent, so obvious? Even over the phone? Thousands of kilometres away? My God!

'Well, it turns out she was right, she *is* fey!' Mammie continued. 'There you were this morning, there by the *Wimpy*. Antjie and I had gone to do a little shopping. There you were with this tiny little woman, and I could see, right from the other side of the car park, you know, that there was something between you. I said to myself, "That must be Kelly!"' She smiled. 'And I was right!'

'But Ma,' I was still puzzled, 'I thought Pa and Ma wouldn't approve, you know. I was so scared, coming here. I was going to leave her at the *Wimpy*, you know, and come and visit you on my own.'

Mammie's look would have wilted a field of sunflowers. 'I would never have forgiven you if you had!' Her tone softened. 'No, my boy, times have changed, you know. And so must we.'

'But Mammie, I never thought that…'

'Yes, Anton, but it's really very simple. You know, I have always been an obedient citizen. That's the way we Afrikaners were brought up, to obey. When Dr Malan, and Strijdom, you know, particularly Dr Vervoerd, B.J. Vorster and P.W. Botha, told us that *apartheid* was correct, I obeyed my leaders like a good citizen.

'When Mr de Klerk said the ANC was now legal and he released Mr Mandela and all the others from prison, I accepted it. When the new president, Mr Mandela - Madiba - showed such forgiveness and respect to those who had held him in prison for all those years… well, I can't deny I was impressed.

'He told us to live together in peace as fellow South Africans, and I, you know, well I obeyed. It's as simple as that. We are all Africans, after all. Where else would Pappie and I belong?'

I looked long and hard at my old mother. Was it just as simple as that?

'And besides, Anton, Kelly is such a charming young woman! Don't let her slip away now, d'you hear me?' She took my hand.

'Yes, Ma…'

* * * * *

After a surprisingly good dinner in the Cumberland Hotel restaurant we relaxed over a last glass of wine at our corner table. In more ways than one, it had been a momentous day. Kelly had a new look in her eyes. At first, I wasn't sure what it meant.

She took a sip and whispered huskily over her wineglass, 'I want to make love to you…' She was looking me straight in the eye. 'I think I'm ready now…'

I could feel a prickling, tingling sensation that began behind my knees and journeyed up the insides of my thighs and through my groin to my solar plexus, as if her eyes had spoken directly to my sex. My pulse was loud in my ears.

Despite the rush of desire, I was determined to play it very unhurriedly, and to let her set the pace. I took a sip.

'Okay… Finish your wine, and then let's go to bed, you beautiful woman, you!'

On our way up the stairs to our room, we had our arms around each other. I resisted the temptation to start any overt foreplay. Kelly was going to call all the shots, and I resolved not to rush her.

Just then, on the top landing, my phone rang. It was Christo.

'*Ja*, Boet!'

'*Hey Poepol!*' Christo sounded very excited.

'What's up?' I was determined that Christo's call was not going to spoil the romantic mood. I kept one arm firmly around Kelly, as we strolled along the corridor.

'Hey, Anton! Where are you, man?'

'In Botswana… on an appeal.'

'You'll never guess it! I've fokken struck gold, my man! Got the fokken jackpot!'

'Why? What's happened?'

'You… news… that…'

I frowned as Christo's voice started to come and go. 'You're breaking up… I'll call you tomorrow.'

'No… fokken … important… talk … now…'

I shrugged and did my best not to look disappointed. Kelly didn't look put out.

'Let him call you on the landline… in the room. I'll go and have a bath…' She winked encouragingly. '*It won't go away*!'

'Hey, Christo, call me on the landline…' We had reached the door of our room.

'*Ja*, okay... Where?'

She unlocked the door and we shuffled inside, still in each other's arms.

'Cumberland Hotel, Lobatse… room twenty-one…' Kelly disengaged herself, scampered across to the little bureau and grabbed a brochure. She held it up for me to read out the number to Christo.

I couldn't hide my annoyance. Christo's call had been ill-timed, to say the least.

'You relax and take your call. I'm going to have a nice, long, deep bath.'

I could feel the romantic mood evaporating. 'What? I thought you were going to… you know… ravish me!' I embraced her fiercely.

Kelly pulled away.

'Wait, you animal! Wait! I said I want you. And I want you without the phone about to ring! Just be patient, luv! We've got all night!' She gave me a reassuring kiss. 'It won't go away. Don't worry! After all, you've waited long enough, a few more minutes won't kill you!' She gave me another kiss.

The phone beside the bed rang. I sat down and answered it. '*Ja*, you were saying…'

'Well, I don't know if you saw the news about that *ou*, Jabu Zulu, the guy in your case?'

'*Ja*, Solly told me last night. Heard about his lucky escape on the radio this morning. Why?' I watched Kelly getting her things from her bag. God, she was beautiful! She went into the bathroom and began running the bath.

'Well, we've got our man! I'm sure of it, fokken hundred per cent sure this time.' Christo was very excited. 'The guy who abducted Zulu is the Castration Murderer, no fokken doubt about it!'

I sat up. 'What makes you so sure? Did he castrate Zulu?'

'No, he didn't manage to castrate him, but he fokken tried.'

'What? And you say you've got him?'

'No, we haven't physically *got* him, as in "have him in custody", but we've got a definite ID. It's the *ou*, Anton, it's blerrie crystal clear, man. It's just a matter of time now and we'll catch him.'

'So, d'you know who he is?'

'*Ja*! Name, ID, mug shot, address, the lot. A white fellow, one of yours. Marthinus Webster, thirty-five. He won't get away this time. I guarantee it. Anyway, I've been told to take over the investigation, you know, my unit.

'Been on it since this morning when they talked to Zulu after he escaped, and realised it was our case. The National Commissioner has personally given me *every* resource I need, and I'm taking him up on it, I'm telling you.'

He paused for breath. 'Old Zulu's just fokken lucky, otherwise he'd have been number seven!'

'But what makes you so sure? Remember the last time? Cupido? You were pretty sure then, weren't you?'

'I'll tell you why I'm sure. Remember, I'm telling you all this because we go back a long fokken way, and you've been with me through this whole thing, *nê*. Also, I think it may have a very real bearing of your perjury case, you know? None of this is for the fokken Press!'

'Of course not! Since when do I…?'

'For your ears only!'

'Of course!' Kelly came out of the bathroom. The water was still running. She quickly came up to me, kissed her fingertip, pressed it against the bulge in my pants, winked and wagged the same finger at me: *You're soon going to be in big trouble… delicious trouble*, it said. Then, she went back to the bathroom.

'Okay, as I was saying. First of all, remember Jabu Zulu has just fokken bribed his way out of a rape conviction. Okay, okay, maybe we can't prove that he actually *bribed* anybody, but you know what I mean, you *mos* know the trial through and through.

'He got off but he was fokken guilty as hell, *nê*. That Lappies Labuschagne is as bent as a fokken nine rand note. If there was any fokken justice in this world, Zulu should have got twenty years.'

'*Ja*, don't I know!' Kelly turned off the water. Her top came off. *Oh, what perfect breasts*!

'Well, that means he fits the profile of the other victims perfectly. The law failed to punish him, so the vigilante will!' He paused. I watched Kelly through the open door of the bathroom. She tested the water, and opened the cold tap. Then she slipped off her jeans. For a moment I remembered how she had nearly pissed herself that morning, and chuckled to myself. Christo's voice dragged my attention back.

'Second, when he was jumped in the underground car park yesterday, he was injected with some or other knockout drug, just like van der Spuy and some of the others.'

Despite the distraction of Christo's call, Kelly's striptease was very arousing. She half-peeled her knickers off her delectable bum, and then leant forward over the bath to turn off the tap, affording me a voyeur's dream view. I was finding it difficult not just to drop the phone on the floor and let myself go.

'Three, he was gagged. Listen to this, *Boet*! He was gagged with red fifty-mill 3-M gaffer tape! D'you hear me? Red, 3-M fokken fifty-millimetre gaffer tape! The same as all the others! D'you hear what I'm saying?'

Kelly was naked now, gingerly getting into the bath, which was obviously still a mite too hot. She saw me watching her, saw me drooling. She frowned, miming annoyance. *Wait*! Then she blew me a kiss, wiggled her hips lasciviously, bent forward and shut the door.

'J... Ja... ja, I hear you. What else?' I sighed involuntarily.

'That's already quite a lot, Anton. But you're right, it's still only circumstantial. Oh yes, he wears size elevens, too. Also circumstantial. But it's not all! Zulu was abducted yesterday afternoon, about three-thirty. The kidnapper seems to have been alone. That also fits, by the way.

'Anyway, it's the same old MO that you know from Cape Town. He knocks Zulu out, chucks him in a combi, and gets out of the underground car park. Sometime before Zulu recovers from the blow to his head, he's been injected with the tranquillizer. Sleeps like a baby.

'And this is the most confidential part, don't you fokken go telling *anyone* this, okay? If the Press gets hold of this, I'm fokked!'

'Of course I won't!'

'Webster uses his old trick of injecting a stimulant to counteract the tranquillizer, an antidote. Anyway, when Zulu wakes up he's on a smallholding somewhere in the *bundu,* the back of beyond near Delmas. Some old deserted farmhouse. This must have been around five-thirty in the evening.

'He wakes up gagged, bound and naked. There is a sort of welded steel gadget, like a makeshift gynaecological couch thing, you know, like a frame with a set of stirrups, in the middle of the room.

'I've been out there today and I've seen it! It's fokken purpose-made! The thing is mounted above a circular saw, you know, and is on fokken wheels, so that it can be driven over the saw, you get me? A custom-built torture chair!

'The thing is just the right height for the *ou's* tackle to get fokken zapped by the saw blade. So when Zulu wakes up he finds himself in a very fokken seriously compromised position, trussed up in this contraption, gagged with the tape, naked with his fokken feet in the stirrups, legs apart - *wydsbeen*, with his family blerrie jewels dangling with a fokken three-hundred millimetre saw blade a few inches in front of them! Remember James Bond in what was it? Goldfinger? Tied to the table with a saw creeping towards his crotch?'

'*Ja…*'

Christo chuckled. 'Okay, same deal, but this is the overhead model!'

For a moment I had completely forgotten about Kelly in the bath. Christo had my undivided attention now.

'So, how did he get away? You say he didn't get his dangly bits removed. What saved him?'

'Well, that's just where Zulu's guardian angel was fokken on the job. What he tells me is that the *ou* threatened him - and this is where it gets interesting for you - he threatens Zulu. He pulls off the gag and switches on a little video camera to record him. Tells him he has to confess or he loses his balls.

'Zulu says at first he told the guy to fok off, but I doubt it - he's too much of a fokken coward. Anyway, then the *ou* switches on the saw. The seat-on-wheels is connected to some little motor so it creeps forward very slowly… The *ou* keeps demanding that Zulu confess.'

'Confess to what? To the rape of Nozipo?'

'Apparently, the *ou* doesn't say. When I questioned Zulu - I spoke to him at the clinic again this afternoon - he was still in a fokken state. He wouldn't say. He refused to speculate. Said it would amount to entrapment. Claims he's as good as gold.

Says there's nothing at all he needs to confess. He didn't know what this guy was on about.'

'Well, is there anything else he could be under suspicion for? A crooked business deal? Is he into drug dealing? You know, those Nigerian cocaine boys can get pretty rough. Maybe he's rubbed some gangster up the wrong way, you know?'

'Of course, we've thought of that, you know, that this Webster *ou* could be a hired hit man or something. I checked with the other police agencies, the Scorpions, fraud squad, drug squad, also the tax people at the Revenue Department, you know, the lot.

'No, the only thing that Zulu seems to have against him is this rape business, of which he's now *mos* been acquitted. On paper, he's as clean as clean.'

'So, he refuses to confess, to whatever it is he's supposed to confess. So, why doesn't Webster drive him through the saw?' I was in my amateur detective mood now, thinking aloud.

'Well, here comes the guardian angel. The frame thing is edging forward, his goolies getting closer and closer to the blerrie saw blade. Just then, there's a fokken power cut. Can you believe it? Webster goes outside to some outbuildings to check out the electrical supply.

'While he's gone, old Zulu manages to free one hand… fokken tears half the skin off his wrist in the process. It's blerrie amazing what fear can do for you. Gives you fokken superhuman strength.

'Anyway, to cut a long story short, he manages to untie himself and make a run for it. Some fellow finds him running down the highway in the twilight, stark naked, blood pouring from his hand, and stops to help.'

'Lucky bastard!' I tried to draw my thoughts together. 'I hear what you say that this crime fits the MO for the castration murders, and all that, and it fucking looks that way. I mean, offhand, I can't think of any other likely explanation.'

'Well, *is* there any other possible blerrie explanation?'

I couldn't think of one. 'I can't imagine Nozipo organising a hit on Zulu, you know. It's not her style at all, and she just wouldn't have the resources.'

'No chance!'

'So, it fits. If Webster has been targeting rapists, particularly rapists that got away scot-free, then Jabu Zulu certainly fits the bill. All I can say is I hope it finally *is* the castration murderer. You deserve it.'

'*Ja*, you said it, *Poepol*! The funny thing is that after all the fokken sweat, all the hours of fokken back-breaking careful detective work, two-and-a-bit years' of it, the *ou* falls out of the blerrie sky. It's not as if we found him, you know. This kidnapping just happened and next thing I know, I've solved my case!

'Anyway, we'll talk more when you get back to Jo'burg. You *mos* owe me a steak! I just thought you should know. I mean, it could affect your case. You know, the State versus Nxumalo.'

'*Ja*, thanks. I'm sure it will affect the case, though I can't say I can predict exactly how, not at this stage anyway! Most important is that you get this fucking Webster *ou* into custody! Don't start celebrating till you've turned the key on him, *Boet*!'

'For sure! Hey, by the way, how's your little darkie?'

I didn't appreciate the attempt at a joke.

'Her name's Kelly! You fucking racially obsessed *poes,* you!'

'Calm down, calm down. I was only teasing! How's Kelly, then?'

'Fucking gorgeous! No, she's okay, fine.'

'Where is she? Did you leave her in Jo'burg?'

'No. She's here. In the bath.'

'You mean you've taken her to Botswana with you? You *are* keen, hey?'

'*Ja*. To be honest, Chris, I enjoy her company, you know.'

'You fokken *poesbedonnerd* idiot! You sure you're not just cunt-struck, heh? You think it's real this time? I mean, really meaningful?'

'*Ja*, I think it could be. Everything just feels right, you know.'

'But what about your old folks, man? I mean they're as *verkramp* as they make them! Blerrie *arch*conservative, for that matter! You know, she's *black* for Chrissake! They're going to have a blerrie fit when they find out!'

'Well, I also thought so, but we had lunch with them in Zeerust today, and they both fell completely in love with her. I don't know what makes me so lucky, but it's true!'

'*Fok me*! She had lunch with *your* parents? A black chick! Fok me with the wrong end of a fokken pineapple!'

When the marathon call finally ended I got off the bed and stretched. I took a deep breath and opened the bathroom door.

Kelly was lying in the bath, eyes closed, floating with only her face and her nipples above the water line. The slight asymmetry of her breasts – the knife scar through the left areola and the off-centred nipple were more apparent in this pose – somehow made her only more perfect. She was so small that her feet barely reached the end of the bath.

I devoured her with my eyes. I knelt by the side of the bath, leant over and kissed her. She passionately returned the kiss. But when I very gently began to stroke her breasts, she firmly took my hand and pushed it away. For a moment I was confused, disappointed.

Her eyes were frank and candid. 'I said it's my turn!'

* * * * *

When the alarm woke me at five forty-five, I was still floating in a heavenly fug. She was wrapped tightly around me as she had been ever since we had finally fallen asleep, and I had to disengage myself to reach the beeping cell phone.

Before I could take stock of my situation Kelly rolled out of bed.

'Bladder!'

I watched her walk to the bathroom, her nakedness almost ethereal in the dawn light. There was the tinkling sound of her on the loo, and then she was back. Without ceremony she pulled off the covers and climbed astride me - the position she had occupied for almost all of last night. When she said she was going to make love to me, I reflected, she meant it quite literally.

Within moments I was ready and she took me into herself and very gently, very sensuously and very lovingly undulated and bore down on me, rolled and surged, smiling at me all the while.

The fact that I knew that this was all totally new to her made it very exceptional and precious. Up until last night she had never in her life made love to anybody. Ever. But since she had got out of the bath last night she had barely stopped.

When she brought me to orgasm, having herself gasped and quivered two or three times, I reflected that she was incredibly good at it already. Then she kissed me and hopped off.

'There you go, lover boy! You've got work to do. You have a meeting with that lawyer fellow in...' she looked at her cell phone, '...forty minutes! You need a shave and a fuckin' good scrub. You reek of my pussy!'

I had barely slept for two consecutive nights, but the spiritual food by which I had been nourished seemed to make up for it. That, and a lot of caffeine and nicotine!

I was on my third cup of coffee when a strikingly good-looking, tall young man in a black three-piece suit with stylish, tied-back dreadlocks walked out to the table in the garden where I was cramming my case notes, getting myself tuned in for the day.

'Mr Venter?' Mathatha Mmino had a rich, pleasant-sounding bass voice. The diamond earring in his left ear glittered in the early morning sun.

'Anton, please!' I stood up and extended my hand. 'You must be Matt? Nice to meet you!'

'And you. It's an honour, Mr Ven… er …Anton. An honour!'

'Sit, sit - unless you'd prefer inside? It's just that I am a social misfit.' I indicated the burning cigarette in my fingers. 'My sort has been banished to the outdoors these days!'

'No, out here is fine. I don't mind if I do, too. I'm also an outcast!' Matt took out a pack and lit one himself, settling down. He opened his briefcase.

'Coffee, please!' he called to the approaching waitress.

It was all over before the lunch recess. After all the anxiety and anticipation, the day had turned out to be a damp squib. The nine o'clock start was delayed, and when the Appeal Court finally convened at around ten thirty, it became apparent that the State lawyers had, through some or other communication breakdown, failed to get all their bits and pieces together in time.

A particular file couldn't be found, and after a long, embarrassing wait, the State counsel had to beg the court's pardon and request yet another postponement.

Babelegi Bogatsu, Matt's senior partner and the third member of Tsotsetsi's defence team, Matt and I adjourned to the Cumberland for a lazy lunch. The case had been postponed till tomorrow, and I had the afternoon off.

Kelly joined the men at the table, and I had the private pleasure of introducing her to the others as my partner. I had to mentally pinch myself to remind myself that this was real - this beautiful woman was now exactly that: my partner. I could see the envy in their eyes. *Yes chaps, she's a doll. And she's mine*!

Afterwards, Kelly and I had no alternative but to go and sleep off the glasses of wine we'd had at lunchtime. Last night's hard labour had also taken its toll on both of us.

At least, that was the intention. In the event, we slept only a little, and made love as much and as passionately as the limitations of my erectile tissue allowed - and even when that was in recovery mode, we couldn't keep our lips and tongues and fingers away from one another's most receptive spots.

It was as if the floodgates had opened, and all the pent-up emotion of the days in Mauritius had come streaming out, uncontrolled and insatiable. Kelly was in a sex-debt situation, a life-long sex-debt situation. Now that she had discovered the repayment method, nothing was going to stop her redressing the negative balance.

Sometime in the middle of the languid, steamy afternoon, while we were dozing, gathering our energy for the next round, Kelly remembered something. She sat up and looked me in the eye.

'So, what was your mate Christo on about? You know; your marathon phone call last night.'

'Oh *ja*, that! Well, he's bloody excited. Looks like he's identified the real castration murderer this time. This is all very confidential, of course. Some guy called Webster, apparently. Says he's hot on the guy's trail.'

'That's good news!' She was nibbling my nipple, moving south. 'Very good…' her lips reached my belly, '…news!' Her mouth was poised, and I could feel her warm breath. 'Hope he gets him soon!' There was a faint quiver of impending resurrection.

'Mmm…'

Twenty-Two

Lunch on Friday was an altogether more subdued affair. The morning at the Court of Appeal had been another total washout. The Attorney General's office had not managed to locate the missing documents and Benjamin Tsotsetsi's appeal against his conviction and sentence had been postponed for another nine months.

His counsel had spent a fruitless morning waiting in an office, waiting, as it turned out, for nothing.

I was furious. 'What a waste of fucking time!'

Lord Douglas-Smith and Sir Virendra Naipaul, who were dining with their wives at a nearby table, turned around and stared at me with frosty disapproval. I pretended not to notice.

'Now you see what we are up against, hey, Anton.' Babelegi Bogatsu was philosophical. 'The whole civil service is like that. They just damn well can't be bothered! Couldn't organise a piss-up in a brewery!'

Matt Mmino chipped in, 'If you're disappointed, just think how Ben Tsotsetsi must be feeling at this moment!'

'D'you mind if we take a different road home?'

'Of course not. Why, d'you want to go via Gaborone?' I unlocked the car.

'Gabs? No thanks, mate! Not my sort of place! I was hoping we could pass through Mochudi. It'll mean going through Gabs anyway, I suppose. The drive to Jo'burg won't be that much longer. In fact, if we take the road via Sikwane, you know, the Sun City road, it'll hardly be any longer at all. It's just, you know, I haven't been there for almost a year.'

'Look, woman! There's no need for explanations!' I dropped the bag into the car and took her into my arms. 'You've got me so bloody tightly wrapped around your little finger that if you want to go via Timbuktu, you know, it's okay with me!' We nearly lost our balance as our embrace almost landed us in the Audi's open boot.

I caught a glimpse of the manager of the Cumberland, looking out of his window at the car park. He shook his head in bemused wonder. The expression on his face was eloquent and couldn't have been plainer: *Those two haven't stopped bloody kafuffling since they arrived!*

The road north passes through the village of Otse, which boasts the hill with the highest elevation in the country. Otse Mountain and some of the surrounding hills have a number of relatively modest but, nevertheless, intriguing climbable faces, and both Kelly and I mentally picked out possible routes on the crags as we drove past. The most northerly peak, Baratani, the Hill of the Lovers, has long vertical faces of what looked like friable sandstone conglomerate.

'Looks like there's a challenge or two to be had there,' I suggested. 'We'll bring climbing gear next time! Never thought of this flat desert as a climbing venue, I must admit!'

'Yeah, for those of us who need climbing gear!' She winked, and changed the subject. 'Any more news from Christo? Has he caught his man yet?'

'Dunno. I haven't spoken to him since his call on Wednesday night.' I punched Christo's number on the cell phone, but his number was *unavailable at the moment*.

It had been three or four years since I had last passed through Gaborone and I was astounded at the explosion of new development, not all of it necessarily attractive or well planned.

It seemed that the city was growing apace, in many directions and styles at once. I noticed that the freeway through the city, the Western Bypass, was as congested as the roads it had meant to relieve.

The number of motor vehicles seemed to have doubled since my last visit. Every third or fourth car was a top of the range model. There were BMW X5's, Range Rovers and Mercedes Benzes all over the place. Clearly, the economy was on the move.

Lining up in traffic for one of the circles, my eye was inadvertently drawn to the side of the road where a drop-dead gorgeous girl was flagging down a mini-bus taxi.

She had stunning, baby-doll looks, a minute top, and jeans so tight they looked as if they had been spray-painted on to her delectable figure. The strategic seams of the jeans disappeared into the most intimate crevices of her body.

She caught my eye, and despite the presence of a woman in the car, gave me an unambiguous look which said: *Whatever the question... the answer's yes!*

I barely resisted that critical extra second and a half that makes all the difference between a casual glance and a serious ogle, and looked at Kelly instead. This was the most beautiful woman in the world, and she was mine. I had no further use of my lifelong habit of window-shopping.

At that moment, there was another. This one was in a short skirt. She had a flouncy, orange hairdo, and her legs seemed to go on forever. I almost hurt my neck dragging my eyes away. Kelly noticed it.

'I saw that.'

'What?'

'You, undressing that girl! You looking for HIV? You could pick it up here in a day if you wanted.'

I gave her hand a squeeze. 'Point taken! But remember the research you did, when you were checking me out? You should know by now that I don't do the casual sex thing.'

'Well, keep your eyes on the fuckin' road then, will ya?'

Soon, we were out of town and heading north on the new dual carriageway, proudly designated the A1.

As the hills of the Kgatleng came into view, a childlike eagerness began to become apparent in Kelly's demeanour. Her eyes sparkled and she leant eagerly forward in her seat, a girl coming home.

Mochudi is set amongst gentle, attractive hills. The beautiful setting has lost a lot of its charm as Mochudi and its neighbouring villages, Morwa, Pilane and Rasesa have developed haphazardly into small disorganised towns, their traditional mud and thatch architecture annihilated by the inexorable advance of cement block, corrugated iron, face brick and ersatz tiles – soulless suburbia.

As the villages have expanded, the organic shapes - twisty roads winding between randomly shaped plots containing rounded buildings - have given way to an unremitting matrix of rectangular yards with cement-coloured rectangular structures, a never-ending grid of grey dusty sameness.

The main road through the village is bordered by endless small businesses - bars and 'liquor restaurants' far outnumbering any other genus. As it was Friday afternoon, the end of the working week, these establishments were already doing brisk trade, groups of drinkers standing around their parked cars in the dusty forecourts, cans and bottles scattered around.

'You know, if there's aught that irks me its how we fuckin' Batswana just chuck rubbish on the ground! Look! The whole fuckin' place is littered with shite!'

She had a point, I reflected. The plastic bags fluttering in the branches of the thorn trees, the sparkle of shattered glass at the bus stop, the carpet of sweet-wrappers, Chibuku *Shake-Shake* beer cartons and endless discarded cans were a poor complement to the statuesque symmetry of Phaphane Hill!

But it wasn't long before we had left Mochudi behind us, and we were back on a highway through in the stark, flat rural landscape that characterises most of the south-east of the country, headed for the border village of Sikwane.

On our way out of town, we had made a short detour and driven through the royal ward past the court, or *kgotla*, seat of the tribal administration, past Pappie's Deborah Retief Memorial Hospital and the Dutch Reformed church, and up to the old colonial school, now the Phutadikobo Museum, with its beautiful, panoramic views of the village that is the proud capital of the Kgatleng District.

Somehow, after Pappie's story the other day and the incredible connection between the Venter and Modise families that had been revealed, I felt that the place was steeped in our personal history, past, present, and future. *Future? God! I hoped so!*

As we left the built-up area, Kelly thought of something. 'Can you stop? At that shop.' She pointed.

'Sure.' I pulled up outside a diminutive general dealer's.

Kelly hopped out and in five minutes returned with a couple of plastic bags with what seemed to be basic provisions. I could make out tea, long-life milk, sugar, bread and other odds and ends through the bags.

We had travelled for less than fifteen minutes from the village outskirts when Kelly put a hand on my knee. Her excitement was palpable.

'Here, luv, can we turn off here?' She pointed to a narrow dirt track off to the right.

I guessed where we were headed. 'Hope it's not as scratchy as it was thirty years ago.'

But the rutted track was far less overgrown. Thirty years of deforestation and the passage of countless vehicles had turned the track into a normal rural dirt road, and the Audi had no problems negotiating its sandy twists and turns.

A few kilometres down the track, Kelly's unconcealed excitement came to a head and she became almost childlike, barely able to contain herself. She indicated a big old morula tree in the distance, and presently a small homestead appeared on the left, beside a large field.

As the Audi turned into the gate of the yard, we were faced with a modest cement-block *two-room*, unplastered and unpainted, but a vast improvement over the tumbledown red-mud hovel Pappie had described, which had previously stood there.

As the car stopped, there was movement in the shade under the morula tree behind the house. Kelly opened the door, jumped out and scampered towards it.

'Mmane!'

When I disembarked I saw Kelly and a skinny, eccentric-looking woman coming towards me. She was dressed in frayed, everyday, peasant work clothes, her hair hidden under a moth-eaten beanie. Her weatherworn skin exaggerated her years - she was, after all, only a few months older than me - and she looked much older than she was.

At a glance, I could tell that she was not quite balanced - her face conveyed an otherworldly, aberrant disposition that accentuated her ragged appearance.

Kelly's animated expression fluently illustrated her excitement and happiness at the reunion. Phatsimo too was obviously excited, although behind the animation her face revealed that there existed within an unusual psyche and a unique personality. In a wild, crazy sort of way she exuded pure joy at the sight of her daughter.

Phatsimo took my extended hand. She held it tightly for a long time, oblivious to her own tuneless humming, as Kelly silently mouthed a comprehensive introduction, combining gestures and carefully enunciated voiceless words.

At some point in the explanation Phatsimo evidently realised that this white person, this *lekgowa*, was not just an acquaintance, the driver of the car, the provider of a lift, a mere stranger - but her daughter's very special friend.

Kelebonye had never before had any sort of gentleman friend, at least none her mother had ever known of, and this introduction was therefore cause for exceptional excitement and happiness. She fervently kissed the back of my hand, then looked up at me with an expression of near wonder, her eyes almost round with awe.

'This is my mother, Anton!' Kelly's face beamed with love and pride.

'*Dumela Mmaago Kelebonye!*' I did my best to make my lips as easy to read as possible. I knew I looked like an ass, and that my atrocious pronunciation was as obvious to her as to a hearing person.

Phatsimo's giggles were insuppressible - like her daughter's. '*Dumela Mokgwenyana!*' The voice was toneless and disembodied, but the mad smile through the broken, discoloured teeth was warm and welcoming, and the crazy laughter full of happiness. She kissed my hand again. I had to admit that being called 'son-in-law' at this early stage was a little intimidating.

Kelly fetched a chair from the house and placed it for me in the swept clearing under the morula tree, while she sat on a little stool and Phatsimo on a rawhide mat on the ground. Wisps of smoke rose lazily from a small fire in the centre of the clearing.

There was an exchange of sign language.

'She's asking if you like the house I built for her.' Kelly was beaming.

'Sure. It's lovely.'

'Yeah, there's a bit to be done yet, plastering, painting, ceilings. But it's a start.'

I was only able to converse with the older woman through Kelly, who interpreted from English to lip-read Setswana and back. For an hour we sat there, making slow progress at small talk, communicating through the barriers of deafness, language, culture and Phatsimo's loony, exuberant eccentricity.

Kelly boiled water on the fire, and served tea and scones from the provisions she had bought in Mochudi. I saw that despite her London accent and her sophisticated, urban ways, Kelly was a deft hand at traditional skills, and I marvelled at the way she adroitly tended the fire and managed to produce the tea in these squalid circumstances without so much as skipping a beat.

Clearly these apparently basic tasks, which urbanites take for granted, require much more skill that is generally appreciated. I watched with admiration as she coaxed flame from the glowing embers, and positioned the kettle precisely to absorb the concentrated heat, so that the water boiled in minutes.

Despite the absence of a table - she had a tin tray balanced on a small stool - there was no ash in the cups, no dust on the scones, and everything was as if Kelly had prepared tea in a city kitchen. I reflected, the traditional fireside skills she had learnt as a child were still with her today. Like learning to ride a bicycle, it was something one never forgot.

Phatsimo looked as happy as could be.

The shadows were lengthening - the sun would be setting presently. 'We must leave soon, luv, we can't be missing the border. It closes at seven.'

'I'm ready anytime, but enjoy the moment with your mom. We've still got plenty of time.'

The relaxed mood changed abruptly when a man entered the compound. He was pushing a bicycle, and I immediately noticed that he was drunk, and that he had an unsavoury demeanour. He looked intently at the Audi as he passed it, then noticed me and came towards us.

'My uncle, Mmane's younger brother, Steven.' Kelly spoke out of the side of her mouth. There was a hint of anxiety in her voice.

Steven sauntered unsteadily towards us. He ignored his niece, and had eyes only for me. '*Dumela Lekgowanyana.*' I stood up, not sure of myself. '*Mphe madi!* I'm want money!' Steven demanded, hand outstretched, '*Geld...Chelete!*'

Kelly immediately flew at him. Her voice was strident, reprimanding. It was clear that she was not going to stand for my being disrespected or insulted, regardless of whether the perpetrator was her elder or not.

'Sorry, Anton! He may be my uncle but he's got no fuckin' manners. He's got no right to speak to you like that, and he knows it, he knows he's out of order. Setswana has very strict etiquette about greetings, an' all. He can't just come in here making demands!'

Steven was not to be diverted however. He had seen the car, worth hundreds of thousands of Pula. He could see the white skin, similarly worth countless thousands. He was not going to be put off getting the price of a drink out of this *lekgowa*, no matter how much his cheeky little city-slicker niece tried to deflect him.

'*Fotsheke! O rata Sekgowa, wena*!' And then, for my benefit, 'You think you are clever, huh? You think you are a white?'

Their interaction descended into an unpleasant exchange of insults and threats.

'Shouldn't I just give him a couple of bucks to shut him up?' I whispered.

'No fuckin' way! I will not have his rudeness rewarded in any shape or form! He's totally out of order, and he fuckin' knows it! Let's get going. It's late!'

Kelly took Phatsimo's arm as we went towards the car. Phatsimo grabbed my hand, squeezing it with concentrated sentiment and looking intently into my eyes. Steven circled behind us like a mongrel cur, snapping at Kelly, who barked back.

I couldn't understand a word, but clearly there was little love lost between them, and despite the age difference, which in normal circumstances would have required her to defer to her elder, it was clear that Kelly was having none of her uncle's bad behaviour.

While Phatsimo said an affectionate farewell to me at the driver's door of the Audi, making it clear to me with her weird gestures that she was happy to have met me and that I should come back soon, the argument between Kelly and Steven reached fever pitch on the other side of the car.

Suddenly, Steven approached her, presumably to whisper a choice insult in her ear, or so it appeared. When he got close to her she became rigid. She abruptly pushed him away from her - two hands in the chest. All her concentrated strength was apparent as he flew backwards, landing on his backside in the soft sand. The violent intensity of her action took us all by surprise. For a moment nobody moved.

Then she dived into the car, slamming the door behind her. There was sheer panic on her face.

'Go! Go!'

I did as I was told. The urgency in her voice was such that I dared not argue, although I could not identify what had suddenly escalated the situation. As we reversed out of the compound, wheels spinning, our last sight was of a bemused, swaying Steven, getting to his feet and making a crude, dismissive gesture with his hand, while beside him, like a child saying goodbye at the railway station, Phatsimo smiled and waved joyfully bouncing unsteadily from one foot to the other.

'You okay, love? What was all that about?'

Kelly was in a state of total shock. She was panting, wild panic in her eyes. I drove on for a while, looking at her with concern. She seemed to be almost beside herself with fear, as if the object of her terror had accompanied us into the car. A kilometre or so from the compound, I stopped the car.

'What is it, Kelly?' I was trying to make sense of it. Sure, Steven had been rude and annoying, but no more than that. I had been dealing with his sort for years. Her reaction seemed totally out of proportion.

I tried to take her into my arms. She resisted me at first, stiff as a board and barely breathing. She went limp and she began weeping piteously, trembling against me.

It was only much later, after we had crossed the border back into South Africa and were on the gravel section between

Derdepoort and Dwaalboom that Kelly seemed to regain her composure.

'Sorry, luv! I mean about what happened back there.'

'What was it? What happened? One minute you were telling him off and the next...'

'Yeah, he was being rude, but my reaction was totally over the top. Not fair on him really. I lost it... right?'

'Yes, one could say you did.'

'It was the smell...' She choked involuntarily at the memory.

'What smell?'

'Did you smell it? ...His breath?'

'I could smell that he'd been drinking, that's all.'

'He'd been drinking *Chibuku*, you know, sorghum beer.'

'And?'

'Well, you remember what I wrote? About the time when I was four... when that old man raped me?'

'Yeah.'

'Remember I said that the smell was what I remembered most vividly... the smell like vomit?'

'Uh-uh.'

'Well, *that* was the smell...'

We entered Jo'burg from the northwest. I was tired. It was just on nine thirty, and the thought of trekking all the way into the city centre to Hillbrow and back again held no attraction for me. On the contrary, the thought of spending the night in my own bed with Kelly in my arms had infinite appeal.

'You coming back to mine, then?'

'What about your kids? They're coming tomorrow, aren't they? Look, luv, the last thing I want to do is to shake up your domestic life, you know? I mean... we've got to take it easy. We may well think we've got something going, but your kids need to be protected from unexpected shocks.'

'They're going to have to find out about you sometime, aren't they?'

'Yeah, but not with me there. You going to have to tell them about us slowly like, and when they've digested it all, you can introduce me to them. They're kids, after all! You got to treat them gently, know what I mean?'

'Okay, point taken.' I appreciated her concern. It was a very favourable sign, her putting the girls' interest before her own like that. It augured well for the future.

'Okay then, will you come home with me and let me make love to you and sleep in my arms, and I'll take you to Hillbrow early in the morning before I collect them?'

'Mmm...'

To say that Esther was surprised would be to greatly understate the truth. In the last six years her Master Anton had never brought a woman home. Well, not that she'd seen, anyway.

I had in fact once, about three years ago, brought a girl called Heidi for a drink and an unsatisfactory romp. We had both been very drunk and she had ended up unintentionally spending the night. Esther had been on her weekend off and had never known about it.

When the Audi arrived back from Botswana, she was not yet asleep and came out in her dressing gown, ready to carry my bags. She nearly fell on her not insubstantial rump when she opened the front door and found her Master Anton and a young African girl in a passionate embrace on the doorstep.

'Esther! Hello. This is Kelly ...er ...Kelebonye. Kelly, this is Esther.'

The women smiled nervously at one another.

'Kelly is er... my friend, Esther. My very good friend!' I gave Kelly a squeeze. 'You'll probably be seeing quite a lot of her.'

Esther's eyes were wide as she went to get the bags out of the car. She tut-tutted to herself and shook her head. Whatever next!

It was pure magic to have her under my roof. It felt so right, so luxuriously comfortable. After a relaxed supper we went to finish off the bottle of red in the lounge, I slouched on the sofa and she on the floor with her head on my thigh. Abdullah Ibrahim wafted gently through the speakers. She looked up at me. When our eyes met I thought of Thomas Hardy… Gabriel and Bathsheba in *Far From the Madding Crowd*:

"And at home by the fire, whenever you look up, there I shall be - and whenever I look up, there will be you."

Though the only fire was in our hearts.

When we went to my bedroom and fell into my double bed, I was the happiest person in the whole world.

Twenty-Three

I eased the Audi into the gateway and reluctantly pushed the buzzer. The house in Honeydew, which I paid for, was much more opulent than my own. The gate slowly slid open, revealing the face-brick mansion, double garage, swimming pool and tennis court, set in rolling lawns and well-tended rose gardens. The paved forecourt had parking space for ten cars.

Rachel came bounding out of the house to meet me. I was sure she was noticeably taller and skinnier than when I last saw her, only three weeks ago. She looked older than her nine years. She was growing like a beanstalk. As I got out of the car, she flew into my arms.

'Daddy, Daddy! Ooh, I've missed you!' Her hug was full of electric intensity.

Margot had always been the less demonstrative one. She strolled towards me, ever casual. With a shock, I realised that she was becoming a young woman. She could easily have passed for fifteen instead of twelve.

'Hi, Margs!'

'Hi, Dad!' She gave me a peck on the cheek.

I went towards the door. Angelica, in a prim housemaid's uniform, came out carrying the girls' weekend luggage, followed by the two enormous Great Danes.

'Morning, Angelica.' The dogs slobbered all over me.

'Morning, Mister Venter.'

'So now this is bladdie half past eight, is it?' It was a declaration of war. Hannah stood on the threshold, her hands on her hips. The frosty scowl - and the depilatory wax around the eyebrows and on her upper lip - detracted from what was essentially a very handsome face.

Her bronze Mediterranean skin and short, black, tightly curled hair gave her something of a classical Greek goddess look. Athena, maybe? The tall, elegant figure had deteriorated over the years and her Jodhpur thighs were much in evidence in the tight stretch-fit pants she was wearing. The fabric was so taut that the orange-peel was clearly visible. Cellulite and hirsutism were her eternal adversaries… and, of course, me.

I looked at my watch. It was eight forty-five. The traffic coming back from Hillbrow had been awful.

'Morning, Hannah. Sorry I'm late.' I was determined not to be drawn into one of our notorious yelling matches. 'In the car, girls. Yes, put those in the boot, Angelica. Thanks.'

'And don't you bring them back late tomorrow, d'you hear me? There's school on Monday! Six… latest!' She turned on her heel and slammed the door shut behind her.

* * * * *

As it happened, they found out soon enough. Much sooner than I had anticipated.

We had driven straight home, only stopping for some supplies and treats at the supermarket on the way, and by ten we were relaxing on the veranda by the pool. It was a bit too chilly to actually swim, and we decided on a game of Rummikub. Margot went into the study to fetch it. She was gone for a few minutes.

'Dad!' She was calling from the study.

'Yes, Margs.'

'Dad… who's this?'

'Who? Where?'

'This… on the computer.'

I suddenly realised what she meant. The Mauritius photos! Of Kelly! I jumped up from the lounger and dashed into the study, my ears hot and glowing. Rachel, sensing the excited tone of her sister's voice, was there ahead of me.

'Yes, who is she, Daddy? Is she your girlfriend? Did you go to Mauritius with her? Is she nice? What's her name? She's black! Where is she from?' Rachel could hardly stop.

'Who is she, Dad? Why do you have all these pictures of her?'

To my horror, she had stopped at one I had taken inside the apartment at Mont Choisy. Kelly was dressed in nothing but one of her tiny G-strings, a bottle of Phoenix in her hand and a lit Marlboro in the corner of her mouth, her beautiful breasts thrust at the lens. She looked quite debauched.

'Does Mom know about her?' Rachel had a knack of getting straight to the point.

'What's she doing here, Dad?' Margot had advanced a few frames to a couple of shots I'd taken of Kelly and me reflected in the window of a bank in Grand Baie. She was standing behind me, peering out from behind my elbow.

In the first picture both her arms were around my waist. Despite the semi-opacity of the reflection, and the poor detail, our togetherness was undeniable. In the second shot, one of her hands had slipped down and was mischievously cupping my crotch. Innocent adult humour, I had thought at the time. Faced with the picture and my two daughters, however, I cringed.

Margot was clicking the mouse, switching back and forth between the two pictures. I grabbed the mouse from her and closed the viewer.

'Well?' Margot looked me straight in the eye. Her inquisitiveness wasn't going to go away.

'Who is she, Daddy?'

Nor was Rachel's. 'Why was she holding your balls?'

'Rachel! Stop being so pathetic!' Margot shook her head and raised her eyes to the ceiling and sighed with exaggerated dramatic emphasis. 'Don't be so stupid. That's what grown-ups *do*!'

'Enough, enough!' I tried not to sound too firm. After all, if there was any fault here it was all my own. 'Her name is Kelly. Let's go outside on to the veranda and I'll try and explain.'

The girls were excited, and I detected no overt hostility. That was a good sign. But I had hoped to approach the subject on my own terms, at my own pace. Now it was all happening at once. I had lost control of the process and was in an utterly compromised position. They could as well have caught me in bed with her.

'I need a pee.' Rachel darted off as Margot and I left the study.

'Is it like… a serious relationship, Dad?'

'Well, let's wait till your sister gets here, then I won't have to say everything twice.'

'Okay, but quickly, before she comes - she's only a child, after all - are you two sleeping together? You know… *screwing*?'

I was bowled over. 'How old are you?'

'Nearly thirteen, why?'

'Well… it's just that…'

'Don't dodge the question, Dad!'

'Yes, well… I suppose so. Yes, we are.'

When she joined us on the veranda a minute later, Rachel had a coy expression on her face. Her hands were behind her back.

'Does Kelly live here?'

'No, love, she lives in her own flat in Hillbrow.'

'Then what are *these* doing here?' Rachel triumphantly produced a pair of tiny red knickers. Kelly must have hung them in the shower this morning. There was no point in asking Rachel why she had used my *en suite* bathroom instead of the one in the passage.

I sat my girls down and tried, without being patronising, to explain how it came to be that Kelly and I had fallen in love. I told them about the chance meeting in court, the short trip to Mauritius, the visit to *Ouma* and *Oupa* in Zeerust, and the last two days in Botswana.

They listened patiently and asked simple, sensible questions. When I finished telling what I thought was a fair, if not too detailed, version of the story, Rachel got up and came and stood in front of me.

'I'm happy for you, Daddy.' She gave me a big hug. 'Where is she now?'

'In Hillbrow, I guess.'

'Well, can't she come here? I want to meet her.'

'Er…'

'Yes, Dad! Can't she come here? Please!'

'No… look. She and I agreed…'

'But, Daddy!'

'Come on, Dad!'

I lost the argument. These young ladies seemed to have complete control over me. Five minutes later Kelly answered her cell phone to hear an unfamiliar voice: 'Hello, Kelly. My name is Rachel, Rachel Zuckerman-Venter. My sister and I would like to meet you, please.'

Margot nudged her. 'Tell her you're Anton Venter's daughter, stupid!'

The conversation ended with Kelly saying, 'Okay, okay! I'll get a cab.'

Anton Venter's daughters were pretty persuasive girls.

After lunch on Sunday, I got back to my notes, preparing for the resumption of Nozipo's case, leaving Kelly teaching the girls to play *morabaraba* – an ancient African game not unlike backgammon.

Normally played by digging a series of little holes in the earth and using pebbles as counters, or 'cows', they were playing on a carved wooden set that I had hanging on the living-room wall, purely as décor. I never realised that it was a board game till Kelly pointed out the fact.

After a brief search I had found the little leather pouch with the shiny black beans that were the counters, and Kelly and the girls had settled down to play.

Both girls sported new hairdos. Kelly had plaited Margot's long reddish curls into thin braids and Rachel's dark hair had been bound with wool into spiky *maphondo*.

Both girls seemed to revel in the African-ness of their new friendship and I thought my daughters looked particularly lovely with this new twist. I wasn't sure I wanted them to go home to Hannah with their hair like that though.

I was mentally preparing myself for their objections later when I would inevitably have to ask them to revert to their usual styles.

I looked across the veranda at the three of them, earnestly bent over their game. I marvelled at the way they had hit it off. Ever since she had arrived on Saturday afternoon Kelly had been the main attraction.

When we had gone out for a steakhouse supper and a walk around the shopping mall, I may as well have stayed home. None of them seemed to notice me. Rachel, particularly, was bowled over by Kelly and seemed determined to monopolise her attention and hold her hand the whole evening.

On Sunday morning Kelly and I were awoken to Margot and Rachel in pyjamas bringing us coffee in bed. The girls seemed to be revelling in their father's new domestic situation, and were determined to promote it actively. We ended up watching part of a movie together on TV, the four of us snuggled together in the double bed.

Breakfast was prepared and the dishes washed by Kelly and the girls. After breakfast it was Kelly who reminded the girls that they had to do their homework, and Kelly who sat with them and answered their questions and checked their spelling.

'What's that you're writing, Kelly?' Margot asked.

'Well, it's sort of homework too.' She shut the blue exercise book. Her body language made it clear that it was not for sharing.

Rachel had to read ten pages of her school reader out loud, and of course, only Kelly was good enough to be the designated listener.

In the event, the girls didn't object at all about undoing their Afro hairstyles. Everyone knew that Hannah was not going to like the idea of my having a new girlfriend, let alone a black girlfriend. That reality seemed to be clear to all of them although nothing was said.

Before I had time to suggest the undoing of the telltale hairdos, Kelly had already started unplaiting Margot's and Rachel was untying her own, getting 'ready for school'. It seemed that a *de facto* conspiracy had come into effect. Without alluding to the core problem, without mentioning Hannah, everyone seemed to know what was going to be needed to keep the peace.

But, as I was to reflect later, things never happen as smoothly as one might hope, and in the event Hannah discovered the truth sooner than any of us would have imagined.

The afternoon was well advanced. Rachel and Margot were bathed and packed and were ready to be dropped home. They were at the bottom of the garden, checking for ripe youngberries in the back hedge.

I was taking a shower in my bathroom at the end of the house. I didn't hear the buzzer ring. I didn't hear Kelly press the button to open the electric gate, the car drive in, the door open and slam shut.

Nor did I hear the dogs barking, and Kelly opening the front door. But when I came out of the shower I heard voices, so I pulled on a pair of jeans and went down the passage to investigate. When I heard the unmistakable sound of Hannah's voice, I froze.

My heart was in my mouth. What was she doing here? Surely, I hadn't misunderstood the arrangement. I was to deliver the girls to Honeydew… 'before six'. She had said nothing about collecting them herself. And now she was here!

They were in the kitchen. Hannah was inspecting the contents of my fridge - something she did whenever she was in the house. I never could work out if she was doing it to check whether the children were being fed healthy food or whether I was spending too much on luxuries... or beer.

Esther dreaded the times when she would arrive in my absence. Hannah would poke about the house, doing a full inspection, and Esther would nervously follow her around, hoping that Hannah wouldn't find fault.

She had been known to simply remove things, things that weren't kosher - bacon for example - and to chuck them away. Once she took a leg of lamb and put it in her car because she 'was entertaining' and 'Anton couldn't possibly need it'.

On another occasion she had come and helped herself to half a dozen bottles of wine, because she was having people for dinner. Hannah, it seemed, could never come to grips with the fact that this was no longer her house.

When I peeked around the door, I could see Kelly, her hands on her hips, standing watching Hannah. Hannah wiped a finger across the top of the fridge and was inspecting it for dust. I pulled back hurriedly, and neither woman saw me.

'So, where's the other girl, the usual one, Esther?'

Esther, the other 'girl', was at least twenty years Hannah's senior.

'I think she has the weekend off.'

Hannah didn't seem to notice that Kelly's accent might betray that she was not the relief housemaid, nor that her jeans, T-shirt and bare feet were not usual housemaid's attire. 'Is the master in?'

'I think Anton's in the shower. Should I call him?'

Hannah raised an eyebrow. These domestics these days were becoming so damned insolent. She would never let Angelica call her by her first name. It wasn't right, and made for poor labour relations. 'No, thank you! I'll wait for him.'

'Can I get you something... tea, coffee... or something else?' Kelly was opening the fridge and Hannah had to move out of the way to give her space.

'Mmm... no, not now.'

Kelly took a bottle of Heineken out of the fridge and was poised to open it.

'I said no! Don't you people ever listen? I don't want a drink. Anyway, I don't drink beer!'

'Okay. I heard you. This is for me.'

Hannah's mouth fell open. Despite the evidence in front of her she was unable to think outside the box. Black women are housemaids. Housemaids don't drink beer in their employers' kitchens.

'Does the master allow you to drink his beer?' Hannah couldn't hide the incredulity in her voice.

'Actually, he prefers Amstel … I'm the Heineken one.'

Kelly was playing Hannah like a fish on a tight line. She pressed home her advantage.

'Come. Let's sit down in the lounge. I'm sure Anton won't be long. The girls are outside in the garden.'

She took up her beer and started in the direction of the sitting room. As she passed Hannah, she stuck out her hand. 'I'm Kelly, by the way. You must be Hannah.' Hannah ignored the hand. The situation was becoming impossible.

'Anton!' The call was loud and shrill, with a faint hint of panic. '*Anton*!'

Kelly felt she had gone far enough. It was time to put Hannah out of her misery. She walked past her and crossed the room to the sliding doors of the veranda. 'Margot, Rachel! Your mother's here…'

Then she walked a few steps towards the bedroom.

'Anton, luv, you out of the shower yet?' Still dressed only in a pair of jeans, I appeared rather suddenly at the end of the passage. She smiled and came to my side.

'Hannah's here to pick up the kids.' She casually touched my arm. 'Sweet of her… It saves us the trip.'

Hannah stood in the middle of the hallway, eyes wide, swallowing like a beached fish.

Twenty-Four

At nine o'clock on Monday morning, when the State versus Nozipo Sibongile Nxumalo reconvened in Court number two, Mr Justice Ephraim Mazibuko looked a much altered man. The violent death of his wife had evidently had a profound effect on him.

He seemed to have aged ten years in as many days. Almost everyone in court noticed this, and people looked at one another when they rose to their feet, as he shuffled into court. Kelly in the public gallery and I at my table exchanged a quizzical look. *Poor man!*

Although it had only been ten days, it felt much longer. Not only had Judge Mazibuko changed, but my life had also altered immeasurably. The court felt a very different place from the one I'd left to have a cup of coffee at the Brasilia with the sexy black chick whom I had been ogling. *Yes, only ten days!*

To compound this strange sensation, the buzz of talk before the start of this morning's proceedings had been of Jabu Zulu, his kidnap and miraculous escape. Although this case was the State versus Nozipo Nxumalo, all and sundry regarded it as Jabu Zulu's case: *Jabu Zulu's Revenge*. Everyone, from the cleaners, the orderlies, the policemen and the clerks to the prosecutor and the registrar, had an opinion, a pet theory, some exclusive inside information.

'Well *I* heard that he hit the guy with a steel pipe and jumped out the window.'

'I heard there were two of them. Did he hit them both?'

'My sources tell me that he actually kicked out the rear window of the combi and jumped on to the highway at a hundred kays an hour.'

The many journalists seemed to be as poorly informed as anyone else.

Clearly in the absence of any hard facts about the kidnap and the subsequent escape, rumour and innuendo were rife. I realised that I knew more about the actual events than anyone else in the room, and my information was already five days old.

Christo was obviously keeping a tight lid on the details of his investigation. I made a mental note to give him a ring. We owed each other some time together.

I finished my summing-up before lunch. It all felt very unsatisfying. There was no continuity, no flow to my arguments. Normally, I would summarise my whole case in the space of a single day, or maybe two. This ten-day recess had introduced a monumental hiccup, a hiatus in the logical structure of my case, and I didn't feel that I had been able to do my client full justice.

Although I said everything I planned to say, the interruption killed the dramatic rhythm, the dynamic phrasing, of my presentation. It just didn't feel right.

Nozipo was not guilty. That much was clear to anybody who had followed the case. The prosecution had set out to prove that Nozipo had deliberately fabricated the allegation of rape, and had calculatingly constructed a web of lies in a premeditated attempt to destroy Jabu Zulu's name and good standing.

Jonas Moyo's arrangement of the facts that made up the case for the State was feeble in comparison to Ishmael Patel's delivery of the same facts when he had used them to defend Jabu Zulu against the rape charge.

In a similar way, my defence of Nozipo was ten times more effective than Ndipo Mokalanga and Neo Motsumi's prosecution of Jabu, though they used the same basic facts as me: no new evidence was to hand, just more time and a more thorough application. Also, I had years more experience than they.

There was simply no case against Nozipo. The media were unanimous.

When the court adjourned early that afternoon for the last time before Judge Mazibuko was to deliver his judgment, not even the prosecutor, Jonas Moyo, believed that a guilty verdict was possible.

When the date for judgment was set for tomorrow, it confirmed everyone's suspicions - even the judge had already made up his mind. Normally, a judgment would be delivered a week or two after the conclusion of argument. Clearly, in this instance, the judge didn't need any more time. Despite my disappointment at the quality of my dramatic performance, I felt supremely confident.

When Kelly came to my table after the court had adjourned I had a sudden sense of *déjà vu*. She was wearing the same skirt and blouse she wore ten days ago when she had come to me and asked what was going on. I smiled when I reminded myself that then I could not have dreamed what I knew now. I was familiar with her deepest, darkest secrets; I intimately knew her warm body and her electric touch.

And now I could look at her and even know what colour G-string she was wearing. After all, I had watched her put it on this morning. In my own bedroom.

Her smile was as beautiful as ever. 'Hey, luv, I'm going to shoot to the office to catch up on a few things. I'll see you tonight.'

'Should I collect you? What time?'

'That would be great. I'll call you.' Her eyes said *I love you*.

I watched her as she walked away. *Utterly beautiful*, I thought as I watched her, my eyes inexorably drawn to the gorgeous, sexy bum. She stopped and turned, and came back to my table.

'Fuckin' pervert!' she whispered. 'I could feel your eyes right in my between!' Her smile was deliciously naughty and I could have had her right there, on the table.

'Here, I almost forgot.' She opened her bag and extracted yet another blue Mauritian exercise book and put it on top of my pile of papers. 'In case you get bored.'

It took me a few hours to get over the empty feeling that had started in court this morning. The conclusion of the case still felt totally unsatisfying. Yet, when I tried to look at it dispassionately, I felt more confident. Surely, the negative emotions I had experienced were no more than a result of the ten-day break and my imminent return to more humdrum cases away from the TV cameras and the limelight.

The more I thought about it, the more certain I was that Nozipo had to be found not guilty. I played the case over in my mind: There was simply no way she could be found guilty. No way!

The house felt empty. The girls were gone and wouldn't be back till the weekend after next. Kelly wouldn't be back till tonight. I was getting spoilt! This had been normal life for me during the last six years, and yet after just one blissful family weekend, I was already finding it unpalatable.

When I went to get myself a Coke from the fridge I caught sight of a bottle of Heineken and remembered yesterday's debacle with Hannah. So much for keeping our affair secret, or at least being discreet!

My initial reaction had been one of annoyance… annoyance with Kelly. Why had she let Hannah in? Why had she confronted her? Surely she would have done better to rush and hide, and to call me to deal with the unexpected arrival of my ex-wife?

As soon as a flustered Hannah had left with the girls, I had turned my discomfiture on Kelly.

'Why did you let her in? Surely you could see what was going to happen!'

'Sorry, luv. I only realised who she was when it was already far too late to do anything about it. Anyfink. Honest. Remember, you had told me you were taking the girls home. We weren't expecting her to come here, were we? When I heard the buzzer I looked out of the window, and you know, to be honest I thought it was a bloke in the car at the gate. You never told me she had such short hair!

'I opened the gate and stepped out of the front door to be polite, like. It was only when she opened the car door that I saw it was a woman. Of course, then I realised what a prat I had been, but it was far too late by then.'

I had been somewhat mollified by her unsolicited confession.

'Then, once she started insulting me, assuming I was the fuckin' maid, I just couldn't resist, know what I mean?'

She was perfectly right, of course. Hannah had behaved totally stupidly and had invited the assault on her arrogant, racist inanity. She deserved everything she got. In retrospect, I enjoyed it more each time I thought of it. The expression on Hannah's face when Kelly called me 'luv' and touched my arm was priceless.

It was probably going to cost a lot in terms of my relationship with the girls, though, I thought. Hannah was bound to find a way of punishing me. Inevitably, it was going to affect the two innocent parties. Kelly and I could handle it, but Margot and Rachel…?

Oh well. Spilt milk and all that.

The blue exercise book beckoned. I picked up the latest instalment of Kelly's serialised autobiography, lit a smoke and put my feet up on the coffee table.

My schooldays were relatively ordinary, and I developed pretty much in line with my peers. I continued to do very well at school, and made a number of good friends. All girls. The only quarter in which my progress was way behind the others was in the area of relationships.

By the time I was sixteen, my best friend Jess was going steady with Ben, Alice was seeing Christopher (and sometimes

Steve) and Mildred was already alternately boasting about her exploits with Pinto on the back seat of his Alfa and agonising over being a day or two late on her periods...

I couldn't even begin to imagine a relationship. Not with a boy, anyway. One night at a party at Jess's parents' house in Streatham I drank too much punch and smoked a bit of ganja and enjoyed myself quite uninhibitedly, dancing blithely with Maggie's elder brother, Quentin.

My carefree enjoyment ended late in the evening when, with the lights low and the music slow, Quentin tried to snatch a quick feel. I ran away and withdrew so far into myself that I stopped going to parties, or to any social gathering where boys were likely to hit on me.

I fitted into my new family very well. Although my mum and dad were old enough to be my grandparents, their only son, Geoffrey, and his wife Fiona provided me with many diversions more suitable for my age. I was also the obvious choice for babysitter for their twins, who were just a year old when I joined the Applebury family. Quite often I would hop on to the tube at Brixton and take the Victoria line up to Finsbury Park and spend the night or the weekend with them.

Despite Geoff's missionary roots, he was a free-spirited soul and something of hippie. He and Fiona loved nothing more than to laze on a beach or mountain meadow, eating good, simple food, drinking cheap Italian red wine and smoking a bit of pot. They seemed to enjoy their life as a young family with innocence and tranquility.

Fiona was a character in her own right. She loved to swim, and most of our holidays together centred on open spaces and lots of water. She was a committed naturist and refused, as a matter of principle, to wear anything when she swam.

Geoff and Fiona were great fun to be with, and Geoff treated me like his little sister. Quite often, they took me along with them on holidays to Wales, or to Holland. One memorable summer we joined friends of theirs on a sailing cruise from Portsmouth to Lundy, the Isle of Man, and back.

The Applebury Juniors, as we teasingly referred to them, loved to take their holidays in Holland and the Baltic, because nudism is much less regulated, and contrived, there than it is in Britain. Fiona was quite capable of spending entire days without putting on a stitch of clothing, and Geoff was not much better.

The first time I went to a beach with them – it was near Tershelling on the Wadden Islands on Holland's North Sea coast – I was terrified. After all that I had been through, the thought of being naked in front of strange people, particularly men, filled me with alarm. Fiona was caring and understanding and did her best to reassure me but, as we walked along the sand that day, I was almost breathless with panic. I was aghast as the sight of hundreds of totally naked people all around me. There were men and women, granddads and toddlers, teens and old crones. I felt as if they were all staring at me.

Geoff found us a spot on the beach and we dumped our gear. He and Fiona stepped out of their clothes as if it was the most natural thing in the world, and got on with helping the twins undress, laying out our towels and setting up the umbrella.

I took an absolute age just to take off my T-shirt. Then I methodically folded it and carefully placed it on my towel. Next came my sandals, and very, very slowly I unbuttoned my jeans.

My nerves were jangling like one of those insistent burglar alarms. My heart was in my mouth. It felt as if I had the eyes of the world on me as I cautiously pulled down my jeans, trying my utmost to feign nonchalance, yet absolutely churning on the inside.

Taking off my bra was even more of an ordeal. My exposed breasts seemed to shout 'Look at me!' to all and sundry. Geoff and Fiona were already settled on their beach towels, smothering the twins in sunscreen.

Now came the most difficult part: my knickers. I ummed and aahed, folding and refolding my jeans, trying to put off the crucial moment. Eventually I ran out of excuses and took the plunge. I took a deep breath.

My knickers hadn't even reached my knees when Geoff looked up from the open cold box and asked, 'Kell, d'you want juice or Coke?'

'Juice please.' I dropped the knickers on top of the jeans, took the drink from him, had a sip and sat down on my towel. The sea was very calm, the beach was very white and the sun was hot.

'Pass me the sunscreen, will ya, Fiona?'

It must have been all of five minutes later that I realised I was naked. It was as if a switch was turned off the instant I removed the last garment. All the angst was forgotten. I was at one with the crowd on the beach. Everyone was naked, and nobody noticed. Nobody cared.

I immediately understood why some folk choose to be naturists. Without their clothes on, people seem unable to be threatening, competitive or even lecherous. Real Garden of Eden Stuff! It's a lesson I've never forgotten.

Right from the start I was interested in sports, and despite my small stature I did well at sprinting, swimming and hockey. Quite by chance I discovered martial arts – Pamela, another ex-South African at Dulwich Girls' School - invited me down to the Brixton recreation centre to watch her at judo. While I was there I saw some kids having a karate lesson in another part of the gym.

The Sensei looked so self-assured, exuded such confidence and poise that I was immediately attracted. Soon I had joined and did karate twice and later four times a week. My mum, who never lost sight of the circumstances in which she had found me, encouraged my interest in self-defence as much as she could.

As a result of my training I never again felt fear in the way I did in Atteridgeville, never worried about walking home in the dark or of being mugged or assaulted. I still don't.

Soon, my fierce enthusiasm for all things academic and a deep desire to be the best at school and to excel at karate meant that my life revolved around the classroom and the dojo. By the time I did my A-levels I had graded to black belt. Later, at uni I would eventually receive my fourth Dan in karate and then change styles and focus on Jeet Kune Do, the style pioneered by the legendary Bruce Lee. I was honoured to be able to study under Sensei Mashimoto Suzuki, probably the most renowned exponent of the style.

It was while I was doing my A-levels that I came close to falling in love. Up to then my fear of men constrained me and I never allowed myself more than the most casual acquaintanceship with a boy.

My French teacher at school, Gertrude Flamini, was about thirty. She was unconventional and foreign and caring and full of fun. I found myself spending much of my free time at her flat, and confided in her more closely that I had done with anyone except my mum.

She made me feel whole in a way that no one else ever had. She was sweet and attractive and attentive and she complimented me and flattered me. I suppose I was infatuated, without admitting it to myself.

One sunny winter's afternoon we were sitting side by side on her sofa, steaming mugs of herbal tea in our hands, huddled over an article in a French art magazine. When she put her arm around me it felt totally natural and comforting. When she kissed me, my pulse raced and my emotions soared, and when she gently fondled my breasts my body shivered inside in a way it had never done before (and never would again... until a certain man took me to Mauritius...)

But when her fingers migrated down my belly and across my pubic hair, panic began to rise, and when she touched my clitoris the panic turned into sheer unmitigated terror, and I fled the flat and never returned.

That was the closest I ever got to being intimate with another human being.

It was quite accidental that I started climbing. It must have been when I was fifteen. My karate lesson was cancelled at short notice one afternoon when Sensei was suddenly called away for a family emergency and, as I wandered around the recreation centre, I joined a group of people watching a climbing competition on the indoor climbing wall.

The climbers were competing on the Red Four route, a series of tiny holds up a section of wall that started at the vertical and canted outwards more and more the higher one got. The last few moves were under a severe overhang, around a lip, and up to the safety of the stance.

None of the competitors was able to complete the route, and the more I watched one after the other fall off at the crux move, the more I was sure that I would be able to do it. I hung around impatiently and as soon as the competition was over I paid my two pounds and got roped up.

I had no climbing shoes of course, and the instructor made me go and wash my feet before he would allow me to climb barefoot. Then he tried to discourage me from trying the Red Four route and insisted that I start on some of the easier sections.

I flew up a couple of the simpler pitches and was adamant that I try the Red Four route, and eventually, with a shrug, he relented. His surprise was total when I scampered up it, barely slowing as I wafted around the overhang that had earlier claimed all the experienced climbers in the competition.

I was totally hooked on climbing from that moment. At least, hooked on the sensation of defying gravity, and feeling the strength of my fingers and arms coming into their own. Of course, when I got to Uni and started climbing for real, out on the crags, in the mists and gales, a totally different addiction set in - a passionate love for wild, remote, airy unexplored places; the more remote and untouched the better.

I managed to get four A-levels, and my grades were good enough for me to be accepted at SOAS - London University's School of Oriental and African Studies where I went to read Sociology and Anthropology.

The ringing of the cell phone dragged me away from London. It was Kelly.

'Hi!'

'Hiya! What you doing?'

'Just got to SOAS.'

'Oh that! You're obviously not busy, then. Still want me to come over?'

'Listen, woman! Don't ask me what I *want*! What I *want* is that you move out of your flat and come here and never bloody leave, that's what I *want*!'

'Is that all, huh?'

'No. A bit of lovemaking won't go amiss... perhaps a massage... maybe a blow job...?'

'You don't half expect a lot! We'll talk about that later, lover boy. Right now, I'm in Braamfontein and want to know if I should get a combi or if you're going to come and fetch me.'

'Give me twenty minutes.'

* * * * *

On Tuesday morning we had to negotiate a scrum in order to get into the Supreme Court building. Jabu Zulu's supporters were back in force, and the anti-abuse lobby too was at full strength.

There were journalists from every imaginable paper, cameramen and anchors with microphones emblazoned with SABC, BBC, CNN, Al-Jazeera, Sky News and Deutsche Welle logos. It was chaos. The police had their hands full.

Once inside the building, Kelly and I still had to navigate the clogged corridors to Court number two. At some point we became separated and it was only later, when proceedings were about to get underway that I saw her squashed into the back corner of the overcrowded public gallery. The air was heavy with anticipation.

To my amazement, the front of the public gallery was occupied by a phalanx of goons in black suits and dark glasses surrounding Jabu Zulu himself. He was dressed in his usual impeccable tailored best. His left hand was still heavily bandaged.

No one would have expected Jabu Zulu to be in court for the judgment. The anticipated verdict - and no one could doubt that Nozipo would be found not guilty: the State didn't have even a prayer of a case - was surely going to cause him further embarrassment.

A not guilty verdict would cast the suspicion of wrongdoing back upon him. He may well have been acquitted of rape, but if Nozipo was not guilty, where did that leave Jabu's credibility? The verdict would, by definition, cast aspersions upon him.

I thought he would have stayed away, and was genuinely surprised to see him there. I tried to catch Kelly's eye, but there was too much movement, just too many distractions.

An orderly appeared. 'Silence in court!'

Mr Justice Ephraim Mazibuko entered the courtroom through the judge's door behind the bench. His mien had deteriorated further, and he appeared neither to have slept nor to have washed since yesterday. His bib was awry and his robe askew on his shoulders.

I looked at the registrar's desk. Annemarie had a tight expression around her mouth. She didn't acknowledge me.

The first part of the judgment was a summary of the charges and a recap of the main arguments. Judge Mazibuko read from notes that fluttered in his trembling hands.

His voice was barely audible, and he drew breath after every couple of words. I told myself that the man was very unwell. I hoped he would get through the task without collapsing.

'The court has... considered the... defence arguments that the... accused was a... paragon of... virtue, and that she... conducted herself... with... modesty and... prudence while... in Mr Zulu's... home.'

He paused for breath. 'A... number of witnesses were able to... attest to... this. However, none... of the said witnesses... were present... on the evening in question... when the accused... was alone in the house... with the said... Mr Zulu.'

I frowned quizzically. The halting voice continued.

'It is common... cause...' He was struggling, '...common cause that the... accused and... Mr Zulu... had... sexual inter... intercourse... on the night in question. The witness, Jabulani Zulu, asserts... that the accused... made overt advances to him. The court is inclined to accept the... witness's version of... the events. We refer to The State versus Jabulani Benedict Zulu... and we quote from the judgment in that case...'

Judge Mazibuko tried to have a sip of water. The glass trembled so violently in his hand that he spilt some on his papers, on the judgment he was reading. There was a pause while Annemarie handed him some tissues to mop up the mess. Then the painful process continued, the judge's voice barely audible as he made slow progress through the document.

As he summarised the defence case, he gave prominence to the claim that Nozipo had spent her sizeable income on charitable works, donating to deserving causes in the Durban area.

He acknowledged that the witnesses had been consistent and had not contradicted one another, and that the receipts presented as evidence appeared genuine.

Then, to everyone's amazement he continued, 'It is clear... to the court that... the witnesses were... coached to... present this... fabricated untruth, along with the... fraudulent documentary... substantiation.

'The court is satisfied... that the prosecution... has conclusively shown that the bulk of... the accused's income... of eight thousand rand per... month was spent in the... acquisition of... cocaine and similar... narcotic substances...'

A cold sensation began to claw at my heart. I could not believe what I was hearing. I looked at the judge in amazement as one after another, the facts of the case were inverted and stood on their head.

Jabu Zulu, in his expensive suit and with his bodyguards in their wrap-around dark glasses all of a sudden seemed to exude a power that pervaded the room like an evil, all-encompassing fog.

Mazibuko had reached the end of his judgment.

'The accused will rise.'

Nozipo rose to her feet. The air was thick with anticipation.

'Nozipo Sibongile Nxumalo... '

The tension in the room was palpable. The weak, halting, monotonous voice droned on. He was speaking faster now, wanting to get it over with.

'...Count number one... Perjury. Guilty... Count number two... Defeating the ends of justice. Guilty. Sentence will be passed on the twentieth of next month. Bail is extended until that date. Court is adjourned.'

Everyone in the courtroom was looking at Nozipo. She was looking at me. I looked at Jabu Zulu. His expression could only be described as a smirk. For a moment, time seemed to be suspended, and nothing moved. There was an eerie silence.

'That's fuckin' bullshit!' shouted a female voice from the back of the public gallery. 'Fuckin' bullshit! How much is he paying you, you fuckin' sellout?' There was commotion as two policemen waded in and dragged the heckler from the room.

Of course, it was Kelly.

Later, that night she sat curled up in the corner of the sofa, watching the TV. I knew better than to try to approach her. She reminded me of a cornered, angry, frightened kitten -

bedraggled and ready to claw anything that came within reach, hissing and spitting with fury.

It had been a testing afternoon. I'd had to put my own feelings on hold. First, there had been bitter, hysterical weeping from Nozipo. She seemed almost to blame me for the outrageous verdict, as if I should have foreseen it, and somehow headed it off.

Then there had been more unruly scenes at the police station where I had tried to calm Kelly down while she performed histrionics, digging a deeper hole for herself.

Initially, the police seemed prepared to release her without charge. But she became so abusive that by the time I finally reached the charge office, they were in the process of charging her with public disorder, resisting arrest and assault on a police officer; restraining her while she lunged at anybody and everybody, shrieking obscene abuse at the top of her voice.

Fortunately, I knew most of the policemen reasonably well - we met frequently in court. Nevertheless it had taken all my negotiating skills and string pulling to get her out of the police station with just a warning.

I was on my third or fourth large whisky. I was slowly coming down. The verdict had been a travesty. Whether Mazibuko had been threatened or paid off was impossible to tell. *Probably both. Like in Columbia, you get offered silver or lead. Choose your currency.*

Oh! Cry, the beloved country!

The SABC news came on the TV. The lead story was the verdict in the Nxumalo case. The presenter faced the camera with the toyi-toying, chanting crowds outside the court in the background.

Banners held aloft read 'Jabu Zulu for President', 'Viva Jabu Zulu, Viva!' and 'No whore will defeat the will of the people'. The noise was deafening.

'In what many regard as an unexpected verdict, Mr Justice Ephraim Mazibuko this afternoon found Nozipo Nxumalo guilty of perjury and of defeating the ends of justice. The case arises from false allegations of rape made by Nxumalo against the prominent business personality and former senior military intelligence official, Mr Jabu Zulu...'

The scene cut to Jabu on the steps of the Johannesburg Supreme court. He was still flanked by his goons, and cameras and microphones were being jabbed at him from every angle. His supporters pressed in from all sides, adding to the jostling, disorganised chaos. Policemen were doing their best to hold back the jubilant crowds.

Kelly spoke for the first time since we had arrived home that evening. Her voice was filled with venom. 'Fuckin' piece of shit!' It rose to a scream, 'You arsehole! Fuckin' bastard!'

'Mr Zulu... Mr Zulu... are you satisfied with the verdict?'

His smile was broad. 'We are very, very satisfied.'

'Is this the end of the saga. Do you plan to bring any further action?'

'You fuckin' arsehole...!'

'I think that the accused, the guilty party, has learned her lesson now... She is a dishonest, immoral, scheming... er... individual. And we hope she receives a suitably long sentence.'

I caught a sudden movement in the corner of my eye and the next instant the television set exploded with a bright flash, a crash and a shower of shattered glass that was flying everywhere. Before I could react, Kelly fled the room. A stone sculpture, a Zimbabwean carved serpentine head, lay in the midst of the wreckage.

'Kelly! Kelly, love.' I ran down the passage and banged on the locked bedroom door. 'Kelly! Kelly!'

There was no answer.

When, in total desperation and rising panic I shoulder-charged the door ten minutes later, the room was empty. The French doors to the patio were wide open.

Kelly was gone.

I was stunned. Yes, I was angry too. Surely there had been a massive miscarriage of justice that was clear. But Kelly's reaction was over the top.

My first thought was for her safety. She was out in Randburg, at night, on foot, unstable and upset. It was not a good situation. I went back to the sitting room, careful not to cut my bare feet on the thousands of small shards of what had once been a seventy-four centimetre Sony Trinitron. I retrieved my cell phone and dialled her number.

I didn't expect her to answer. She was clearly still too upset and unhinged. As the thought passed through my mind, I heard her phone ring. It was still in the kitchen where she had left it earlier. So much for that!

I spent the next two hours slowly driving up and down every street in Randburg, Rivonia and surrounding suburbs. I checked the bus stops, the shopping malls, a couple of pubs, and every street corner. Eventually, depressed, worried, and very sad and tired, I went back to my empty house.

Much later, unable to sleep, I stumbled on the blue exercise book that I had been reading yesterday.

Halfway through my first semester at SOAS Mum and Dad agreed that I was spending too much time on the number sixty-eight bus - my commute from Herne Hill was a good hour and a half each way - and they helped me find a shared flat just off the Tottenham Court Road, near Bedford Square, within easy walking distance of my lectures in Russell Square.

My roommate, Belinda Montgomery, was nineteen and hailed from Trinidad. She was full of cheerful enthusiasm and Caribbean joie de vivre and we became good friends very quickly. She had only been in the UK for a few years - most of which she had spent in Manchester - and was in many ways still finding her feet in London, and I revelled in my role as her guide and protector.

She was something of a party animal, however, and I found it difficult to share her enthusiasm for the university social scene. After a few tries at getting me to join her, she relented and we agreed to disagree.

On Friday and Saturday nights, if I didn't go home to Mum and Dad, I would busy myself with my studies or go down to the gym, and she would party till the early hours. We respected each other's space, and the arrangement worked fine.

In her West Indian and very un-British way, Belinda was able to talk extremely candidly about herself, and we had only been together a few days when she confided in me that she had been raped by her uncle, her mother's older brother, when she was just thirteen.

She had fallen pregnant and had an abortion. To my surprise she seemed to have weathered her ordeal very well, and unlike me, apparently bore no obvious scars from the events, and could discuss them very matter-of-factly.

She seemed to have very little anger towards her uncle, whom she regarded as a social inadequate, a victim himself, rather than an evil criminal. It gave me a different perspective with which to view my own trauma, and from that moment I started a long, slow process of trying to take myself a little less seriously, at least in terms of resisting the temptation to indulge in self-pity.

Nevertheless, I found I couldn't bare myself to her as easily, and only managed to hint at the things I had been through.

It wasn't long, however, before an event occurred that would radicalise Belinda and bring her much closer to my way of thinking. It happened one Friday evening.

Belinda burst into the flat. She was breathless and very excited. 'Hey, Kelly! Guess what? Maurice Wentzel has asked me out. You know, that good-looking blond hunk, you know, in Socio. I've been eyeing him for weeks and I thought he didn't notice. Thought maybe he didn't like black girls, know what I mean? Anyway, today he comes up to me and he's like, I say! Would you fancy going out with me? God's truth, he asked me on a date! Some do at the rugby club. I'm so excited! What d'you think?'

I didn't think much of Maurice Wentzel's type. Upper-class twit. He had an air about him that screamed narcissism at the top of its voice.

'I vote you give him a miss, Bee. Looks like your typical womanising arsehole to me.'

'But, Kelly! He's so cute! And sexy! And he looks rich! Just look at the clothes he wears, you know, what would you call it? Kind of posh–grunge, you know? Corduroy, tweed and leather, you know... gentry.'

'Ah, give it a miss, luv. Please! He'll shag you tonight and tell all his mates, and never look at you again. Mark my words.'

Belinda was suddenly very haughty. 'One thing I never do is let a man sleep with me on the first date. Won't compromise on that!'

'Good for you! But I still say give it a miss.'

But eventually our 'agree to disagree' principle prevailed, and an excited Belinda left the flat later that evening, dressed to the nines and in high hopes. I settled down to write an assignment paper on urban anthropology, trying unsuccessfully not to feel like a total nerd.

I was fast asleep when Belinda woke me at around six. She was in a desperate state. She had been bleeding from a cut lip, and there was dried blood on her cheek, her neck and all over her top.

Her left eye was swollen shut and looked like a piece of raw meat. She stank of vomit and there was some in her hair. She was in tears.

''What happened, luv?' I was still half-asleep, trying to take it all in. 'What's happened?'

'The bastard... he...' Belinda could hardly talk. Her cut and bruised lip was swollen to twice its normal size. She had obviously drunk quite a lot, and was also clearly in shock.

I jumped out of bed and started fussing over her. I grabbed our little first-aid kit from the bathroom and started to clean up her face. As an afterthought, I put on the kettle. The true Brit in me... in a crisis, always make a cup of tea!

While I tidied up the mess on her face, and wiped the sick out of her hair with a damp facecloth, she calmed down enough to tell me what had happened.

The first part of the evening had gone well enough, except that Maurice seemed to have more time for his mates than for his date. Poor Belinda was stuck with a group of prissy upper-class females who seemed totally used to being treated this way by their men folk.

They didn't do much to make Belinda feel welcome or to ease her awkwardness at being the only dark face at the club, and in desperation she ended up quaffing every drink that was put in front of her. That had not stood her in good stead later.

'He bloody ignores me the whole evening, and I'm well, like, that was a waste of time. So after the party, like, I ask him to bring me home..' The action of speaking had opened the split in her lip again and the bleeding had restarted. 'Maurice... he's really drunk, you know, like, damn belligerent. He just bloody refuses.

'So, I'm like... Okay, see ya. I'll get a cab. He's like No, get in, okay, I'll take you home. But then he drives bloody north, not to here.' She was crying again, and I had to try and stop the bleeding.

'All the way, I'm like, take me home, take me home! He's just driving fast as hell. Ignores me!' The emotions overwhelmed her, and for a while all I could do was to cradle her and rock her like a child.

After a couple of minutes she had calmed down and could continue. 'We get to his flat. Hampstead, I think. I don't want to get out of the car, but he like begs me, you know, like, I'm really spoiling his evening or something.

'I'm, like, trying to tell him, you know, like, it's too late now. I'm, like, you think you can ignore me the whole evening, and now you expect me to be bloody polite? He's not having any of it. Turns on the bloody charm, like. Says he's sorry, just come in for, like, one cup of coffee and he'll take me home. He's, like, I need some caffeine, love, can't drive all the way to Bloomsbury in this state, what! He's like all apologetic and stuff. So like a fool I fall for it.

'The moment I'm inside the flat and he's, like, shut the door, he suddenly changes, you know. He starts grabbing my tits and that. I'm, like, take your bloody hands off, mate, and he's, like, fuck you, you tart, who do you think you are?'

Belinda started to sob and I had to comfort her again while she calmed down again.

'So, he's like chasing me around the flat, lik,e trying to get his hands up my skirt and grabbing my punani, and I'm, like, pushing him away and trying to get to the door. I'm, like, you know, ready to run.

'He gets me in the kitchen, and manages to, like, corner me. I push him off as hard as I can and the bastard bloody slaps me, like, hard!'

She touched her swollen cheek. 'He's, like, he's, like, you fucking black slut. Bitch! I'm going to shag you whatever you say, you little black whore. Then I start to get scared. He's like so bloody violent, and angry!'

She started crying again. 'Why was he angry? What had I done to him?' She blew her nose and had a sip of tea. 'Anyway, he forces me, like, over the kitchen table, and starts trying to pull off my knickers, like, and then we end up just plain fighting. But he's strong, you know.'

She paused to let me dab the bleeding lip. 'Doesn't manage to get me into his bedroom though! I'm like no! no! as loud and as clear as I bloody can. My last attempt at resistance...I lock my legs together to try to stop him from getting my knickers off, like. But he just punches me in the face... in the mouth and in the eye... He ends up shagging me on the bloody kitchen floor... shagging me and hitting me and calling me a fucking stupid little black bitch! ...under the bloody table.

'I'm, like, you bastard! You bastard! And he's just thumping me. Shagging me like there's no tomorrow. And then he's hammering me with his fist and he's, like, bitch... bitch... fucking bitch... you whore...cunt... black cunt, bitch, shit cunt slut. Then, he just bloody comes right inside me, and he's too strong and I'm too pissed to fight him off. And then the bastard vomits all over my face.'

I had reached the end of the exercise book.

Twenty-Five

I tossed and turned all night. I hardly slept. Kelly's outburst was so unlike anything I had ever seen her do, but then I reminded myself, I had known her less than two weeks, and there was much of her complex persona that I still had to encounter.

I was worried sick about her. Jo'burg is not the place for a young woman in an unbalanced emotional state to take to the streets alone at night. Okay, I accepted that she may well have a black belt in kung fu or karate, or whatever, but still, the bad guys have guns and stuff.

The bit I'd read about her friend in London being raped didn't help my state of mind either. Shit! Is the male race as bad as that? I reflected that I must have led a pretty sheltered life.

I never encountered these things except in the Press, and occasionally in the courts. Never at first hand like this. Poor Kelly, and many other women, seemed destined to relate to males only on unimaginably horrific terms.

Somehow, the realisation that she trusted me enough to open herself to me as she had done made me feel all the more responsible for her well-being, all the more angst-ridden and apprehensive about her present condition and whereabouts.

During the long night, when I wasn't worrying about Kelly, I was agonising over Nozipo and her bitter disappointment. I wondered what sentence she would receive. I suspected that it wouldn't be a very severe one.

After all, the conviction was totally unsafe, and a harsh sentence would just add to the overall erroneousness of the judgment and strengthen our hand for the appeal - and an appeal there most certainly would be. That much I had assured Nozipo.

I was also worried for Ephraim Mazibuko. Poor man must have been in fear of his life to do what he did. He had a lot to lose. A lifetime's reputation forfeited at a stroke. I knew him well enough to be sure the judgment had been forced out of him. All this only a few days after the chap's wife is murdered.

I was up before dawn. I kicked myself that I had never bothered to get Kelly's landline number. I would at least have been able to check if she had managed to get home. That's if she would have answered. In her present state, I doubted it.

While I was shaving, I had a brainwave, and darted back into my bedroom and opened the wardrobe - the one I had told her she could use. Her few things, a couple of T-shirts, jeans, some knickers, a small cosmetic bag, and some odds and ends, were still there. I couldn't see her sandals. Perhaps she had had the good sense to put them on. She had clearly left as she was, in jeans and T-shirt.

Her rucksack was also there, on the floor of the wardrobe. I took it and sat down on the bed to search. Maybe I'd find some sort of clue, a return address, an *if found please return to* …something, anything.

What I did find gave me no comfort at all: her keys. There, in a zipped pocket of the rucksack was the bunch of keys I'd seen her take out of her bag as I dropped her off when we got back from Mauritius. Her flat keys. So, even if I had found her home phone number, it would just ring and ring.

In her rucksack I also found another exercise book, one of the pack of six she had bought at the supermarket in Mont Choisy. I glanced at the first page. No, I hadn't read this one yet. I put it aside for later.

I hadn't been to the office - not to sit at my desk and do some work anyway - since before the Mauritius trip. Abby was there as usual.

'Hi, Abby, you okay?'

'Fine, Anton.' As ever, she was concerned in her endearingly maternal way. 'You must be disappointed about Nozipo. Sorry, hey!'

'*Ja*. Something very fishy going on there, Abby, and I'm fairly sure that Jabu fellow knows something about it!'

'Sounds that way to me, too. Oh yes, Anton, Mr Mokoena asked me to tell you that he's gone to see a client in Welkom this morning, and he'll probably only see you tomorrow.' I marvelled how Abby addressed both partners to their face by their first name, but referred to us as Mister Mokoena, or Mister Venter in our absence. Typical of the unique and rather unconventional nature of our little firm, I thought.

Later that morning, I struggled to concentrate. There were piles of papers on my desk: correspondence and administrative things that had to be attended to. A number of case files also needed my attention. But Kelly's absence worried me and I couldn't settle down.

I picked up the directory and looked up SAWAA. The number rang and rang, and eventually reverted to voicemail.

'Hello! You have reached South African Women Against Abuse.' The recorded voice was not Kelly's - a South African accent. 'We are unable to take your call at the moment. Please leave your name and number after the tone…'

'Hi, this is Anton Venter. Could Maggie please contact me on …' I gave my cell and office numbers. As an afterthought I added, 'It's fairly urgent!'

Damn! Why hadn't I any other way of finding her? Of course, I could go to the flat in Hillbrow. At least I knew the building. I was fairly sure that one of the other residents would be able to point me in the right direction, to tell me her floor and flat number. But, I thought, *what's the use? If I've got her fucking keys, she can't be there, can she*?

Suddenly, I thought of her cell phone. Yes! As soon as I got home I would search that for the numbers of likely friends or relatives or somebody, anybody who may have an idea where she could have gone.

As the morning wore on I gradually managed to put aside thoughts of Kelly and to push on with some work. I even managed to remember that I had social responsibilities beyond her. I picked up my phone and dialled Christo.

'*Ja Poepol! Wat sê jy?*'

'*Nee… niks, fokkol.* How's the investigation?'

'*Ja*! It's moving. But what about your trial, hey? I've been meaning to phone you. Fokken shit story, man. No one I spoke to thought that chick was going to come out guilty, man! What the fok happened? Mr Venter losing his touch, or what?'

'Shit, Christo, I don't know what to say. Truth be told I think the judge was threatened, you know, his wife *mos* got murdered a couple of weeks back. I think they went for him while he was vulnerable, you know?'

'*Ja*. Man, this country is fokken going down the drain, know what I mean?'

I sighed. '*Ja.*' There was a pregnant pause… 'And your investigation… Mr Webster. You close to getting him?'

Christo's tone changed. He sounded guarded. 'Very fokken close! Let me not fokken jinx it by talking too much, but it could be, like, soon, very soon! I'll keep you posted, though. Hey! What about your little dark… er… I mean your chick…whatsit? …Kelly!'

I was hurting too much to admit to Christo that she had run off, that I had no idea where she was, or where I stood with her.

'No fine… she's okay, first class!'

Christo sounded busy. There were voices in the background. 'Hey, Anton, a steak and a couple of cold ones, *nê*? Soon?'

'Sure, Chris. You just give me a shout when you're free.'

Just before I left the office, Abby put through a call from SAWAA.

'Anton Venter?' I was pulling on what must have been my fiftieth cigarette of the day. Stress always made me smoke more.

'Hi, this is Maggie Seboko, at SAWAA. I'm returning your call.'

'Hi, Maggie. Thanks! Yes, I was trying to get in touch with Kelebonye Modise.'

'Kelly? I'm not sure.' She sounded a bit hesitant. 'I mean, aren't you Anton... I mean, the guy she...?'

'*Ja*, that's me. I'm the guy she's been seeing. It's just... I... I haven't seen her since last night and I don't know where she's got to.'

Maggie sounded surprised. 'Isn't she answering her cell?'

'No... well... in fact she left it at my house.' I felt I had to be a bit less mysterious. 'Actually, she was very upset last night; the Jabu Zulu thing, you know?'

'Yeah, I'm sure. We were all very angry.'

'Anyway, I'm a bit worried. I'm not sure where she's gone. I don't think she's at her flat either. I mean, she left her flat keys behind.'

'Don't worry, Anton. Our Kelly's been known to throw a wobbly from time to time. She'll be okay. Probably gone to her cousin's.'

'Who's that? Where?'

'Thandi... somewhere in Soweto, I think. Don't know exactly.'

As I neared home, my anticipation rose. Kelly was sure to be there, waiting for me. Maybe a little sheepish about the smashed TV, but hey! What's a TV set between lovers, between soul mates?

But she wasn't there.

The thousands of pieces of glass had been vacuumed up, but the screenless Trinitron was still on its stand, blind and dumb, looking utterly stupid - a vainglorious monument to useless consumerism. Esther was sullen and stiff and had '*I could have told you so*' written in italic, underlined, bold capitals on her frown.

I ignored her implied admonishments and rushed to find Kelly's cell phone. It was still in the kitchen where she had left it. It had switched itself off - probably a low battery.

Eagerly, I switched it on, ready to press the buttons that would give me her last-dialled numbers. Surely one of those would be a friend, a relative, someone who may have an idea where Kelly might go when she went walkabout.

Instead the screen said: "*enter PIN*". I tried the default 1, 2, 3, 4, hatch; but that wasn't it. What a let-down!

After a supper of beer, snacks and yet more cigarettes I tired of pacing restlessly around the house. The blue exercise book I found in her rucksack yesterday was still on the bedside table. I fetched myself another Amstel, found an ashtray, kicked off my shoes, lay down on the bed and began to read.

Belinda eventually dozed off for a couple of hours. When she awoke she was sober and sore all over.

She sounded panicked. 'Kelly! We got to get to the police. I mean, the longer I wait, the more likely they won't believe I was raped.'

'Hey Bee, is it worth it? I mean.'

'What d'you mean, worth it? I'm damn sure it's worth it. I'm going to lay charges against the bastard. He can't be allowed to get away with it.'

'Let me tell you, Bee, I haven't told you this before. I don't know what it was like in Trinidad when your uncle, you know...' I had to steady myself. We were getting into difficult territory. 'When I was twelve, I was, you know, gang-raped by three blokes.'

There was sudden compassion in her eyes. 'No!'

'Yeah, and let me tell you, girl, the examination by the district surgeon and the questioning by the police was almost worse than the bloody rape.'

Belinda's raised eyebrow suggested some scepticism.

'Okay, you don't believe me? Let's go down the police station now then. First, they'll tell you were probably asking for it.

"What, you went into his flat?" They'll say it was your fault. Then they'll send you to the quack who'll treat you like a leper and will shove a fuckin' cold stainless steel speculum up your pussy and poke about with swabs in your depths.

'I'm telling you, Bee, you'll have to go through the whole dehumanising process and at the end of it you'll be at the mercy of the inefficiency of the police and the Crown Prosecution Service.

'And Maurice will probably be able to talk his way out of it. If it ever gets to court, which I seriously doubt, he'll have his expensive lawyers, paid for by his rich daddy, and they'll tear you to pieces on the stand and you'll end up looking like an evil, low-class whore-slut who seduced their poor, unsuspecting, innocent boy.

'Remember, it'll be your word against his in the end. Who d'you think they're going to believe? Huh? They going to side with a black foreign chick, who wears short skirts and lace knickers, or with one of their own? He won't ever be convicted. Mark my words!'

Belinda was listening.

'I've got a better suggestion.'

''What?' Belinda wasn't sure.

'Let's teach the bastard a lesson... ourselves, like!'

I had her full attention now. Her face lit up. 'How?'

'I'll explain, but first, have you got his home number?'

She shook her head. 'Only his mobile.'

I picked up the directory and looked up Wentzel. 'What's it... Maurice?'

'Maurice Anthony... M A Wentzel.'

There was more than a full page of Wentzels, but only two M A Wentzels: one in Pimlico and the other at 13 Crown Crescent, Hampstead. I dialled the Hampstead number, and winked at Belinda.

A man with a posh accent answered. I put on my civil servant voice.

'Is that Maurice Anthony Wentzel?'

'No, this is his friend, Roger... Roger Phipps-Jones... Maurice is... er... a trifle under the weather at the mo', actually, on his knees speaking to God on the great white telephone. Can I give him a message?'

'Yes, I wonder if you could please tell him that WPC Andrews called from Bloomsbury police station. Er... we are investigating a complaint of sexual assault and may require him to come down to the station at a later time to be interviewed.

'If you could be so kind as to ask him to stay near the phone? We'll call when we need him. Oh yes... and tell him our advice is that he should not leave the London area for the time being. Will you?'

'Gosh! I say!'

'Thank you so much!'

Belinda was giggling. She was getting better already.

By four that afternoon we were ready. Belinda sent Maurice a text message: 'I may withdraw the charges if you come and apologise. I will be in all evening. We need to talk it over.'

We waited, trembling with anticipation.

The scene was set. We had spent the day assembling a complex list of props and accessories. Everything was ready, and we had rehearsed our roles over and over.

Thirty minutes later, when the buzzer sounded, we gave each other a last wink. Let's do it! Belinda went to the intercom. 'Yes?'

'Oh, hello. Belinda? This is Maurice.' He pronounced it the English way: Morris.

She pressed the button. It would take him only a few seconds to climb the two flights of stairs to our flat. I took up my position behind the door.

There was a knock. I nodded at Belinda, and she opened the door.

Maurice only managed to get one stride into the flat before he was down. I hit him twice... a side uraken uchi, or back fist, to the temple, then, as he swayed, pivoting on one heel, a shotei uchi, or palm-heel strike, to the base of the nose, and he was on his way to the floor.

By the time he hit the plastic drop-sheet that we had laid out over the carpet, he was out like a light. We rushed into action. First, we stripped him completely naked. Then, together we managed to lift him on to the small kitchen table, which we had placed in the middle of the room, laying him across the width of it, his head and shoulders overhanging one edge, and his bum and legs the other.

Quickly, Belinda gagged him with gaffer tape, and then we securely taped his wrists to the table legs, as far down as they would go. We did the same to his ankles. We pulled his knees as wide apart as we could, and secured them to the tops of the table legs with tape slings.

For good measure, we also taped his torso to the table with big, long swathes of tape so that there was no way he would be able to wriggle about later.

When he came to, about ten minutes later, we had suited up. The aprons we wore were part of a considerable collection of items we had managed to 'borrow' from one of the labs at the London School of Hygiene and Tropical Medicine around the corner. Our latex gloves, surgical masks and other odds and ends we had bought at the local Boots.

It didn't take Maurice long to absorb the seriousness of his situation. Within seconds of opening his eyes, the stark terror in his face made it clear that he was fully aware of his acutely vulnerable circumstance.

Belinda spoke. 'Hi Maurice, remember me?'

She went around the table to a point where he could see her clearly. 'You must remember me! Surely! Just look at what you did to my eye. See that? Remember that? Remember our little romantic moment under your kitchen table?'

Maurice was patently petrified. He made unintelligible noises through his nose. His eyes were bulging with terror.

I took over. 'Maurice, we don't appreciate what you did to Belinda last night. Rape is not nice, Maurice, not nice, is it?'

I waited for him to make some more muffled noises. 'Belinda thought she would spare you the embarrassment of a court case. Very considerate of her, don't you think?'

He looked about frantically. His muscles bulged, and his breath came in snotty gasps. It was clear that he had tried to exert all his strength against his bonds and had realised that any attempt to break loose was futile. Gaffer tape is fucking strong!

I continued, 'Maurice, God gave men genitals so that they would be able to express tender, gentle love and affection to their wives and to their lovers. To make love, and to procreate.. D'you understand?

'Not to use as weapons! Not to use as implements of torture to hurt women! We think people who don't know how to use their genitals perhaps don't deserve to keep them.'

I leant over so that my face was right close up against his. 'Are you with me?' His eyes looked as if they were about to pop out of their sockets. He was breathing in short, shallow, panting breaths. The mucus in his nose gurgled back and forth.

I straightened up and went to join Belinda on the other side of the table, between his diverged knees. Maurice could barely see us. He had to strain his head upward and forward to be able to see just our faces.

He had no way of seeing our hands, or what we were doing with them. We made sure that he could hear the metallic clatter of our surgical bits and pieces that we had placed within easy reach on a small cabinet.

'You ready, Belinda?' I asked.

'Any time.'

'Sure you want to go ahead with this?'

'Damn sure!' There was real vehemence in her voice.

'Maurice...' I took hold of his penis and gently stretched the limp member to its full length. 'You ready to say goodbye to this?'

The muffled wail through the snotty nose was pitiful.

'Was that a yes?' I turned to Belinda. 'Did he say yes?'

'Guess it must have been yes... sure sounded like it!' Belinda was playing her part to perfection.

I grabbed his scrotum in my other hand, a little less gently. 'And these?' I juggled the testicles up and down, testing their weight.

The snotty nasal wail was pathetic.

'Okay... scalpel!' I turned to Belinda, hand outstretched. Maurice strained his head forward with a monumental effort to see what we were doing. I ensured that my hand was just within his field of vision. Belinda placed a surgical scalpel in my hand. It still had the protective paper cover on the blade, and I removed it, holding it high enough for him to see my every move.

'All right, then, let's do this!' I tried to sound as businesslike as possible, but was having real problems containing my laughter. I could see Belinda was in the same state, approaching the giggles. I gave her a stern look. Let's not mess up now!

Maurice's whine was high-pitched and drawn out. One nostril bubbled with snot. His face was a bright, fluorescent pink, and veins stood out on his forehead.

The next series of moves were what we had rehearsed earlier. I hoped we would get it right.

I took Maurice's scrotum firmly in my left hand. I quietly put down the scalpel and exchanged it for a cube of ice from the kidney bowl on the cabinet.

Belinda opened the little incubator, also 'borrowed' from the lab, and removed a large syringe filled with pig's blood. The incubator had been set to thirty-eight degrees, roughly body temperature. It contained not only the syringe of pig's blood, but also some extra blood in a beaker, and our masterpiece... The Thing!

The Thing was the focus of the operation, and had taken a lot of time and effort to make.

We had had a busy day. Not only had we done over the lab at the School of Tropical Medicine to get the incubator, aprons, kidney bowls and so on, gone shopping for syringes, scalpels, gloves and masks at the chemist's, but we had also gone down to the market in the Atlantic Road, in Brixton.

Before getting on the tube, I phoned a friend of mine, an old Nigerian woman whom I knew from my school days. Auntie Mabel worked in a butcher's that specialised in providing the West Indian and West African residents of Brixton with some of the more unusual cuts of meat: goat's eyes, sheep's intestines, tripe, that sort of thing.

They had to keep a fairly low profile so as not to draw the attention of the council's health inspectors, but nevertheless managed to provide their customers with most of their un-British requirements.

The Brixton market is almost directly above the tube station. So, within two minutes of getting off the tube we were in Auntie Mabel's back room, inspecting our order.

Auntie Mabel also supplied the necessaries for various voodoo rituals and suchlike, and never asked questions.

On the phone, I had asked her to find us a cockerel, and to give us the skin and the innards. She had also prepared us a pair of pig's testicles, some pig liver, and a pint of fresh pig's blood. All for less than five quid!

Within ten minutes we had been back on the tube with our unconventional groceries, hugging ourselves with delicious anticipation. When we arrived at the flat, we had sat down and carefully constructed The Thing.

First, we carved a sausage-shaped piece of the liver. Then, with needle and thread, we carefully sewed the chicken skin to cover it, fashioning a foreskin at one end, and a scrotum at the other. Into the scrotum we put the testicles and some of the innards, and decorated the open end - the part that would look as if it had been cut from his groin - with bits and pieces of the cockerel's intestines. They looked just like veins and arteries and stuff.

We smiled at our handiwork. It looked pretty realistic. Before placing the gruesome item into the incubator, we snipped a few blonde hairs from a cheap doll we bought from a stall, and carefully dipped the ends one by one into some superglue, and then fixed them to the scrotum.

With the addition of the blonde pubic hairs the construction looked as real as made no difference... definitely real enough to fool a terrified rapist! A last touch was to pour some pig's blood into the scrotum and to carefully leave it to warm to body temperature.

I jumped as the phone rang. Could it be Kelly?

It was Christo.

'*Ja*, Chris! What's up?'

'Hey, Anton! Webster's just struck again... in the last couple of hours.' He sounded very keyed up.

'What? Where?'

'He attacked the same *ou*, that Jabu Zulu, again. This time he fokken cut off his goolies! Swear to God!'

'What? You say Webster attacked Zulu again?'

'*Ja*! That's what I'm saying. Only this time, he's put him in the hospital, in a coma, without a piel, or balls, man!'

'Fuck me! Where did this happen? You say a couple of hours ago?'

'*Ja*, around seven this evening. At African Diamond Corporation in Auckland Park - same place as the last attack. Only this time Webster somehow got into his office, and fokken tied him to his chair. *Ja*, and before you ask, he did use fokken red gaffer tape - fifty mil - just like all the other murders.'

I was stunned. For a moment I had forgotten the gruesome story I had been reading. This was now… this was real… not some elaborate, twisted, sick practical joke.

'The Castration Murderer? You sure?'

'Fokken sure! Only this time, something went wrong. He didn't kill the *ou*.'

'What d'you mean?'

'Well, he rigged up a system that was going to finish Zulu off, but a security guard somehow managed to save him in the nick of time.'

'Slow down… Start at the beginning.'

'Okay. I'm just waiting for the forensics guys to come back to me. If they call, I'm going to have to cut you off.'

'Okay, that's fine.'

'We found some blood, probably Webster's, he must have hurt himself breaking in, or whatever. We having it checked out, too.'

'Busy night, huh?'

'Blerrie busy. Anyway, seems like Webster somehow gets into the building sometime this evening, makes his way up to the eighth floor, the top floor. How he does this without being seen I can't fokken tell you. There's blerrie security cameras all over the place, in the lifts, on the landings. We're still trying to work it out.'

'But he gets into Jabu's office?'

'*Ja*. Office, my foot! A blerrie suite, you know, there's a gym, a fokken sauna and a spa, and a cocktail lounge, a couple of offices, a little bedroom. Takes up half of the top floor. Also, got a roof garden, the lot.' Christo paused for breath. 'Then, he must have knocked Zulu out and tied him to the chair.'

'Okay…'

'Then he rigs a thing up with piano wire. You *mos* remember van der Spuy, *nê*?'

'Of course. Have you checked if it's the same piano wire? What was it? Some Japanese brand?'

'Yamaha. No, that's one of the things we're still waiting for forensics to come back to us. But I'll fokken bet you a million bucks that it is the same piano wire!

'Anyway, Webster does the same sort of thing as with van der Spuy, only, this time he's in a rush. One noose is around the *ou*'s balls and piel, and the second wire is around his neck. The other end of each blerrie wire is tied to one of the weights from the gym. Twenty fokken kilos!'

'Jesus!'

'*Ja*. So, he hangs the weights over the railings of the roof garden, and secures them with a separate piece of wire. Then, he uses the same trick he used in Cape Town two years ago, you know, little syringe barrels with the piano wire threaded through, and with different concentrations of acid. You still with me?'

'*Ja*, I get the picture, the acid corrodes the anchor wires, one at a time.'

'Exactly! When the wire burns through, the fokken twenty-kilo weight goes plummeting over the railing. After a fall of ten metres, or so, it jerks tight and… goodbye balletjies, goodbye dick!'

'*Net so*! Exactly!'

'So what stopped the second wire? What saved his neck?'

'Well, that's where this *ou* is so lucky. Apparently, there's this security guard patrolling the grounds and he hears a thump, as the weight hits the earth in the flowerbeds.

'Of course, he's unaware that there is a fokken piece of meat attached! Anyway, he alerts his boss. When they go upstairs to check, they find that Zulu has fokken locked himself in. That's what's still puzzling me. The office is locked from the inside!'

I was trying to imagine it. 'Webster must have found a way out somehow. Did he abseil down from the roof garden? Did you guys find a rope?'

'No, no rope. But anyway, you guessed the other part, the security guys force the door and remove the second noose, the one around his neck, just in time.'

'So, how did Webster get in? Isn't the place heavily guarded?'

'*Ja*. Hey hang on, Anton.' There was muffled talk in the background. 'Got to go. Forensics have some news.'

I was intrigued by the whole thing. 'Call me later?'

'Okay.'

I put down the phone with a sense of horror. I was surrounded on all sides with castration stories - Christo with Webster's attack on one side, live, real and immediate, and the story of two girls taking their macabre revenge eight years ago in a London flat on the other.

And, oh! Where was she? I ached for her to be with me, to be safe. In my arms.

I lit another cigarette and picked up the book.

We were ready! I had Maurice's scrotum in one hand, and an ice cube in the other. The last thing Maurice had seen me holding was the scalpel, and no doubt he thought I was still holding it.. Belinda was ready, too.

In her right hand she had the large syringe of warm pig's blood, pointed upwards, ready to simulate a cut artery. With thumb and forefinger of her left hand she carefully held his foreskin at the ready.

Two smaller syringes lay within easy reach - also without a needle of course. They were filled with Nali, a fiery peri-peri sauce from Malawi; the hottest chilli sauce I've ever tasted. The label on the bottle says 'Friends Beware' and they mean it!

We looked at each other. My eyes counted... one... two... THREE!

I tugged and squeezed Maurice's balls really hard. The pain would hopefully confuse him and allow our little charade to achieve its full impact. At the same moment I circumscribed his entire groin with the ice, exactly as I would have done with the scalpel had I been cutting off his genitals.

I grabbed the syringe of chilli sauce, tucked it under his foreskin and squirted some Nali on to his glans, trying to ensure that a few drips got into the little mouth where the pain would be most acute.

As I finished 'sawing off' his genitals with the ice cube, Belinda began to squeeze off rhythmic squirts of blood with the big syringe. The blood went all over the place - on to Maurice's naked chest, all around the 'wound', on to our aprons, even on to my mask.

It was spectacular!

Before he could settle, she shoved the other syringe of Nali up his arse and squeezed the trigger. I poured the rest of the blood from the beaker on to our gloves and the last drops over The Thing in its dish.

Maurice stopped whining for an instant. He had just been castrated and emasculated, and he waited with bated breath for the agony that seemed only seconds away.

To complete the performance, I carefully picked up our painstakingly constructed Thing from its kidney bowl and came around the table to Maurice's face.

He was ashen-pale. His breathing was very shallow. Every fibre of his body was listening to the pain as the peri-peri sauce began to gnaw into his urethra and rectum. I was sure he was vividly imagining that the pain originated from a gaping wound that had once been his genitals.

My gloves were covered in blood. I held up the dripping Thing in front of his horrified eyes.

'There you go, Maurice. At least the women of the world will be able to sleep peacefully now, won't they?' He looked as if the fear alone would kill him. I smeared the open end, the chicken-intestine-end of the Thing across his face. Then with my other hand, I squeezed out the pig's testicles for him to see.

'Well, there goes the family! Generations of fine breeding... wasted!'

Belinda brought a bucket and I dropped the lot into it with a gesture of finality.

The job was done. Maurice was riding a wave of well-deserved anguish that would leave him with no permanent damage except to his ego. I felt good. If only every rapist could experience what he was experiencing now!

As a finale, we placed the bucket under his crotch. The plastic bag of water that we had taped to the underside of the table was pricked with a pin, and a steady drip-drip began into the bucket... musical accompaniment for Maurice's deep soul-searching meditation session.

Then it was just a matter of stripping off gloves, aprons and masks, collecting our overnight bags and letting ourselves out of the flat.

'Goodbye, Maurice... Have a good death!'

I took a break. Phew!

I had a much-needed shit, and then took a walk outside in the garden to let the fresh air clear my head. It was getting late, almost midnight. I looked up at the sky, the stars barely visible through the urban light pollution. Where are you? Please come home!

My heart leapt. My phone was ringing. I sprinted across the lawn to the open French doors of the bedroom and dived for the phone.

But it was only Christo. I tried to hide my disappointment. 'News?'

'*Ja*!' There were background noises - vehicle noises. 'We're on our way to get Webster. We've got a positive sighting. He's under surveillance, and we're going to get him. We'll have him in the next thirty minutes!'

'Great!'

'Got to go...'

'Good luck. Keep me posted.'

'Aren't you going to bed?'

'No, I'm too excited. Even if I do, keep me posted, anyway.'

'Okay!'

I knew there was no point in trying to sleep. There was just too much happening in my head. Kelly, Kelly's story, Webster, Jabu in a coma. I was spinning.

I made myself some coffee, emptied out the ashtray, fetched a fresh pack of Marlboro and settled down once more.

When we entered our flat together on Sunday evening after a pleasant weekend in Cambridge, we knew what we were going to find.

Maurice Wentzel was still taped to the table.. He was still gagged, still naked, as we had left him. During the long, frightening dark hours of Saturday night he had managed to rock the table enough to tip it over, knocking over the bucket in the process.

This was probably not a clever thing to do, as it meant that he spent the rest of the weekend on his face in a widening puddle of his own pee, pig's blood and chicken entrails. The table was upside down on his back, and his arms and legs, still taped to the table legs, pointed uncomfortably up in the air behind him, like a skydiver endlessly practicing an exaggerated 'arch' posture.

He cut a splendidly pathetic figure. The smell of urine and slightly off offal that permeated the room was a very fitting accompaniment for him. Mercifully, he had managed to resist having a shit. Mercifully for us, that is. We would have to clean up all this mess!

When the door opened and the light came on, he looked up from the dropsheet covered floor, utter despair on his face. Belinda burst out laughing.

'Well, Maurice… How was the weekend, huh? You've enjoyed yerself, then, darlin'?'

'I imagine he's probably had a bit of a think,' I said. 'Haven't you, Maurice?'

He made pathetic grunting noises through the tape. I continued, 'Now, if you're a very good boy and promise not to make a noise and to disturb the neighbours, I'm going to take off the gag.' I knelt down in front of him. He whimpered and looked up at me with big, sad, blue, bloodshot eyes.

'No noise?'

He eagerly signalled assent with his eyes. When I ripped off the tape it pulled at the stubble that had grown in our absence, and he yelped inadvertently. Strong stuff, gaffer tape!

'Okay, Maurice, we're going to let you go home now. But first, Belinda wants to ask you just a few little questions... okay?'

Maurice's voice was a croak. 'Wa... w... water... please... water...'

Belinda was unmoved. 'You'll get your water. You can go and have a beer even. A trough full of beer. Just a moment.' She paused, and took a small mini-tape recorder from her bag - one of those that executives liked to use to dictate their letters - and pressed some buttons on it. Then she held it in front of him so it would pick up every single word he said.

'Maurice, what would you call what you did to me on Friday night?'

Maurice looked confused.

'How would you describe it? A shag? ...Making love?'

Maurice didn't know what to say.

Belinda's voice had an edge. 'Would you call it rape?'

Maurice's resistance levels were very low. 'Ye... yes.'

'Sorry, you understand that I need you to say out the whole sentence.'

The dry voice croaked, 'I... raped you. On Friday... I raped you... I...'

'You can do better than that, can't you?'

He made a supreme effort. 'I, Maurice Anthony Wentzel, admit that I raped and assaulted you... er... Belinda Montgomery, on Friday night.'

Belinda looked satisfied. 'Was that the right thing to do?'

'No!' The voice was desperate.

'Say again...'

'No, it wasn't the right thing to do.'

Belinda pointed at her black eye. She waited till she was sure he had focused on it. 'Did you do the right thing when you punched me and called me a fucking stupid little black bitch?'

'No... I'm sorry...'

'What was that? Say that again...'

'I'm sorry... I...'

'That's what I want to hear, Maurice, that's what I want to hear!' Belinda switched off the tape recorder. She was enjoying her revenge, and so was I.

'Now, before we let you go, tell us what you're going to do about having been illegally detained for the weekend. You planning to go to the police, maybe... to your daddy's lawyer?'

'I swear... just let me go... I'm sorry... I'll never...'

I stepped in. I bent down and put my lips to his ear. 'If you do, Maurice, if you do... Oh, Maurice! I believe you know what will happen, don't you?'

Maurice nodded.

'And another thing. If either of us ever hears that you have shown the slightest disrespect to a woman again, I mean any woman, ever...' I paused until he nodded.

'Then, we're going to cut them off for real! D'you understand me, Maurice?'

'Yes, ma'am.'

I had reached the end. There was nothing more written in the book. I was stunned. There was a creepy, crawling sensation on my skin and I had sudden palpitations.

I couldn't deny that there was a similarity between Kelly's story and the real castration murders. Okay, I had to admit that the modus operandi was very different. Kelly and Belinda had done it - or pretended to do it - with their bare hands, not with some elaborate mechanical contraption like Webster preferred to use.

But still…

For a moment, the hair on my neck was on end. But then, I reminded myself: the kidnap of Jabu Zulu occurred when Kelly was sitting next to me on the plane from Mauritius. End of story!

Yet why do I find myself at the intersection of two different castration stories? Why me? Why tonight?

Oh, where are you? I love you so…!

I had been sitting in the study for hours. I was cold and stiff. My mouth tasted like a vulture's crotch, but I lit another Marlboro anyway, and continued staring at the wall. The phone rang. It was five past three in the morning. This time I didn't dare hope it could be her.

Sure enough, it wasn't.

'We got him, Anton! He's in the slammer!'

Twenty-Six

I didn't sleep at all. When the first light of dawn began to creep through the curtains, and the twitter of birds started to filter into my exhausted brain, I stretched and got up off the chair. I went for a pee, and made myself a strong cup of coffee. Then I took my cell phone and Kelly's bunch of keys and went out to the car.

Esther had just emerged from her annexe and looked at me with deep concern. 'Are you okay, Mister Anton? You don't look well at all.'

I could only manage a grunt. 'I'm fine.'

As I drove out of the gate, I heard her say, 'Don't worry, she'll come back…'

I hoped she was right.

I wasn't really sure why I wanted to go to her flat. If I had her keys, then surely she couldn't be there? But, I argued, maybe she was. Maybe she had a spare key. Maybe she had asked the caretaker to unlock for her with a master key. Maybe a neighbour had her spare key for emergencies. Maybe she had broken in and fitted a new lock.

The closer I got to Hillbrow, the more sure I became that I would find her there. Embarrassed, contrite, beautiful… forgiven. My body ached with the thought of Kelly melting into my arms.

I found parking easily enough. Hillbrow at dawn was pretty quiet. It reminded me of the morning I had collected her to go to Botswana. Grey, desolate, and windblown. *God! That was less than a week ago*! It felt like ages.

The floor to ceiling windows in the lobby were all cracked. The lift was out of order, and I aimlessly started up the filthy, dingy stairs. None of the people I saw looked at all approachable. There was one guy asleep on the first landing and an entire family on the second.

A desperado in a black trench coat was following me up the stairs, making me feel very white, very northern suburbs, and very vulnerable.

My state of sleep deprivation was such that I acted totally out of character, and instead of trying to outpace the suspicious-looking fellow in the coat, I turned and waited for him to catch up with me.

'*Heyta*!'

'*Yebo*. You look lost, man!'

'Hey, I'm looking for this chick… Kelly… you know, short, like this… dreads… very pretty…'

'*Ja*! I see her, bro'…'

'D'you know her flat?'

'Try twelve.' He pointed up the stairs.

'Ta, man!'

'Sure!'

I was breaking out in a sweat by the time I reached twelve. The three packs of cigarettes I'd smoked since I'd last slept were taking their toll, and I was short of breath. As I came out of the fetid, dark stairwell on to the twelfth floor lobby, I almost bumped into a middle-aged woman, dressed in office clothes, who was about to head down.

'Excuse me… I'm looking for Kelly Modise.'

'Twelve-oh-two. I don't think she's there though.' She was halfway down the first flight.

'Thanks!'

I found 1202 easily enough. I knocked and waited a minute, then tried the keys till I found the one that fitted. Before I turned the key I inadvertently depressed the handle, and the door opened. It wasn't locked.

It was pretty dark inside. The heavy curtains were drawn, and there was a mustiness that told me immediately that she was not in. I tried one light switch, then another. The power seemed to be off. That might explain the non-functioning lift, and the dark stairwell, I thought.

I cursorily peered into the sitting room, and peeked into the two bedrooms. One was more of a storeroom, but the other seemed to be in use. It was very sparsely furnished - more a nun's cell than a young professional woman's bedroom. The narrow steel-framed bed and small bedside cabinet barely took up any space, making the tiny room look cavernous.

The small kitchen was pretty tidy. There was not much in the fridge. The milk had gone sour, and was giving off a bad smell. I took it out and poured it down the sink.

I was about to open the curtain to let in the morning light when my phone rang. It was Christo.

'Hey, *Poepol*! So, I come to your house so you can fokken congratulate me and give me a cup of coffee, maybe even breakfast, and old Esther here tells me you're out! What's up? It's not even six thirty!'

'Hey sorry, Christo… had to shoot off early…' I felt guilty. Guilty and lonely. 'I'm in Hillbrow… where can we meet? I'll buy you breakfast.'

'Fok, I don't know. There's a place in Hyde Park that opens twenty-four hours… *Burger*-something.'

'*Ja*, okay, I know it. Twenty minutes, okay?'

'Okay.'

I locked the flat and started down the stairs. Then, on second thoughts, I went back and unlocked the door, leaving it as I had found it.

The restaurant was a typical twenty-four hour American-style franchise joint. The sort of place where the coffee was pale, the chips anaemic, and the Coke watered down. Christo was there, waiting for me.

'So what takes you to Hillbrow at fokken six in the morning? Taking the chick home, hey?' Christo winked.

I let it go. It was a good enough reason and it avoided unpalatable explanations.

We ordered full *Prairie breakfasts*, with all the trimmings; in the hope that maybe one of the items would have some flavour.

'So, tell me about Marthinus Webster. You say you've got him?'

'*Ja*! We've got him. He's in cells at Midrand at the moment. I'm scheduled to get a shot at interrogating him at eight.' He mechanically checked his watch. 'In the meantime they're just doing the routine stuff, you know: name, address, next of kin. Soften him up for the real questions.'

'So, what have you got on him?'

'The fokken lot, *Boet*!' I noticed that Christo sounded much more confident than when they arrested Sylvester Cupido, the tattooed Cape Town queen, two weeks ago.

'It's him, all right. Last night, when we arrested him, he had an assortment of stuff in his house - the red gaffer tape, size eleven blerrie shoes - not Hi-Tecs, though. Maybe they wore out. Various chemicals, including some sulphuric acid and other *kak*. We're still sifting through his place. Will take us a couple more days till we've got all the stuff, but so far it looks fokken hundred per cent!'

'Sounds good!'

'Oh yes, nearly blerrie forgot. Webster's wife drives, guess what.'

'I don't know… a beige Hilux?'

'Fokken right! A two thousand and five model, my boy! Not only that, it's got holes for a winch on the front bumper. Remember? Your winch!' Despite his obvious state of exhaustion Christo sounded elated.

'*Ja*, I remember.'

The full *Prairie breakfasts* arrived. The eggs, hash browns, toast and chips were pale, and the sausages and hamburger patties were grey - as predicted. The cheese was tartrazine orange, and the bacon was an improbable pink. The cappuccino tasted like dishwater with foam. I called for *Tabasco* - anything to mask the greasy sameness.

We ate in silence for a while. Both of us were no longer as young as we used to be, and were feeling the strain of not having been to bed. Christo broke the silence.

'You *mos* know, *Boet*.' He had a sentimental tone to his voice. 'It's blerrie important to me that I can discuss this case with you.'

'Sure.'

'And you know, I blerrie appreciate it the way I can phone you to discuss the case, even in the middle of the night, like last night. Means a lot to me.'

I looked up from my tasteless hash browns.

Christo was almost dreamy. 'I mean, it really has fokkol to do with you, and by rights I shouldn't be talking to anyone outside the force - sorry, these days we *mos* have to call it the police *service* - about the investigation. It's just, you know, we go back a long fokken way, and I trust your judgment. You understand?'

'Sure, Chris, and I appreciate it. I do. Anyway, this fucking castration thing has bloody fascinated me for what? Two, two and a half years? I'm as excited as you are!'

'And you's *mos* my bes' buddy.'

Later, we stood outside, leaning against the Audi so that I could have a smoke.

'Old Jabu Zulu's fokken lucky, that's all I can say.'

I looked at him slightly puzzled. 'Lucky?'

'*Ja*.'

'What d'you mean "lucky"? The *ou's* just lost his fucking manhood!'

'True, but at least he's blerrie alive. You can't say that for any of Webster's other six victims, can you?'

'You have a point.'

'*Ja*. I think that this time Webster didn't have time to plan properly. It was a rushed job.'

I raised an eyebrow. 'How?'

'Well, first of all, the other six murders were all different, all distinctive. And all clinically executed. This one is different.

It's a sort of half-baked rehash of the Cape Town thing, of the van der Spuy murder. You know, the sulphuric acid and the syringe barrels on the piano wires. All the others each had something original, something unique.'

'True.' Christo had a point.

'Okay. I grant you that the MO the other day in Delmas was pretty unique. That one sort of fits the pattern. But he cocked up big time and the fokken saw contraption didn't work, did it?'

'And Zulu escaped.'

'Right! Now - I mean last night - he has a second stab at Zulu and cocks up again! Blerrie injures himself, bleeding all over the floor and leaving us a DNA sample as big as a fokken house. Could just as well have left us his blerrie ID book!'

'Also, he rushes his preparations, goes into action with a half-baked plan, and the security guards come and rescue his victim.'

'True.'

'No, I'm telling you, *Boet*, he's lost his touch. He could manage six, but not seven. Strange, hey? I'm telling you, something made Webster cock up.'

I nodded and took another drag. Christo went on. 'Just wait till old Jabu Zulu regains consciousness. He's going to have a fokken story to tell! He's going to be able to give evidence against Webster that will put him away for fokken life, many times over!'

Christo kicked some pebbles with the toe of his shoe. 'Went to see him yesterday afternoon. He's at the Morningside in intensive care.'

I looked up, surprised. 'Zulu?! I thought you said he was still in a coma.'

'No, he is. I went to chat to one of the doctors.'

'What's the prognosis? When do they think he'll be likely to come round?'

'*Ag*, you never can tell. Could be today, could be never. But they're hopeful, you know. It's not as if the *ou* suffered brain damage or anything.'

I was still half-awake. 'I'm not so sure about that. From the way the bastard behaved towards women one would think his brain was in his dick. And that was bloody well terminally damaged, wasn't it?'

Christo chuckled. 'What was that one I heard the other day? Oh *ja*: God gave man a brain and a penis, but not enough blood to operate them both at the same time!'

'Maybe now he'll have enough blood to operate his brain full-time!'

'*Ja*,' said Christo. 'Maybe he'll also learn to respect his wife now, hey? Man, Anton, that made me mad, you know, when he stood up in blerrie court and admitted in front of his wife that he'd been fokken screwing that niece of his. What a complete *doos*!

'Anyway, as I was saying, I went to the Morningside yesterday, and there's one thing I can't quite understand.'

'What?' I was alert, despite my state of exhaustion.

'Man, you know, a curious thing. The bruise on the temple, the blow that knocked him out.?'

'*Ja*.'

'The doctor says he's fokken sure it was made with a fist; you know, he reckons he can see the individual contusions where the knuckles landed…'

'Well, what's so mysterious about that?' I was puzzled. 'If Webster knocked him out with a punch to the temple, surely it's possible that the knuckles left their individual marks?'

'*Ja*, true! But that's not the point. I've *mos* seen Webster's hands, you know, he's got blerrie farmer's hands, big, like fokken shovels.' Christo looked me in the eye. 'These knuckle marks, the bruises, are much too fokken close together.'

He furrowed his brow. 'Like it was a much *smaller* fist, you know?'

He looked at his watch. 'Fok! Is that the time? I've got to go! See you, *Poepol*!'

'Cheers, *Blikpiel*!'

I sat in the car for a long moment after Christo had driven away. My tired, dulled brain was scurrying around in ever-tightening circles, spiralling into a dark, deep hole.

I started the Audi and headed back towards Hillbrow at speed.

The power was back on in Kelly's building, and I risked the lift. I couldn't face the stairs again. The inside of it was revolting and smelt of stale urine. There were slightly less stale puddles on the floor.

There was a fresh blood smear on one wall. The inspection schedule, in its little glass case above the buttons, attested to the fact that the last six-monthly safety inspection by Waygood Otis had been conducted in July, 1995.

The original reason I decided to come back to her flat was to search for phone numbers, friends, relatives, contacts, anyone who could possibly help me locate her. But on the way from Hyde Park, a whole new thought process had begun in my head.

I switched on the lights and opened the living room curtains, then went back and switched off the lights when I saw the bright sun streaming into the room. I settled down on a hard chair by the phone - a phone-fax combination - on the floor.

The room was very sparsely furnished. The bare floor, a few un-upholstered chrome and PVC chairs, and a small chrome and glass table hardly added up to home sweet home.

There were no pictures on the walls, no colour to breach the harsh, cold and very clinical textures. Nowhere could I see anything to remind me of the warm, vivacious, beautiful woman that I had so recently held in my arms.

The room was clearly used as a gym for martial arts training - definitely never as a warm and friendly place to socialise, to entertain friends for dinner. There was a small exercise mat on the floor, a set of dumbbells in the corner and a heavy punch bag hanging from a bolt in the ceiling.

Against the wall on a low stand was a weightlifter's set; a bar with removable blue circular weights of varying sizes on each end. I noticed that it was lopsided: one of the clamps was lying on the floor, and the largest weight was missing from one end.

I started looking for an address book, a note pad, anything that might hold a clue. I pressed the *redial* button on the phone, and watched the machine dial the SAWAA number I had looked up yesterday.

Dammit!

After a moment, I reached some sort of decision point. I took out my cell phone and started to scroll through the numbers. It was at times like these that I was glad that I was an inveterate hoarder. A hoarder of information, particularly phone numbers. As I scrolled I saw names to which I could no longer put a face. Memorabilia of chance encounters over the years.

Then I saw it. *Vuyo Songo*. I dialled.

'Detective Sergeant Songo. Can I help you?'

'Hey, howzit, Songo? Anton Venter, you know, Christo Januarie's friend. You remember?'

'Of course, Mr Venter. You were with us that evening on Devil's Peak!'

'Right! The very same!'

'What can I do for you?'

'Congratulations! I heard you introduce yourself as detective *sergeant*! Well done!'

'Thank you, sir!'

'I don't know if you can help me, man, you know, old Christo Januarie sort of occasionally uses me as a sounding board, you know.'

'Yes, he used to speak highly of you.'

'Well, I'm sort of following a hunch. Are you still with the unit? The castration unit?'

'No, not for a year now. I've been posted to fraud, white-collar stuff, financial crime, you know?'

I couldn't hide my disappointment. '*Ag* well, anyway.'

'What was it you wanted? Maybe I can still help.'

'No, I was just thinking. You remember the car hire records you had? The beige Hilux?'

'Sure. Avis, Hertz, Imperial, Budget. We did the lot.'

'Exactly. You wouldn't know where I might get hold of them, would you?' I felt slightly ridiculous. It was none of my business, and I had absolutely no right to be putting Songo in this situation.

'Sure! Lynette is still with the unit. She's got all that stuff. I'm sure it won't take her five minutes to dig it up for you. Look, Mr Venter, I'll get back to you. Is this your number?'

'Yes, but hey, Songo, but you don't have to…'

'Don't worry, Mr Venter. Any friend of Detective Inspector Januarie is a friend of mine!' He chuckled, then suddenly seemed to have a thought. 'You haven't perhaps got a fax number, have you? That information you want is all on paper, you know? Hard copy. Much easier to fax than to email, you know what I mean?'

'Yes. I'm actually right next to a fax.' I searched the instrument and found the number written on the little label under the handset. 'Hey, Songo, you got a pencil?'

No sooner had I ended the call to Songo than Christo rang. I answered, my thoughts in a gloomy pit.

'Hey, Anton, fokken strange thing. Webster's just confessed.'

Suddenly, the darkness lifted. 'That's great! You sure?'

'*Ja*! But only to the kidnap. You know the Delmas escapade, the attempted assault with the circular saw.'

'What about the other attack on Zulu? And the other murders?'

'*Ja*, well that's just the point! As soon as Webster realised that we were trying to pin the whole serial killer thing - the Castration Murders - on him he blurted out his confession.'

'What?' I was confused. 'Explain.'

'*Ja*. He says he was hired by some guys who are mixed up with illicit diamond trading. We've heard of them. Guys who deal in stones that are smuggled out of the Jwaneng mine in Botswana.'

I was trying to focus.

Christo went on, 'Apparently all this time Jabu Zulu has been dealing in illegal diamonds on the side. This while he's a fokken director of African Diamond Corp, you know?'

'Uh-huh.' I was trying to take it all in.

'Well, apparently old Zulu blerrie double-crossed them and was holding a few million rands worth of uncut gems that belonged to them. Webster was supposed to frighten Jabu into admitting that he had the stones. That's what the circular saw was for.'

'So, are you saying he had nothing to do with Wednesday's attack at the office, with the castration thing? Nothing to do with van der Spuy, and all the others? He was just a hired hit man?'

'Fokken looks like it, man, Anton! I'm back to fokken square one!' He sounded bitter. 'Blerrie fokken square fokken one!'

'Jesus!' My mind began to race again.

'Webster's even got a fokken cast-iron alibi for Wednesday evening, when Jabu Zulu was attacked in his office. We've checked it out. He was with his parents in fokken Bloemfontein on Wednesday night! 'Strue!'

As we were talking, I had aimlessly wandered into the spare bedroom, the one that Kelly seemed to use as a storeroom. There was a sturdy table in the middle of the room, like a workbench. I tried the door to the built-in cupboard. It was locked.

I could hear someone talking to Christo in the background. 'Just hold on a minute, Anton.'

'Okay.'

I dug in my pocket for the bunch of keys. The second one I tried fitted.

'Thanks, thanks. Hey, *Boet,* you still there?'

'*Ja*, I'm here.' I had managed to open the cupboard.

'*Ja*, more bad news. The blood, you know, the blood we thought was Webster's, in Zulu's office?

'Uh-huh.'

'Well, it's not! The forensics *ou* has just given me the report. Analysis: type O.

'What's this?' Christo was reading from the paper he had just been given. 'Hey, Anton, listen to this! It says here, mitochondrial indicators: female, San and Bantu maternal antecedents. Are you hearing this? The blood was left by a fokken woman!'

The phone in the living room was ringing. Before I had taken two steps, the fax took over, and began its squeaking and whirring.

'D'you hear me?'

My throat was tight. I could barely make a sound. '*Ja*.' It was a croak.

'Wait, here it's got database cross matches. Fok! …Fok me!'

'What?'

'Cross match sample reference blah blah… one hundred per cent match… Hey, Anton! Remember the skin sample, the one from the Mpumalanga murder? The one we found under the victim's fingernail?

'*Ja*!'

'It's her! It's the same fokken DNA!'

I was looking at a well-organised tool cupboard. There was an assortment of power tools and good quality hand tools on a purpose-made rack on the inside of the cupboard door. A selection of climbing gear and a climbing rope hung from the rail.

'You still there?'

I grunted.

'Are you thinking what I'm thinking?' Christo was excited.

I wasn't thinking at all. My brain had frozen.

Christo continued regardless. 'The fokken Castration Murderer is a fokken *woman*! …A *woman*! Fok me! …Fok me with the wrong end of a blerrie pineapple!'

'Mmm.' I looked around the room. There was a very large, red-handled screwdriver on the floor beside the workbench. When I bent down to pick it up, I noticed a padlocked steel toolbox on the floor. I dragged it out from under the workbench and found a key that fitted the padlock.

As I turned the key I realised that the padlock wasn't locked. I looked at it more closely. It was twisted and had been forced open, probably with the screwdriver. The fax machine in the next room beeped. I left the toolbox to go and collect the incoming fax.

'Oh yes, forgot to tell you.' Christo was still on the line. 'My guys found footprints in the flowerbeds by the side of Jabu's building. True as God, size eleven blerrie Hi-Tecs. Doesn't make any fokken sense.'

Christo was clearly confused. 'Also traces of talcum powder on the *outside* of the fokken building. You know, climber's chalk. Looks like whoever she was *climbed* up the *outside*. Must be a fokken good climber!

'There were also more bloodstains on the wall and on the window ledges, like she climbed *down*, as well.' He paused. 'But who was wearing the blerrie size elevens? Were there two of them? Does she work alone? Are there *two* Castration Murderers?'

I had the fax in my hand. I walked back to the toolbox in the spare room as my eyes scanned the pages. They were the car hire records for Cape Town the week van der Spuy had died. Records for the hire of 2005 beige Toyota Hilux four-by-fours.

There, halfway down the second page.

My heart was ice.

K. Applebury.

Christo was saying something but I couldn't hear him. I opened the toolbox. It was very neatly packed.

Size eleven Hi-Tec North Ridge boots. Inside the boots, like specialised inner-soles, was a pair of size five climber's EBs.

Yes, Christo. She does work alone.

Five rolls of red gaffer tape - 3-M - fifty millimetre. A spool of Yamaha piano wire. A brown glass bottle 'Sulphuric Acid conc. B.P.'. A plastic bag of small syringes. A tray of glass vials, some missing: 'Hexabarbitol, 15ml'.

A scrapbook at the bottom of the toolbox caught my eye. I extracted it. It was full of hundreds of newspaper cuttings. I scanned some of the headings: *MOTHER OF 13-YEAR- OLD BITTER AS RAPE CHARGES WITHDRAWN... CHILD RAPE CASE COLLAPSES. DLAMINI FREED... RAPE VICTIM, 10, FOUND MURDERED... CASTRATION MURDERER STRIKES AGAIN... JABU ZULU NOT GUILTY OF RAPE...*

'Hello… hello… Anton! You there...? …Hello? …Hello…?'

My cell phone lay on the floor.

In a daze I walked into the other bedroom. Her bedroom. The heavy curtains were still drawn, and it was dark. I turned on the light.

Kelly was sitting on the narrow bed. Her shoulders were hunched and her hands were imprisoned between her knees, her feet neatly side by side on the floor. Her head was inclined forward and, if she was looking at anything at all, it was at the tips of her toes.

I noticed inconsequentially that her toenails had been painted blue. She seemed shrunken, as if even her spirit had crumpled in on itself. She didn't react to the door, to the light… to me.

There was a humming in my ears, which seemed to have been blocked by a sudden, perilous increase in blood pressure. Vainly, I tried to take in the reality before me. She hadn't been here earlier, but now she was. I considered the fact with incomprehension.

I stood immobile, staring dumbly at the top of her head. I noticed that she had a grubby bloodstained bandage on her left hand. She was wearing a watch. I'd never seen her wear one before.

In the next room, my cell phone began to ring. The vibration alert was on as always. The phone must have been laying on a bad, hollow bit of the concrete floor, and the buzz... buzz... buzz noise of the vibration alert sounded like a jackhammer and seemed to echo through the whole building, almost drowning out the ringing.

Neither Kelly nor I moved. The phone rang and buzzed, buzzed and rang, and then finally fell silent.

My mind was racing, but numb at the same time, as if the cognitive spiral had turned so far into itself that it had short-circuited. Despite the frantic mental activity, I wasn't thinking at all. It was as if my head had filled with hot cotton wool.

For an instant, I was back in the Wynberg police mortuary looking down on the cold, bloodied corpse of Johannes Jacobus van der Spuy. The grimace, the congealed blood on the teeth, the eyes wide with terror.

The black hole where his balls had been! His dick in a stainless steel kidney bowl covered in sand and pine needles!

I looked at the top of her head. Could this tiny, shrunken frame sitting immobile on the bed in front of me be capable of the most horrendous evil?

And there had been five others, each as brutal and pitiless as the other. Then, the Jabu Zulu thing.

I noticed she was shivering. Apart from that, she had not moved at all.

Completely involuntarily, the picture of the twelve-year-old in Atterigeville burst on to my mental video screen. A darkening room, a cold cement floor, a dying child naked in a pool of blood, the guffawing insolence of the rapists.

Suddenly, the feeling changed. I felt her embrace, the last time I had held her, the other morning before that terrible day in court. I felt the quiver of her body as she came, felt the electric intensity of her clinch as I had ejaculated, gushing my love into her.

The juxtaposition of the disparate feelings I was experiencing was as incomprehensible to me as the sight of her blue toenails. I was unable to even try to make sense of it.

The cell phone began its buzzing and ringing again. On the third or fourth ring, Kelly very slowly raised her head and looked straight at me. Her eyes were swimming, and all I could see of them was the reflection of the room in the wetness.

'Aren't you going to answer that?' Her voice was small, barely audible. It had an unusual quality in it that instantly reminded me of the taxi on the way to Plaisance Airport, when she had confessed her love. She had said, *'Please God, don't you ever leave me, Anton. Don't you ever leave me… no matter what… what … tell me you won't… no matter what… Oh, Anton! …Love…'*

And I had answered, 'I'll never leave you, Kelly… never! I love you… I love you… I love you!'

The buzzing cell phone was still ringing. She held my eye. I took a deep breath. Like the last breath a desperado takes as he steps off the rooftop. Like the last breath before he puts the shotgun barrel into his mouth. A very deep, life-changing breath.

'No, fuck it,' I said. 'Let it ring. It'll only be Christo wanting to take you away from me.'

She glanced at her watch, like someone waiting on the platform for the train to arrive. Then she looked at me for a long moment. There was an air of unutterable sadness about her, absolute vulnerability. As I watched, the tears welled up and began to cascade down her cheeks.

'It's too late for that, mate.' Her voice was tiny, as if she were very far away. 'Far, far too late….' She sat up, rising out of her hunched posture, and looked at me with a kind of defiance. There was a faint, reflective glint at her throat, as if the tears had trickled under her chin.

She looked at her watch again. 'Get the fuck out of here while you can.' Her tone was much gentler than the words suggested, much more tender. She couldn't hide that. But there was a hint of urgency in her voice. 'Please…'

As she looked up she quickly glanced - guiltily almost - over her shoulder, at the curtained window. My eyes followed hers. I crossed the room and yanked open the curtain.

The room was like millions of others in cheap high-rise blocks all over the world in that the outside wall was, in fact, a large steel window frame. The lower apertures were filled with asbestos panels and the rest with glass. I had opened the left-hand curtain, allowing the dazzling morning sunlight into the room. I opened the window and looked out.

My sleep-deprived brain slowly took in what I saw. It didn't make any sense at first.

I had opened the left-hand window. To my right was another one, also open. A metre or two below it, swinging languidly over forty-metres of empty space, was the missing weight from the set in the living room - a blue circular chunk of steel with '25 kg' embossed on the side.

It was hanging on a thin, shiny piece of wire. Piano wire. The other end was tied to the latch of the open window. Halfway up the wire was a small syringe barrel. The wire was threaded through the little hole in the bottom.

A second piece of wire led from the weight to the open window. It was slack and loosely spiralled, as if it had recently been taken from a spool, and it moved lazily in the breeze.

As I leant out of my window, looking across the short space to the other window, my uncomprehending eyes followed the slack wire to where it disappeared: into the room through the open casement.

I withdrew my head and could make out the wire where it entered the room under the hem of the curtain, at the head of her bed. There was a loose coil of the wire on the bed, directly behind her. From where I had been standing at the door, I hadn't seen it. Now, with the curtain open, it glinted brightly in the morning sunlight.

From the coil on the bed, the shiny wire curled up against her back, between her shoulder blades, and disappeared under her dreadlocks.

She was looking at her watch.

The instant my tired brain worked out what it was I was looking at, things began to move very quickly. There was a sudden twang and then the rushing, whistling sound of the wire uncoiling off the bed, faster and faster.

It was all very fast, but somehow I saw it all in slow motion.

I launched myself forward, diving through the air, my fingers straining, striving, stretching out to somehow grab the wire on the bed before the last coil whipped towards the window.

But even as I flew across the small room, I knew I had reacted too late.

Glossary

Ausi	Elder sister (from ou sus)
Balletjies	Testicles
Blikpiel	Tin-dick
Bogadi	Bride Price
Bojale	Female initiation rite
Charwal-chemise	Asian-style pants and shift outfit
Dominie	Pastor, Reverend
Doos	Cunt
Eina	Ouch
Fotsheke	Voetsek – Go to hell
Goedgedaan	Well done
Jou ma se moer	Your mother's cunt
Kaalgat	Buck naked
Kaaskop	Shaven head (Lit: 'Cheese head')
Kaffir	Nigger
Kak	Shit
Kefir	Unbeliever
Laager	Stockade
Lekgowa	White person
Lekgowanyana	Little white person
Mmamosadinyana	The little queen, Elizabeth II
Mbaqanga	'60s Township Jive
Meid	Girl
Moer	Cunt
Moffie	Homo, Poofter
Mokgwenyana	Son-in-law
Mos	After all, indeed
Muti	Witchcraft, magic potion
Nê?	Not so?

Oom	Uncle
Ou	Bloke
Piel	Penis
Poepol	Arsehole
Poes	Cunt
Poesbedonnerd	Cunt-struck
Punani	Vagina
Skattie	Little treasure
Sussie	Little sister
Toe	Please